Love Harder

STONE STEPS
PUBLISHING

Stone Steps Publishing: September 2016

ISBN 978-0997992601

Love Harder

by

Vivian Franks

Dedicated to my family and friends
for appreciating and supporting my talents.

Chapter 1

The rising tide rolls up over the sand, swallowing up the manicured feet of Mika Jones. Mika curls back her toes, watching as the water just misses kissing her flesh before making its retreat. Her gaze rests on the ocean before her. She is mesmerized by its vast emptiness, and she envisions ghost ships filled with explorers like Magellan, Raleigh, and Columbus—men who had the courage to leave behind all they knew for a life of the unknown. Mika had no idea if any of these travelers were ever near this non-descript beach; she never paid much attention in history, but that didn't matter to her. Not here. Not now. The water creeps back to her feet, enveloping her toes before she can move.

A man's voice invades this world. "Mika?"

The open sea fades, suddenly replaced with the reality of her husband's Mercedes.

"Mika? Hello?" Todd Jones, 44, kept one hand on the wheel while nudging his daydreaming wife with the other.

Mika shook clear the final images of her beach retreat.

"I'm sorry, what?"

"What time is dinner at Lisa's?" He could tell that it wasn't registering with her. "On Saturday? Jesus, you talked to her about it." He accelerated to make it through a yellow light at McDowell and Scottsdale roads.

"I don't know." She looked down at her toes, which only moments ago had been dancing with the waters of a distant sea.

Todd rolled his eyes. He knew that her response was born of a lack of caring, not knowledge. And it was true.

At the age of 40, Mika cared about very few things. She worked hard at her job while managing their household affairs, doing the shopping and cooking, and making sure the bills were paid. She was heavily involved in the booster club for her son's high school swim team, and she and her husband ran with an active group of couples. She did everything with the fervor of someone who was passionately involved, something she had done since she was forced to care for her father when she was only 10-years-old.

She did everything well. But despite how she made it look, she didn't truly care about any of it. She wouldn't admit this to anyone, though, because she didn't know it herself. Not yet.

"I'll text her. I think she said eight." Mika took out her phone and sent a text to her friend, partly to get the answer, partly to distract her from the silence of driving home with Todd. They had been sharing his car since hers died on the freeway two month ago. Todd, a financial planner, crunched the numbers and didn't think the value of the car justified putting any more money into it. And even though he agreed that they should get a new car, they had yet to do so. Instead, Mika drove Todd to work in the morning, and then she picked him up if she didn't need to be somewhere for their son Ryan and the swim team. On those days, Todd would take the bus, even though Mika thought it was foolish.

"Let's just get a car. We have the money," she had told him last Wednesday when he took the bus home.

"I'm fine," he replied, but Mika knew that what he really meant was that he didn't want to spend the money if he didn't have to.

So, that's where they were. They drove home together, some days in silence, others with Todd complaining about some government ineptitude. Only occasionally were they actually engaged in a conversation. This ride was mostly in silence, but she put forth at least a minimal amount of effort.

"I have a booster meeting at 6:30 tonight," Mika said, staring at her phone, trying to will a response to her text.

"Okay."

And that was Mika's ride home with her husband, just like most every other one.

* * *

Desert Horizon High School was generally considered one of the better public schools in Scottsdale. Great test scores, championship sports programs, and active parents who never tired of discussing the scholarship offers their sweet little angels had just received. Mika was one of these, but she never felt like she quite belonged.

She pulled into the parking lot and saw the new display on the side of the building: "We are better without bullying." She stared at it, thought about it, and shook her head. *What a stupid idea*, she thought. *Of course we're better without bullying; it's like saying the country is better without poverty.*

Mika entered the gymnasium, where a dozen other moms and a few dads were meeting. She worked well with the dads. Straight forward. No drama. But the moms were like pets on parade, she thought. Fake breasts on display in baby doll tees and tight dresses. Full makeup and bleached hair. Stiletto heels and spray-tanned, long legs. This was not Mika's element. Mika was beautiful. She had age-defying skin that made other women jealous, and it took little makeup to highlight her cheekbones and eyes. She often tied her thick auburn hair into a ponytail, even in public settings. Yet, she always felt inferior to these women. Her natural breasts didn't stand at attention like the manufactured ones that bounced around town, and her curvy hips accentuated any outfit she wore. She wasn't fat, but she carried a little more weight than she wanted. She didn't quite have a muffin top, but Todd once called it that, and she never forgot it. She could have worn contact lenses, but she chose to wear black rimmed, quirky glasses, partly because she liked them, partly to mirror her displeasure with her looks.

Her body had been a frequent topic of conversation between her and Todd. Last year, they had been at the neighborhood 4th of July party. As the evening progressed, alcohol took over and she and Todd ended up in the hot tub with Lisa and Gary Cousins, their close friends. Their sons, Ryan and Mark, had been best friends since 8th grade.

"I don't care. I'm just going to do it. Come on, Mika," Lisa said, as she removed her bikini top, revealing a pair of silicone-filled, C cup breasts, which seemed to float on top of the water.

"Mee-ka! Mee-ka!" chanted Gary.

"I don't know. She doesn't quite measure up," laughed Todd.

"Really?" Mika tried to laugh it off, but it irritated her. Another woman might have been suspicious of her husband sitting in a hot tub with a topless beauty, but not Mika. For all his faults, Todd didn't have it in him to cheat.

"Gary, what did those cost you?" Todd asked, nodding to Lisa's enhanced breasts.

"I don't know. Six or seven?"

"Closer to seven," Lisa corrected. "They're not cheap, like that slut whore Laney."

Lisa noticed the frustrated look on Mika's face.

"Hey, it's not for everyone. If I had what Mika has, I wouldn't have done it." Lisa glided over to Mika and caressed her breasts, laughing. "Seriously, these are nice."

"Thank you." She meant it, not only for the compliment but also for the touch; it had been more than a month since she and Todd had been physical. Lisa's unexpected touch, combined with several vodka tonics, made her nipples erect.

"But they could be better, and when you can afford it, why wouldn't you do it?" Todd asked. He also moved in on Mika. "Not that I'm not happy just the same." He kissed Mika, and she returned the gesture. Todd didn't notice how perfunctory it truly was.

Now she sat in the Desert Horizon gym among a dozen swim parents, Lisa at her side.

"Did you see the new sign? Love it!" Lisa said as one of the other parents started talking about fundraising.

"Are you serious?" Mika said without looking at her. "It's fucking stupid."

"What? What's wrong with it?"

"It doesn't say anything. It's just window dressing without…." She saw the lost look on Lisa's face and knew that once again her voice was in the minority. "Never mind. It's not horrible; I just think it's pointless."

The other parents began to talk louder as a cue to Mika and Lisa that they needed to be quiet. All it really did was irritate Mika even more, but she quieted down and listened to their conversation about fundraising, travel expenses, and equipment for next season. Too expensive. Too cheap. Not enough profit margin. Inequality. Too much work. Mika sat back and watched. This was her son's senior year, and with just a month left in the season, she didn't have an interest in what they did next year. She and Lisa were in charge of the end-of-the-year gala next month, so mostly she was here to report on the event. It was not like her to sit back and keep quiet, and everyone in the room noticed her silence until a discussion arose regarding the color of the new sweatshirts.

"Can we do something a little different next year?" complained one parent. "I'm sick of forest green."

Several other parents agreed, and the discussion escalated, like an avalanche rolling downhill and headed straight for Mika. "White gets too dirty." "Lets do something colorful." "Boys won't wear pink." Each comment and suggestion seemed to be designed to ignite one of Mika's diatribes. It was as if they were daring her to not express an opinion. Mika's stomach knotted, and she felt her heart rate increase. And then, her internal avalanche gave way.

"Are you kidding me?" she blurted.

"You don't like orange?" asked Lisa.

"Yes, I like orange just fine, but it's not one of our school colors."

"But we want to do something different," said Tammy McGill, one of the few who felt comfortable arguing with Mika. "It doesn't always have to be forest green."

Mika took a calming breath. "Yes, it does, because it's part of our school colors. This is a team. In the history of team sports, they have a color and stick with it."

"I kind of like orange," Lisa butted in.

"It doesn't matter what *you* like." Her volume increased as she leaned forward, but she resisted the urge to stand and pounce on the group. She felt her heart beat faster. *Shit, don't get worked up*, she thought. *What do you care?* She forced a laugh. "It's not a matter of what we want. It's the team. You go with team. Orange is asinine. Yes, the whole concept of a team colors might be stupid, but it's what we do. You can still do something different, but you have to stick with the green somehow. Green on grey. Green on white...."

"But white gets too dirty," proclaimed one mom.

"Yes, I know. I'm just giving ideas. Look, I've said my piece. Do what you want. I won't be here next year." Mika leaned back, acting defeated, but knowing that she probably had convinced a few people. Everyone was silent for a moment before someone spoke up.

"I kind of like the green and gray idea."

* * *

Mika sat in bed that night, searching the channels for something to watch. Todd came in, gnawing on a piece of beef jerky.

"Why do you do that?" The irritation in her voice was potent.

"It's tasty."

"It is now. Not so much when you wake up three hours from now with heartburn."

"Not tonight. I can feel it." Todd disappeared into the bathroom. "How was the meeting?"

"The usual," she sighed.

"I don't get why you go. It's a total waste of your time."

She rolled her eyes. "Thanks." She settled on CNN and dropped the remote.

Todd stood in the doorway, talking around the toothbrush in his mouth. He wore his usual sleepwear: black boxer briefs. At one time, Todd had a decent build, and parts of it were still there in his shoulders, which Mika had always found attractive. A small tire had started to develop around his waist about ten years ago, but Todd had always kept it in check. Mika noticed that the tire had taken up permanent residence in the past year.

"It's nothing against you, but your time is too valuable to give to people who don't appreciate it." He disappeared again, and Mika could hear him spit into the sink, which he always did with unnecessary force.

"It's for Ryan, so it's not a waste of time," she said as Todd joined her in bed. "Speaking of Ryan, is he home yet?"

"No. I told him to be home by 11. They're studying, or so he says."

"With Emily?" Mika was not fond of her son's girlfriend. She found her to be too controlling of her only child.

"Yes. Hey, no!" Todd frantically felt around the sheets for the remote control. Todd was a conservative, and he despised the mainstream news networks, especially CNN. Mika was far more middle-of-the-road, but she liked to think that she kept an open mind, something that Todd referred to as "being weak."

"Come on. I want to see if there's any more about that fire in Wyoming. Lisa's cousin lives nearby."

"Well you won't find anything here. They only tell you what the government wants you to hear. Turn to Fox." He found the remote under her leg and switched the channel. She didn't really care where the news came from, so she should have just let the discussion die. She wasn't that disciplined.

"So the government is covering up something about a forest fire in Wyoming? Did they start it?" She giggled.

"You're such an idiot. This administration has proven to be capable of just about anything."

"Why would they start a forest fire? What could they possible gain from doing that? And don't call me an idiot." She slapped him on the leg, which carried a sting, but Todd would never admit it. "Why can't I have an opinion that's not yours without being an idiot?"

Todd slid under the sheets and prepared to go to sleep. His arrogance, which at one time Mika found sexy, made her want to smother him with his pillow.

"Because when you ignore the facts, that's just stupid," he said, fluffing his pillow behind his head. "Okay, you're not stupid, but ignoring the truth and facts is stupid."

"What facts? There's a fire in Wyoming that's burning more than 1,000 acres. Those are the facts."

"Listen, I don't want to argue about this anymore. I just don't always believe everything I'm told, that's all."

"And I do?"

Todd tried to make amends, but couldn't avoid being condescending. "Of course you don't. Can I go to sleep now?"

She responded with silence and turned off the television before her story update came on. Mika stared into the darkness, trying to fall asleep. She felt small, dwarfed by the heavy breathing of her husband. Her mind traveled through time, back to her youth, trying to remember her dreams and how she thought she might end up. She could not remember how she pictured her future, but she knew it was not here. She spent 30 minutes clicking back to different ages and events: her 4th birthday party at the park, babysitting for the twins next door in 7th grade, working at the senior center her senior year. She found a lot of images, but no dreams, hopes, or desires. Her eyes closed, but as she started to fall asleep she felt Todd's hand fumble for hers. He took her wrist and pulled her hand to his erection, as he had done countless nights before. This was an ancient compromise that had become routine. Todd was the first man Mika had sex with, and the thought of putting his penis in her mouth, at the age of 21, made her sick. The issue had not been brought up in almost 20 years, but there had been times when Mika had reconsidered it. When Lisa told some of her stories about her sexual activities, the thought of it aroused Mika, but an unidentified resentment of Todd kept her from changing their arrangement. So on nights like this, when Todd had a difficult time sleeping, he took her hand so she could jerk him off. Without thinking about it, without any feeling or emotion, Mika pleasured her husband before going to sleep.

Chapter 2

"Any chance we can look for a car this weekend," Mika asked as she turned into the parking lot of Todd's office.

"Maybe," he said nonchalantly, looking around his feet to make sure he hadn't dropped anything before he left for work. "I have to do a little work, and then we have the dinner. We'll see." She pulled the car up to the curb. What she wanted to do was slow down and push him out. He leaned across the car, kissed her on the cheek, and left.

Mika watched him walk away in his very safe, charcoal grey suit that he had purchased on clearance at Nordstrom's three years ago. *That stupid, fucking suit*, she thought. Todd appreciated nice clothes, but he had an overwhelming sense of value. In most cases, Mika appreciated this about her husband. They had money to spend on very nice things, but partly because they didn't spend frivolously on day-to-day items. Today, however, it pissed her off, certainly a byproduct of the car situation.

Mika and Todd lived in an upscale home in north Scottsdale, a house they had bought after their brief stint in marriage counseling. It was one of the few times that Todd didn't stress about the value—a failed and misguided effort to appease Mika—but he complained every time he paid the mortgage for the next two years. Todd's office was about 15 minutes away on the border of north Phoenix and Scottsdale, but Mika worked in south Scottsdale about 25 miles away. Fortunately the 101 connected most of the route between their two offices. She pulled into the MedCare parking lot and flashed her badge to open the security gate.

The MedCare campus consisted of a state-of-the-art smoked glass building nestled among several acres of natural desert. Today, the rolling, puffy clouds created a beautiful performance in the building's reflection. MedCare had its own park and walking trail, which were used for both business conversations and lunchtime fitness efforts, usually between October and April when the Arizona sun wasn't so intense. Mika was an account manager in the Wellness Division, a role she had accepted four years ago after returning to the workforce. In recent years, insurance companies had started promoting programs to encourage healthy living rather than just responding when illness set in. She helped design incentives and competitions for those insured by MedCare. Customers who documented a certain number of hours at the gym could qualify for any number of prizes, usually gift cards or small electronics. MedCare had its own elaborate program, which was immediately evident to anyone entering the building.

Mika held her key card to the foyer doors and passed into the lobby, which was framed by a towering glass wall that showcased a gym with high-tech treadmills, stationary bikes, free weights and other workout equipment. At the end of the lobby were two large rooms where fitness classes were held. The standard was yoga, but the latest trends were always being added, from Zumba to a recent revival of jazzercise. The gym's prominent location in the lobby was Mika's idea. The traditional school of thought was to keep the workout facility tucked away on a higher floor, but Mika made a name for herself by challenging this plan. Two years prior, Mika's supervisor, Tanya Halvord, invited Mika to join her at a meeting with the directors who were discussing plans for the new fitness facility. Mika wasn't officially the second-in-command for the department, but everyone viewed her as such. Tanya had come to trust Mika's instincts and appreciated her thought process, and she wanted Mika there to defend their ideas.

* * *

Mika sat in a comfy leather chair at the large cherry conference table with Tanya and seven other directors from sales, technology and finance; she held a confident exterior, but she was uncomfortable at this table. She knew some of these people on an informal level, especially Don Hicks from sales, but had never been in a room with this many supervisors. *I should fake a phone call and bail,* she thought, but then the meeting abruptly started with the silent entrance of Dominik Moon, vice president of operations. Dominik was a small man in his mid-50s, demure in nature, but the room responded whenever he entered.

"Alright, let's finish this," Dominik said as he stood at the head of the table as if not expecting to stay long.

Kelly Hanson, assistant director for operations, consulted with her laptop, and the monitors on the wall flickered on. Mika watched several diagrams and three-dimensional representations roll through the screen as Kelly narrated the different options.

"Right now, we are down to the first floor or the second floor," Kelly said, "but I think we have agreed on the second floor." Mika glanced at Tanya, who shot back a discouraged look.

Don Hicks' booming voice stole the room. "That's right, Dominik. Sales supports this plan."

Of course they support this plan, Mika thought. The sales division is currently on the ground floor—no wait for the elevator, access to the garden courtyard and walking path, and down the hall from the cafeteria. Mika's dislike for Don predated this meeting. She had worked with him on a few accounts, and she considered him a pompous ass. At 6 feet 4 inches, Don was a large man who towered over people with his height and overweight frame. One of Don's sales tactics was to brag about his new Lexus or extensive traveling; he figured that if people knew that he was successful, it would increase his chance of landing the deal. If that didn't work, he would get close to people when talking, and his towering size would intimidate. In both cases, Mika hated him. His little blond mustache and large front teeth only enhanced the rat-like image that Mika had of him. He had recently been promoted to director, but spoke as if he had authority over his peers.

"It displaces fewer people, and it makes better use of prime space in the building," Don said. It was quiet for a moment. *Certainly everyone sees through his bullshit,* Mika thought. No one did, or more accurately, no one cared. The gym was a nice addition, and they didn't care where it went if it didn't directly affect them.

Dominik looked around the room. "Anyone else?"

The others followed with silent nods or an indifferent "sure" or "yes." Mika felt her heart rate increase. She looked to Tanya, expecting her to speak up. Tanya returned the look right, suggesting that the ball was in Mika's hands.

"Okay then, thank you...." Dominik started.

"Wait!" Mika startled everyone. The directors had already started thinking about different issues before being brought back to the room by this relatively unknown voice. Don was the most surprised.

"Why aren't we using the first floor?"

"Well, as I just said, and as has been outlined at previous meetings—which you did not attend—it would require moving more people. And we have better use for that space than a gym," Don said in his condescending manner. He reminded Mika of Todd in that moment.

"What do you mean by 'better use of space'?" Mika asked, her displeasure starting to become assertiveness.

"It's the lobby of our building. It's the first thing people see. What's it going to say when they see our employees sweating in shorts and a tank top?"

"First, I don't think anyone still wears tank tops to the gym." Mika laughed, alone as usual. Don continued.

"It's not a very professional image. Now, I think we are all in agreement here...."

"No we're not. I don't agree." Mika looked around the room and caught a few people smiling, including Dominik Moon. While Don was a valuable member of the company, most people found him annoying, even his supervisors.

"Why are we putting in a workout facility to begin with?" Mika asked. No one answered until Tanya saved her.

"Healthy employees save us money," Tanya said. "They take less time off from work, they are more productive when they are here, and they visit the doctor less frequently."

"Which also saves us money," said one of the finance directors, who had remained uninvolved until now.

"Right," said Mika. "But none of that happens if no one uses the facility."

"Really?" Don asked. "No one can find the second floor?"

"If we want to encourage employees to work out, hit them in the face with it right when they come in," she argued. "No one's going to go to the second floor unless they are going to the gym. On the second floor, it's out of sight, out of mind. It will be a ghost town, I promise you. But if I come in and see it in the morning, it's in my head and I am more likely to schedule a workout for that day. Or when I'm leaving and see people I know going to the gym, I'm more likely to join them."

Several heads in the room nodded. "It's the lobby of a professional complex. We have clients, CEOs, feds and state agencies who enter this building every day, and you want them to see a gym?"

"You're worried about perception? Okay, let's talk about that. Public perception is that we are a bunch of greedy, unethical bottom-dwellers," Mika said. Dominik Moon raised an eye at her. Tanya slid her hand onto Mika's knee, cuing her to tone it down. Mika proceeded without caution.

"I'm sorry, but it's true. Every story on the news about lost benefits or denied claims furthers the notion that we don't care about people. I get what we do, but the reality is that the insurance industry now sits at the bottom of the pool with accident attorneys and used car salesmen."

"Now, come on," Don interrupted, but he couldn't get another word out.

"Isn't that why we spend millions of dollars trying to keep the government off our back?" Mika continued. "Isn't that one reason why we started the Wellness Division?" She looked around the room to see a few heads nodding in agreement.

"We make a profit, but we are also serious about health and wellness, right?" Mika had an annoying habit of turning a statement into a rhetorical question. It was a secret weapon she used to close a deal; she forced you to begin agreeing, and then it was over. "Is that what we're about?" Everyone but Don expressed agreement.

"Then shouldn't that be the first impression people have when they come here, that health and wellness *is* our business and it is a priority?"

Don succumbed to the favor of the other suits in the room and nodded. "Right," he said, even though he was fuming underneath. Mika felt Tanya's hand pat her on the knee. Mika looked to Dominik Moon and said, "Well, *now* I think we are all in agreement." He smiled, nodded at her, and quietly exited the room.

The workout facility was a hit, and employees could often be found getting in a workout at various parts of the day.

* * *

Mika passed through the MedCare lobby, but today the gym was empty.

"Mika!" She turned to find Tanya hurrying to catch up with her. "You ready?"

"We'll see," she replied. Mika hadn't given much thought to today, but she could see the tension in Tanya's face. As they entered the elevator, Mika noticed the same uneasiness on the faces of several other passengers. What would typically be a ride filled with small talk and laughter was today eerily silent. For the first time since the announcement, Mika started to feel that maybe she should be nervous.

Chapter 3

Mika and Tanya entered the MedCare learning center, a large auditorium used for training sessions and, on a rare occasion, a staff meeting. Today was not a training session.

MedCare, like much of the rest of the nation, had recently experienced tough times. Two years ago, right after the workout facility issue, MedCare experienced losses for three consecutive quarters. The next four quarters leveled out, but the company was not turning much of a profit, which made shareholders nervous. The Board of Directors approved an organizational audit of the company, which entailed bringing in outsiders to evaluate MedCare's operations with a fine-tooth comb and make recommendations to eliminate redundancies, improve efficiency, and reduce financial waste. Today they would meet the interlopers, Century Consulting.

"Here we go," Tanya said, squeezing Mika's hand. "We'll talk at lunch today." Tanya moved down toward the front with the other directors. Even though she had not given this much thought, Mika knew why Tanya was nervous. Despite her argument that MedCare was about health and wellness, that was really bullshit. They were about profits *from* health and wellness, and her department was probably most expendable when it came time to cutting costs. They had already seen their budget cut twice in the past nine months.

Mika took a seat on the aisle, slightly away from the hundred or so directors and supervisors. She felt more comfortable by herself and thought that she could remain anonymous if she were not in the crowd. However, from a speaker's point of view looking at the crowd, she stood out like a sore thumb. Down below she saw Dominik Moon, other high-ranking suits, and a few unknowns shaking hands, making introductions, and engaging in small talk. Mika figured the unknowns to be members of the Century team.

Her phone vibrated, and she looked to see a text from Ryan. Before she could read it, she was interrupted.

"Well, this is going to be painful," said a voice from behind. She turned to find that someone had taken a seat behind her. A man was leaning forward, as if he had already established some intimate connection with her and needed to keep their conversation private. When Mika moved past her surprise, she saw that he had incredibly good looks, highlighted by chestnut eyes that sparkled with his ivory smile. His steel-gray hair misguided people to initially believe he was much older than his actual age of 38. Mika had not seen him before. *Bad time to be new to the company,* she thought. She tried to shake off his good looks and smiled politely.

"Yeah," she said. She started to turn back around, but he spoke again.

"Are you worried?"

Shit, why is he talking to me? Mika hated small talk, no matter how good looking a guy was.

"I don't know. Not really."

"That's a good attitude. I mean, what the hell do these people know, right?" He laughed, trying to engage her in a smile. She didn't oblige. "What have you heard about them?"

I guess we're having a conversation. "Not much. They come in, spend some time with us, make us sweat for a few months while they determine if we're worthy of keeping our jobs."

"Do we have a nickname for them yet?"

"It depends on who you ask."

"Like...?"

"Storm troopers."

"Storm troopers," he chuckled.

"You know, from Star Wars. But that's from the comptrollers."

"What else?"

"The death squad. Trolls. Baby killers. Anal crabs. The Gestapo...."

"Anal crabs? Wow!" He leaned back, taking that one in, slightly amused.

Why am I still talking to this guy, she asked herself. Something about his smile kept her involved. "Not my favorite, but we'll see," she said. "Maybe it fits."

"Let's hope not." He stood and straightened his light grey suit jacket. He set his hand on her shoulder, almost as a way of thanking her for her time. "Well, thanks for sharing. Maybe we can chat more later." He smiled that damn smile again and then headed down the stairs. She watched him join the suits at the front of the room. Faces lit up as people saw her mystery man, and they shook his hand or patted him on the shoulder. Dominik Moon even shook his hand and whispered in his ear before motioning for everyone to sit down.

Shit, Mika thought as she started to realize his identity. *Just don't be the boss, she thought. Dear God, just be an assistant or something.*

Dominik Moon stood at the podium, silently bringing the meeting to a start.

"I know this is a stressful time for all of us. Uncertainty can bring that," he said with a dryness that was surprisingly reassuring. "MedCare has faced tough times, and we have endured. But for our own long-term health, we must stop and evaluate where we are so we can move forward with certainty. But you know why we're here, so I don't need to rehash the past. I just want to stress how important this process is, and how important it is for everyone in this room to be supportive."

Please just be an assistant.

"Let me turn this over to the team from Century Consulting. This will be their home for the next few months, so lets consider them part of our family."

Maybe he's the driver! He drove the damn company van....

"At this time, I am going to turn it over to Jayce Beckett from Century Consulting."

For Mika, time stopped as Dominik Moon stepped aside. She waited for this Jayce Beckett to stand. Members of the Century team smiled at each other before—finally—he stood. The gray-haired, chestnut-eyed mystery man with the ivory smile approached the microphone.

Fuck!

Chapter 4

Jayce Beckett was a gifted speaker. He was natural and spontaneous in his delivery, and he displayed a great sense of humor. After a round of applause that was more than polite but far from enthusiastic, Jayce looked around the room and smiled.

"Now, now, that's not necessary," he said, putting on humility like a standup comedian setting up his punch line. "Especially since I know you don't mean it." He laughed, and the audience followed suit, relieving some of the tension that suffocated the room.

Mika stared him down from her private corner, seething. *Oh, so you're the funny one?* She hated him for what she perceived to be a trick several moments ago. She hated him because he caught her off guard with his good looks. And she hated him because he had charisma, which Mika considered to be the devil's blend of charm and wit that allowed people to skate by on style over substance. She had seen it too often with some of the best salesmen, usually men who could engage their customers, lure them in with their smiles and winks, and then once the deal is signed, leave them somehow feeling less than satisfied. Mika had spoken with Jayce for only a few moments, and she was definitely less than satisfied.

"We are very excited to be here at MedCare," he continued. "We know what a rich tradition MedCare has for not only taking care of its customers, but also for taking care of its employees. And yet, I know—we all know—that our presence makes some of you nervous."

You make me sick.

"I assure you that the reason we are here is to allow MedCare to continue to prosper, to continue to provide for its employees. We have no preconceived notions about how to do that, and we have no plans for eliminating anyone or anything. We come with one goal…"

To smile pretty and be an asshole.

"…to help you achieve your potential. Yes, in the end that might mean that your leadership has to make some tough decisions, but it also might just mean that some things are done differently. Now, most of you have not been through a process like this before, but obviously we have. So, don't worry, I already know about the secret signals you will give to alert your colleagues of our presence." He pretended to make a phone call: "The bathroom is flooded. I repeat, the bathroom is flooded." Everyone laughed. "And I'm sure many of you already have nicknames for us." He looked toward Mika and winked.

Did he just wink at me? Go fuck yourself with that wink!

"Keep doing those things. I get it. And as a fun little challenge, I am willing to buy lunch for the department that comes up with the best nickname for us." Several subdued laughs rang from the crowd. "Well, to be accurate, I'm going to expense the lunch to Mr. Moon, so…." The laughs grew as he smiled at Dominik Moon, who also chuckled. "Alright, let me introduce my team so you know who we are. First, we have Ray Blanchard." Ray, a stocky man whose bald crown shined atop the stretch of hair that wrapped around his head, stood and acknowledged the polite round of applause. Mika's phone vibrated, and she read a text from Tanya.

TH: K, if we're getting fired, this guy can do it. HOT!"

MJ: NOT!

Jayce continued to introduce the other members of his team, but Mika had stopped listening. She read through a few other text messages, including the one from her son.

RJ: Going to Emily's after practice.

MJ: Not tonight. Dinner.

As she waited for his acknowledgment, another text came from Tanya.

TH: You're sitting 2 far away. Or you're sick. HOT!

Mika considered a reply, but didn't want to devote any more of her life to Jayce Beckett. Then, Ryan's response came.

RJ: What? Why?

She contemplated her response. Ryan's question was legitimate; they were not a family that typically ate dinner together, not since he had entered high school anyway. Ryan's practice schedule and Todd's growing client list kept everyone on different schedules, and Mika was secretly okay with that.

MJ: Because.

As she finished typing, her colleagues noisily stood, talking in hushed tones with each other as they filed out of their rows. She looked down to see Jayce Beckett and his team talking with different directors and executives, including Don Hicks. She tried to exit the room quickly but ended up stuck in a logjam of people headed for the doors. Mika stared intently at her phone, trying to avoid getting caught up in a conversation with those around her. She didn't want to hear everyone's predictions about what the future held, nor did she want to hear the likely comments about the charming Jayce Beckett. Just as she reached the doorway, someone tugged at her arm from behind. She turned to see Tanya, and they exited together. Tanya pulled her aside in the corridor.

"Not hot? Seriously?"

"He's not."

Tanya stared at her, dumbfounded.

"Okay. Yes, he's okay looking—"

"Okay?"

"—but I don't find arrogance attractive."

"You thought he was arrogant?"

"Yes. Maybe that's not the right word... he just rubbed me the wrong way."

"Can't you just separate—" but before Tanya could finish, they were interrupted by a familiar voice.

"Excuse me."

Mika turned to find herself once again face-to-face with Jayce Beckett.

"I'm sorry to interrupt, I just wanted to introduce myself. I'm Jayce Beckett." He smiled and twinkled his eyes in a way that made Mika want to kick him in the teeth.

"I'm Tanya Halvord, from Wellness."

"Wellness, interesting concept for a medical insurance company," he smiled.

Mika took a small step back, hoping she could just slip away.

"I know, right? And if you recommend cutting us, you're going to have to deal with Mika here."

No, no, don't say my name.

Jayce turned to Mika and extended his hand. "Mika?"

Shit! She reluctantly shook his hand. His long, narrow fingers were strong but delicate, and they swallowed her entire hand. Mika tried to pull away as soon as their hands touched, but he held on firmly for what Mika felt was an eternity. She knew this routine: establish a physical connection by holding the shake for an extra moment, smile wide and twinkle those eyes. It made people feel important, but it wasn't going to work on her. She smiled and looked in his eyes as she had done with every professional introduction, but quickly withdrew both.

"Mika Jones, also with Wellness," she said, and he finally let go of her hand.

"Mika, nice to meet you, formally. I hope I didn't offend you earlier by not introducing myself."

"No, of course not. Why would I be offended?" *Damn right, I was offended.* "If anything, I probably offended you." *Not that I care.*

"No, no, not at all. As I said, this is what I do, so I know what happens. It's just nice to get a chance to talk to people before they know who I am, even if it means being called a venereal disease." He laughed, trying to relieve Mika of any tension she may have from the incident.

"I am so sorry about that." *No I'm not. You are an anal crab.*

"Like I said, no need. Well, I need to get back to the team, but I look forward to talking with you again. I can't wait to hear about wellness." He winked at Mika again before retreating back through the auditorium doors.

Damn it! Stop winking at me!

Mika turned back and was startled to find a very confused Tanya, whom Mika had almost forgotten about.

"Venereal disease?" Tanya escorted her down the corridor toward the elevators. "What the hell happened?"

Chapter 5

Mika stood barefoot in her kitchen, grating a block of white cheddar cheese. Behind her, steam rose from a pot of boiling macaroni. Her three-cheese and artichoke macaroni dish was her go-to comfort food, and tonight she needed comfort. Mika had spent the morning with Tanya, recounting her exchange with Jayce Beckett— twice—and then listening to her team speculate on many issues. Would they be downsized? Would they be eliminated? What should they all say to send a consistent message? Will they get to speak with Jayce, and if so, will he take off his shirt? It was the same type of gossipy drivel that Mika avoided in college, and today's dose was enough to send her straight to a dinner of unapologetic carbs, gooey cheese, and artichokes.

Todd was upstairs responding to emails on his computer, providing Mika with some solitude. She tried to focus on sliding the block of cheese against the stainless steel grater, but her thoughts kept bringing her back to the same image: Jayce Beckett's wink. Had he not sat behind her and tricked her into saying the things she did, perhaps the wink would not bother her as much. But, she viewed it as a nail in his coffin, and she couldn't get it out of her head.

"Hi, Mom." Ryan's voice startled her, and she almost took off a chunk of skin in the grater. Still, Mika was glad to hear her son's voice. She needed the distraction to clear her mind of today's events. She looked up, but her natural smile quickly became work to maintain when she saw Emily by his side.

"Hi, Mrs. Jones," she said, as the two sat on stools at the kitchen island.

"How are you, Emily?" she asked, still forcing a smile.

"Good, thanks. Wow, that's a lot," she said, peering into a bowl of cheese resting between her and Mika.

"Emily's going to stay for dinner, okay?" Ryan asked, pinching a small amount of cheese and dropping it into his mouth.

Great. Just great.

"Great, that's great. How was practice?"

Ryan shrugged. "Okay."

"Just okay?"

"I don't know. It was practice." He took more cheese and dropped it into Emily's open hand.

"How's Mark's hand?"

Mark Cousins swam freestyle for Desert Horizon High School, and he had finished third in state the previous season in the 100 free. He was also the anchor for the medley relay team, and Ryan swam breaststroke. Ryan had a relatively late start to swimming, picking it up as a freshman to satisfy his parents' demand that he be a part of something in high school after deciding to give up baseball. He and Mark had been best friends at the time, two lost souls who found each other during 8th grade lunch, sharing sandwiches and their love for *Arrested Development* and *The Office*. Mark had been swimming since he was five, and he was a natural in the water. Despite his athletic superiority, he was always supportive of Ryan, who had never risen to Mark's level. Ryan was just good enough to compete at State in the breaststroke, and he had earned a spot on the relay team. All had been good between the two until Emily entered the scene this past summer. Mika noticed that the more time Ryan spent with Emily, the less Mark's name came up. Two weeks before school started, Mark broke his hand at a party, which put his swim season at risk.

"I guess it's better," Ryan said, clearly disinterested in continuing this path of conversation.

"I heard he'll be back in the water next week. Lucky us," Emily said, the last few words soaked in sarcasm.

I wasn't talking to you, Mika thought.

"Good. Hopefully you guys will be at full strength against Hamilton." A timer beeped, and Mika dumped the cooked pasta into a colander in the sink. The steam rose to her face, and she felt her pores open, releasing some of the tension that had been building.

"Where's Dad?" Ryan asked.

"Where do you think? Go tell him that dinner will be ready in ten minutes." Mika quickly regretted her words as Ryan kissed his girlfriend on the shoulder and ran upstairs to his father's den, leaving her alone with Emily. She moved to the stove and prepared a roux, spooning flour into a saucepan of melted butter.

As Mika whisked she could feel Emily watching her in awkward silence. Emily finally spoke.

"Can I help with anything?"

"No, I've got it. Thank you."

"Do you always use butter for your roux?"

"Yes...." She was surprised that Emily knew what she was doing. "You know what a roux is? Do you cook?"

"When I have to. My mom was sick a lot, so we watched a lot of Food Network together. I started doing some of the cooking, and I just copied some of what I saw on TV."

"Who's your favorite chef? Emeril?"

"Umm, I don't know who that is."

"He's a chef. The 'Bam!' guy."

"I don't think he's on anymore."

Mika frowned as she realized that the last time she watched a cooking show was when Ryan was a baby. "So, who do you like?"

"I don't know. I like Alton Brown because he explains a lot. I've used some of Giada's recipes. My dad loves Italian, so you know." Mika nodded, but she didn't know either of those names. She started piling cheese into the saucepan. Silence again, which Mika broke this time.

"What was wrong?"

"What do you mean?"

"With your mom? Is she okay?"

"She has lupus. It took awhile to figure out. She was down a lot." Ryan re-entered the kitchen.

Mika stopped stirring the cheese and looked at Emily for the first time tonight. "How is she?"

"She's good. She manages it most of the time. Now that they know what she's dealing with, she can manage it better."

"Dad said to start without him," Ryan said, draping his arms around Emily. Emily stood up and quietly nudged Ryan toward the living room. He tried to hide his smile, but Mika caught it.

"Call when dinner's ready," he said, pulling Emily into the next room.

Mika smelled something burning and quickly returned to her sauce, rescuing it from the heat before it became a complete disaster. She stirred in the remainder of the cheese, and she was sad. She had only met Emily's mother once at last year's swim banquet, and she had no idea that she had anything wrong with her. It's not like they lived in a small town where everyone knew one another's business, but she felt guilty just the same, as if she should have been there to help in some way. Guilty that even though she didn't want to do anything to validate her son's relationship with Emily—like meeting her parents—she should have reached out to establish a connection. Guilty that she had been blessed with a healthy body and family but didn't always appreciate it. And Mika felt guilty that Emily had to watch her mother suffer, much like she had done with her own mother.

Chapter 6

The Wellness Division windows faced west, revealing the picturesque Papago Mountains, a series of red sandstone buttes that grew out of the desert sand. They weren't very tall, but they made a beautiful impression on the landscape. Mika could see the dust clouds forming way in the distance behind them, and she wondered whether or not they would roll in and bring them rain. The desert heat had extended into late October with high temperatures still in the 90s, and Mika was eager for some relief. The skies had teased her in the past few weeks, but they never delivered any rain.

She sat at her desk, sitting tall on her ergonomic balance ball chair as she returned her attention to an email from a client. Whereas most departments were a series of cubicles defined by low partitions, the Wellness Division was much more cutting-edge contemporary with its open concept. Shortly after starting the department, Tanya decided that it should represent the very wellness that they intended to promote. She eliminated the traditional desks and partitions, replacing them with conference tables where several employees could sit with their laptops. This not only encouraged collaboration, she argued, but also prevented the mind from feeling closed in. The office also included several new-age wellness items, including the ergonomic ball chair that Mika sat upon.

Mika liked the office setup; she found it invigorating to be a part of a team, and she felt empowered whenever she entered the open space. Until today.

She had written a "6" on a Post-It and affixed it to the top of her laptop. This represented the number of days MedCare had been held hostage by the intruders from Century. If a company could have a libido, MedCare's had been stifled by Jayce Beckett and his team.

People tried to put the process out of their minds, and most departments did a good job of looking like it was business as usual. But as the meeting times with Century grew closer, so did the anxiety. Emotions were less stable. What was a joke last week wasn't quite as funny today. Just being cordial required a little more energy. It was like MedCare was experiencing PMS, and today was the Wellness Division's time for cramping and bloating.

Now, the usual buzz of energy in the office had been stifled. Everyone smiled and was pleasant, but Mika could feel the tension. She noticed it in the way a coworker sat hunched at her computer, or the way someone's eyes darted around the room while talking on the phone. Their scheduled meetings with a representative from Century were today, and for most of the women in the office, the silver lining was a chance to sit across from Jayce Beckett; Mika dreaded the thought.

She sent her email, and then stared at her screen, lost in an empty thought. She didn't want to be here today, but she was stuck, quite literally. Mika was without a car so Todd could drive north to see a client. She had started an online search for car reviews when her Fitness Challenge dinged with a request. One of their products was an intra-office social media outlet, where employees could challenge each other to different workouts. They knew that people who exercise with a partner or group often stayed more committed to their fitness plans, so this provided an opportunity for coworkers to encourage each other. Tanya and Mika developed the program from scratch, and it was one of their more successful products. Mika clicked on the envelope icon; it was from Sheri in IT, and she was challenging the entire wellness team to attend her yoga class after work.

"Hope to see you at 5:30 for a rigorous and therapeutic session of yoga! Namaste –Sheri"

She clicked "maybe" and sent her reply. Mika wasn't a fan of yoga. She wanted to be, but Todd had squelched her budding enthusiasm last year. Whenever Todd realized that he needed to lose a few pounds, he would start on a fitness kick. Cycling. Hiking. Running. Racquetball. Todd did them all, and initially Mika joined him. She had stopped a few years back, though, for two reasons. First,

Todd was uber competitive, keeping track of times and scores in what Mika considered an unhealthy manner. When they hiked, he kept time and constantly reminded Mika that she needed to "pick it up" so they could beat their best. When they played racquetball, he was clearly the dominant player, but he never praised her for any improvement. When they cycled, there was no time to stop to check out an open house or a beautiful view. He played hard, which she respected, but it wasn't for her. More importantly, though, Mika had stopped working out with her husband because she didn't feel that he wanted her there as a workout partner; he wanted her to lose weight or tone up for his own satisfaction.

After Sheri had become a certified yoga instructor 18 months ago, she started inviting employees to her classes. Mika had ignored the invites for the first few months, but as she heard different people talk about the class, she became intrigued. *Maybe this could be my niche*, she thought. After work one day, she stopped at a Lululemon and picked up a mat, some yoga pants and a tank. She told Todd about it at dinner, and her excitement grew. That night, Todd crawled onto her side of the bed and initiated a rare night of sex. They rolled around in their usual fashion before she ended up naked and on top of him. After they both came, she slowed down her rhythm, still making use of his erection and thinking about getting him going for a second round. Todd slid his hands along her sweaty thighs, around the curves of her hips and finally resting on her ass. He squeezed.

"I can't imagine how hot you'll be when you start doing yoga," he said with a little smutty laugh.

Mika's slowing rhythm came to a quick stop, and she rolled off of him. She knew that if she confronted him on this comment, he would get defensive and say that she was misreading a compliment. Maybe she was, she thought, but it didn't change how she felt. And with that, her enthusiasm for yoga ended. Since buying her mat just over a year ago, she had attended just four classes, and she did so strictly out of support for the program. Her outfit still sat in a duffle bag in her locker.

Mika looked at the clock and saw that her Century meeting was in 15 minutes. *Here we go*, she thought as she logged out of her computer. *Be smart.* She left the department and headed for the elevator. Her hands felt clammy, so she made a quick turn into the bathroom. As she washed her hands, she stared at herself in the mirror. She lifted her chin to make sure she had blended her foundation, something she constantly worried about because it was such a pet peeve of hers with other women. She was happy with her makeup, and overall, she felt she looked good.

He better not wink at me.

Mika headed for the elevator and pushed the button for the 9th floor. Her hands still felt sweaty, her heart started to race, and it pissed her off.

Why are you so nervous? Fuck him.

The elevator doors opened, and Tanya exited.

"How did it go?" Mika asked in a lowered voice. She held the door open with her hand as she and Tanya had a close, hushed conversation.

"It was fine. Just relax."

"What did they ask?"

"Just some basic stuff. Describe your day. Who do you interact with the most? Who do you need to interact with more? What's your biggest challenge? Seriously, it's kind of an interesting conversation."

"Who was there?" *I hope it's not him.*

"That's the part that sucked. Jayce wasn't there. It was Ray, the balding guy with the wrap-around."

Thank fucking God! Mika immediately felt her heart rate slow down, and she stepped into the elevator.

"Find me when you're finished," Tanya said as the doors closed.

Her hands were still a little sticky, but Mika was more relaxed and confident as she rode to the 9th floor. She stopped focusing on her nerves and looked forward to defending her department and their work. She smiled as she walked past a series of conference rooms. *Let's do this!*

She came to the end of the hallway to room F. The door was partly open. She didn't know whether to wait for someone to come get her or just go in, but she used her sudden burst of confidence to knock on the door and take a step in.

"Hello?"

The room was empty save for a stack of files, a legal pad, and a laptop resting on the eight-foot cherry wood table that ran the length of the room. She stepped to the table and strained to see if she could read anything on the legal pad. She was interrupted by a familiar voice.

"Good afternoon." It wasn't Ray.

She turned to find Jayce Beckett entering the room and reaching for a handshake.

"Are your ready to do this?" He smiled.

Fuck.

Chapter 7

Mika sat across from her gray-haired adversary. She had been rattled when he first entered, but she was able to recover and now sat with confidence. She noticed that Jayce was relaxed, perhaps too relaxed, and this irritated her even more.

"Mika Jones." He gave a smile, which she did not return.

"Mr. Beckett."

"Jayce, please."

You smug son of a bitch. Let's see if I can rattle him a bit.

"Okay," she agreed without saying his name.

"Well, I know you've been explained the process, but do you have any questions?"

"No, not really." She was determined to give him as little as possible. Jayce's eyes narrowed, as if analyzing her.

"Okay then. Well, I'm going to ask some questions, but this isn't an inquisition," he laughed.

She intentionally joined his laughter so she would appear less bitchy. "It's close, though, right?"

Jayce recoiled a little. "No, it's not like that at all. I'm really looking for a conversation. I want to hear your perspective."

"But it's you asking me questions, right?"

"Right."

"So you're here in an official capacity, and you're asking me—all of us—questions. Then you're going to come to some conclusions about how we operate, where we waste money, how and when we are inefficient, things like that. Right?" He nodded. "It may lack the blood and guts of medieval times, but some capitalist might not see a difference between this and an inquisition."

Jayce leaned back and studied her again. "Okay, so maybe this is an inquisition."

Mika let out a condescending chuckle. "See, there you go." *One for me,* she thought.

Jayce placed his hands on the table, as if surrendering. "But, for the record, we also point out areas of strength and examples of efficiency and excellence."

"I'm sure you do. Mr. Beckett."

"Jayce."

"I know."

Jayce stood and took a few steps to a hook on the wall. Mika now noticed his suit, which was not only a beautiful dark gray that nicely complemented his chestnut eyes and steel-grey hair, it was also tightly trimmed and accentuated his great shape.

"I need to get comfortable if you're going to keep roughing me up," he said as he removed his jacket and hung it on the hook. Mika saw that his fitted white shirt pulled at his broad shoulders and round biceps.

Stop it! Focus on something else. She turned her attention to the wood grain of the table.

"So, tell me about the Wellness Division," Jayce said, returning to his seat.

"What do you want to know?"

"What would you like me to know?"

"I want you to know that we are an important part of this company, that it can be easy to look at us as dispensable when evaluating the bottom line." Mika was setting aside her dislike for Jayce, as well as her admiration for his tight shirt. Now she was getting into her zone.

Jayce wrote down a quick word on his legal pad, but Mika couldn't see what it was. "Tell me more about that," he said. And Mika did. She spent the next 15 minutes repeating a monologue she had given more than a dozen times. She talked about the need to balance capital growth with customer advocacy. She cited obesity and declining health rates, and connected poor health management with long-term cost increases. She pointed out the hypocrisy of any company in the health industry that fails to actually promote healthy living. And when she was finished, she felt invigorated and satisfied in saying everything that needed to be said. Mika looked across the table at his legal pad and saw that Jayce hadn't added more to the one word he had written earlier. *What the hell?*

"You're dead on. You don't have to defend your work to me."

She gave him a confused and irritated look. "You're the one who is going to recommend cuts. You're exactly the person I need to show our value to."

"First, this isn't just about cuts. It's about making recommendations about—."

"—how to operate better," she interrupted. "The good, the bad. Yeah, I got that."

"But you don't believe me?" He smiled, but something in his eyes gave Mika the impression that he was disappointed. She withdrew her claws for the moment.

"It's not that I don't believe *you*. It's just that this is business. I get it. We have an obligation to our shareholders. If our profits had been setting records this past year, you wouldn't be here, would you?"

Jayce nodded. "Probably not."

"I just wish it was about more than that."

Jayce started to write something, but then stopped. He leaned back in his chair.

"So, how did you get here?" he asked. Mika wasn't completely sure of his question, so she tried to be funny.

"I took the elevator."

Jayce just stared at her.

Okay, that was stupid, she thought. But then Jayce smiled, picked up his pen and started writing.

"Took the elevator... funniest line today. I'm writing that down. Seriously, how did you end up working in Wellness? What was your background that brought you here?"

Mika thought for a moment. She wasn't ready for this question. "I don't know. I just ended up here." And the truth was, she didn't remember the details, only that this was not something she had planned. When Ryan was in 7th grade, her marriage had slipped into a dark period filled with animosity and bitterness. In one of their couple's sessions, the marriage counselor had suggested that she return to work to regain some footing and confidence. Before Ryan, she had been an account representative for Federal Express, and fourteen years later she was interviewing with Tanya for a position they had just created. She couldn't remember who told her about the opening or how she came in contact with Tanya, only that it seemed to just happen amidst the tornado of sadness and anger that was consuming her life.

"Nobody just ends up somewhere," he said. He seemed to want to probe more, but then changed his tone. "That's alright. I'm just fascinated by how some things come to be."

"So what was the second thing?"

"What do you mean?"

"You said, '*First*, this isn't about cuts.' Was there a 'second'?"

He thought for a moment, and Mika noticed the little crinkle that formed between his eyes.

Damn it, Mika! Stop it!

"Oh, right. I was going to say that I know you have value. I believe in preventative medicine, and I try to live it. I try to eat well and take care of myself."

That's obvious… stop it, Mika!

"I know that how I live and feel when I am 60 or 70 depends on what I do now, so I get it. Personally, I believe in what you do. I know the importance of what you do. And for the record, I know the value of Mika Jones."

She laughed, nervously. "You do?"

"Yes, your name has come up on more than one occasion here. You are well-regarded by your colleagues."

What? Who the hell mentioned my name? Is he kidding?

Mika felt her face turn red. "Oh, I'm not so sure about that."

"Trust me." He winked at her.

Oh please, don't do that….

Jayce straightened up and pulled his legal pad closer to his body. "Alright, I do have some other questions I need to ask. Okay?"

"Of course." And Mika answered his questions about department goals, her typical day, her interactions with others, office policies and protocol, and program descriptions. She spoke with comfort and passion, and when he said they were finished, Mika saw that their meeting had run 32 minutes past the hour that had been scheduled.

"I'm sorry. I probably rambled a bit there," she said, as they both stood.

"Not at all," he said, extending his hand, a smile, and sparkle in his eye. "I enjoyed hearing what you had to say." He winked.

Wait! Did I get suckered again? Did I tell him too much? That fucking wink!

She reached across and shook his hand, making sure not to notice how his skin felt against hers.

"Thank you, Mr. Beckett."

Chapter 8

"I think I screwed us," Mika said, sitting across from Tanya at a nearby Starbucks.

"You didn't screw us," Tanya said with confidence while emptying a sugar packet into her coffee.

Mika wasn't so sure.

After leaving Conference Room F an hour earlier, Mika's emotions swirled. Her blood initially buzzed from talking about her job and her opinions, and she felt she had effectively expressed herself. But each step away from the conference room was a step into a pit of doubt and paranoia. She worried that he had used his charm and good looks to get her to lower her guard and make a mistake that she couldn't identify.

Why did he enjoy hearing what I had to say? No matter what he says, he is going to cut programs. That's the goal, right? Did I give him ammunition? And why does he keep winking at me? What the hell did I say?

As soon as she had exited the elevator, Tanya whisked her away to their local Starbucks, where they now sat.

"What the hell did you say?" Tanya asked.

Mika sipped her iced green tea and tried to replay the conversation in her mind, but she was so flustered that she couldn't remember the specific words she had used.

"I don't know. Same old stuff, you know? I talked about moral purpose and giving something tangible." She slid her fingers to the back of her neck, applying a little pressure to release some of her tension. "I talked about the Virgin Active study and Dr. Glazer's article...."

Tanya almost spit out her coffee. "You talked to him about that? Why would you bring that up?"

"I don't know. We were talking, and he's just really easy to talk to. I kind of mentioned it as a joke."

"And because he's hot."

"No, seriously. I don't know. I only mentioned it."

"You just decided to bring up that exercise increases blood circulation in your penis and vagina, which can lead to better sex? That just came out of nowhere?"

"I didn't say it like that," Mika said, defensively.

"What words did you use? Pubic area?"

"No."

"Vajayjay? Box? Girly bits?" Tanya enjoyed egging her on.

"No! I don't know exactly. It was about 20 seconds of a 90-minute meeting. It was no big deal"

"How did he respond? Did he blush? Did he smile? Was he aroused?"

"I wasn't paying attention." Mika was getting flustered.

"Bull. And I still don't understand why you got him while the rest of us had the Wrap Around."

"Because he's an asshole, that's why. He's messing with me."

"He's probably not an asshole."

"Really? He tricked me in the lecture hall—."

"—Or you just opened your mouth more than you should have to a complete stranger" Tanya interrupted.

Mika ignored her comment. "And then he catches me off guard so I will say things that I shouldn't say."

Tanya saw the concern on Mika's face and turned serious. She took Mika's hands and looked into her eyes. "I'm sure we have nothing to worry about. The department is where it is today because of you, and nothing you could have said can ruin that. You know your stuff, and you're the best person to speak for us."

"I don't know why, but I just hate that guy. Really."

As they drove back to the MedCare office, Mika noticed the clouds moving in over the Valley.

"Shit, it's going to rain. Any chance you can give me a ride home today? Todd has the car."

"Sorry. I'm just dropping you off. I have an appointment across town that's going to run late. When are you going to get a new car?"

"Don't ask. I'll figure something out."

They turned into the MedCare campus. Tanya rolled down her window and activated the gate with her security badge. "Catch a ride with Sheri. She lives your way."

"No she doesn't. She lives in Mesa."

"When did she move?"

"About a year ago. Besides, her car smells like dog."

Tanya pulled the car up to the curb, and Mika opened her door. "See you tomorrow, if I decide to come in," Mika laughed.

"Hey, I'm sure you did great. Relax."

"Thanks." Mika closed the door and ascended the wide steps to the entrance. She was tired of reflecting on her conversation with Jayce Beckett, and tired of hyper-focusing on the words she could remember using. She knew that it would continue if she returned to her office, so she made a detour to the sales department to meet with a few of the agents. She spent an hour getting updates on two new accounts they were recruiting. She and the agents exchanged some ideas about what the clients needed, and she took notes on what she needed for their next meeting. It was the type of mental activity Mika needed to stop thinking about her meeting with Jayce. She left the sales department feeling much more balanced and positive than she had an hour before.

Fuck Jayce Beckett, she thought. *I kicked ass. I kick ass. The Wellness Division kicks ass, and if he says otherwise, I'll kick his ass.*

Mika entered the Wellness Division and immediately noticed that it was empty. It was the end of the day, but it was unusual for everyone to be gone. She was relieved. Even though she was in better spirits, Mika didn't want to have another discussion about her meeting. She checked her watch; if she hurried, she could catch the 5:15 bus.

She grabbed a few files from her workspace and tossed them into her black leather Tumi computer bag. She started to pack up her laptop when she noticed that her Fitness Challenge was open.

Come on, Sheri. I already responded.

She went to close it, but she stopped cold as she read the invitation. She reread it twice more.

"I would love to see you at the 5:30 yoga class! See you there… Jayce Beckett."

Chapter 9

Mika was an emotional mess again, only this time it was resulting in a focused tornado of anger ready to land on Jayce Beckett. She rode the elevator to the first floor, rehearsing her impending confrontation.

Aren't you supposed to come in here to help us be a better company? Where does harassing me fit in that job description? Why the hell are you inviting me to yoga? Is that some kind of attempt at hitting on me? Why don't we ask Dominik Moon what he thinks of it? We'll just downward-facing-dog your sweet ass out of here.

The elevator doors opened, and she saw her target standing in front of one of the fitness rooms, talking with Sheri. She almost didn't recognize him in his basketball shorts and tight t-shirt as she marched toward him.

There you are, fuck face.

"Mika Jones," he said, and his ivory smile almost knocked her off course.

"You made it," Sheri added, but Mika didn't really hear her.

"Mr. Beckett, may I have a word with you?" It was more of a demand than a question as she walked off to the side of the hallway. He followed.

"You're not dressed for yoga," he said, innocently.

"No, I'm not. I'm trying to figure out what you have against me?"

"What do you mean?"

"First there was your little stunt before I knew who you were. Then, everyone else gets interviewed by the Wrap Ar... by someone else on your team, but you pop in on me at the last second. And now you're sending me personal invitations to yoga class. I'm not sure what you're trying to do, but I would like you to leave me alone."

Jayce looked at her, started to speak, and then stopped. He ran his fingers through his hair and then let out a small laugh.

"What?"

"I invited the whole Wellness Division." He gestured to the fitness room behind him.

Mika looked past him and saw several of her colleagues stretching inside the fitness room. Now she was definitely blown off course and at a loss for words.

Oh my God. That's why the office was empty. I'm a fucking dumb ass!

"After we interviewed your team today, I decided to try your fitness challenge. If I had known it would upset you so much, I really wouldn't have done it. I'm truly sorry."

Mika was humiliated and wanted to disappear, yet she was grounded somewhat by the compassionate tone in his voice.

"I am such a bitch."

Jayce let out a hearty laugh, and he put his hand on her shoulder.

"No, that's okay," he said, but she didn't hear it because his touch had shut down her other senses. She didn't hear anything, she couldn't smell, and her vision blurred. She only felt the pressure of his five fingers as they pressed lightly into her shoulder, carrying with them the same compassion of his voice. She felt intoxicated, but pushed hard to sober up before she fell down drunk. She stepped back out of his reach, and Jayce's face came back into focus.

"No. I'm so sorry. I'm just having a rough day, and I shouldn't have taken it out on you."

"No worries. We all have those. You know what's good for stress?"

Wine? A good fuck?

"Yoga," he continued. "Someone mentioned that in a meeting today." He chuckled. "Do you have your clothes?"

She still had clothes in her locker "just in case." Mika didn't want him to know that she was indeed able to join the class; she just wanted to go home.

"Um, yes. They're in my locker," she muttered. *Shit! Why did I just say that?*

"Great," he said. "I'll see you inside then." He turned and entered the fitness room. Through the glass wall, Mika watched his broad shoulders as they struggled to stay inside his t-shirt.

This sucks.

She stood frozen, torn between two worlds: one where she walks into the locker room and changes clothes, and the other where she exits the building and walks the entire 26 miles home. She didn't want to do yoga; she didn't want to do anything. But if she left, she knew that she would have to explain tomorrow why she wasn't there. She was angry again. Angry that she admitted that she had clothes in her locker. Angry that she was worried about her job. Angry that she was going to have to take the bus. Angry that Jayce Beckett had such great arms to match his eyes and smile. Much to her dismay, her feet steered her into the women's locker room.

She took her cloth duffel bag from her locker and withdrew her pants and top, staring at them as if waiting for them to say, "Put us back in the bag and let's get out of here." She quickly changed, not because she was in a rush to get to class, but because she was never comfortable being naked around others. Even as a child at sleepovers, she would lock herself in the bathroom and then step into the tub before changing. She wasn't that extreme anymore, but the issue still lingered.

Mika folded her skirt and blouse and shoved them inside her bag. *I'll just wear my yoga clothes home.* She turned and faced the mirror. Typically, she wouldn't mind what she saw. Her black yoga pants accentuated well-defined calves and a nice curve up along the hips. Her capped-sleeve shirt was form-fitting, highlighting c-cup breasts that still had some bounce. Despite some softness that had developed in her arms, her triceps and shoulders still had slight definition. But today Mika could only see the soft bits of flesh here and there that she wished were tighter. She spread her fingers and pressed her hands down her sides, as if the skin might stay stretched if she did it slowly enough.

Blah!

She lifted her arms to see if she had any stubble showing. She didn't see any, but she retrieved a disposable razor from her bag and gave each pit a quick swipe anyway before shoving her bag into her locker and proceeding to the fitness room.

The yoga class was near full, which was unusual. Mika looked around the room and quickly counted six women who were likely there simply to spend time with Jayce Beckett. *Losers*, she thought, taking a mat and maneuvering to a vacant spot in the back. She was three mats away from Jayce, who nodded at her. Mika's stomach instinctively sucked in and tightened, which immediately embarrassed her. *What the hell are you doing? Forget about him.* She focused on stretching, and she felt little pops and tugs from places deep inside, making her realize just how long it had been since she exercised. *Okay, this is going to suck.*

Sheri dimmed the lights and took control of the room, which to this point had been a blend of those genuinely getting ready to work out mixed with some high school wannabes whispering about the hot guy in the room.

"Welcome," Sheri said in a surprising low and soothing voice that contradicted the exuberance and energy that defined her during the day, and the disconnect bothered Mika. "Let's start with sukhasana," she said, and Mika followed everyone's lead into a sitting position with her legs crossed. "I see a lot of new faces here, so please remember that this journey is about you."

Stop with the voice, already!

"Do what you can do, make the necessary accommodations, and honor where you are right now. Let's close our eyes and establish your intentions for today. It could be increased strength, flexibility, peace, or whatever it is you want from today."

I want you to shut up.

"Let's take a few deep breaths, filling your belly," Sheri continued, and Mika could hear the heavy exhales from across the room. She wasn't comfortable enough to produce a similar noise. "And with your last exhale, send those intentions out to the universe."

The deep breathing had calmed Mika. *All right, I'm going to do this*, Mika thought, and she followed Sheri's lead sun salutations. She reached over her head, folded into uttanasana followed by a half lift into ardha uttanasana, and then dropped into plank position before lowering herself and then lifting into cobra. What should have been a fluid, rhythmic posture was clunky and awkward for Mika, and while she wanted to avoid thinking about Jayce Beckett, it was difficult as she regularly peeked around the room to see if she was holding her pose correctly.

On the fourth sun salutation, Mika was feeling more confident until Sheri came around and placed her hand on Mika's lower back, gently suggesting that it straighten during the half-lift. She immediately felt the strain in her hamstrings.

Ouch! Shit, that hurts!

The class continued with motion and poses that became increasingly more challenging for Mika, and she felt her body shaking and sweating. The middle part of the class became a dance between Sheri's instructions and Mika's thoughts.

"Try to touch the ceiling as you reach your arm up and behind you."

Go fuck yourself.

"Try to get lower to the ground, like you're sitting in a chair."

I really hate you.

"As you hold this pose, your legs will eventually get used to it and will stop shaking."

Nobody likes you!!

Midway through class, Sheri directed the class into child's pose.

"This is your safety position," she said. "When you need a break, this is where you go. We all have those moments, and it's okay. Listen to your body and spirit."

I'm not going there, Mika told herself. Despite the difficulty she had with the first half of class, she was committed to do it all without letting up, partly to challenge herself, but mostly because she wasn't about to let Jayce Beckett see her taking a break.

Mika continued to struggle during the second half of class, especially in the half moon and full boat, but for the most part she did well, and there were a few moments where she stopped cursing Sheri and found herself lost in her own body. At one point in downward facing dog, the room disappeared; the rush of blood through her muscles and the sound of her heartbeat consumed her. She forgot about her clients, Todd, the lack of a car, her meeting with Jayce Beckett, and even Jayce Beckett himself. Of course, he wasn't completely gone. Toward the end of the session, when twisting toward the back of the room for marichi's pose, he passed through her line of sight, and she couldn't help but notice the definition in his arms and the tattoo on his calf. But this glimpse was miniscule as Mika ended the class with a pace and rhythm that suited her, and she wasn't going to let anyone distract her from this personal journey, which was perhaps one of the few she had ever taken in her life.

When the 50-minute class ended, Mika managed to escape the room without making eye contact with anyone, especially not Jayce. She was in an odd state of clarity and peace, and she wanted to preserve it for as long as possible; engaging with any of her colleagues would have certainly killed her buzz. She was much sweatier than she anticipated, but still opted to wear the yoga outfit home. She threw on a cotton hoody, grabbed her duffel bag, and hurried out of the locker room just as most of the class was exiting the yoga room.

Mika stood just inside the entry doors of the MedCare lobby, staring at yet another miserable addition to her day: it was raining.

Shit piss, she thought, a phrase her father had used frequently. Mika never understood the expression, but figured it was probably the result of a language barrier when her father had learned English as a young adult. Still, the phrase lived within Mika and occasionally revealed itself.

Other employees started passing her on their way out of the building. She could ask for a ride, but Mika hated inconveniencing people. Plus, she wasn't in the mood to be trapped in someone else's car and forced into making small talk. Besides being uncomfortable, she also didn't like depending on people. The rain wasn't heavy, and she thought about waiting it out, but the next bus was in 12 minutes. If she missed it, she would be stuck for another 20 minutes. Mika pushed through the doors, put her head down, and quickly marched down the steps. When she reached the main driveway, her march turned into a short-stepped run. The raindrops were light but quickly dotted her shoulders and misted her hair and face. She made it to the street, turned right, and hopped over a few puddles during her trek to the bus stop two blocks away.

She took shelter under the small steel awning and sat down. She planted herself in front of a large ad for a realtor that sat behind a plastic sheet littered with a several pieces of gum and had the word "boobies" scratched into it. She dusted the water from her hair, wiped her face, and took a deep breath. Raindrops splashed in a shallow puddle that was forming on the street just in front of the covered structure. She watched the little ripples made by each drop, and they reminded her of her beach. Her mind started to drift there, and she could see the water rolling up the sand toward her feet, but before she could fall away completely into her secret haven, car tires crushed through the rain puddle and ended her trip. Mika looked up, expecting to see the city bus; instead, she found a black minivan. She didn't recognize the car, and she couldn't make out the driver through the rain-spotted windows.

Please just go, whoever you are.

As Mika stood to get a better look, the window rolled down, revealing a grey-haired, attractive man.

Shit piss.

"Can I give you a ride?" Jayce Beckett called out with a smile.

Chapter 10

Mika sat in the leather passenger seat of Jayce Beckett's minivan, and she could only think two things: *Why did I accept his ride, and why the hell didn't I change my clothes?*

She had kept telling herself to just take the bus, but her mouth betrayed her and she accepted the ride from Jayce.

"So, where are we going?" he asked. He held his finger over the GPS screen, waiting to enter her address. Mika noticed that he had changed back into his suit, but his shirt collar hung open a button, freeing him from the bondage of his tie.

"8712 E. Benton. I can just tell you where to go."

He laughed. "I'm a little afraid of that." Mika didn't get the joke at first, until she saw him grinning at her. She relaxed a little.

"Yes," she laughed. "I can be good at that."

"I have no doubt about that." He finished entering her address, and the navigator voice started directing him. "That's Julia."

"I'm sorry?"

"The GPS voice. Her name is Julia."

"You named your GPS?" *Okay, maybe he's weird.*

"The first time we had a rental car with GPS, about two years ago in Seattle, the team had a competition to give it a name. The winner was Julia Roberts, so we could joke about Julia Roberts giving us directions. We spent the whole month calling her Julia Roberts. Things like 'thank you, Julia Roberts,' and 'are you sure that's the best way, Julia Roberts?'"

"Why Julia Roberts? Because you had a crush on her?"

"Well, I wouldn't exactly call it a crush. Let's just say I have respect and admiration for her talent."

"And she's beautiful."

"Yeah, that too." They both chuckled in unison.

"So there you go. Now you name all of your GPS robot voices Julia Roberts." *Okay, he is weird.* "That might be one a step away from stalking," she said in a playful manner.

"No. It's not Julia Roberts anymore. Just Julia."

"I'm sure Julia Roberts is disappointed to hear that she's been fired."

He laughed, seemingly a bit reluctant to explain, but he did. "I spend my time travelling to new cities. Even when I work with some of the same team, I often get into town first, and I don't know anyone. When I get into the rental car, the GPS voice is always the same; it's the one person I know, even though it's not a real person."

A little weird, but kind of cute, Mika thought.

"Now that I'm actually saying this out loud, I'm realizing it sounds a little weird," he laughed.

"No, it's not weird. Unless you talk to it… her. That might be a little odd."

"No, no. I mean, when I'm lonely there's some dirty talk, but… you know." Mika and Jayce again chuckled in unison.

Why the hell are we talking about this? And why am I still keeping it going? "Well, I doubt there's a need for that when you're driving a minivan."

"Ouch." Jayce feigned being hurt. "You go straight for the heart."

"I'm just saying that it's an interesting choice for someone who is clearly not a soccer mom."

"The minivan is a sweet ride."

"Right."

"If I go to the mall in this, pull out a diaper bag… well, let's just say I'm quite popular," he smiled.

Mika had a quick vision of Jayce in jeans and a tight t-shirt carrying a diaper bag, and her body quivered. She looked over and noticed, for the first time, that he wasn't wearing a ring. *Is he single, or does he take off his ring?*

"Really, though," Jayce continued, "the company makes our reservations, and as long as it gets me where I need to go, I don't care what kind of car it is."

"Julia" gave a direction to turn left in 500 feet.

"That's not the best way, Julia Roberts, but okay," Mika said with a mockingly serious tone.

"Really?" Jayce asked, reaching to pause the GPS.

"No, it's fine. An hour ago, this would have been faster. But go that way. I don't want to come between you and Julia."

"Well, I'm sure she's glad to hear that." They stopped at a red light, and the sound of the windshield wipers filled the air between them. Jayce took a quick look at his phone, and Mika saw that he grinned a little. *Girlfriend?* The silence had been there for only a moment, but it made Mika uncomfortable. She wanted to apologize again for yelling at him, but she also didn't want to revisit the event.

"How did you like the class?" she asked, watching the rain dribble down her window.

"Yoga? That was great. It really is an amazing feature to have at work. How long have you been taking class?"

Mika thought about making something up, but then couldn't figure out why she would do so. "That was my fifth class. Couldn't you tell?"

"What? Are you serious?"

"Don't mock me. I know; I'm horrible."

"I'm not mocking. You were seriously pretty good, from what I saw."

Were you watching me? "Obviously, you weren't looking closely enough."

"Look, I'm far from an expert, but if that was your fifth class, you were pretty damn good."

"For someone in her fifth class." Mika really wasn't begging for compliments, but she was afraid it was coming across that way.

"Well, you can't expect to be as good as someone who has been doing it for years. You have to go with where you are, and where you are is a lot better than other people I've seen who are just starting."

Mika forced a thank you, partly hoping they would stop talking about her, partly because she wasn't used to getting this type of support.

"What about you? I don't see a lot of men in class."

"I like it. Well, I've come to appreciate it. I live out of a hotel room, so I have to find things to do to stay in shape that don't require a gym. Hotel gyms are aren't always the best, and I don't always have time to find one. My sister is a yoga instructor; she taught me a few things I can do in my hotel room."

Don't respond to that. Don't think about commenting. Don't think.

"So, what's your story? Car in the shop, or are you just a big fan of public transportation?"

Mika laughed, and she could see that it caught Jayce by surprise.

"No, it's kind of a long story."

Jayce reeled back his playful tone. "I'm sorry. I didn't mean to pry."

"Oh, don't worry about that," she said, and she proceeded to tell him the story of her car, including the financial details and how she was waiting for a trip to a dealership like most women anticipate a vacation. She talked about the types of cars she was considering and how leather seats were a feature she wanted, but knew it might be a deal breaker because of the cost.

As Jayce pulled up in front of her house, Mika realized that she had been talking for about 15 minutes without any reservation. *What the hell have I been talking about? Why do I talk so much around this guy?*

"Is this it?" Jayce asked.

"Yes, with the windows in the garage," she said, pointing to the house across the street. She opened the door and took a step out. "Thank you so much for the ride. You really didn't have to."

"Well, I don't usually like to deprive people of riding the bus, but I thought I might take a chance that you would appreciate it."

"Definitely." There was an awkward silence for the first time since they started talking. "But seriously, thank you."

"My pleasure," he smiled that damn smile.

Don't wink. Don't you wink at me. She looked away to avoid eye contact. She closed the door, not noticing that the rain was falling softly on her head and building momentum. She tapped on the window, and he rolled it down.

"Is everything okay?" he asked.

"You know, I feel like I just rambled on and on, so I'm sorry if I bored you with all that."

"Don't apologize. I really enjoyed the conversation. Now get inside. It's raining." He winked at her and rolled up his window. She stepped over the water that flowed in the gutter and onto the sidewalk. She faced her house but wanted to look back. She heard his wet tires roll away. The rain started to come down harder, quickly drenching her hair and clouding her vision as the rain bounced from her cheeks. Rather than hurry inside, she stood there and let the rain have its way with her. A knot tightened in her stomach as she stared at her house, an immediate salvation from the downpour, yet one she didn't want to enter.

Chapter 11

Mika tossed her duffle bag on her bed and proceeded to the bathroom, leaving a trail of water in her wake. She grabbed a towel and wiped her face. Looking in the mirror, she laughed at her miserable condition: soaked clothes, ringlets taking over her normally wavy hair, bits of mascara resting on her cheeks.

Beautiful, she thought, and then she heard a buzzing coming from the other room. She draped the towel over her head as she returned to the bedroom. She fished around the inside of her duffel bag and found her phone. There were two text messages; the first was from Todd.

TJ: Stuck in traffic. Home in an hour. Hope you made it
       home ok.

She debated a no response, but she was afraid he would follow up with a phone call. He rarely did so, but if this were one of those times, she wasn't in the mood.

MJ: I'm home.

The simpler the better, she figured. The next text was from Ryan.

RJ: No practice. Going to Emily's for dinner.

The knot in her stomach started to return. Mika fought her initial urge to tell him no, but she knew that she needed to handle the Emily situation with strategy, not emotion. Ryan had been a relatively easy teenager, so far. He maintained good grades, was a hard-working athlete, and had been a bit of a homebody. While other teenagers craved the social world outside the arms of their parents, Ryan had spent most of his freshman and sophomore weekends at home. The times he did go out, it was with Mark Cousins, and they were usually home by 9 pm. The past year, however, Ryan started becoming more social because of Mark, who was able to use his swim success as social collateral. But even then, Ryan always kept his mom in the loop by texting her whenever he went somewhere, and as far she knew he never lied about it. Even when Ryan and Mark ended up drinking at a party last March, he called Mika for a ride and apologized the entire way home. But ever since Ryan had started dating Emily, things had changed. He was more distant, and Mika was feeling him slip away, which was made worse by the fact that in less than a year he would be away at college. She always knew this would be difficult, but her anxiety was expanding exponentially as she tasted more and more of his absence. While Mika would certainly miss seeing her only child every day, she was more fearful of life alone with Todd.

When Ryan was 3-years-old, Mika and Todd had started trying for a second child. Todd was one of three boys, and he wanted Ryan to have the same brotherly experiences he had. In contrast, Mika was an only-child, and after her father's death she was terribly alone. She didn't want the same for her son.

Ryan had come easily—way too easily—so they never anticipated having problems conceiving a second time. In the beginning, they approached the issue without thought; Mika simply ended her birth control prescription, and they went about their sexual life whenever the mood hit them. After six months, however, Mika started to stress and took the more formal approach of monitoring her ovulation patterns and scheduling intercourse around her most fertile times. This led to some of the more liberal sexual activity of their lives, including sex in the back of their car several times at locations between their offices, a few times on the top floor of Paradise Valley Mall parking garage, and once in the parking lot of a Joann Fabric. She still dreads going to that mall as it resuscitates the disappointment she felt from their lack of success.

After a year of trying for a sibling for Ryan, they had started more intense—and creative—measures. She stopped drinking caffeine, avoided starches, and generally ate a more healthy diet, except after each failed pregnancy test. Then, she would drive through a Wendy's for a large order of fries and a Frosty, consumed between lonely crying fits in her car. Todd had his sperm tested, and his boys were plentiful and mobile, which he bragged about in a joking way for months: "My boys can move. They're all over the place!" Never once did he notice that each little joke was a tiny dagger in Mika's heart. She also explored non-traditional routes: she ate coconut, wore pearls, burned sandalwood incense, and ate bananas for dessert. She taped 11 coriander seeds to her left thigh, and when that didn't work, she crushed coriander seeds and put them into Todd's coffee, but Todd refused to drink her craziness. "I don't need any help, remember?" One evening she even filled her bedroom with phallic and vaginal symbols, from bowls of cucumbers and bananas to conch shells and vases of lilies. She had found a cheap poster of Georgia O'Keefe's Grey Line and hung it over the bed. She turned the room into an ode to human genitals, and when Todd entered to find her naked body glistening from the flickering flames of three penis candles, he broke out laughing. Mika joined in, relaxing for the first time in months. They slipped under the covers and made love, and Mika sold herself on the idea that this would definitely be the start of a second child. She was wrong.

Eventually, they stopped talking about growing their family, and the thought of it was eventually wiped clear from Mika's mind. *Maybe it was a sign that this is how things are supposed to be,* she thought. A year ago, Todd and Gary went in together for vasectomies, which they timed so they could recover while watching March Madness. "I think I'm officially past going through another diaper phase," he had declared.

Now, Mika stared at the text from her only child, another reminder that he was slipping into his own world. She replied.

MJ: Ok. Have fun. Be home by 10:30, plz. Love you.

She dropped the phone on her bed and entered the bathroom. She was still cold from the soaking she took while standing in the rain, so she turned on the shower, peeled off her clothes, and stood before the mirror, waiting for the water to get hot. She studied her naked figure in the mirror. She scrutinized her middle and pinched the skin on the side of her waist.

C plus, she thought. Normally, she would give herself a 'B', but today she was being hypercritical because she worried how her colleagues viewed her during yoga. More specifically, she worried about how Jayce Beckett had seen her.

Why did he have to see me like this?

Her disgust was furthered when she saw Todd's shaving residue covering the bowl of the sink.

Damn it! How difficult is it to rinse the sink?

It was one of the on-going battles between them, and Mika considered his actions intentional, almost as a statement: "It's my house, I can do what I want."

The steam from the shower started to cloud the edges of the mirror; she rounded the corner and stepped into the walk-in shower, which consisted of a partial wall and an interior of Travertine. She stood under the overhead rainfall showerhead, grabbed the hand-held attachment and started spraying herself with the hot water, immediately sending shivers to each area of her body before the heat took over and warmed her blood. She let the hot water pour through her hair and down her face while she mindlessly moved the hand held up and down her thighs and across her stomach. She thought about her car ride home with Jayce.

He said he enjoyed the conversation? Why would he say that? I talked my ass off about stupid stuff. He has to think than I'm an idiot. Her heel covered most of the drain, and the water started to build around her feet. She stared at the shallow pool, moving in and out as water fell from above, and quickly the water turned to the tides, and her feet were under sand. She drifted back to her fictional beach.

Mika stands in the sand, just at the edge where the water rolls over her feet. A cool breeze presses against her face, and she takes a few steps back. She looks up and down the beach, seeing nothing but white sand sandwiched between the crystal blue water and lively green foliage. Mika's not sure where this beach is, but it is hers. She returns her attention to the sea, where an ancient ship floats a few hundred yards away. She studies it, waiting for signs of life. Magellan, perhaps? Raleigh? She takes a few steps forward until she is ankle deep in the water. A figure appears on deck with his back toward her, and Mika's body instantly warms. She feels a tingling in her groin, and it expands throughout her body. The figure wears tattered white pants and a tight t-shirt that seems to be hanging on by its last thread. She recognizes the shoulders, and she knows the gray hair. He turns, revealing the smooth face of Jayce Beckett. He looks to her and waves. Again, her vagina throbs.

Back in her shower, Mika stood with her eyes closed and the sprayer nestled between her legs. She held it just right so that the pulsing jet spray intermittingly hit her clit, sending warm vibrations throughout her midsection.

On the beach, Mika smiles and returns the wave. Jayce says something, but she can't make out what. The ship is closer now, too close for reality, but not close enough for Mika. She glides into the water until she is waste deep. Jayce leans against the railing, his well-defined triceps shining in the sun. Again he speaks. "I enjoyed our conversation." Mika smiles and is about to respond when someone grabs her from behind. It all disappears—the beach, the ship, Jayce....

"Well, hello," Todd said as his naked body rubs against Mika's. She drops the sprayer, like a thief ditches the evidence when the police arrive.

"You're home?" Mika asked, trying to disguise her disappointment as surprise.

"I told you an hour," he said, kissing her wet nipples, "but I got lucky with some lights."

Mika was surprised to realize that she had been in the shower for almost 30 minutes. She moved her foot, letting the built up water exit down the drain.

"This is a nice surprise," Todd said, moving his kisses to her mouth. He pressed her against the shower wall and slid his hands down her body, starting with her breasts. He pinched her already hard nipples, and while this wasn't the situation she craved, she let her body respond in a purely physical way. He slid his hands down her sides, avoiding her backside as he had recently trained himself to do, and his body followed until his face was buried in her crotch. He nibbled at her, sending pulses down Mika's legs. Mika's body responded positively to the familiar routine. When Todd spun her around, bent her forward and went at her from behind, she came quickly.

Mika's mind, however, was back at the beach.

Chapter 12

Beep. Beep. Beep.

Mika laid in bed, listening to the alarm clock release its annoying call as it did every morning. But today, she didn't reach for it. She couldn't. That movement would require using her core muscles to pull herself up a few inches, and she was in too much pain from yesterday's yoga class.

Beep. Beep. Beep.

Todd nudged her, hard. She still couldn't move, and she couldn't help but chuckle at the sight of her lying in bed and unable to perform such a simple function.

"God damn it," Todd grumbled, rolling over her and slapping his hand on the clock.

"Sorry," she laughed.

He rolled off her and onto his back. "What the hell's wrong with you? Are you sick?"

"No, I'm in pain," and she laughed again, but this time even that movement was too much and sent pain through her sides.

Todd leaned up and looked at her, concerned. "What kind of pain?"

"I took a yoga class yesterday, and I guess I went all out."

"Oh," he said with a tone of relief in his voice. "Well good for you. That's a good pain."

"If you say so."

"Where does it hurt? Here?" He touched her side, tickling her just enough to make her body tighten and again sending a pain screaming through her muscles.

"Stop!" Mika tried to slide out of his way.

"Stop what? This…?" He pursued her again, laughing. Mika summoned all of her aching muscles to roll off the bed, hitting the ground with a thud. Todd's face stared down at her from above.

"Are you okay?"

"Asshole." She was annoyed, but smiling as again she couldn't help but see the humor of her suffering.

Todd got off the bed and helped her up.

"I'm sorry, really." He carefully slid his hand around her side, trying to navigate to an area where he could grab her without causing more pain. "You need to drink a lot of water."

"Or vodka," she said, getting to her feet.

The rest of the morning was spent in her typical fashion, only at a much slower pace: shower, a short breakfast, and a ride to work from Todd. The only difference this morning was that every movement, from sitting in a chair to climbing the stairs to picking up her purse, was a reminder of muscles that she had forgotten she had.

* * *

Mika stared at her computer screen, examining some figures from a wellness plan proposal for Dyal Communications, a prospective client. Her numbers were a little higher than requested, but she felt they were justified and wanted to discuss them with Brooke, the sales agent on the deal.

She needed to use her arms to slowly push herself out of her chair, and she grabbed her laptop and proceeded to the door.

"Where are you going?" Tanya stood in her doorway, holding a cup of coffee.

"I need to go talk to Brooke about a contract."

"Why don't you just call her? You've been in and out of the office all morning. It's like watching a ping pong ball."

It was true. Mika had made seven trips away from her desk this morning: three to accounting, two to the archives, one to sales, and one to the cafeteria. Most of them were all tasks that she would have made over the phone. But not today.

Mika laughed and then winced. "I have to keep moving." She held her sides, delicately. "I went a little too hard at yoga yesterday. The longer I sit in my chair, the harder it is to get up."

"Aaahh," Tanya smiled. "No pain, no gain, right?"

"I sure as hell hope so." She left the office, and went straight for the elevator, smiling at people as she passed. It was true, the longer she sat in her chair, the more her muscles tightened and the more pain she felt with the slightest adjustment in her chair. While walking, she could stretch to minimize the pain. What was also true was that every time she went to the elevator, she hoped to run into Jayce. She would casually look to her left and right, expecting—and hoping— to catch a glimpse of him coming out of a random office. And when the elevator doors opened, for that split second before she could see inside, she envisioned Jayce standing on the other side, only to be disappointed each time. Even her trip to the cafeteria to get a bottle of water was a disguised attempt to run into him, as she had water available in the workroom on her floor.

Now she faced the elevator doors for the eighth time today. Mika pushed the down button, and caught herself checking her hair in the wavy reflection on the shiny elevator doors.

What the hell are you doing? You're not going to see him. And so what if you do?

The elevator dinged, and the energy that buzzed through her stomach quickly dissipated when she discovered that it was empty. She took a lonely ride to the sales department, where she found Brooke working at her desk.

"Mika? What's going on?"

"My numbers are a little high for Dyal, but I wanted to show you what I was thinking." Mika sat down, slowly, next to Brooke and opened her laptop. "Can I have a few minutes?"

"Sure, but you could have just called."

"I know. Long story."

She opened her spreadsheets and began to explain the details of her proposal. Brooke played devil's advocate on behalf of the client, and the two of them agreed on the figures that wouldn't work and the ones they could sell. As Mika typed a few notes, Brooke's phone rang, and she answered it.

"This is Brooke." Her eyes narrowed, confused for a moment as she listened to the caller. "Actually, she is." She handed the phone to Mika, indicating that it was for her.

It must be Tanya, Mika thought.

She took the receiver and continued typing. "This is Mika Jones."

"Well, hello, Mika Jones. This is Jayce Beckett. I hope you don't mind that I tracked you down."

Mika wasn't exactly sure what he said next. She looked at Brooke, trying to see if she had any kind of reaction to Jayce calling for her. Did she even know it was Jayce? If Brooke had any interest in the call, she didn't show it as she read an email.

"Ok, I will see you in an hour," Jayce said. Mika didn't respond right away, and she was starting to recognize her own silence when Jayce's voice drifted into her ear. "Mika?"

"Right. Sorry." She turned slightly in her chair, like a teenager trying to hide her conversation from a parent. "When are we meeting?"

"In an hour, in the conference room, if that's okay. We can schedule for another time if that's better for you."

"No, no. That's fine. I will see you then."

"Great. Looking forward to it."

Mika handed the phone back to Brooke, and tried to return to work. She focused on the spreadsheet on her laptop, but she only saw a bunch of numbers floating without context. She struggled to make sense of the screen and worried that Brooke would notice that she was completely lost.

"Well, I'm okay with those changes, but let me know if they won't work," Brooke said, barely looking away from her own computer.

Mika was dizzy. *Are we done? Did we finish the changes?* She could see her notes, but couldn't comprehend what she had written just moments ago. Assuming they were finished, she carefully stood to leave. Her legs wobbled, and she leaned on the edge of the desk to stabilize herself.

"Are you okay?" Brooke asked.

Mika managed a small laugh. "Yes, just a little sore. I'll send this to you when I'm finished."

"Great. Good to see you, Mika."

Mika stared at the elevator doors. *What does he want? He's going to call me out on something I said yesterday. Shit! Shit! But he said he was looking forward to seeing me. Why would he say that?*

The elevator doors opened, and Mika joined three other people she didn't recognize. She managed a "hello" as she took her spot near the back. The buzz inside her head mirrored the hum of the elevator as it travelled to the eighth and tenth floors. When the last person exited, the doors closed, leaving Mika standing alone desperately trying to not think about Jayce Beckett.

Don't let this guy get to you. You know your shit. He's just a guy. A hot guy with a killer smile and great shoulders.

The elevator took flight again, racing down to the first floor and picking up more passengers. Mika travelled up and down three times before realizing she had never pushed the button for the floor of her office.

When she finally arrived at her desk, she found two bottles of water waiting for her.

Thanks, Tanya.

She opened one and drank half of it in one gulp. She looked at the clock on her computer; she needed to leave in 25 minutes to meet with Jayce.

Make it 20 minutes, she told herself as she remembered how slowly she was moving. She finished off the rest of the water, opened the second bottle, and slowly made her way to Tanya's office.

Tanya was the only one with an actual office, but like the rest of the division, it was an open concept without a door and just a partial glass wall to give her limited privacy. As she approached, Mika could see that Tanya was at her desk and talking on the phone. She stopped and started to turn, but she was so slow in doing so that she caught Tanya motioning for her to come in. She made her way to the opening that would be a door and leaned against the edge. She drank some more water as Tanya finished her call.

"Yes, I understand." Tanya rolled her eyes at Mika and continued her conversation, but Mika didn't hear much of it. She was wrapped in her own thoughts.

Should I tell her about my ride home? Was that really stupid? She's going to think I'm an idiot. Or she'll make some snide comment about how he wants me. What if he does want me? Of course he doesn't want me. What difference does it make? You're married, idiot. Dear God, am I in high school again?

"Mika?"

Tanya was off the phone and had apparently asked Mika a question, but Mika had no idea what it was.

"Are you okay?"

"Yeah, sorry. I was just thinking...." She drifted off again, but this time to nowhere in particular, to that empty space between reality and daydreaming. Mika wasn't even aware that Tanya had come to her until she felt Tanya's arm around her shoulders.

"Sit down," she said, leading Mika into a chair. "Maybe you should go home."

"No, no need," she replied, coming back to reality. "I have a meeting."

"Push it to tomorrow. Seriously. Maybe your body is in some kind of yoga shock."

"It's with Jayce Beckett."

"You shouldn't... what?"

"My meeting is with Jayce Beckett."

"Another one? What does he want?" Tanya leaned against her desk, appearing to slip into her own state of shock.

"That's what I was hoping you could tell me. You're the head of the department. Did he call you?"

"No. I haven't heard a thing."

"Is this normal?"

"I don't know; I've never been involved with this kind of thing. I'm sure it's no big deal. He probably just needs to follow up on some questions. What did you tell him yesterday?"

"I told you, I don't really remember. I felt like I rambled." *When he gave me a ride home....*

"That's right," Tanya said, returning to her desk and sounding less concerned. "You were too busy checking out his shoulders."

"Right... wait, no!"

"So you did notice. Nice, right?"

"Maybe."

"Maybe my ass," Tanya picked up the phone and started to dial. "Find me when you're finished."

Chapter 13

Mika exited the elevator and made her way toward Jayce's conference room office. She was feeling better about the meeting because she was back to being angry. She wasn't exactly angry with Jayce, just at the feeling of being out of control. She hated the knots in her stomach and the inability to complete a thought. She hated feeling incompetent and like a schoolgirl. As she watched the numbers climb in the elevator, enough of this anger coalesced into a jolt that knocked Mika back into a right frame of mind.

Now, she sat outside the conference room door thinking not about what she might have said to Jayce the previous day, but about what she was going to say to him today. She organized her thoughts into facts, figures, and philosophy. This focused energy revitalized her, almost making her forget how sore her muscles still were. She felt confident and indestructible. But then she had a horrible realization: *I have to pee.* She had consumed 60 ounces of water in the past two hours and it was time to pay the piper. Mika eyed the restrooms down the hall and checked her watch. She had a few minutes. *Crap. Better hurry....* She struggled to get out of the chair, at first leaning on her right arm to push herself up, then the left. She eventually stood, and as she turned to her left, the door to the conference room opened. *Oh shit. No!* The wrap around guy exited, almost bumping into Mika.

"Excuse me," Wrap Around said. "I didn't see you."

Jayce's voice followed as he appeared in the doorway. "Mika, good to see you again. Come on in."

Before she could object, Jayce was back in his office, and Wrap Around was halfway down the hallway. In any other situation like this, Mika would excuse herself and be a few minutes late, but for some reason she didn't this time. *Damn it!*

She entered the office, closing the door behind her.

"I'll be just a second," Jayce said as he quickly typed something on his computer. Mika slowly lowered herself into a chair, desperate not to reveal her pain and to not pee in her pants. Settled in, Mika did whatever she could to find comfort.

It's okay. This will be short. You can hold it. Don't think about it. Just find something else to think about, Mika. The Wellness Division. Think about your plan. Don't let him get the upper hand. What's he making me wait for, anyway? This is a little rude, right? Look at him, sitting there. His hands look strong. I hadn't noticed that before. Shit! Stop!

Jayce closed his computer and smiled at Mika. "I'm sorry, that was a little rude. Thank you for waiting."

"No, nothing to worry about. It wasn't rude."

"Thank you, I appreciate that. Now, I wanted to ask you some questions about…" he started, but Mika interrupted him.

"I'm sorry, can I just say something?" Before Jayce could agree or disagree, she continued. "If this is about yesterday, I'm glad, because I feel like I just rambled and talked forever, and I probably didn't make any sense. So I would love the chance to clarify anything I said yesterday."

Jayce looked confused. "You didn't ramble yesterday. Actually, you were quite articulate."

I was? "Oh. Well, thank you." Between the need to pee and Jayce's disarming sincerity, Mika had lost her angry edge that she so wanted to bring to this conversation.

"I actually spent a lot of time thinking about your division, and I have few follow up questions."

He smiled at her, but didn't say anything. *Did he ask me a question? Am I supposed to say something?*

"Okay?" he asked.

"Sure, go for it."

"The plans that you design for clients usually include incentives for employees who get regular wellness checks. Annual physicals. Blood tests. Mammograms. Things like that. But what percentage of employees take advantage of those incentives?"

"It depends on the company."

"Could you estimate an average, or perhaps a range?"

It's in the reports we prepared for you. I could be peeing while you read them. "It's tough to say an average. A new company starting with a program might be about 10 percent, mostly because people aren't aware of it yet. In year three or four of the program, we hope that gets closer to 35 percent. It also depends on the culture of the organization. The more it's promoted and the better the incentives, the higher the participation rate. It also depends on the ratio of males-females. Women go to the doctor far more often."

Jayce leaned back. "Thirty-five percent? That just seems low."

"Well, when you consider the national average of men ages 30-50 who participate in annual wellness activities is about seven percent, and women is about 20 percent, it's a fairly good number." *Holy hell, I have to pee.*

"Seven percent? I'm speaking personally here, I just don't get that."

"People live in denial. Most people either don't believe that anything bad is going to happen to them, or they don't want to know if there is something wrong."

"That's just foreign to me. If something is wrong, I want to know... are you okay?" Mika was gripping the arm of her chair, holding back a wave of urine that was close to escaping. The urge subsided, slightly.

"I'm fine." *For now.*

"Well, this just seems like a huge issue."

"It is a huge issue. You're not a woman—"

"Thank you for noticing." He smiled that smile at her. She wanted to enjoy it, but she dismissed it so she could move on quickly and hopefully make it to the bathroom.

"If you ever work in an office where someone is diagnosed with breast cancer, she usually keeps it to herself in the beginning. Fear. Embarrassment. Whatever. It's hush-hush for a while before she starts talking about it. Now, women have been dealing with the intricacies of their bodies since they entered puberty; we've lived most of our lives knowing about the dangers we face. But life happens, and you go a few months longer than you should without a checkup, maybe even a year or two. But when a friend or colleague is diagnosed with cancer, it becomes one big support group for each other, giving reminders about getting checked and sharing articles about diet."

Jayce scratched his head. "I don't see men doing that."

"No, they probably don't. But the point is that everyone has some kind of trigger that makes them pay attention." She paused. "There are people living toxic lifestyles—smoking, alcoholism, obesity—and they don't want to admit it."

"Or they don't even see it," Jayce interrupted.

"Exactly. People live with signs that something is wrong all the time. Fatigue. Headaches. Weight gain. Anxiety. They tell themselves that it's nothing, and eventually they get used to it, and they assume it's normal. But at some point, they hopefully will open their eyes and see that there might just be a problem in their life. If it's bad enough, they have no choice but to confront their problem. We want to make sure that when they do, a clear avenue exists for dealing with it. The sad thing is that this lucid moment in a person's life can be so short that even a $40 copay could push someone back into a state of denial. So you're right, 35 percent might not be very high number, but the important thing is to have a system in place that helps people get there when they are ready."

As she spoke, her energy rose, as did her urge to pee. She couldn't hold it anymore. "Can we be done?" Jayce was confused by her abrupt request, but before he could say anything, Mika let out a sound that was half laugh, half cry. "I really, really have to use the restroom."

"What? Yes! Go! Go! You should have said something earlier."

Mika struggled to get out of her chair, and Jayce hurried around to help her, firmly grasping the back of her arm.

"I know. I just felt stupid for some reason." Out of her chair, she remained slightly hunched over as she shuffled to the door. "I'll be right back."

"I'll wait right here," he said.

Mika crossed the hall and entered the bathroom, using all of her mental capacity to control her muscles and prevent her bladder from emptying in the hall. Once she was in the stall and seated, her muscles slowly relaxed, allowing her urine to flow out with such force that

Mika was sure it could knock over a small child. Once she could regain use of her brain for actual thought, she started beating herself up.

I'm such an idiot. Why didn't I just go before? He surely thinks I'm a fool. Maybe if I wait in here long enough, he will have another meeting and I won't see him. How long would I need? 10 minutes? 20 minutes? Wait, how long have I been in here? Hurry up, pee! He's going to think I'm some kind of bladder freak!

She cleaned up and checked herself in the mirror several times before leaving. She slowly pushed against the bathroom door, opening it just enough to see if he was in the hallway, or better yet, his office door was closed. It was not. *Shit. Just go back. Everyone pees.* Mika crossed the corridor and entered the office, putting on a false front of confidence as she leaned against the doorframe.

"Thank you. I'm so sorry about that," she said.

Jayce looked up from his phone. "No worries. Everyone pees, right? Although, I don't think I've ever seen someone in that much pain before." He gave her a teasing smile, which again eased any tension that rested within Mika's body. She laughed, embarrassed to share but still willing to do so.

"Actually, I can barely move. I am in so much pain."

Despite her laugh, Jayce looked concerned and stood. "Is everything okay?"

"Yes, I'm just stupid."

Jayce waited for an explanation.

"Yoga." Mika started laughing, which made her sides hurt even more. Jayce joined in, coming around to her side of the table.

"Make sure you drink plenty of water."

"Why do you think I had to go to the bathroom so badly? Someone hands me a bottle of water everywhere I go."

Jayce leaned against the conference table, smiling at her.

What's he doing? "What?"

"So the wellness champion hasn't been practicing wellness that much?" He winked at her.

Mika thought about getting defensive, fabricating the other ways that she stays active and how this was just the first time she had done yoga in awhile. But in the end, she just smiled and hung her head.

"Not really. But I am starting. Really."

"I'm just giving you a hard time. Thanks for coming down on short notice. You gave me what I needed."

"That was it? Are you sure?"

"Yes, I was intrigued by the human behavior component. What motivates people to act, or not to act? It's fascinating."

"I guess it is." Mika pulled herself away from the doorframe, unsure of her next step. *Should I shake his hand?* "Let me know if you need anything else."

"Definitely." He extended his hand, and she placed hers inside his long, strong fingers. She felt each tip as it pressed into her skin. She made eye contact like she was conditioned to do, but abandoned it quickly before she became lost in his eyes. As she turned to leave, he spoke again.

"So how is the car search going?"

Mika was confused as she had momentarily forgotten that she had shared her car troubles with him.

"Oh, yeah. Nothing since yesterday evening. Have bus pass, will travel."

"Well, if you need a ride again, let me know." He handed her a business card. She could see handwritten numbers on the back. "My cell phone is on the back, in case I'm lost somewhere in the building."

Be cool. Don't be a jerk.

"That's really kind of you, but really not necessary. You have other things to do than chauffer me around."

"Don't tell anyone this, but not really." He laughed. "Look, I enjoy getting to see different parts of the cities I am in, so this gives me a reason to head your way. And I really did enjoy the conversation."

Mika tried to process this and struggled for an appropriate response, but she had nothing to say. She didn't even have a thought. Jayce took an awkward step back before returning to his chair.

"It's just an offer. I know how much you love the bus, but if you're not into public transit today, I'm available. If not, don't worry about it." He smiled as he sat behind the table.

Say something nice, you idiot.

"Thank you. Maybe. We'll see." She left his office and made her way to the elevator in a fog. When Mika returned to her office, she treated his business card as a winning lottery ticket, checking it frequently to make sure it was real. After meeting with Tanya to explain the details of her meeting—minus the phone number—she spent the rest of the afternoon trying to forget the card. She tucked it away in her purse, which she placed on the window ledge as the rain drizzled along the glass and created a peaceful backdrop. She participated in two conferences calls with sales teams and clients and worked on proposals. In between each task, her mind wandered back to Jayce's offer, and she debated whether or not to take him up on it: *It's not appropriate. What's not appropriate? Todd took the car and now I'm the one who has to take the bus? It's not like we're doing anything? I'm married, what's the big deal. Would I care if Todd got a ride home from a beautiful woman? Probably. Maybe not.*

Her final conference call ended at 4:55 pm, and she was now at the tipping point. She had changed her mind several times over the past few hours, but now she needed to make the call. Or not make the call if she was going to make the 5:25 pm bus pickup.

This is stupid.

Mika shut down her computer, grabbed her purse, and left the office with a few pleasant good nights to her remaining colleagues. The early wave for going home had started, so several people waited outside the elevator doors. Mika stood toward the back to avoid having a conversation with anyone. She faced away from the crowd, staring across the corridor, out the window, and into the rain. Thoughts of running through the rain, hopping from one tree canopy to the next filled her head.

It hurts to run, but I can just suck it up, she thought. *But I don't want to.*

Her phone rang. It was Todd, but she declined the call. She didn't want to talk to him, not now. The elevator doors opened, but she stepped aside as others filled the elevator. She retrieved Jayce's card from her purse, and she studied his number for a moment. She entered the numbers on her phone and took a deep breath before pressing the dial button. She listened to it ring four times and was ready to hang up when Jayce's voice filled her ear.

"Hello?"

"Is this Jayce Beckett?"

"Yes, this is Jayce."

"Hi. This is Mika Jones, we met earlier—"

"Well, hello, Mika Jones." She could almost hear him smiling on the other end, or maybe she wanted to believe that he was smiling. "Is it raining?"

"Yes, but if it's a problem, it's no big deal."

"Not a problem at all. What time will you be ready to go?"

"Anytime, really. Whatever is good for you."

"I have a few things to finish up here. I'll pick you up out front in… about 15 minutes? How does that sound?"

"Sounds great. See you then." She hung up and instantly looked around to see if anyone had heard her conversation. Mika returned to the elevator, slightly stunned and filled with buyer's remorse. *Abort. Abort. Call him back. Just take the bus. What are you doing?*

She continued this inner debate into the elevator, down to the lobby, into the locker room while she primped her hair, and out to the lobby, where she stood inside the entry doors and watched cars leave the rain-soaked parking lot. *What if someone sees me getting in his car?* She studied each car as it drove past, trying to identify the driver, but she couldn't discern any faces through the rain. *Call him back and cancel, just to be safe.* She really wanted to take out her phone, but she didn't. Instead, she watched the parking garage and waited for his minivan to emerge. When it finally did, she smiled and passed through the lobby doors and into the steady rainfall. She descended the steps, keeping her eyes on the approaching chariot crawling along the driveway. Mika stopped and waited at the curb, where another car suddenly stopped. *Keep moving. Keep moving.* But the car didn't move, making Mika grow even more restless as this car was in her way. She gave a subtle wave to the minivan, just in case Jayce didn't recognize her. When she realized the car in front of her wasn't moving, she decided to walk to Jayce but was stopped by Todd's voice.

"Come on, get in!"

Mika's head spun, and she almost fell backwards when she realized that the car in front of her was her husband's, and through the rolled down passenger window, she could see her husband repeating himself.

"Mika! Let's go."

She opened the passenger door, and as she started to get in, she stopped and gave one last look to the minivan. She couldn't see his face, but she tried to send him an "I'm sorry" with hers.

Chapter 14

Mika slid into the passenger seat of her husband's car and pulled the door closed.

"That was good timing," Todd said, checking his mirror for an opening to pull away.

"What are you doing here?"

"We had to cut our meeting short. Tony's kid broke his arm at school. I was heading home when I realized I could get here before you got on the bus."

"That was nice," she said, pretending to look at herself in the vanity mirror. She was really watching the minivan behind them as it pulled away from the curb and headed for the gate. Todd followed, pulling in line behind Jayce.

"You know, I felt guilty about the rain and all. You did it yesterday, and to walk to the bus in this mess would have sucked." He reached over and patted her on the knee, which slightly alarmed her.

This was one of those moments that Mika hated because Todd was being sincere. One of her frustrations with him was his lack of consistency. Be a jerk, be a gentleman... whatever, but don't go back and forth so much.

"You should have called. You almost missed me," she said, putting her wet hand on his.

"I did, but it went to voicemail."

"Really? I didn't hear it ring." Mika remembered dodging the call, but she couldn't remember if it was before or after she called Jayce, and then she wondered what would have happened if Todd had seen her getting into Jayce's minivan. How would she explain it? Would Todd accept it as something innocent? He wasn't typically a jealous person. Her thoughts were interrupted by a car horn.

"Come on, minivan!" Todd honked the horn again. Jayce was ahead of them, ready to turn right, but he hadn't done so. "What's this guy doing? Let's go."

"Relax, he's being cautious. It's raining." She removed her glasses and found a relatively dry patch on her sleeve to wipe them on.

"But he could have turned five minutes ago. Fucking minivans."

"I hear they're a sweet ride." She smiled at her inside joke.

"Well, if you want to get a minivan tomorrow, we can do that." Jayce finally turned, and Mika watched his car disappear into the drenched sea of traffic. It wasn't until moments later when Todd found an opening in traffic that she realized what he had said.

"What?"

"Let's go car shopping tomorrow."

"Ryan has regionals."

"We'll go after. He should be done by one or two, right?"

"Probably. Alright then." Mika was excited, but she tried to temper it. She had been down this road before, and something always seemed to get in the way. She heard her phone vibrate in her purse. *Shit. What if it's him? Why would it be him? It could be him.*

"So, you want to look at minivans then?" Todd said, sarcastically. She didn't hear him. Instead, she was carefully taking her phone from her purse, holding it at an angle so that if the text were from him and possibly used the words "sex" or "fuck" only she would see it. It wasn't and it didn't. It was from Lisa.

LC: Pick up some vodka.

What? "Oh shit! I forgot about Lisa."

"What's going on?"

"I completely forgot that we're meeting tonight to work on the gala." Mika and Lisa were planning the end-of-the-year gala for the swim team, a black tie affair that was far more pretentious than it needed to be.

"Thank God that's almost over with. Let me guess, vodka?"

"Do we have any? I think we have a bottle, but I'm not sure."

"I don't know, but I'll stop. You know, if you have to drink to get through something, maybe it's not worth your time."

"Todd."

"What are you going to do with all of your free time once swim is finished? Cure cancer?"

"Why not." It was a question she tried to avoid because her lack of an answer scared her. What she wanted to do at that moment was drift away into her own world, but she was afraid that Todd might somehow suspect that she had been thinking about the strong hands of another man. Instead, she engaged him in a conversation about his work, and Todd talked about the market, Obama's incompetency, and the stupidity of one of his partners. He only paused for a moment to stop at the drive thru liquor store for a bottle of Ketel One Vodka, her favorite, and he ordered a case of Guinness.

"I'll have Gary come over while you two work."

"Or, you could come help us."

"I didn't sign up to volunteer for a reason." He handed her the vodka, which she tucked beneath her feet, and he placed the beer behind her seat. "Once you start helping, they never stop taking advantage of you."

"There's only one event left, and then Ryan's graduating. Somehow, I think you could lend a hand on this one and not get sucked in for any other duty."

"Pass." He laughed, pulling back into traffic, and they drove the remaining mile home in silence.

At home, Mika turned on the oven and put in a dish of leftover lasagna and garlic bread. She hurried upstairs and changed into jeans and a sweatshirt. She thought for a moment about rinsing the sink of Todd's toothpaste spit, but then walked away. *Fuck it.* As the lasagna heated, Mika opened the bottle of Ketel One and poured herself a shot. She sipped it, and it felt clean and smooth on her tongue, where she let it rest before sliding it down her throat. She went to the pantry for some paper plates, where she also found another half-full bottle of Ketel One. *Damn it!* She wished she had checked before opening the new bottle.

She checked the oven, and then called Ryan. He answered on the third ring.

"Hey, Mom. What's going on?"

"Nothing. Just getting ready for a quick dinner. Where are you?" She knew the answer.

"I'm at Emily's. We're on our way to see a movie."

"You have a race in the morning."

"Really? Are you sure?"

Mika typically appreciated his sarcasm, but not now. Todd entered the kitchen, and opened the oven. He gave Mika a "thumbs up."

"Don't give me shit, Ryan. It's regionals," she said sharply.

"I know, Mom. I know. I'll be home by 10:30. I'll be fine."

Mika rolled her eyes at Todd, hoping for some support. He waved her off, telling her to not push it.

She relented. "10:30. Got it?"

"Got it." He hung up, and Mika tossed her phone on the counter. She took another sip of vodka.

"He'll be fine. He's been there before," Todd said, pulling the dish from the oven.

"I hope so. I just don't want to hear him complaining about it if he does poorly tomorrow."

"Well, he makes his own choices, and he can live with the results. It's the best thing we can show him as parents," Todd said as he again opened the oven door. He stuck a fork into the lasagna and shoveled a load into his mouth. Mika pulled the dish away from him before he could send his fork back in. She prepared two plates, and they ate standing at the counter, talking about the travel details for the morning.

An hour later, Mika sat at Lisa's Tuscan-style dining table. Lisa sat across from her, nursing a glass of cranberry juice and vodka. Two other moms were with them, Jenni and Stacey. They were freshman moms, and they were being sucked into this job for next year. They had no idea what the gala involved, so they mostly took notes and tossed an occasional "What a great idea."

This year's event was a casino night, as it had been for the past six years. Most of the larger details—location, personnel, and equipment rentals—were already in place; now they were wrapping up all of the little details, which was tedious. As they itemized the list of prizes they had already received as donations, Mika's phone vibrated. It was a text from a number she didn't recognize.

JB: Can you tell me of a great coffee place near Tempe?

Mika stared at it. *What is that number?* And then the phone vibrated in her hand.

JB: btw it's Jayce

She looked again, making sure this was real, and it vibrated a third time.

JB: Beckett

Before she could do anything, it vibrated four more times.

JB: From Century Consulting

JB: Working with your company right now

JB: We met yesterday

JB: And today

Mika smiled and almost laughed out loud.

"What's going on over there?" Lisa asked. "Your phone is blowing up tonight."

Mika stumbled in her reply. "It's Ryan. He's going to the movies."

"Ryan went out too? I told Mark he better not be late or I will beat him."

"I know, but he'll be fine," Mika said, but she wasn't really paying attention. Her mind was searching for coffee places on the north side of town, and she typed.

MJ: Plantation Jane's. University and McClintock.
        Tempe

Mika set her phone down and took a long sip of her vodka. Mika had only been there once or twice because it wasn't really in her neck of the woods, but she remembered liking it. One of the new moms asked how the prizes are given out.

"It's a raffle," Lisa explained. "We make sure every swimmer gets something." Mika smiled as she spoke, not at Lisa's comments but at what she was going to do next. She picked up her phone and copied his staccato style.

MJ: From Mika

MJ: Jones

MJ: MedCare

MJ: Wellness Division

She set the phone in her lap and tried to get involved in the conversation about how to give out prizes in a way other than a raffle, but she could only focus on her phone and the anticipated buzz in her lap. Finally it came, and she looked down.

JB: LOL. Thank you!

Chapter 15

Mika was bundled up at the Mona Plummer Aquatic Center at Arizona State University. The rain had stopped in the middle of the night, and it was a chilly morning, a welcome relief from the heat and hopefully a sign that the cooler weather was here to stay. The Desert Horizon parents had taken control of the west section of the bleachers, hovering above the pool deck where their swimmers had established their own makeshift campground of duffel bags, jackets and towels. Mika sat bundled in a Desert Horizon green blanket, holding her phone in one hand and a coffee from Plantation Jane's in the other, which had spurred an argument with Todd because it was 10 minutes out of their way. Lisa sat next to her while Todd and Gary stood on the deck below with the swimmers.

Mika was exhausted as a result of four hours of sleep. Jayce's "Thank you" was the final text she had received from him, but she had been on edge for most of the evening waiting for another. And when she was in bed trying to fall asleep, all she could think about were the texts.

Why did he text me? What was he doing? Did he really want a coffee place, or did he just want to contact me? Should I have sent him another text? Should I have ignored him? Why am I so consumed by this? It's probably nothing, just a guy in town trying to find a good coffee place. Who looks for a coffee place on a Friday night? Is he gay? He can't be gay. Please don't be gay. Why do I care? I'm married. I'm lying in my bed next to my husband, thinking about another guy. This can't be good.

Her mind ran through this cycle several times before tiring, but just as she started to fall asleep, she thought she heard her phone vibrate, thus reigniting her brain. Her best guess was that she finally conked out around 3 am. When she awoke, she was even stiffer than the previous morning, but this time she tried to own it. After struggling out of bed, she fell into a few yoga poses to help stretch and get some blood flow into her muscles. She was still tender, but better able to move.

"How is Ryan feeling? Good?" Lisa asked while scanning the crowd of swimmers below.

"I think so. I just don't know where his head is lately."

"He's a good kid."

"Thanks. How is Mark doing?"

"You mean besides the black eye? He's good."

"What?" Mika searched the swimmers below before finding Mark, who was talking with Gary and Todd. When he turned his face, she could see the swollen and bruised cheek.

"What happened?"

"He won't tell me."

"He won't tell you?"

"Well, he says he was over at Tom's house goofing around and he tripped and hit his face on the corner of the couch, but it's bullshit. I heard someone mention a party this morning, but nobody is saying anything. Look down there. It's weird."

Mika studied the collection of swimmers, and Lisa was right. There seemed to be a hushed energy, even in the way the swimmers stood and talked with each other. It appeared, Mika noticed, that while people were around Mark, no one was really talking to him. And then she noticed Ryan and Emily leaning against the fence at the edge of the camp, talking with a few other teammates. Ryan seemed to be standing a little taller, or was it her imagination? Was this one of those moments where she realized that he was becoming a man and she was late in noticing?

"I'll see what Ryan knows." She was angry that Ryan wasn't with him now. "Although lately he doesn't seem to know anything if it doesn't involve Emily."

Lisa laughed. "Young love."

"I just don't want him being that guy who ditches his friends when a girl comes into the picture."

"And you also don't want him being that guy who won't ever ditch his friends to be with his girl," Lisa countered.

Mika thought about this while looking at Ryan, then to Mark, and then to Todd and Gary. "No, I guess not."

"My God, look at him," Lisa said. Mika followed her line of sight to one of the coaches from another school. Early thirties. Strong physique in a tight t-shirt. From the bleachers Mika could see his white smile contrasting with the tan that most swim coaches have. He was a good-looking man, but Mika kept quiet. He was no Jayce.

"If Mark weren't a senior, we would be transferring schools next year."

Mika laughed, but was uncomfortable with where the conversation might lead, so she tried to change the subject.

"So, I think the gala is looking good."

"The gala wouldn't need any planning at all if he were our coach. We could just set up an empty room, and everyone would stare at his ass. Look at that ass."

"You're funny."

"Even Gary would like that ass. And we had four years of old man Davey. Life's not fair." She opened her thermos, filled her cup with coffee, and then offered to refresh Mika's.

"No, it's not." She removed the lid from her cup and let Lisa refill it. She knew that Lisa would never have an affair, but she talked about other men a lot. She deeply wanted to ask her, *if you had the chance right now, would you do everything you say you would with him?*

Mika saw Ryan walking along the far side of the dive pool with Emily. He removed his jacket, handed it to her, and they kissed. Amidst the buzzers, cheering, and her own internal strife, she missed the announcement for his heat to report to the pool.

"Let's go, Ryan!" Lisa yelled. Neither noticed that Todd and Gary had made their way into the bleachers and were sitting behind them. Todd placed his hands on Mika's shoulders, and she panicked and dropped her phone into her purse. Hide the evidence.

"I think he's ready," Todd said. "He feels good."

"I hope so," Mika responded. "I'm not sure where his head's been lately."

"You worry too much," Todd said.

Jesus, can't you just let me be without criticizing me? "I know."

They watched as Ryan and the other swimmers stood behind their starting blocks. Ryan did his little bounce steps while he shook out his arms. As they waited, Emily came and sat next to Mika, which generated a small knot in Mika's stomach.

"Hi," Mika said, trying to sound genuine.

"He feels good," Emily said. "Not sure if I believe him."

Mika wasn't sure how to respond, as she didn't really want to discuss the inner workings of her son with his girlfriend. "So, how was the movie?"

"What?" Emily thought for a moment. "Oh right. It was sold out, so we just hung out."

What started as uncomfortable small talk was now a bad taste in Mika's mouth. *Did he lie to me? Did this girl make him lie to me? Were they having sex?* But before she could continue these thoughts, the firing gun sounded, and Mika's competitive spirit kicked in.

"Let's go, Ryan. Push it!" She and the others watched as Ryan glided through the water, and he reached the first turn a half body length ahead of his closest competitor. This extended to a full body length by the second turn. Mika ignored her muscular pain as she jumped up and down and hung on Lisa's shoulder.

"Holy shit! Go! Go!" Ryan ended up winning the heat by almost two body-lengths, and he set a personal best by 1.5 seconds.

"Where did that come from?" Todd asked. "Come on." He helped heard the group down to the deck, where they met Ryan, who was all smiles and drying himself with his towel. Mika met him first as she embraced his wet body. He hugged back, but slid out of her grip.

"Mom, come on," he said as he continued to dry himself. Emily joined him and tossed his jacket around his shoulders. He placed his arm around her and kissed her. Todd moved in with his arm extended, and they bumped fists.

"That was PB, right?" Todd asked. Ryan nodded, and Todd and Gary raised their arms in celebration. "I told you he felt good. Personal best!"

Lisa leaned in and kissed him on the cheek. "Whatever you did last night, do it again before state!"

Mika was caught off guard by this comment, and she diverted her eyes to watch Emily and Ryan respond with an awkward laugh.

They spent the rest of the morning watching Mark as he easily won his two events, black eye and all, and they cheered like crazy as the relay team took a commanding lead and never lost it. Mika wanted to celebrate the victory, but she was struggling with the lack of interaction between Mark and her son. She had spent so much energy trying to balance her joy for her son's accomplishment and her concern for what was happening in his life that she had completely forgotten that Todd had committed to shopping for a car when this was all over. She and Todd were in the car before he said anything about it.

"Alright, are you ready?"

"Ready for what?"

"You've been bugging me about a car for weeks, and now you've forgotten about it?"

"Oh my God, that's right."

"We could just go home if you don't want to go," Todd smiled.

"If you take me home right now, I will make it painful for you."

"I'll choose car shopping."

"Smart man."

As they drove to the dealership, they talked about Ryan's chances at state and their surprise over his performance today. Throughout the conversation, Mika couldn't help but think, *bugging you about getting a car? Bugging you? I need a car. We need two cars.* But things were good at the moment, so she knew better than to express her feelings.

They walked around the showroom of the Chapman Mercedes dealership, despite Mika's questioning why they were going with a Mercedes.

"I liked my Volvo," she said. "They're less expensive."

"Or we could just get a minivan," Todd quipped.

"I'm fine with anything with four wheels and an engine," she said, which was almost true. Mika grew up in a house without a lot of money, and while she had become accustomed to new purchases of a better quality, she was still a little embarrassed by excess. Mercedes, in her mind, was excess. They searched the SUVs, and after looking over each car, she immediately went to the sticker price. Fortunately, the cost of the entry-level model matched her appreciation for the car, but even then it was more than she felt needed to be spent. She sat in the passenger seat of a charcoal gray GLK-Class SUV and said emphatically, "I like it."

"I think we should go with the M-Class," Todd said, looking over the feature list of Mika's pick.

"That's another ten grand," she said. "That's stupid."

"Closer to fifteen, but it has better features. The surround camera is awesome. Come on."

Mika didn't budge. "I don't care about the surround camera. Even this car is more than I need. I would be happy with a Toyota. Yes, even a minivan. As long as it has strong safety ratings, I really don't care at this point." Todd closed in on her and kissed her on the neck, which confused her.

"You deserve the best," he said.

"Well, then that would be the G-Class," she argued, knowing full well that he would never spring for a G-Class.

Todd laughed, trapped by his own reasoning. "Okay, maybe not the very best. Look, this is about value. If we can get a slightly-used M-Class, it will drop the price. It will be a better value."

Mika's phone buzzed in her hand, but she ignored it.

"I get that, but if we did the same with one of these, it would be even cheaper."

"This isn't just a decision you make on a whim. I don't want to leave with a huge case of buyer's remorse."

"You worry too much." Mika said with a biting tone that contradicted her smile.

"Yeah, but I worry about things that are important," he said, condescendingly.

Mika just shook her head. "This one is cheaper."

"Cheaper, but not a better value. With what you get for the M class, it will be worth it."

"He's right," said a young, sharply-dressed salesman who had quietly approached.

"See," Todd said.

"The problem is that we don't have any pre-owned right now. Not here anyway. But I can check with the other dealers."

"Could you?" Todd asked, and they exchanged handshakes and introductions. The salesman shook hands with Mika, but she didn't catch his name, mostly because she didn't care. Todd and the salesman walked over to one of the M-Class cars, comparing notes on its features and the sticker price.

"I'll stay right here," Mika said to their backs.

I just want a fucking car. Any car. But she decided it wasn't worth her time to argue about it. Her phone vibrated again, and this time she looked at it and saw a text picture of a cup of coffee from Plantation Jane's, followed by another text.

JB: Good call. Thx.

She smiled, and thought about responding with a smiley face, but deleted it.

MJ: I know.

She sat in the car and placed her right foot on the dashboard, forgetting where she was as she awaited another text. Moments later, it came.

JB: Any other recommendations?

MJ: What are you looking for?

As she sent that last one, she recognized that it was a potentially dangerous question.

JB: Pizza?

MJ: I don't like pizza

JB: What?! Who doesn't like pizza??

MJ: Me

There was a break before his next response, and Mika could see Todd heading into the salesman's office.

JB: That's interesting.

What does he mean by that? Why's that interesting?

MJ: It is?

JB: No ☺

Mika laughed out loud, and then stifled herself as she realized that she was sitting alone in an SUV on the showroom floor of a Mercedes dealership. Then came the next and final text of the night.

JB: But good job on the coffee. You're my go-to in case I need something else

She thought long and hard about her response. *Certainly? Of course? With pleasure? No, definitely not 'with pleasure.' Good night?* None of these made her comfortable, so she kept it simple.

MJ: Kk

Chapter 16

Mika drove herself to work on Monday, but not in a new car that she could call her own. They had spent an hour and half at the dealership on Saturday but left empty-handed. They couldn't get the right car at the right price, Todd said, but there were a few leases that might be turned in early, so maybe this week. Mika wouldn't hold her breath. Today she drove Todd's car alone because he was attending an overnight conference, and one of his partners agreed to pick him up. The conference was only 20 miles from their house, but it was company-sponsored and all employees were required to stay at the hotel for two nights. Mika thought it was silly, but it meant three days of having a car to her self. She felt liberated, like a teenager driving alone for the first time, as she pulled through a Starbuck's drive thru for an iced green tea.

When she arrived at work, she got out of the car and moved with much more ease than the last time she was here. Even though she still had a little tightness in her thighs and hips, it felt good—good enough to motivate her to use her previously never-opened yoga DVD on Sunday, and she was intending to join the yoga class after work today since she wouldn't be in a rush to get home. She had debated going to Lululemon to buy a new outfit just in case she needed to look good in class, but she finally convinced herself to drop her infatuation with Jayce Beckett. It wasn't easy.

She had several meetings to start the morning, including one with the entire division and one that was off-site during lunch. All of this was enough to keep her mind engaged and off of the man from Century Consulting. But when she returned after lunch, it was more busy work, and she had to resist the urge to wander for no reason. Twice she almost went down to Sales before forcing herself to just pick up the phone. And when she was thirsty, she was at the elevator headed for the cafeteria before she turned around and retrieved a bottle of water from the division's refrigerator. It had not been easy, but she made it through the day without seeking Jayce or checking her phone for his texts.

After work Mika went to the locker room and dressed for yoga class. She had cleared her head of Jayce and was only focused on the workout. She was still sore from the first class, but she was determined to do better this time. She pulled her hair back into a ponytail, shoved her bag into a locker, and made her way to the movement room, where she was the first to arrive. *Shit.* She ended up talking to Sheri while they waited for class to start. She told Sheri about Ryan's swim meet, which made Sheri super excited, more than Mika thought she should be since she had never met Ryan. Sheri eventually moved on to another person who had entered the room, and Mika looked out the glass wall of this room and through the glass wall of the gym. There she saw Jayce jogging on a treadmill. He was talking to Donna, or Dana, or something like that from Adjustments, who was on the treadmill next to him. She was laughing and appeared to be trying too hard to keep up with Jayce.

I see. It's just who he is. I was the flavor of the day. It made her feel a little better, as it would be easier to forget him. Before she could turn away, Jayce looked Mika's way and smiled. He made a gesture, either a wave or a salute of some kind. Mika wanted to pretend like she didn't see it, but she returned a small wave.

Damn it.

Fortunately, Sheri started the class, and Mika was able to focus on her body as she worked through the progression of poses and movements. Many of them were the same from the previous class, and Mika still struggled, which irritated her because she was foolish enough to believe that she would come in today and rock it. She used her frustration, though, to stay focused and work even harder. This time she spent less time cursing Sheri and more time listening.

"We do these poses several times," Sheri said as they started their second rotation of Warrior poses, "so you can improve each time. It's like a second chance to push a little more, make some adjustments, or just to get a better feel for the rhythm." Toward the end of the class, they moved into pigeon pose, which was new to Mika. She felt the stretch and burn in her hips as her left leg curled in front of her and her right leg stretched back. She struggled to collapse forward on her chest, as some of the other people were able to do.

"There is strength in *holding* some of our poses," Sheri said. "But sometimes there is strength in letting go. Pigeon is about letting go and not fighting it."

Holy shit, Mika thought as she tried to "let go." It was easily the most difficult pose for her.

After 50 minutes of stretching and twisting and holding, she was again drenched. Her pulse raced and her skin felt hot as she remained on her back in shavasana with her arms relaxed at her sides. She listened to her heartbeat and tried to slow it with several deep, controlled breaths. She realized that in this little space, she was hearing herself and nothing else. She felt strong. When she finally lifted her head, she was the last in the room. She slowly stood, took a cleansing breath and then made her way to the locker room. She felt strange. At first, she thought it was a headache, but it wasn't pain. She felt, for lack of a better description, awake. She saw things—the door, the carpet, the wood benches—all with unusual clarity. She almost didn't hear Sheri as she passed the vanity mirrors in the locker room.

"Nice work, Mika," Sheri told her as they crossed paths.

Mika said her "thank you" with a simple smile since she was afraid that using her voice would crack this strange and delightful state. She removed her bag and clothes from her locker, debated whether or not to change, and then saw that she had several text messages. She thought about ignoring them, but couldn't resist the instinct. She fished her glasses from her purse. The first was from Ryan.

RJ: Will be home by 10.

Of course.

The next was from Todd.

TJ: Forgot my phone charger. Can you bring it?

No. Maybe. Damn it… ok.

The next two were from Lisa. The first asked if Mika had heard from the banquet manager for the swimming gala. *No.* The next asked if she wanted to meet for a drink. *Maybe.*

Mika changed back into her work clothes, shoved her yoga outfit into her Vera Bradley duffle bag, and left the locker room.

As she exited the building, her phone vibrated. At first look, she thought that the text was from Lisa, asking her again to get a cocktail, but then she saw it wasn't Lisa's name on her screen. It was a number. It was *his* number.

JB: Plantation Jane's. Care to meet?

She stood on the entry steps, her head down and staring at her phone. She scrolled up to the previous messages to make sure that this was indeed from Jayce. It was.

Shit. Is this for real?

Before she could gather a complete thought, she had already sent a response.

MJ: Kk

She held the phone even tighter, stared a little harder, wondering where the "Kk" came from. Did she really type that? Can she undo it? Did she enter some kind of alternate universe through a yoga pose? She was so lost in the text that she didn't hear Don Hicks' booming voice behind her.

"Mika?"

She heard it the third time, and when she turned she was so startled by his towering figure standing right behind her that she dropped her phone. Don made a motion to pick it up, and she panicked that he would see the text and know immediately what was going on, even though she herself didn't know. She quickly bent down and pushed past his arms to retrieve the phone.

"I got it! Thanks though," she said, phone in hand and straightening up.

"Are you okay? You look a little out of it," Don asked with a directness that lacked sympathy.

"I'm fine. Just took a yoga class. You know how it is," she said, and then followed instinctively with a jab. "Or maybe you don't, I guess." She smiled, and he returned a polite grin that failed to mask his contempt.

"I sent you an email about a new client, Kondike—an electronics group in Seattle. Can we meet this week?"

"Of course. I'll check my calendar."

"I included some times that work for me. Let me know which one is best." He nodded a goodbye and walked past her toward the parking garage.

She watched him lumber down the sidewalk. *Asshole.* She waited behind, partly because she didn't want to risk talking to him again, partly because she was paranoid that they would pull out of the garage together. She feared that he would notice her turning in a direction away from her house, even though he would have no idea how she typically went home, nor would he have any idea that she was heading to Plantation Jane's.

Chapter 17

Mika sat in her husband's car in the parking lot of Plantation Jane's, a stand-alone building in the front of a large strip mall that contained a family-owned jewelry store and a pet resort.

She was trying to find the right mental state before entering the coffee shop. Her drive had been filled with internal dialogue trying to analyze why he wanted to meet, and most importantly, why he wanted to meet here. Was this about business? If so, then why meet here? More questions about the wellness program? Maybe he wanted an inside scoop on Sales. *Did he meet with Don Hicks and wants me to help plot his death? Maybe he wants to apologize for being a jerk. But, he wasn't really being a jerk. Maybe he wants to give me a heads up about getting fired. Maybe he just wants sex.* She tried to avoid this last thought, but it did enter her mind a few times. Mika wanted any kind of answer, as it would help frame her attitude when she entered the building. But no answer came, and it wasn't until she was exiting her car that she asked herself the most important question: *Why did you agree to come?*

Before she could even begin to analyze her own intentions, her phone buzzed with a text message.

JB: In the back, around the corner. Still in?

She thought for a second before replying.

MJ: Almost there.

Yes, I'm in. I am so fucking in.

She took a deep breath and found her bearings. Her purpose, for now, was to discover the answers to her questions. Just as when she enters a meeting with a new client, she could now enter with confidence and purpose. It was, of course, a façade, but it allowed her to keep walking forward. She did her best not to look suspicious as she scanned the parking lot for familiar cars. Plantation Jane's was far enough from her home that the only car she recognized was Jayce's minivan, but she figured that with her luck, she would see someone she knew. How would it look if she were seen meeting a strange man for coffee, especially an incredibly handsome stranger? She entered the coffee house, which had a large storefront made of bamboo and plywood palm frond cutouts. A few people stood in line, but none of them were Jayce. She proceeded cautiously through the sitting area, which consisted of three sections divided by partial walls to create intimate sittings.

She passed the first section of leather sofas and armchairs, and she nervously scanned several faces to make sure she didn't know any of them. She could see straight ahead past the eye-level wall and saw that she didn't know anyone in that group of tables either. *He said he was in the back.* She walked along the divider to the doorway that lacked actual doors, turned the corner, and found Jayce sitting at the last table, his back to the wall. He looked up from his phone and smiled at Mika. Her stomach tightened, and she felt her heart rate elevate.

Shit. What are you doing here, Mika?

Mika returned the smile as she approached the table, passing an elderly couple enjoying their coffee in silence.

"How are you?" he asked as he stood and extended his hand. She placed her hand in his, and he held it for an extended time as they both started to sit.

"I'm good, thank you."

She felt dirty hiding in the back corner of a coffee house, miles from her home with a beautiful man, but she was glad he had chosen this location. She was glad that she could sit with her back to the rest of the room, which provided an additional level of security.

"You didn't order anything, did you?" he asked.

Mika realized the irony in the fact that she had not even thought about it. "No, but maybe I'll get something in a bit."

"Well, I took a chance and ordered some tea and coffee."

It was only then that Mika noticed three cups on the table. Jayce pointed to the two in the center of the table. "I wasn't sure if you were coffee or tea, so this one is hazelnut, and this is a dragon fruit green tea."

He's good.

"But I have no idea what dragon fruit is," he laughed. "The lady at the counter said it was delicious."

"The lady at the counter?" she teased him. "I think they're called baristas." She took the tea and sipped it.

Why are you teasing him?

"Yes, I think you're right, but I feel pretentious using it in a sentence. And I'm not sure she is technically a barista. She might just be a cashier."

"Just a cashier?" Mika quickly interjected. "So you think you're better than her because she's *just* a cashier?" She smiled, but inside she was a mess. *Just shut up! He might not know you're joking.*

Jayce blushed slightly and laughed. "I can tell I'm going to be in trouble with you." He sipped his coffee and winked at her from behind his coffee cup.

What does that mean? Shit. He thinks you're a bitch. Recover. Say you were joking.

"You might just be."

What? Why did you say that? It's time to go.

But Mika didn't leave. Instead, she tried to relax in her chair, but without much success. She sat with a knotted stomach and tense legs. She sipped her tea and agreed with the lady at the counter; it was delicious.

"If you're going to drink the tea, the bathroom is around the corner. Feel free to go at any time during our conversation," Jayce said, emphasizing the "at any time" with hand gestures.

Mika smiled. "Don't worry, I will."

They sat in silence for a moment, two strangers on opposite sides of a small table, and yet Mika didn't feel like they were strangers. The silence drove Mika crazy. *Why are we here?* Finally, she spoke. "So what's the conversation about? Human behavior? Participation rates?"

"It's about whatever you want to talk about."

"You called this meeting. Don't you have questions about something?"

Jayce looked around the room, and Mika could tell he was thinking. For the first time, he didn't have a quick response. For the first time, he looked a little vulnerable. His finger circled the rim of his cup, and then he interwove his fingers together and leaned forward. He looked directly across at Mika and smiled a nervous smile.

No. No. Don't smile like that.

"First, I don't know that this should be called a meeting. I'm not sure what to call it, but I don't think it should be called a meeting."

"Then what would you call it?"

"I don't know. Two people having a conversation." He took a quick look around the room before settling back on her. "Here's my thing. I travel from place to place. I'm in. I'm out. I never get a chance to really know people. I have to keep a professional distance, or people just see me as the enemy. Whatever, it's a fairly isolated job."

"But what about the Wrap Around?" *Oh shit! Why did you say that?* She stammered to correct herself, but was at a loss for words. Jayce's eyes narrowed as he tried to figure out what she was talking about. He grinned.

"His hair, I get it. Right. Don't get me wrong. I have friends, but I meet all these people everywhere I go, and I never really get to know them. We're those guys that ask questions and have nicknames like 'The Wrap Around' and, what was it, 'anal crabs'?"

"I'm so sorry about that...."

"Don't be. But my point is this, I find you fascinating. I talk to people all day long, and it's all interesting. But talking to you, I enjoy it. You're a breath of fresh air."

Mika could feel herself blush, and she quickly took a sip of tea to hide it. Apparently Jayce could tell, and started to retreat.

"I'm sorry, I just thought it would be nice to have an actual conversation like we did in the car the other day. I thought about calling you to my office again, but that would start looking bad to my partners, and probably to yours as well. I'm realizing now, though, that this was probably a bad idea. I don't want to compromise my position, and I'm sure this is awkward for you, being married and all."

He took a long pull from his coffee, as one does when getting ready to leave. Time stopped as he drank, and a dozen thoughts raced through Mika's mind.

I shouldn't be here. He's right; this is bad. Could I get fired for this? Could he? What if Todd walked in, or Ryan? What would we talk about? He thinks I'm a breath of fresh air? We didn't have a conversation the other day; I babbled on. Why am I fascinating? I really should go.

But one trumped all of these thoughts: *I want to talk to him. Not because I need something from him. Not because I need to sell him on our wellness program. Not because we're organizing a swim event together. Not because he's my husband. I want to talk to him because I enjoy it.*

Jayce positioned himself to stand. "The tea was good?"

"So, what do you want to talk about?"

Jayce stopped just as he was about get up. He gave her a quizzical look.

"I don't want to put you in an uncomfortable situation," he started to say, but she stopped him.

"It's fine. Let's talk."

"Are you sure?"

"Well, I don't think I could live with myself knowing that you were driving around town with no one to talk to except for your minivan."

He smiled that smile. "So you're taking pity on me?"

"A little. Rumor has it that you have anal crabs."

"That's what I hear," he said, settling back into his chair.

Chapter 18

Mika checked the dashboard clock again, making sure she had seen it correctly the first two times: 9:20 pm. She couldn't believe that she had spent more than two hours talking with Jayce. Her head tingled as she tried to process the night.

Their conversation had begun with a simple question from Jayce.

* * *

"How did you get here?"

"Here? Right now? It's going to take me some time to process that one. I'm still not sure."

"No, I mean MedCare. You didn't really answer it earlier," he replied. "And yes, *this* might be a topic for another day."

She explained some of the less personal details. Accounting major. Account manager for Federal Express. Pregnant. Stay-at-home mom while Todd built his client base. Playdates. School volunteer. PTO president. When Ryan was in eighth grade, a parent from her former PTO days called her about a part-time job at MedCare, and she and Tanya connected immediately in the interview. What she kept from Jayce was that she had taken the interview because she had been preparing for a life without Todd. Todd had reluctantly agreed to marriage counseling, but Mika wasn't sure it would do any good. She took her counselor's advice and found a job, hoping it would help keep her mind off her problems. She also knew it would help her be more financially stable in case she and Todd ended their marriage. Mika sometimes questioned whether or not they had ever landed together on the right page and whether or not Todd had really made any changes. She wondered if maybe she just caved and found it easier to be passive than to fight.

"And what about you," Mika asked with a bit of forcefulness. She didn't want to leave the evening feeling that she had rambled like she did last time.

Mika had listened intently as Jayce shared how he was born in Cape Girardeau, a small town on the Mississippi River, but grew up in Seattle. He majored in finance at Missouri State and worked for Boeing for five years before getting his Master's degree from the University of Virginia. One of his professors at UVA had gone to college with Bryan McDouggal, the CEO of Century, and he recommended Jayce for his current job, which he has held for seven years.

Mika would later cringe when she recalled her reaction and the next question.

"So how old are you?" She had been trying hard not to study his face too much while he spoke. If she looked into his beautiful chestnut eyes for too long, she could no longer focus on what he was saying, nor could she remember what she was trying to say. His skin was smooth with no signs of wrinkles, yet his gray hair told a different story.

"I'm 38."

"Really? Went a little prematurely grey, then?" Mika smiled, feeling comfortable enough to joke, but then immediately panicked. *What the fuck, Mika?*

Jayce laughed. "Yeah, a little. It started turning when I was at Virginia. By the time I was 30, I was left with this."

"Did you get that from your dad?"

"I don't know," he said, nonchalantly. He paused. "But once I was able to accept it, I found that it kind of helped. People think I'm a little older than I am, which tends to give me more credibility when I first join a project. I guess it gives people the sense that I'm experienced."

Mika disregarded her initial thoughts on what to say next. *Everyone loves an experienced man. And what about personally? Are you "experienced"? Does the carpet match the drapes?* Instead, she went with something simple but equally uncomfortable.

"Well, I like it." *I like it? So what if I like it?*

"Well, thank you," he said, and he smiled the smile that used to anger her, but was now close to making her wet.

* * *

Mika pulled her car into the garage, grabbed her duffle bag, and entered the kitchen. She was surprised to find Ryan sitting at the counter. His face was buried in his phone.

"You're home early," she said, dropping her duffle on the counter.

"I told you I would be home by ten. Where were you?"

Mika had already forgotten how late it was, and she checked the clock on the microwave to see that it was 9:50 pm.

"I took a yoga class, and then I had dinner with Tanya." She was pissed that she said this because she had not yet eaten and was starving. Would her cover be blown if she went to the refrigerator right now? "Did you eat?"

"Yes," he said, not looking up from his phone.

"What did you have?"

"In & Out."

Mika sighed. "Put the phone down."

Ryan complied. "What?"

"How about some complete sentences? Maybe a conversation?"

"What? I told you I went to In & Out." His tone could have been taken as defiant, but it was based in genuine confusion. He gave up trying to question his mom. "Mother, I went to the restaurant called In & Out. It was a delicious meal."

Mika had grown tired of trying to coach her son on her expectations. When she called him out on things like his one-word answers, he always seemed to be sincerely ignorant of her complaint, which frustrated Mika because she knew he wasn't stupid. However, he always complied, so she learned to just accept that he had eventually done what was asked and moved on with her conversation.

"How was school?"

And as Mika predicted, Ryan came through. "Okay. We had a substitute for physics. The dude was crazy, and he reeked of cigarettes. We walked into the room and BAM! He just stunk."

"That's gross." Mika had forgotten her concerns about eating and took a bowl of grapes from the refrigerator. She placed it between them, and she and Ryan alternated picking grapes from the bowl.

"I know. I don't know why anyone smokes."

"Did you get your essay back?"

"Yes." His voice rose. "She gave me a B."

"And how do you feel about that?" She had learned not to press too much on his grades. Ryan had high expectations for himself and knew when he hadn't done his best, but if his mom expressed any disappointment, he went the other way and became content with falling short of his goal. English wasn't his strongest area, so she figured he would be happy with the B.

"I should have done better."

"Why do you say that?"

"I rushed through the book and waited too long to edit it. I had a bunch of stupid errors that cost me an A."

"That's too bad," Mika said, trying to suppress her irritation. She opened the bottle of vodka that she had left on the counter and poured a drink. *You rushed because you're spending so much time with Emily.* Now that Emily was in her head, she knew she should support that part of her son's life. "So, how is Emily?"

"She's good," he said, but he sounded distracted.

"That's it? Just good?" *Please let there be trouble brewing. Did you realize that she's too clingy? Wait, did she break up with you? Little bitch.*

"Yeah, there's just some drama going on with some friends. It's really pissing us off."

Us? Oh well.

"What's going on? Which friends...," she started before he cut her off.

"Granola, Mom."

Shit. This was their code word for an issue that wasn't going to be discussed. When Mika and Todd were attending marriage counseling, she worried about how their issues would affect Ryan. Mika overcompensated by talking too much to Ryan. She had brought Ryan to a session, and the counselor negotiated a saying that meant, "Mom, I really don't want to talk about this right now." She could press him on issues, but as soon as he said, "I want some granola," she had to back off. She always honored it, and Ryan didn't over use it. In the past few years, he would just say "granola" and she knew what it meant.

"Okay. Okay," she said, sipping her vodka tonic. "I hope it ends well." She heard her phone vibrate. "So, have you thought about getting a job after the swim season?" She fished around the bottom of her purse.

"A little, but it's kind of limiting when I don't have a car."

She pulled out her phone and saw that she had missed seven text messages. The most recent one was one word from Jayce.

JB: Thanks ☺

She smiled. She hadn't heard Ryan's comment. "So, what are you thinking? Job?"

Ryan repeated himself, a little irritated. "Yes, but it sucks not having a car."

"You're telling me that?" Mika laughed.

"Seriously Mom, how am I supposed to get to a job? Ride my bike?"

This last comment got to Mika. She had ridden her bike everywhere until she was 20, and she had always tried to balance giving her son everything she could with an appreciation for everything he had, which could be difficult living in north Scottsdale. This is why she and Todd were able to agree on at least one thing.

"You know the plan. When you can pay for the insurance and gas, your father will buy you a car."

"But I need a job before I can do that. And for a good job, I need a car." Ryan finished the last of the grapes and took the bowl to the sink. "I'm not going to work at In & Out," he said. Mika knew that his calm demeanor was covering his deep frustration. Mika had always admired his ability to stay even-keel; he rarely raised his voice, even when he was upset. This allowed them to continue conversations that probably would fall apart in other families.

"Well if you want it bad enough, you'll figure something out."

Ryan laughed. "You and Emily. You're killing me."

"Well if she said the same thing, she can't be all bad," Mika laughed.

Oh no. You did not just say that! Fortunately, Ryan had returned to his phone and apparently didn't analyze what his mother had just said.

"I know. You're conspiring against me. Did you talk to Dad? He called like four or five times."

Shit. "No, he sent me a text." She returned to her phone and saw that he had sent six texts after the first one about his phone charger.

> TJ: Hello?
> TJ: Forgot my charger.
> TJ: HELLO??
> TJ: Bring it in the morning, plz.
> TJ: Where are you?
> TJ: Battery almost dead....

When she finished reading, she found Ryan taking a sip of her drink.

"Hey!" she snapped.

"It was just a little sip," he grinned.

"And I'll show you just a little kick in the ass."

Ryan laughed, told his mom "good night" and ran upstairs. Mika did a quick calculation and determined what time she would need to leave to take the phone charger to Todd, and then she returned to Jayce's text. Again, she smiled.

> MJ: No, thank you.

Realizing that she had the bed to herself gave her an additional level of pleasure, and she decided to pour herself another vodka tonic and take it with her to bed. As she took her first step up the stairs, she was reminded for the first time in several hours that her body hated her. Lifting each leg the eight inches necessary to get to the next step was a chore, and she couldn't help but laugh at herself.

After changing into a large t-shirt and her boy short panties, she slipped into bed. Mika stretched her legs wide under the sheets, not just because it felt good, because she could. She was feeling great for many reasons: the awakening of her muscles from yoga, two vodka tonics without dinner, the night to herself, and—of course—her conversation with Jayce. Unlike last time, she wasn't kicking herself for what she had said. There were awkward moments, like her comment about his grey hair, but they didn't linger inside her head. She closed her eyes and saw his engaging eyes behind his warm laugh. They were like a magnet drawing her in, and then she saw his hands. His long, strong fingers held his coffee cup with an interesting balance of confidence and tenderness. And as his fingers manipulated the cup, her own hands had slipped down between her legs, massaging her inner thigh before sliding inside her underwear and caressing her sweet spot. Mika arched her back as she felt the pleasure of her own fingers, and she came quicker than she had in a long time, perhaps ever.

Chapter 19

Even though Mika awoke an hour earlier than her typical time, she was invigorated. She moved with energy, as if she had slept for a week, and her head held a slight buzz. She had forgotten about her bedtime self-pleasure until she realized how relaxed she felt, and she was slightly embarrassed. She took one quick look in the mirror, hoping to see some progress—which she knew was impossible after just two yoga classes—yet she was hopeful anyway.

Standing in the shower, the hot water washed away her elevated state as she started to map out her morning, beginning with her drive to bring Todd his phone charger. Then she remembered that she needed to schedule a meeting with Don Hicks, and by the time she left the shower she was back to feeling flat. She dried her hair, dressed, and hurried downstairs just in time to see Ryan as he headed out the front door.

"Can I give you a ride?" she asked. She knew the answer but asked anyway.

"Emily's here."

"How about dinner tonight?" Before he could say no, she added, "You *and* Emily?"

"Sure. I'll see if she can go." He closed the door behind him, and Mika went into the kitchen.

It will be fun, Mika thought, trying to convince herself. She took a strawberry Nutri-Grain bar from the pantry and quickly devoured half of it while she poured a glass of cranberry juice. She drank, took another bite, and then looked around at the empty kitchen. She sighed.

She drove to the Pointe Hilton where Todd was staying, and she felt good that it was far enough away from Plantation Jane's. She hadn't thought of Jayce until this moment. She wasn't sure if it was guilt, but she was relieved to know that there was no way Todd could have seen her drinking tea with another man last night. And this thought made her realize—for the second consecutive day—that she needed to put Jayce Beckett out of her head. She scanned the radio, searching for the perfect song to occupy her mind, but she couldn't settle on one. She drove for 20 minutes, listening to 20-second clips of more than 50 songs from just about every decade, from *Every Rose Has Its Thorns* to *Teenage Dream* to *In the Air Tonight* to *Strawberry Fields*. In between songs bites, she worked on her story about why she never replied to his text messages yesterday. Between the song search and creating an alibi, her mind was occupied enough to quickly pass the time, and she was in the Marriott parking lot before she knew it.

Mika entered the hotel lobby of white stucco and Saltillo tile, and debated whether to just drop off the phone charger at the front desk or to call his room. She decided to call his room.

"Can you ring Todd Jones' room, please?" she asked the young female clerk at the front desk. "I'm his wife."

As the clerk explained that she would need to go to the courtesy phone and request his room, Mika realized how this could look: a wife trying to catch her husband with another woman. She chuckled inside as she thanked the clerk. *Thank you, front desk lady*, she thought, smiling as she remembered the barista conversation from last night.

Mika found the courtesy phones and requested her husband's room. Todd picked up on the third ring.

"Hello?"

"I'm here. What room are you in?"

"Finally! I'm running late, so just wait in the lobby." He hung up before she could respond. Mika strolled over to the elevators and sat on the edge of a large leather chair. Her thoughts returned to the idea of catching Todd with another woman. She knew he would never cheat, but she wondered how often it does happen. The elevator dinged, and a man and woman exited. They were dressed professionally and didn't appear to be a couple, but the thought entered her mind. *Did they have sex last night? Are they married? Did she enjoy it?* She watched them disappear down the hallway, and the other elevator dinged. Todd exited with a few other men, one of whom she recognized from his office. He motioned to his partners that he would catch up as he marched toward Mika. She stood, expecting to hug him out of habit, but instead she just stood there.

"Thank God," he said, taking the charging cable. "Why didn't you respond last night?"

She replied quickly. "I went to yoga and put my phone in my duffel bag. I completely forgot and left the bag in the car. By the time I got it, your phone was already dead." *Did I say that too quickly? Was it too rehearsed?*

"Why didn't you call the hotel? I had no idea if you were coming," he said with his condescending voice.

"I don't know. I wasn't thinking," she said. *Fight or flight? Flight.* "I'm so sorry."

"I was worried," he said, relaxing a bit, but not completely.

Mika felt a little guilty, but was offended by the hint of anger still in his voice. *Fight.* "Then why didn't *you* call from the hotel phone?"

"What difference would it make? You didn't have your phone with you, right?"

"You could have called the house, or Ryan. Right?" She stared at him, and he looked odd, almost uncomfortable. It was a strange, new look on him, one that she hadn't seen before. *Did he have a woman in his room? Please tell me you were having an affair.*

"I don't know our number. Or yours. Or Ryan's," he admitted.

She cocked her head a few degrees. "What?"

Todd laughed. Mika realized that he wasn't uncomfortable; he was embarrassed. "I don't know our phone numbers. They're in my phone. I just press your name. I don't know if I even have the home number in there. We never use it. Who knows their home number anymore?"

Mika laughed with him. "I know our numbers."

Todd challenged her on this, and she quickly rattled off all of their phone numbers. She stood before him, victorious.

"Okay, so I'm an idiot," he said.

"As long as we're all in agreement," she laughed. "How's the conference?"

Todd rolled his eyes. "The same. Dinner is tonight. Are you going to make it?"

Mika usually attended the final night's dinner, as did many of the other spouses, but she was relieved that she had other plans.

"I told Ryan that I would take him out. And Emily."

"That's probably more fun." He looked at his watch, and then held up his phone charger. "Thank you. I have to run. I'll touch base with you later." He hurried down the hall and disappeared around the corner. Mika left the lobby, not realizing that she and her husband had never touched.

Mika spent much of the morning on the phone negotiating a trouble-shooting session between a client and her go-to guy from the I.T. department, Jesse. She also confirmed a meeting with Don Hicks for the afternoon. She didn't want to meet with him today, but he only gave her three options: today or two different times on Friday. It was better to get it over with than to dread the experience for the next several days. As Mika finished typing some notes from her troubleshooting experience, Tanya interrupted.

"I'm heading down to the cafeteria. Care to join me?"

It was good timing; Mika was hungry. It was earlier than her usual craving, but then she realized that her day had started an hour earlier than normal.

"I'll meet you down there," Mika said. "Give me ten minutes."

Mika finished her notes, sent Jesse the I.T. guy a thank you email, and left the office. Waiting for the elevator, it was the first time she had slowed down since arriving at work. It was also the first time that she had thought about Jayce, which she did when she caught herself looking down the hall with the hope of seeing him. And while this began as a nice thought, it suddenly made her nervous as she thought ahead to her lunch with Tanya. Most of her conversations lately had revolved around the Century team and the future of the Wellness Division. Would she be able to keep a poker face if Tanya started down that path? Would she accidentally let something slip, thus revealing her rendezvous with the gray-haired stud? And while these thoughts made her want to expel Jayce from her mind, her heart raced when the elevator doors opened and she saw a head of gray hair among the four people in the car. Thankfully, it was not Jayce.

As Mika rode the elevator to the lobby floor, her phone vibrated. She saw that she had two messages. The first was from Todd, which came an hour ago.

TJ: Charged and back in business. Thanks!

The second and most recent was from Ryan.

RJ: Emily can't do dinner. Mom is sick and dad is out of town. Mind if I stay with her? Maybe dinner tomorrow?

Mika's heart sank, for several reasons. While she was disappointed that she wouldn't be having dinner with her son, she was instantly taken back to her own childhood.

* * *

Regina Bublik, a Ukrainian immigrant who valued her education and making sure that others did too, had been a preschool teacher in Tucson. When Mika was eight years old, her mother started complaining that she would occasionally see flashes of light in her right eye. After several months of visits to an optometrist, two different ophthalmologists, and finally an oncologist at the University of Arizona Medical Center, she was diagnosed with ocular cancer. A tumor had formed in the back of her eye, and while they treated her with chemotherapy to minimize the spread of cancer cells, she ultimately lost her eye.

Even at the age of 8, Mika noticed the affection between her mother and father through this difficult time. Her father, Denny, was a roofer who worked long, laboring hours, but he never failed to be there when she needed him. After full days baking his soul on rooftops under the Arizona sun, he still came home to make dinner and clean the house. Mika became his sidekick, enjoying most of her time in the kitchen next to her dad—washing and shredding lettuce, boiling water, and cutting vegetables. She wanted to help her mother, but most of the time the best thing to do was to let her be, so she turned to assisting her father, a larger-than life figure who was carrying their world on his shoulders.

After chemotherapy, Regina eventually returned to her old self, with the exception of an eye patch. Even though she had a glass eye, Regina hated it and insisted on wearing the patch. Whether it was for vanity or as a badge of honor, Mika would never know for sure. Two years later, Regina returned to the doctor complaining of great fatigue. The cancer had reappeared and spread to her lymph nodes, her lungs, and her pancreas. It was such a rapid growth that Regina's case would later be mentioned in two studies in the Arizona Medical Journals. They tried several types of treatments, which did nothing more than to put the family closer to bankruptcy. Mika watched as her mother lost weight and hair, almost becoming a different person over a nine-month period. And during this stretch, she not only saw her father as a dad, but as a human. His eyes were often red from crying, which he would never let Mika see, and he seldom ate. Yet, he worked hard to maintain a positive environment. He and Mika still made dinner together, and when Regina would go to bed early in the evening, he made sure to spend time with Mika. Often, that meant putting his arm around her while they watched TV. It didn't matter to Mika what they watched; she could escape the pain of her real world sitting on the sofa under her father's arm while watching *Dallas*, *Magnum P.I.*, and *Cheers*.

Toward the end of her 5th grade year, Mika was in class comparing fractions when she was called out of class. She packed her backpack and went to the office, where she found her father. He took her hand, and they left in silence, which is how they remained until they reached the hospital. They walked through the dingy hallways to her mother's room. Denny knelt down and put his hands on her shoulders. His eyes were glassy and red, and Mika could see the pain behind the strength he had mustered for this moment. Throughout the rest of her life, whenever she thought of her father, these eyes were the ones she most often remembered.

"Be strong," he said, and he hugged her.

They entered the hospital room. One wall was lit with horizontal slits of light that came through the partially closed venetian blinds, and along the other wall, her mother's bed lay in the shadows. Tubes delivered medication and fluids into her withered arms, and she wore her eye patch and her signature scarf over her head. Regina's eyes were closed, and Mika feared that she was too late. She approached carefully. Her stomach knotted. She felt her eyes swell, and a tear rolled down her cheek. She turned to her father, who indicated that she should keep going. When Mika reached the bed, her mother opened her eyes and smiled.

Mika felt her mother's cold hand take hers.

"How was school?" Regina struggled to say.

Mika just shrugged.

"Mika...." Her father's voice encouraged her from behind.

"It's okay," her mother said.

"We're comparing fractions," Mika finally said. "It's easy."

"For you, yes. You are very smart."

She looked into her mother's good eye, and saw a different pain than she had seen in her father. She couldn't define it at the time, but her father's pain was that of a man losing the love of his life, a man who knew that his daughter was losing her mother. He was a man struggling to know how he would hold his future together. Regina's eyes, however, were filled with a future that she would never have with her daughter. Her first love, her first heartbreak, graduation, talks of politics over coffee, a wedding, a career, grandchildren... all the moments they would never share were painfully present in her gaze. Mika's tears took over and she collapsed onto her mother's hollow chest. Her head rested under her mother's chin, and she could feel her shallow breath on her ear while Regina's hand caressed Mika's.

"You are so beautiful," her mother whispered. "I am so proud of you."

"I love you, Mommy," Mika returned between sobs. Regina's hand moved to Mika's back, and she dragged her fingers back and forth between Mika's shoulders, a move that never failed to calm her daughter, and this was no exception.

Regina whispered into Mika's ear. "Always work hard, my sweet, but love harder, and take care of him." Mika knew that the "him" was her father, the nearly broken man leaning against the wall with his head down.

Mika's mother continued breathing for two more days, but she never stayed awake long enough to utter another word. Mika carried her mother's final words as commands, but deep down she always felt that she had failed her mother on one of them.

* * *

The elevator reached the lobby floor, and she read her son's text again.

      RJ: Emily can't do dinner. Mom is sick and dad is out of town. Mind if I stay with her? Maybe dinner tomorrow?

She replied with the only words she could.

      MJ: Of course.

Chapter 20

Mika sat in one of the sales department's conference rooms, tense and irritated as Don Hicks outlined the specs on his new client.

Her lunch with Tanya had been uneventful. She never brought up the topic of Century Consulting or Jayce Beckett. Instead, Tanya wanted her opinion about some investments she was considering making. Tanya was single and childless and—combined with a few inheritances—had amassed a decent nest egg. She was considering investing in a friend's restaurant as a silent partner, which Mika thought was a horrible idea. She didn't tell her not to do it, but instead posed many of the negatives that she knew to be true about restaurant investments and then left it to Tanya to decide for herself. She sensed that Tanya was looking to do something different with her money, something that gave her a feeling of ownership, but she valued Mika's opinion enough to reweigh her options. Mika enjoyed the lunch primarily because it took her mind completely away from Jayce, her family, and MedCare, even though they sat in the company cafeteria.

But now, she was back in her corporate world listening to one of her least favorite people, his assistant, and a few people from I.T. and finance. While Don's arrogance irritated her, she was also fuming that he had been 10 minutes late to the meeting that *he* had initiated. She took notes in the profile package that he had prepared, trying to look for odd numbers or conditions that might complicate a program design. She didn't see any yet. Kondike was a large technology plant that manufactured micro conductors, and their proprietary invention—some type of screen that Mika didn't understand or care about—had helped them experience exponential growth in the past four years. Like many companies, they offered their employees a choice of healthcare plans, and hopefully MedCare would be one of them. She wondered why this meeting was so important as it appeared to be a relatively standard package design opportunity. Then it became apparent. As Don rehashed figures from the company profile, the conference room door opened. Dominik Moon entered, followed by Jayce Beckett.

Oh shit. Mika's body was at war with itself. Her first instinct was to smile, but she fought that urge as her stomach tightened.

"I'm sorry we're late," Dominik said in his unassuming tone.

"Don't worry about it all," Don said, too eagerly. "I'm just going over the profile."

"Everyone remembers Jayce Beckett with Century, right?" Dominik asked, and everyone nodded. Jayce smiled as he scanned the faces in the room. He ended with Mika. *No, don't do that!* She quickly darted her eyes back into the meaningless pages of the Klondike profile. *Did anyone notice us looking at each other?*

"Nice to see you again," Don said as he shook Jayce's hand. They all took a seat. Jayce sat at one end, slightly behind Mika, which made her a little more comfortable since she could look at Don without the distraction of Jayce's beautiful face.

"So what we need is a solid package that will not only get us the deal, but also drives their employees to choose MedCare."

No shit, Mika thought. *I needed to be here so you can show off for Jayce? He's smart enough to know that you are full of crap.*

"So Mika, the wellness piece needs to be top-notch on this one, okay?"

Oh my God, I want to punch you in the fucking face.

"Mika? Hello?" Don was chuckling while looking at Dominik and Jayce, as if he were a king amused by one of his peasants. Mika forgot about Jayce.

"Right, top-notch program. Unlike the other programs we design, which, I'm assuming, are less than top-notch?" Mika said.

Don became visibly annoyed, and he stood up in his traditional way of using his size to intimidate. "That's not what I'm saying, Mika. It's just that Kondike would be our third largest client, so I think you can see why we should give it that extra attention. Details, you know?"

"I don't know how you operate, Don, but we give all of our clients that extra attention, regardless of their size." She could hear Don sigh heavily as she flipped through the profile. "Now about those details, I don't see an existing behavior analysis in the profile. Did I miss it?" She looked up to see Don nervously shuffling papers. Mika and Don both knew that this information wasn't always included in the initial client profile, but Don had been so focused on impressing his invited guests that he forgot and started to scramble. For some reason, Mika took pity on him.

"Don't worry about it," she said. "I know you usually send it later."

She could see Don regain his composure, and she turned just enough to see Jayce. He sat, expressionless, but for the brief moment when their eyes met, she could sense a smile.

"Yes, that's right," Don said, his voice retaking control of the room. "But if you want it now, I will have it sent up."

They spent the next 90 minutes discussing initial product proposals and timelines. Dominik and Jayce stayed for the first 20 minutes before excusing themselves.

"Thank you, Don," Dominik said as he stood. "Fine job," he said to the group.

"Thank you," Jayce said, with a simple smile as he scanned the table. He ended with Mika, and he winked.

No! She felt flush, and now it was Mika who was scrambling. After Jayce left, all she could think about was the potential impact of his wink. *Did anyone see that?* She envisioned Don telling his partners about Jayce's lascivious wink and people whispering behind her on the elevator. The knot in her stomach tightened. But then she thought, *I've seen him wink at other people; it's his thing.* She hadn't actually seen him wink at anyone else, but she tried to convince herself that she had. She felt that all eyes were on her, and she mustered the courage to look up from her notepad. Her muscles relaxed slightly as she saw everyone engaged in their conversations and taking notes. *Just relax and keep going,* she told herself. She took two controlled breaths, and within a few minutes she was back in the conversation.

Chapter 21

It was nearly six o'clock, and Mika was still at her desk. After her meeting with Don Hicks, she had retrieved the information that was missing from the meeting and then spent the remainder of the afternoon sorting data and getting started on the plan for Kondike. Except for a few interruptions, she had stayed relatively focused on the new client, and when she had finally stopped to look at the time, she had already missed the start of yoga. She considered going to class late, but decided to close out some emails instead.

She closed her laptop, looked around at the empty office, and sighed. *Same as home,* she thought. She left the office and contemplated her evening now that Ryan was out of the picture. She could go home for a quiet evening of whatever was left in the refrigerator, or she could stop at Spinato's for a chopped salad and a glass of wine. What was nagging at her, though, was a level of guilt over missing Todd's company dinner. Even though she would be late, she felt that it would be a nice gesture to go now that she was free for the night. She continued this internal debate out to her car, each time looking for a logical reason why she should not go to Todd's dinner. She sat in her car, key in the ignition, and waited, almost hoping that the car would just drive to wherever it was that she was supposed to go. And then her phone vibrated with a text. It was Jayce.

JB: Car trouble?

She smiled, but was confused.

MJ: No? Where are you?

JB: Look to your left.

She looked out her window, across the two empty spaces next to her, and there sat Jayce in his sweet ride of a mini van. Mika smiled, and then she sent a reply.

MJ: Just trying to decide what to do for dinner.

She watched as he read the text and typed his response. Mika laughed as she realized how silly it was for them not to just get out of the car and talk, but this was more fun. And safe.

JB: Sadly, I'm headed to Plantation Jane's. I'm addicted.

Mika read his response, and instantly she knew where she wanted to go tonight. She wasn't sure, however, if this was an invitation. Then another message came.

JB: Care to join me?

She looked up from her phone and over to Jayce. She smiled and nodded.

JB: Follow me.

Anywhere, she thought, and she started the car and followed his minivan to their coffee hideaway. Her heart raced along the way. What started as an evening of undesirable options was now filled with excitement. As she pulled into the parking lot, her energy tempered a bit as some of her fears returned. She again scanned the parking lot for familiar cars. She felt better not seeing any that she recognized, but she was still nervous and sent a text to Jayce.

MJ: Go in without me.

She figured she would wait until he was in and had time to order before she entered. She sat in her car, looking for something to do to kill a few minutes when Jayce responded.

JB: Iced tea? Food?

Mika contemplated her response. She was starving, but she wasn't comfortable eating in front of him. Plus, she had never eaten here, so she didn't really know what was on the menu.

MJ: Sure, and whatever.

Mika typed a message for Ryan.

MJ: Love you. Let me know when you are headed home.

Just as she hit send, another message came from Jayce.

JB: Okay. They have a lot of whatever. I'll sit where we did last time.

Mika smiled, and decided to send Todd a message.

MJ: Hope the dinner is going well.

She didn't know why she felt the need to send it. Possibly, it was from guilt. Possibly, it was a pre-emptive strike because if he texted her while she was with Jayce, it would be okay to ignore since she had already sent him a message. Mika stared at the interior of her husband's car—the dash, the stereo, the cup holder—and then to the fake palm tree exterior of Plantation Jane's.

What am I doing here?

She contemplated restarting the car and just driving away, but then her phone buzzed.

JB: Same table as last night.

Mika abandoned her thoughts of going home, stuffed her phone in her purse, and headed inside, where she proceeded through the dining area with her head slightly down, eyes straight ahead and avoiding eye contact with anyone. She turned into the secluded corner, where Jayce sat in the same seat as last time. He smiled as he lifted his coffee cup. Mika took her seat quickly and then as she grabbed her cup of tea, she noticed several small white plates with a variety of baked goods.

"I wasn't sure what you meant by 'whatever,' but I assumed it meant high carbs. There's a chocolate chip scone, an oatmeal cookie, and a blueberry muffin, which is supposed to be just the best."

"So says the counter lady?"

"Exactly."

Her hunger overrode her fear of having food stuck in her teeth, and Mika took a small corner from the scone, which quickly crumbled on her tongue. They sat in silence for a moment. Mika wanted to talk about his visit to today's meeting, but wasn't sure how to ask if she kicked ass without sounding arrogant. As if he were reading her mind, Jayce brought it up.

"I really want to avoid talking about MedCare with you," he said, leaning forward. "It's important that we don't talk about it, but I just want you to know that you did a great job today."

Right. Was that before or after you winked at me?

"Thank you," she replied as she placed another chunk of the scone into her mouth.

"I don't want to pretend like I know you that well, but I don't think you realize how good you are," he said, this time leaning back into a more relaxed pose. "People listen to you."

What the fuck? Mika was unprepared for such a compliment, so she tried to dismiss it. "Except for Don Hicks."

"I have no comment on Don Hicks."

"I'll take that as an agreement that he is an ass," she smiled.

"Nope. I have no comment on Don Hicks. I have no comment on Dominik Moon. I have no comment," he smiled.

"Got it. No MedCare talk." She washed down her last bite with some tea. "Okay, so let's talk about you. I don't see a ring. Not married?"

"No." He smiled in a way that made his eyes appear distant despite the perpetual sparkle.

"Why not?" *Shit, Mika! Can you be more obnoxious?* "I'm sorry, that was a little rude."

He laughed. "No, not at all. I just haven't found the right person yet. Travelling makes it difficult."

"I can imagine. Although, there is something to be said about long-distance relationships."

"Really? Like what?"

Mika realized she was heading into a deep subject, and she tried to backpedal. "Oh, you know, it's easy to get caught up in routines. Kids. Work. Taking care of the house. You can lose sight of yourself a bit. Having some time to yourself can be a healthy thing, and it can make you appreciate the time when you are together."

"Does your husband travel a lot?"

Shit. I don't want to talk about Todd right now.

"A little. Not much. He's at an in-town conference right now, so I've had a few days to myself."

"And a few days with the car."

"Right, and the car." *Okay, how do I get out of this conversation?*

"Good. So you get that alone time you need then. That's good."

Mika just smiled and nodded. *Sure, whatever.* "So, what do you do when you aren't doing this?"

"What do you mean by *this?*"

"You know, your job. Talking to your car. Meeting strange women for coffee."

"First, I never said you were strange. I may have thought it, but I never said it." They laughed. "I do typical stuff. I like to stay active, so I run and hike when I can, and if there's a pool around, I swim."

"My son's a swimmer."

"I know, you told me. He has state coming up, right?

"Right." Mika felt a little foolish, and she feared forgetting what else they had already talked about.

"I swam in high school until my senior year."

"Were you any good?" *Of course you were good. How could that body not be good in the water?*

"I was okay. I couldn't put in the time to practice everyday, so I reached my ceiling a little early."

"So why did you stop your senior year?" Mika shoved a larger piece of scone in her mouth.

"I just had a lot of things going on with my family, and since I couldn't really commit to it, I decided it wasn't worth investing my time." He reached for a piece of the muffin, and as he did, Mika read that maybe she should change the subject.

"So what else do you do besides take care of yourself?"

"Well, I really like movies."

"What kinds?"

"All kinds, really. Not horror so much, but pretty much everything else."

"Like *The Notebook*?" She smiled. Lisa had made her see *The Notebook* because it was "the best movie ever." Mika couldn't stand it.

He grinned. "I did see the Notebook."

"And...?"

"It had its moments."

The two continued to nibble at the pastries as they discussed the movie. Mika found Ryan Gosling's character to be a little creepy, and Jayce appreciated the story of two soul mates eventually ending up together, something he wasn't sure was real but wanted to believe existed. They spent the next forty-five minutes talking about other movies, from *Shawshank Redemption* to *Moulin Rouge* to the *Rocky* movies, with occasional detours about vacations (in particular Mexico via *Shawshank Redemption*) and societal violence (via *Rocky*). They ended with their top 5 celebrity crushes: Nicole Kidman, Jennifer Lopez, Katie Holmes, Scarlett Johansen, and Salma Hayek for Jayce, and Jon Hamm, Christian Bale, Usher, Paul Rudd, and Brad Pitt (but only from *Legends of the Fall*) for Mika. They debated the merits of each, often making fun of the selection (Paul Rudd? "He makes me laugh."). When they finished, Mika looked down and saw three empty plates.

So much for not eating.

She looked across the table at Jayce, and he was studying her. She wiped a napkin across her mouth in case she had food lodged somewhere.

"Can I ask you a personal question?" he asked.

"Well, I did just tell you that I find Paul Rudd oddly sexy, so sure," she laughed.

"Did you stay in your car because you didn't want to be seen walking in here with me?" He smiled in an odd, almost sympathetic way.

How do I answer this? Shit, just be honest.

"Yes. But it's nothing personal."

"I know. I mean, I think I know."

"It's just... I don't know, weird." *How eloquent, Mika.*

He leaned back and stared at the coffee cup before him. He drummed his fingers nervously on the table.

"Are you okay," Mika asked, suddenly feeling a little uncomfortable.

He didn't look up, and his lips moved as they tried to express his thought. Finally, words came out. "I'm in a little bit of trouble here."

"What kind of trouble? Are you pregnant?" She laughed at her own joke.

"No," he smiled. "I'm not pregnant." He finally looked up, and his eyes locked on hers. "I'm having a really difficult time not thinking about you."

What?

"The moment I walked into that auditorium, I noticed you. Obviously, I saw this beautiful woman sitting there, and you are far more beautiful than you know. But there was something about the way you sat there, an understated confidence, maybe, that made me want to talk to you. Which was a mistake."

Mika's head was swimming, and all she could utter was, "It was?"

"Yes, because I have spent every day since then wanting to talk to you. I take a few extra trips to the elevator each day hoping to bump into you, just to hear your voice or see your smile. And this--" he gestured back and forth between the two of them sitting at the table, "this I really enjoy. Probably too much."

Mika sat back and pulled her eyes away from his. *Holy shit. What the hell am I supposed to do with this?* She was speechless, and she couldn't garner many thoughts either. Finally, she could only state the obvious, "I'm married."

"I know. You're married." Jayce leaned back and sighed. "But I don't care."

She looked at him. He smiled, and all she could feel was panic. *Oh. My. God.*

He gave a defeated smile. "I told you, I'm in trouble."

Mika struggled to put together a response, but she couldn't. Finally, she took her purse and said, "I need to go."

"Of course," Jayce said. "I'm sorry..."

"No, don't be sorry," she said, and she knocked over the chair as she turned to leave. She reached down to get it and fumbled twice before finally getting it back on four legs. Mika left without looking back, and her wobbly legs barely carried her back to her car. Her hand shook as she opened the car door. She got in, started the car, and with the lights from the dash illuminating her face, she could finally verbalize a thought.

"Shit piss."

Chapter 22

Mika turned off the radio and drove home in silence. Her mind raced from one incomplete thought to the next.

I'm a horrible person. Did he just say he wanted to fuck me? Is that what he meant? How did I end up here? Will anyone be able to tell that I was just propositioned? Why would he say that to me? I could never do that... could I? I'm an idiot; I must have misunderstood him. Why didn't I wear a better bra? Did he even notice? Mika, stop thinking. Just stop!

As she pulled into her driveway, she saw that the lights were on, which meant that Ryan was home. It also meant that she needed to push all of these thoughts aside. While she tried to clear her head of what had just happened, she couldn't wipe away the feeling that lay hidden deep beneath her heart—the feeling of happiness that came from being with Jayce Beckett, and the pleasure of knowing that he wanted her in a physical way.

She entered the house and dropped her purse on the kitchen counter. She could hear the television in the next room, and she followed the sound to find Ryan asleep on the couch. She returned to the kitchen, looked around at the familiar surroundings, and felt lost. She went to the pantry for the bottle of vodka, but then changed her mind.

Even that's not going to help. Mika went to the refrigerator, reached past Todd's Guinness for a plastic bottle of cranberry juice, and took a long pull. She turned off the lights and returned to the living room. As she turned off the television, she found it odd that he had been watching the Food Network. Ryan awoke at the sound of silence.

"Hey, I was watching that." He pushed himself onto his elbows as Mika sat on the edge of the couch.

"You're home earlier than I expected," she said.

"It wasn't good. She was in pain, and I felt like I was in the way," he said.

Two hours ago, Mika would have seen this as an opportunity to speculate about the health of his relationship with Emily. Two hours ago, she would have crafted a follow-up question that hinted at them breaking up. Two hours ago, her heart would have tingled at the thought of discontent between her son and his girlfriend. But now, she could only muster one thought.

"Well, good to see you." She patted him on the knee, and for the first time that she could remember, she sat in awkward silence with her son.

"Are you okay?" Ryan asked, and Mika turned to see him studying her.

Oh shit. Shit. "Sure, why?"

"You just seem a little out of it."

"I'm just really tired," she managed to say. "I might have a cold coming on." She massaged her throat, pretending it was a little tender.

"Go to bed, then," Ryan said, as if he were the parent.

"You too," Mika replied, and she leaned over and kissed him on the forehead.

"Thanks, Mom. I appreciate you giving me your cold a few days before state finals," he smiled.

Mika had already forgotten the lie she had told less than a minute ago, and she almost gave it away before catching herself. "Oh right! Sorry." She offered a "good night" as she went upstairs, and she could hear the television turn on.

As she undressed in her bathroom, she heard her phone vibrate.

Do not look at it, she told herself, and she continued to get ready for bed, all the while trying to push away thoughts about the evening. She scrubbed her face several minutes longer than usual, brushed her hair longer than normal, and applied lotion to her arms, which wasn't a typical part of her routine—anything to distract her from returning to her bed and picking up her phone. Eventually she ended up in bed and quickly placed her phone out of reach on the nightstand. She stretched her arms and legs and took a deep breath.

Fuck.

She tried thinking about work and her new project. She tried thinking about the swim gala. She tried thinking about the ceiling fan that rotated above her. But all she could think about was Jayce's mouth and what it would feel like to kiss his lips. After several minutes, she gave in and reached for her phone. She slowly turned it over and was both happy and disappointed that it was from Lisa.

LC: We need to meet. Tomorrow?

Mika responded with "Kk" and then dropped her phone next to her. She spent the next several hours trying to fall asleep, but instead she tossed and turned, flipping into new positions, different pillow combinations, and different fan speeds in the hope that something would allow her to fall asleep. Finally, just after 1 am, she decided to use her unproductive energy and do some yoga. In the empty space next to her bed, she started in table position, took some deep breaths and went into cat's stretch. She wasn't following any prescribed routine; rather, she just went into poses as she remembered them. She focused on working all of her muscles, keeping her arms, torso and legs engaged in such moves as warrior's pose, hoping to exhaust her muscles so she could fall asleep. She tried collapsing into pigeon, but her hips were too tight to let her chest fall to the floor. Fifteen minutes later, she was already sweating and her heart rate was elevated. She placed her feet together and slowly lowered herself into the balancing butterfly. She wobbled in the squatted position as she tried to balance her toes; she found her balance, but it was work and her quadriceps shook, eventually knocking her out of the pose. Her breathing was heavy, and she moved into child's pose. Sitting back on her knees with her arms stretched out in front of her, she took several slow, intentional breaths with her diaphragm doing the work. For the first time since she left Plantation Jayne's her mind started to clear, and before she knew it, Mika fell asleep in child's pose.

Chapter 23

Mika awoke to the sound of her alarm, and was lying on the floor next to her bed. After realizing where she was and remembering how she got there, she found her phone on the bed, silenced the alarm, and immediately checked for a text message. There was one, but it was again from Lisa.

LC: We need to meet. Don't forget!

Mika was disappointed, not only because she didn't receive a message from Jayce but also because she just wanted to be done with the swim team.

MJ: Kk. Will call after work

As she showered and got ready for work, she convinced herself that meeting with Lisa would be a good thing. Working through the minutia of the gala would keep Jayce Beckett out of her mind. She hoped. Plus, Todd would be home tonight. Mika always enjoyed her days of solitude when her husband was away, but this year's absence brought an additional level of comfort and satisfaction.

Mika vowed not to check her phone for messages that morning, a commitment she broke three times before leaving the house. As she entered the kitchen, she caught Ryan as he was leaving for school.

"Dinner tonight?" she asked. "Dad will be home."

"Maybe," he said. "I'll let you know."

She sighed as he closed the door behind him. She looked around at the silent kitchen, and her stomach knotted at the thought of being alone in this empty house next year. Alone with her husband. The only way to shake the feeling was to get on with her day. Mika headed for work, stopping at a Starbucks for an iced tea. She had debated going out of her way to stop at Plantation Jane's, but unlike her lack of follow through with the phone, she decided it was best to go somewhere else. As she waited in the drive thru, her phone vibrated. She didn't want to check it, and she had the most surprising—and depressing—thought: *Please let it be from Todd.* She tried to ignore it, but as she pulled up to the window, she grabbed her phone and looked at the screen. It was from Jayce.

JB: Sorry for making you uncomfortable. That's the last thing I want to do.

Mika stared at the screen. *Don't reply. Don't reply.* She sat there long enough to forget where she was, and the server at the drive thru window called to her twice before Mika finally turned to see an outstretched hand holding a tall green tea.

"Are you okay?" the woman asked.

"Yes, thank you. Just thinking, sorry." She took the tea and pulled forward. She wondered how she must have looked if someone was compelled to ask if she was okay, which led her to think how nice it was for her to ask. And then she smiled and wondered if the kind lady was technically a "barista" or a "woman at the window."

Damn it! Don't....

She pulled off into a bank of empty parking spaces, picked up her phone and typed a response.

MJ: No worries. ☺

Mika drove to work and spent the day in a strange mental place that was neither here nor there. She was happy that she and Jayce had communicated that morning, even as minimal as it was, and yet she wanted no further thought of the man from Century. She spent most of the day at her desk, which was such an unusual event that Tanya approached her and asked if everything was okay.

"I'm fine," Mika asked, barely looking up from a spreadsheet that she had already looked over last week. "Why?"

"Just making sure. You seem a little down."

"I'm good," Mika said, forcing herself to look at Tanya with a smile. "I just want to get ahead on the Kondike account." *Please don't talk to me anymore,* she thought as she returned to the spreadsheet. Unfortunately, she felt Tanya's hand on her shoulder.

"I know what you're worried about," Tanya said in a lowered voice.

No you don't.

"Those guys from Century have us all on edge."

No kidding?

"You don't have to prove yourself," Tanya said. "Jayce Beckett is too smart not to see your value."

Please go. Just. Please. Go.

Mika muttered a "thanks." Tanya patted her on the back and returned to her office.

She tried to make this be her final thought of Jayce, yet he still lingered in her head as she plotted ways to avoid running into him. When she ate lunch, she bought a prepackaged turkey sandwich so she could jump past the people waiting for the hot-served entrees. She took the sandwich back to her office, keeping her eyes buried in a folder just in case Jayce was in the vicinity. Even her trips to the bathroom felt like covert spy missions: *Get in. Get out. No casualties.*

By the day's end, Mika had accomplished quite a bit on the Kondike proposal, but she had also accomplished a lot of nothing as she double-checked figures on programs already in place. Now that the day was over, she faced a dilemma: her hips and lower back were wrecked from sitting at her desk and spending the previous night on the floor. She wanted desperately to take a yoga class before going home, but she was afraid that she would see Jayce. She looked around the office and realized that she was the only one there. Some of her fire returned at the thought of leaving one lonely place and going directly to another.

Fuck him. I'm doing what I want to do.

Mika left the office, purposely holding her head high as she walked down the hallway. She rode the elevator to the first floor, and crossed the lobby to the women's locker room. She didn't see Jayce, and while she had mustered up some bravado, she was relieved because deep down she knew that his presence would have torn it all away. She changed quickly and entered the yoga class just after it had started.

"Nice to see you, Mika," Sheri whispered. "There's some space over there." She pointed to the side of the room against the wall. Mika made her way past people on their backs in shavasana. She tried not to trip over anyone as she quickly scanned the room. No Jayce. Mika felt the muscles in her shoulders relax, and she found her space against the wall. While her muscles relaxed, her mind did not. Mika spent the class working extra hard to stay focused on her breathing, but it never lasted long. When she wasn't thinking about Jayce, she was thinking about Todd coming home and Ryan leaving. She was unstable several times, and Sheri came over twice to help her with her pose.

"Don't forget, you can always go into child's pose if it's too much," she said to the class but with extra attention thrown Mika's way.

I don't need child's pose!

This began another internal dialogue that kept her from focusing on her body.

Then what do you need?

I don't know.

Do you need Jayce?

No! Why would I need Jayce?

Todd?

No. I don't need anyone! Shut up and focus!

She took two long, controlled breaths as she slid from cobra into downward facing dog. And then she hit herself with the final question.

Well, then what do you want?

She took another breath, filling her lungs as her diaphragm expanded.

I don't know.

And that became the lasting thought that carried her through to the end of class.

Chapter 24

Mika finished the class feeling drained, both physically and emotionally. Despite her earlier thoughts, she just wanted to go home and get on with her life. As she pulled into her driveway, her phone vibrated.

Now? Are you kidding me?

She looked at the phone, but it was from Lisa.

LC: Let me know when you can come over

Mika had not forgotten, as she was still hoping it would keep her distracted.

MJ: Got it. After dinner.

Shit. Mika had not considered dinner for her family. She entered the kitchen with the expectation of foraging through the refrigerator but instead was hit with the scent of seafood, and she found Todd, Ryan and Emily cooking.

"Hey, Hun," Todd said, sautéing shrimp at the stove.

"Hi, Mrs. Jones," Emily said, tossing cut grape tomatoes into a large salad. Mika saw Ryan tending a steaming pot of boiling water and pasta.

"What's going on?" Mika asked, setting her bags down next to the door.

"We got out early," Todd said without looking up from the shrimp.

"So you decided to cook?" Mika was caught off guard. Todd was actually a decent cook, but he only did so on special occasions or if Mika pestered him. She made her way over to the stove.

"Well, I was talking to Gary, and he said you and Lisa were working tonight. Plus, you got up early to bring me my charger yesterday, so I thought it would be nice if I took care of dinner." He gave her a cheesy, sincere smile, one she hadn't seen from him in a long time.

"It was my idea," Ryan chimed in.

"No it wasn't," Emily corrected.

"Well, it was kind of a collaboration," he smiled.

"Nope. Not at all." Emily laughed, and Mika was surprised that she actually enjoyed the exchange between her son and his girlfriend. Perhaps she was just glad to see him regardless of the situation.

"Go change," Todd said, giving his pan a shake. "Dinner will be ready in five minutes."

"Well, alright then," Mika said with some spirit that came more from surprise than joy. She kissed Ryan on the back of the head as she passed him and went upstairs.

In her room, she found Todd's shirt and tie crumpled on the chair and his suitcase on the bed, unopened, which had always been an issue for her. Whenever she traveled, Mika made a point of emptying her suitcase before doing anything else. She considered it an extension of the trip. When it was done, then she was really home and could relax. Todd had a different approach, which usually resulted in Mika taking care of his travel items and laundry. It was just a carry-on, but the suitcase served as a reminder that while what was happening in the kitchen was a pleasant surprise, it was not what she wanted. If Todd's helpfulness were a more consistent part of their life together-- something that she could rely on--she might have a different appreciation for it. But when it showed up like a random shooting star, it wasn't enough for her to enjoy. Still, she wanted to try, if for no other reason so she wouldn't feel like an unappreciative bitch.

"Mom!" Ryan's voice called from downstairs. "Dinner!"

Mika quickly stripped off her clothes and put on jeans and a slightly tattered Calvin Klein t-shirt.

She hurried downstairs and joined the table.

"This is nice," she said, looking at a plate of shrimp scampi and a salad. It was Todd's go-to for cooking, and even though Mika wasn't a huge fan of shrimp, she acknowledged that it was good.

"Thanks," Todd said through a mouth full of linguini.

She ate a bite of salad, and as she chewed, remembered that Emily was there. Mika watched as Emily wrapped a fork with noodles. She was intrigued that this young woman elicited such strong emotions from her. Emily looked up, and Mika felt guilty for staring.

"So, how's your mom doing," Mika asked.

Emily shrugged. "Better today, but not great."

"She's out of bed though," Ryan added.

"Well, that's good. Give her my best." Mika immediately felt stupid, as she had only met Emily's mother once.

"I will," Emily responded. "Thank you for asking. I'm hopeful that she can make it to state on Saturday."

"I didn't realize that you were racing?" Mika said, confused.

"I'm not, but she wants to support the team."

"And me," Ryan chimed in with a mouth filled with shrimp. "She loves me."

"Ryan…," Mika started to admonish him but was interrupted by Emily.

"She does. She just thinks he is so *adorable*." Emily made a comical face on the last word, and Ryan smiled with a false image of arrogance.

Mika suddenly felt uncomfortable at her own dinner table. She wanted to love the fact that another parent appreciated her son, and she wanted to love watching her son in a fun relationship, but it still left a bad taste in her mouth. Fortunately, Todd kept the silence from growing.

"Are you ready for Saturday?" he asked, leaning back in his chair as if this question demanded all of his attention.

"I'm good," Ryan said. "Not much more I can do."

"Bullshit," Todd said as a matter of fact. "Stay sharp up here," and he tapped his head.

"I know. I got it."

"How is Mark's eye?" Mika asked, and she immediately felt the tension between Ryan and Emily.

"Good, I guess," Ryan answered, barely looking up from his plate. Mika saw him shoot a glance at Emily, and he changed the subject.

"Any chance I can borrow the car this weekend?"

Todd started to respond, but Mika wasn't listening.

Come on. Don't be one of those guys who ditches his friends when a girl comes around.

She kept trying to think about how to bring Mark back into the conversation, but she lost herself in her own thoughts, which eventually found their way back to Jayce and his beautiful face. Fortunately, her husband intervened before she journeyed too far down that path.

"Mika? Hello?" Todd was leaning forward, looking irritated.

"I'm sorry, what?"

"That's probably okay, right?"

Mika had no idea what he was asking, but she was afraid to let on that she wasn't paying attention.

"Yes, I think so," she said.

"Sweet! Thanks," Ryan said.

Mika snuck a look at Todd, but he was looking at his phone.

I need to get out of here, Mika thought, not because she didn't want to be with her family, but because she didn't want to sit with them and try to suppress thoughts of Jayce. It was too much for her to handle. She took in one last bite of salad, stacked her plates, and stood.

"This was nice, but I need to get over to Lisa's." She scooped up her plate and utensils, and then took a look at all of the dishes on the table. *Crap.* She knew Todd wouldn't touch them, and she didn't want to come home to a sink full of dirty dishes. "Ryan, will you take care of the kitchen?"

"What? But I helped cook?"

This angered Mika, as they had never operated under the "I cook, you clean" policy; she had always done both. "So what?"

"We'll take care of it," Emily said, and she reached for Ryan's hand.

Mika momentarily set aside her dislike for their relationship and gave a sincere, "Thank you." She took her plates to the sink and set them next to the dirty pots and utensils, washed her hands, and dried them on her jeans.

Lisa's house wasn't far, but it seemed much farther than usual as she thought about Jayce. More specifically, she thought about how to *not* think about him. His face would appear, and she would tell herself to stop. Then she envisioned his strong hands on his coffee cup. She would catch herself and try to think of anything else. *Did the Lipinski's paint their house? Is that a new bush in the Hubert yard?* But like an imaginary ninja patrolling her brain, Jayce seemed to have a counter move for each of her evasive thoughts. She was relieved to pull into the driveway at Lisa's house. *Lisa will keep me distracted.*

It started successfully. She readily accepted a vodka tonic from Lisa, and the two of them delved into their event notebooks, checking off and sharing what was done for the gala. They took about 30 minutes to review all of the vendor contracts and confirm checks, and then Lisa was ready for another drink.

"So, how's Ryan doing," she asked, pouring herself a drink that was mostly vodka with very little tonic. "I haven't seen him in awhile."

"I know, right? What happened between those two?"

Lisa shrugged, pouring some more vodka into Mika's glass. "Ah, they're busy being seniors," she said, not sounding concerned.

"He just seems to spend all of his time with Emily."

"That too," Lisa laughed.

"I just hate for him to be that guy, you know."

"Have you seen her little body? If he wanted to spend more time with Mark than her, then I would be worried."

Mika thought about this, and apparently Lisa could see the concern on her face. "Don't worry about it. He's a teenager. It's what they do."

Mika knew that there was some truth in this, but still couldn't help being bothered by the intensity of their relationship. Mika followed Lisa back to the dining room table.

"We haven't talked much ourselves," she said. "How's that audit thing at work?"

Shit! Don't bring him up. "The audit thing?" Mika wasn't sure why she felt the need to play dumb, but she did.

"That company coming in and looking at everything."

"Oh, right. Century. It's good, I guess."

"Have they talked to you yet?"

"Um, a few times, I guess." Mika mindlessly flipped through her notebook, hoping it would redirect them to the gala.

"Well, how was it? Are you worried?"

"Worried? About what?" *Please stop asking me questions.*

"About your job. Isn't that the danger for everyone, that you could lose your job?"

"No, I'm not worried. I think it's good."

"Well, if you get in trouble, you could just fuck one of them!" She let out a vodka-enhanced laugh.

Mika forced a smile. "That's not going to happen. Now let's get back to this before we're too drunk."

They returned to their lists, checking on the room arrangement and casino details. But as Lisa talked and read notes, Mika could only hear Lisa's previous words. *You could fuck one of them.* And everything they discussed dragged her one step further into the world of Jayce, no matter how hard she fought it. As they talked about tables, she thought about Jayce at the conference table during their first meeting. When they discussed the black jack tables, she pictured Jayce dealing and his hands elegantly sliding cards across the table. And when they got to food and beverage, she could only think of Plantation Jane's.

She looked across at Lisa, who was making adjustments to a room map, and Mika felt angry. Angry that she couldn't concentrate. Angry that she felt out of control. Angry that Jayce had done this to her. And partly angry that he hadn't texted her since that morning. *That fucker!*

She took her phone and sent Jayce a message.

MJ: Plantation Jane's?

Before she could even start writing her own list of things to do, her phone vibrated. It was Jayce.

JB: When?

She looked at the time; it was 8:45 pm. She and Lisa still had work to do, but she was mentally done.

"All I have left is to go through the list of prizes. I'll do this at home and send it to you, okay?"

Lisa kept writing. "Okay. Heading home to your hubby? Going to show him what he's been missing?" Lisa smiled.

Dear God! "Something like that." She typed her reply to Jayce.

MJ: 20 minutes?

Lisa finished writing, slammed close her notebook, and looked at Mika. "When this gala shit is over, we're going out and getting wrecked!"

"Deal," Mika said as her phone vibrated in her hand.

JB: Perfect.

Chapter 25

Mika sat in her car in the parking lot of Plantation Jane's. There were more cars than she expected, and she was second-guessing her decision to come.

Her trip here had been filled with fiery internal conversations of how she was going to put Jayce Beckett in his place. *You're real smooth, aren't you? Who do you think you are coming on to a married woman?* She had never really settled on an approach, and she was even more uncertain now that she was moments away from facing him. She almost changed her mind, but then realized she needed to do this if she were to properly function ever again.

As she walked through the parking lot, she didn't see his minivan. *Maybe he chickened out*, she thought, but then she saw his car turn into the parking lot. His headlights hit her like a spotlight as she stood outside the entrance, trapping her against the building. *Shit!* Not only was a possible exit thwarted, she was reminded that she was wearing her jeans and an old t-shirt. It was nothing horrible, but not what she wanted to be seen in. Not by him. She entered quickly and proceeded to their usual table, where she took her seat with her back to entrance. Her stomach tightened.

What are you doing here, Mika? What the hell are you going to say? Look, Jayce, you're a son of a bitch and I don't ever want to talk to you again? Or maybe Lisa's right; I should just fuck him. No, you can't. Holy shit, stop. This guy is trouble. Jayce, I don't know who the fuck you think you are, but I'm reporting you to Dominik tomorrow. You can't just tell a married woman that you want to have sex with her, asshole!

Her thoughts were interrupted by Jayce's hand, which lightly touched her shoulder as he passed by and sat across from her.

"Hi," she said with a meekness that drastically contradicted her emotions.

"Hello," he said with a reserved smile. "Nothing to drink?"

"No, I'm fine," she said. "I don't have much time."

He leaned forward, setting his elbows on the table and resting his chin on his hands. Mika thought he looked exhausted.

"Well, I'm guessing that this is kind of a goodbye," he said with a knowing grin.

"What makes you say that," Mika asked.

He lifted his chin as if his battery had been recharged. "You mean it's not?"

Mika tried to recall all of her previous thoughts, looking for some of the fire that had driven her here. It was gone.

"Look, I'm married. I don't do this, whatever this is." She looked into his eyes and almost lost herself in their clarity. She darted her eyes away.

"I get it," he said. "It's probably better this way."

"Well, I think so," she said. *Wait, what?* "But why do you say it like that?"

"I was a little useless at work today," he chuckled. "It took all of my energy not to send you a text, and twice as much effort not to check for one from you. I had to carefully navigate the building to do whatever I could to not see you today."

Mika tried to hide her smile, but wasn't successful.

"It's not funny," he said. "I just don't get it."

"Wow," Mika teased. "You really know how to compliment a girl."

He laughed. "No, no. You know what I mean, right?"

And she did know what he meant. She had found men attractive before, and she had even had a few "what if I weren't married" thoughts, but nothing like this.

"I haven't had this type of attraction to someone before, not this quickly," he continued, "and I don't know what to do with it."

They sat in awkward silence, and Mika wished that she had a drink so she could fidget with the cup. Finally, she said simply, "I'm married."

He looked at her, and she immediately looked down at her hands. He leaned forward, and placed his hand on hers.

Oh dear God! "No, don't," she said. The touch of his hand against hers sent an electric charge through her body, causing the hair to stand up on the back of her neck. His fingers caressed the back of her hand, and he gently massaged her index finger. *Oh dear God.*

"I know; you're married," he said in a low voice. "But life is short, and I would regret not telling you this. You are an amazingly beautiful woman, and you have me captivated in every way possible." He continued to caress her fingers. "And if you don't have people in your life telling you that, then that is a crime."

What? All thoughts were gone from her head, and it was all she could do to not look at him. Her only available sense was the touch of his skin against hers, and then that went away. He stood, and she managed to look up.

"I'll leave first this time. I won't bother you anymore." He held her gaze for a moment, and then drifted away, leaving Mika sitting alone in the back of Plantation Jane's. She almost left a minute after him, but then figured that she should wait. She looked at the time on her phone and decided to wait five minutes, which surprisingly passed quickly. She told herself that she had done the right thing, but she kept asking herself, *How did I get here? How did this happen? Why did this happen?*

After five minutes had passed, she made her way back to her car, careful not to make eye contact with anyone for fear that it was obvious that she had just missed having an affair. She hurried to her car, climbed in, placed the keys in the ignition, and then just sat. The glow of the dashboard washed over her, and she hoped that it would consume her so that she could be anywhere but here, anywhere but headed home. Several times, she reached to put the car in reverse, but each time she wasn't ready. She tried to muster the focus to go home, but the opening of the passenger door startled her. *Oh God!* Her heart stopped as she thought she was being robbed. She fumbled for her door handle, but kept missing it. The intruder was now in her car, but instead of finding a seedy crime figure seated next to her, she saw Jayce. The dashboard lights hit his eyes like the moon on a lake.

"What are you doing?" she asked.

"I said I wouldn't bother you," he said, softly, "but I lied." He leaned forward, placed his hand on the side of her face, and planted his lips against hers.

Chapter 26

Mika sat in her car, which was now parked in her garage. She was still numb from her encounter 25 minutes ago.

Her initial fear of being robbed had immediately turned to confusion when she saw that it was Jayce who had slid into the passenger seat of her car. She remembered asking him what he was doing, and then he closed the door. The rest was a blur. His fingertips had pressed against her cheek, and all tension left her body. His eyes twinkled like the night sky as his face closed in on hers, and she remembered thinking, *Wait! What's going on?* All thoughts died, though, as his soft lips touched hers. She could remember his scent, an amber-woody aroma that rose from his neck, and she could remember the warmth of his tongue as it entered her mouth and met with hers.

She had no way of knowing for sure how long they had kissed. A minute? Maybe two? It could have been days, for all she knew. He had pulled away quietly, and when she opened her eyes, he smiled.

"I would have regretted not doing that," he had said, then opened the car door. "I'd like to do it again, but that's up to you."

He left, leaving Mika in stunned silence. Sitting there alone in her husband's car in the parking lot of a coffee shop, Mika was a melted pile of flesh. But, she had never felt more alive. Her hands trembled as she put the car in reverse. A police officer surely would have pulled her over if he had seen how she occasionally drifted out of her lane as she drove home.

Which is where she now was, trying to find the courage to go inside. She pulled down the vanity mirror and checked her face.

Shit.

His end-of-the-day stubble had slightly irritated the skin around her lips, leaving it a little red. Or was it her imagination? She lightly patted the area with her fingertips, hoping that increasing the blood flow might help. It didn't, and she examined herself again, trying to determine if it was only noticeable to her because she was looking.

She quietly entered the house, and much to her relief, the downstairs was empty. She went directly to the kitchen sink, pumped foaming soap into her hands and washed her face. She repeated this twice, hoping it would also wash away any thoughts of the evening. As she patted her face dry with a paper towel, she remembered his cologne. Mika tried to smell her own face, and her lack of success only drove her back to the sink to re-wash her face, this time with a little more soap.

This time she noticed that the dishes were clean and put away. She opened the dishwasher, and even that was empty. Mika looked around the dimly lit kitchen, and for some reason she focused on the breakfast table, which they had purchased at a garage sale ten years ago. She argued with Todd about their ability to get it home safely, but he removed one of the back seats of the their van, disassembled the legs, and tied the back door partially closed. They had driven 10 miles below the speed limit all the way home. She had looked back in the van, saw the table wedged in and Ryan holding the legs across his lap, and she had to admit that he was right. As she remembered this and then looked at the family photos hanging on the wall, the euphoria she felt earlier was quickly being replaced with shame and guilt. Her legs weakened and her stomach tightened. She leaned against the counter and closed her eyes because she couldn't look at anything without feeling even worse.

You didn't do anything, she told herself repeatedly. *He did it, not you.*

"Mom?"

Mika let out a loud gasp and opened her eyes to see Ryan standing at the bottom of the stairs.

"Are you okay?"

Be calm! Be calm!

"Yes, sure. Sorry. I was just thinking," she stammered. She hoped he wouldn't come in, but he did. She took a coffee mug from the cupboard and filled it with tap water, and kept it near her mouth as much as possible to hide any evidence that another man's lips had been on hers. Ryan went straight to the refrigerator and removed a large bottle of apple juice.

"Are you sure? You look, I don't know… sick?" He drank directly from the bottle.

Despite her state of panic and weakness, she thought quickly and replied, "I think I had a little too much to drink at Lisa's." Ryan just nodded as if it made perfect sense.

Now leave.

He didn't. "We cleaned up," he said, fishing for a compliment.

"I see that," she said, holding the mug in front of her mouth as if it were hot coffee on a winter day. "It looks great. Thank you." And then she added, "Thank Emily too."

"I will." He took another pull from the apple juice and returned the bottle to the refrigerator.

They shared the kitchen in unusual silence, and Mika felt like he wanted to say something.

"Are *you* okay," she asked.

He looked uncomfortable, but answered with a nod. "I'm fine." With his demeanor, she was expecting him to say "granola," but instead he said, "I'm going to bed," and he went upstairs.

That was weird! Was it weird, or is it just me?

Mika finished her water, set the mug in the sink, and slowly made her way upstairs thinking only one thing. *Please be asleep. Please be asleep.* She carefully opened her bedroom door, and discovered Todd lightly snoring on his half of the bed. *Thank God.* She saw his empty suitcase against the wall as she darted quickly into the bathroom, sliding the pocket door closed behind her. Mika stripped off her clothes, and as she reached for her pajamas, she stopped and looked at herself in the mirror. Her naked figure stared back at her, and while her body was clean, she felt dirty. She turned on the shower and entered immediately without waiting for it to turn hot. The cold water shocked her system, and her skin tightened until the warmth arrived. She stood under the stream, letting it hit her face and run down the front of her body. The water bounced off her cheeks, blurring her vision, and she lost herself in her thoughts. She thought of her guilt of betraying her family. She thought of having to face Ryan if he ever found out. She thought of her parents and their commitment to each other. She thought of how disappointed her mother would be, and Mika started to cry. Yet, none of these thoughts could erase the fact that Jayce's touch electrified her in a way that nothing ever had, and it terrified her.

Chapter 27

Mika stared out the passenger window as Todd drove her to work the next morning. Her gaze vacillated between the phone in her lap and at nothing in particular—just random objects and street signs blurring past her. She was tired from a lack of sleep, and she had settled into a nice place where she was no longer thinking about anything.

"Are you taking class tonight?" Todd asked as they turned into the MedCare parking lot.

"I don't know. Maybe." She knew that she wasn't because she didn't bring her clothes, but she didn't want to commit to anything he might suggest.

"Well, when should I pick you up?" She could sense the irritation that he was trying to suppress.

"I'll let you know."

"When?"

Now she was irritated, and she raised her voice. "After lunch. Let me see how my morning goes, and I'll let you know after lunch."

"I don't know why you're getting so upset. I need to plan my day so I know when to be here." He had that condescending tone that made Mika want to punch him.

"And I'm tired of planning my day around not having a fucking car!" They had pulled up next to the curb near the entrance.

"Jesus! Will you just relax? We're getting you a car."

She wanted to tell him to fuck off, but she knew deep down that her attitude was more about her than him. "Go ahead and plan your day. I'll just get a ride," she said simply, and she got out of the car. As she climbed the steps, she heard a slight squeal from his tires as he pulled away, causing a few heads to turn from others around her. *Nice.*

Mika felt fortunate that her morning was filled with meetings, even if one of them was with Don Hicks. She unpacked her laptop and files for the day, read a few emails—one of which was from Tanya asking her to go to lunch—and she checked her phone for what she vowed would be the last time. She wasn't checking in hopes that Jayce had sent her a message, but just to confirm that he had not. Even though he had said that he wouldn't bother her and then moments later kissed her, her instinct told her that it really was her move, a situation that gave her both comfort and angst.

Mika poured her focus into her work and had a productive morning. She even tolerated Don Hicks as he tried to explain to her the importance of her own department. "That's a nice way of putting it," she told him when he finally stopped talking.

Now she sat across from Tanya at Pita Jungle, but it was not the relief that she had hoped for. Mika had looked forward to the companionship and the chance to talk about anything. Even though they had lunch together just over a week ago, so much had happened that it felt like forever. Unfortunately, Tanya set the course into uncomfortable territory.

"So, what's going on? How are you?"

"What do you mean?"

Tanya leaned forward, and Mika appreciated her genuine concern. "You seem a little off lately. Is everything okay?"

It was here that Mika realized how much trouble she was going to have dealing with this situation: she couldn't talk to anyone, no matter how desperately she needed to. Lisa was her closest friend, but they were family friends, and she didn't really trust Lisa's perspective. Tanya was her closest colleague, but she couldn't share this with her. So once again she felt alone.

"I'm fine," she said, but she knew that wouldn't be enough to satisfy Tanya. "I'm just tired lately. I haven't been sleeping well."

"Have you been to the doctor?"

"No, I'm good." Again, she fished for a statement that would end her interrogation. "I've just been busy with Ryan's swim team. The gala is next week."

Tanya leaned back a little. "Well, if you need some Ambien, I can get you some. My brother brought me some from Mexico."

Mika smiled for the first time all morning. "Don't you think it's odd that we work for an insurance company and you're offering me prescription meds from Mexico?"

Tanya laughed, and with that their conversation turned to her financial decisions and the restaurant investment.

"I just don't know why you would put your money into something you know nothing about," Mika said. "Especially with the possibility that we won't have jobs soon." *Uh oh. Don't go there.*

"We're good," Tanya said with assurance. "We're not going anywhere."

Mika smiled. "You never know what's going to happen."

"You're right. You never know. But I don't want to live my life on just one path. Opportunities come up, and if we never consider them, then maybe we're closing ourselves off to a better life. I'm just afraid that that's going to be me."

Mika didn't respond, and Tanya continued to talk about the restaurant investment throughout the remainder of lunch.

Mika spent the rest of the afternoon working on program reports and the Kondike plan while trying to avoid looking at the clock. The end of the day would mean trying to get a ride home, or burying her pride and calling Todd. He had already sent one text asking if she needed him, and she had told him no. Now, as the office started to empty and she was ready to go home, she was starting to regret that decision. Tanya had left early, and she really didn't feel comfortable asking any of her other colleagues from the Wellness Division. She wasn't necessarily close to them, and she felt like she would need to explain why she needed a lift.

She packed her laptop, put away her work, and made her way to the lobby. She felt like a lost child at the mall, not sure where to turn. She wandered to the fitness room and saw Sheri leading a class. She could ask her, but she lived in a different direction. Also, Mika knew her just well enough that she might get too comfortable and spill the details of Jayce Beckett. She walked outside, hoping someone might see her and insist on giving her a ride. She went back inside, sat on a bench, and just watched as people left, usually side-by-side embroiled in conversation. Mika checked the clock on her phone, and she spent just enough time debating whether or not she could still catch the bus that she actually missed the final pick up. She finally decided that she had but one choice. She called Jayce.

Chapter 28

Mika walked out to the bus stop, questioning her sanity. Jayce had answered on the third ring, just as Mika was getting ready to hang up.

"I didn't think I would hear from you."

"I didn't either. I feel really stupid asking, but can you give me a ride."

"Where to?"

"My house."

"Interesting." His voice had made it sound like he was amused.

"Never mind. You don't have to."

"I'm still in the office, so give me five minutes."

"Oh," Mika had said as she turned around, half expecting him to be standing nearby.

"I'll meet you in the lobby?"

"Sure," Mika had said, still looking around and hoping to find the face that matched the voice. "No. Not the lobby. How about at the bus stop?"

Mika waited at the place where he had first picked her up on that rainy day, and she contemplated why she had called him. She had no intention of getting physical with him. Did she? She wasn't entirely certain, but she did know that his kiss last night—his entire presence, for that matter—had turned her upside down, and she needed to talk about it with someone. The only person that she actually could talk to about this was Jayce.

Mika sat on the bench and waited, feeling stuck between two worlds: one with her husband, a man she knew she didn't want, and the other with Jayce, a man she wanted but knew she shouldn't. She felt alone with nowhere to turn, which was not a new feeling for her.

*　*　*

Mika and Todd had met when she was a 21-year-old intern at Wescott Financial. She was in her final semester of college, a requirement of her major even though she had already received a job offer from her current employer, Federal Express. Because she wasn't getting paid, Mika found it difficult to motivate herself to put in the 15 hours each week that she needed, but one of the junior planners had started to catch her attention.

Todd was primarily an assistant to a team of advisors, helping them with research and preparing reports, but he was eager to impress and start building his own client base. Wescott occupied the entire second floor of a four-story building, and it consisted of a web of cubicles and conference rooms. Todd roamed the floor with just enough confidence to be called cocky. In Mika's third week with the company, he approached her while she sorted client profiles from a former advisor who had just moved to another state.

"Hey intern," Todd said, leaning on her desk. "Anything look interesting in there?"

She should have been annoyed by the "hey intern" comment, but something in his voice made her laugh.

"Not exactly," she said. "Just double checking the account types."

"Well, keep up the good work," he smiled. "I'm going to let the bosses know that you're doing a great job."

"Thanks. I appreciate that," she joked as he did some weird half-shuffle, half-dance away from the desk.

This type of exchange went on for a few weeks, and Mika soon found herself looking forward to it. One day she had just entered the office when Todd slipped in next to her.

"You're coming with me," he said, taking her by the arm. "We have a meeting."

"Um, okay," she said. "What kind of meeting?"

"Don't worry about it." He escorted her to the conference room, where two advisors were working. "I'm going to a meeting, and I thought I would take the intern." Their look of indifference apparently was also their approval. Todd led Mika out of the building, and they walked down the street. It was the first time that Todd hadn't said anything to her when they were together. She broke the silence.

"I do have a name, you know?"

"I know. It's Mika," he smiled, not missing a step. "But 'intern' sounds a little more mysterious, don't you think?"

She chuckled. "I think it makes you sound a little more pompous, don't you think?"

"Ouch," he smiled, and he directed her into Brownie's Deli, a tiny mom and pop deli and sandwich shop. He took a small table against the wall and next to the cooler filled with cans of soda. She sat opposite of him, but she looked confused.

"The meeting is here?" she asked.

"This *is* the meeting." He smiled.

Mika looked around, as if she would find clarity from one of the other tables.

"What do you mean?"

An older lady, whom Mika would later discover to be the sister of the owner, brought them two menus and two glasses of water. "How are you today, Todd?" she asked.

"Just great. And you?"

"You know me. I can't complain," the waitress responded. "Well, I could, but no one cares. Let me know when you're ready," and she disappeared behind the counter.

Todd looked at Mika and grinned. "I'm taking you out to lunch."

"What about the meeting?"

"Right, it's a lunch meeting."

Mika cocked an eye. "Wow. That's pretty bold."

Todd took that as a compliment. "I know."

Mika found herself amused by the junior advisor sitting across from her. Between working 35 hours a week entering data at Federal Express and preparing for her final year of school, Mika had little time to socialize. This was her first "date" in more than a year, and she appreciated his energy and companionship, something she had lacked since her father's accident when she was 17-years-old.

"This place is my favorite," he said, handing her a menu. "They have a fantastic bagel sandwich. I get it every time."

Mika ordered a chicken salad on wheat, which she enjoyed while sharing college stories with Todd. He had graduated a year earlier, and had taken some of the same courses that she was taking now. He asked about her family, but she skirted the issue by talking about his. She didn't want to have the death of her parents set the tone for a potential relationship. She had seen what she perceived as pity in the eyes of a relative stranger whenever she told her story, and she couldn't handle it. They finished eating, and despite Mika's protest, Todd paid for lunch. They walked back to the office a little closer than when they had left. Before they re-entered the building, he stopped her, and she thought he might try to kiss her. Instead, he offered a subtle smile, one that betrayed his brash persona and revealed some vulnerability.

"I had a great time, and I hope you don't mind if I ask you out again."

"Well, technically you didn't ask me out this time," she smiled.

"True," he blushed. "So, I would love to ask you out again for the first time then."

She smiled and gave him her phone number, which he only needed to repeat twice to memorize. He called her the next day, and that Friday night he took her to The Fish House, an upper-end restaurant that Mika was definitely not accustomed to. Mika was sure that Todd was trying to impress her, and she didn't want to disappoint him, so she talked up the restaurant. She would have been just as happy at any number of middle-of-the-road eateries, but she liked his company and appreciated his drive for success. They dated exclusively for the next two years, and while there were many good times, including their spontaneous road trips to the beach or the mountains, they were also prone to arguing. One contentious subject was the amount of time he spent working, even when they were on vacation. After Todd had bought his first mobile phone, he was constantly taking and making calls to clients and colleagues. This frustrated Mika, but she recognized that his work ethic was one of the qualities that she initially liked about him, so she convinced herself that it was part of the package.

They also fought—frequently—about political issues. It began with little moments, like Todd chastising her for giving a dollar to someone on the street. He began with relatively innocuous statements like, "You're not really helping them," but as he became more comfortable in the relationship, he would toss out "lazy pigs" and "you're such a fucking bleeding heart." Mika learned that there was no point in arguing, so she would just fuel his fire with a "thank you." The relationship remained positive as long as Mika was able to dance around inflammatory issues, which she became very good at. They broke up once for about a week, but through Todd's persistence, they reconciled. Mika became good at accepting the blame for many of their issues, and she figured that if she worked harder, the relationship would work. So she continued the dance.

Their last fight, however, had been too much. Mika and Todd had been discussing moving in together. She was resisting the idea because she felt that her parents wouldn't approve if they were still alive, but—as Todd had logically explained—it made sense financially. They had been looking at apartments during the day, which was stressful; he wanted a place with status while she wanted something more economically practical. On top of that, Mika wasn't feeling well to begin with. After an exhausting day of looking for a home, they went to a party with a group that mostly consisted of Todd's friends and colleagues.

"Can we just stop in and say hi," Mika asked. "I'm beat."

"We'll see how it goes."

She sighed. "An hour? Is that enough time?"

"I said we'd see."

They followed their usual routine of grabbing a few drinks and mixing as a couple before splitting off and finding their own crowds. This night, Todd connected with one of his partners, and they smoked cigars in the yard while talking about portfolios and difficult clients. Mika quickly gravitated to Nancy Gomez, Mika's voice of reason in this conservative crowd. Nancy worked briefly with Todd at Wescott and was now an auditor with the state. Mika and Nancy had crossed paths a few times when was Mika was fulfilling her intern hours at Wescott, but they had become party friends at these events. Tonight, Nancy was with someone new, a good-looking blond in his early thirties.

"This is Roger McComb," Nancy said. "He just moved here from Arkansas."

"The land of Clinton," Mika mused. "Don't say that too loudly around here."

"I'm not too worried," he smiled. "But I'll try to play it safe."

Nancy mockingly spoke in a hushed voice, and said, "He actually worked with Bill."

Mika was intrigued. She was a fan of the new President, or—more specifically—she wanted him to succeed. However, this was not a dialogue she could have with her partner, so the opportunity excited her. They spent almost an hour talking about Arkansas' education reform package, for which Roger was a consultant. He was a policy designer, and with parents who were educators, his interests went in that direction. Mika was mentally engaged in a way that she hadn't been in a long time, and it didn't hurt that Roger was attractive and kind, offering to refill their drinks when they were empty. Her curiosity got the best of her, and she had started trying to determine if he and Nancy were "together" when Todd joined them.

"Hey, hey, why's everyone so serious?" Todd asked, clearly relaxed from a few beers. He noticed Roger and introduced himself.

"I'm Roger. Nice to meet you."

"Roger just moved here and works downtown with me," Nancy explained. "We were talking about education reform." Mika wished that she hadn't said that.

"Simple," Todd said. "Privatize it."

"Well, that's one idea," Roger replied cautiously, apparently well aware that arguing politics at a party usually doesn't end well.

"It's the only way," Todd said with his usually cockiness. "We overspend, money is wasted, and we get poor results."

Roger gave a disarming smile. "Well, I don't know that you could say that we overspend."

"Sure I can."

Nancy interjected, "Roger helped write Clinton's education reform plan in Arkansas."

Todd let out a wicked chuckle, another symptom of his alcohol intake. "Clinton's an idiot!" he bellowed, loudly enough that a few heads turned from around the room. Mika's stomach tightened.

"Todd, don't be rude," Mika said, taking his arm.

"I'm not being rude," he said, pulling away from her grasp. "He's a moron! He's going to ruin the economy."

"I don't know how you can call him a moron," Roger said, looking like a man who knew that he shouldn't argue, yet couldn't help himself. "He's a Rhodes Scholar. He's very smart."

"So he's a Rhodes Scholar. He's educated, but that doesn't mean he's smart."

They spent 45 minutes discussing elements of President Clinton's political agenda, especially education reform. Most of this involved Todd making inflammatory statements, which were contradicted with facts and statistics by Roger. Each time that Roger said, "Well, research actually shows that…" Mika fell a little bit more in love with him. She enjoyed watching Todd get flustered as his arguments were unmasked as nothing more than the unfounded insults that they were. Unfortunately, his frustration was infused with alcohol, which created a toxic cocktail of nastiness.

"So you drank the fucking Kool Aid," he yelled. "Just like all the other liberal demo-dicks."

"Hey!" Mika said.

Roger laughed, in an almost condescending type of way that had been Todd's area of expertise.

"Don't fucking laugh at me," Todd said, and he took an aggressive step forward. Mika saw Nancy's eyes panic. Mika took a step forward.

"Todd, don't."

He pushed her away. "Don't tell me what the fuck to do, Mika." A small crowd had started paying attention, which embarrassed and angered Mika.

"God damn it, Todd," she said through gritted teeth while she took his arm. "Knock it off."

Roger put up his hands as a type of surrender. "Hey man, I wasn't laughing at you. I just thought we were having a good little debate here. I was enjoying hearing your perspective."

"Todd, be done with it," Mika said.

She felt his arm relax slightly. He turned and said, "Let's go." She watched him march through the crowd, making disparaging remarks about "the fucking democrat" along the way. She looked to Nancy and then to Roger. Embarrassed, she simply smiled and followed Todd out the door.

They drove in silence for several miles before Todd started with "what a fucking idiot." After tearing into Roger for a few minutes, he turned on Mika, who had decided it was best to just keep quiet. "And why the fuck didn't you defend me? Because you believe that shit. I don't know how you can be so smart and so stupid at the same time." (In marriage counseling 13 years later, he would argue that this statement should have been taken as a compliment.) He continued his tirade as they stopped at a red light. Mika had stopped listening. She was trying to find a place in her head that was anywhere but here. When she couldn't find a mental escape, she opted for another. Just before the light turned green, Mika opened the door and got out.

"What are you doing?" Todd yelled. "The light's green!"

Mika walked along the sidewalk, and Todd drove slowly next to her with the passenger window rolled down. His initial pleas of "Come on, Mika" eventually turned to "Get in the fucking car!" Mika never responded. After two blocks and several horns blaring from cars trying to pass, Todd gave up. "Fine!" And he sped away. Just as his taillights were out of sight, Mika cried. She thought about calling someone for a ride, but she didn't have her mobile phone with her. Todd had purchased it for her the week prior, and she had not yet made it a habit to carry it everywhere. She resigned herself to walking the three miles to her apartment, and she cried the entire way. She cried because she missed her mom and dad. She cried because she somehow felt that she wasn't living life as she should, and because she didn't know how that should be. She cried because she had ditched her shoes in the parking lot of a 7-11 and had walked barefoot for more than a mile. She cried because she felt like she was getting sick and this wasn't going to help. And she cried because of Todd, for all that he had said and the fact that even he didn't stay behind to make sure that she got home okay. Every tear seemed to relieve a bit of the tension that had built from every argument—actual and suppressed—during their three-year courtship. While her vision was blurred from the crying, Mika had a new sense of clarity by the time she had reached home: she wanted to change her life, beginning with Todd.

The next morning, she called Todd and left him a very simple message. "I can't do this anymore. Please don't call me." And he didn't, not for two weeks. Every day was a new challenge. She shed several tears for the first few days, but each day thereafter brought her new strength. She didn't know what life had in store for her, but she told herself that it would be good. Her road to independence hit a speed bump when Todd called after a week and left a lengthy message, apologizing and wanting to see her again. She ignored it, and he called twice more in the next three days, leaving a simple message on the second call: "Hey intern, call me." She had committed herself to not responding. She knew that if she didn't make a clean break, she wouldn't have the strength to keep going. But life had already thrown Mika two giant curveballs with the deaths of her parents, and she was getting ready to face another.

Almost three weeks after calling Todd and telling him that she was done, Mika sat alone on her bed. She saw that he had called twice that morning while she was at the pharmacy. She didn't want to return his call, and her stomach tightened at the thought of doing so.

But I can't do this alone. I can't, she told herself.

There in her room, Mika felt stuck between two worlds. In one hand, she held her phone with Todd's number flashing on the caller id, and in the other she held a pregnancy test that was positive. She had started to wonder about her condition a few days ago, but had only confirmed it that morning. And while she didn't have a lot of time to process it, abortion was not an option; she had experienced enough death in her life to live with the thought of causing another. Since their breakup, Mika had told herself many times that she was a strong and confident woman, that she deserved more than what Todd was offering, and that she could handle all that life offered. She wanted to accept all of those encouraging words, but sitting on her bed with a positive pregnancy test staring at her, she knew that she never really believed any of it.

* * *

Mika now sat at a bus stop, once again torn by two potential worlds. She was confused by how she had ended up here, and she contemplated getting up and walking away. She would just walk, disappearing into the McDowell Mountains and only stopping when her legs could not take another step. Before she could decide for or against this action, Jayce's minivan pulled alongside the curb in front of her.

Chapter 29

Mika sat in silence next to Jayce, partly unsure of what to say, partly embarrassed by the situation. Jayce finally spoke.

"Where are we going?"

That's a hell of a question.

"Home. My home," she said, and she started to give the address when he reminded her that it was already in his GPS.

"Julia knows everything," he smiled.

This is weird! Why is this so weird? We've talked so many times, and I can't think of anything to say. Say something! "Gotta love Julia Roberts." *Oh my God! You're an idiot!*

After she had finished berating herself, she realized that Jayce had not gotten on the freeway, and was instead pulling into an empty parking lot of a little league baseball field. The car stopped.

"What are we doing here?" she asked.

"Are you okay?" He looked at her, and she could see that he was asking a genuine question. She almost lost herself in his sparkling brown eyes, briefly forgetting about the world and her life. She quickly came back to reality, and so did all of the confusion and pain, and she surprised herself by bursting into tears.

"I don't know," she sobbed. "I don't know." She felt Jayce's hand rest on her shoulder, and he gave it a slight squeeze. Her sobbing turned to laughter as she realized how ridiculous it was to be sitting here crying in front of a man she barely knew. "I'm sorry. This is stupid."

Jayce laughed as well, but mostly out of discomfort. "I don't know what you're looking for here, but I don't want to complicate things for you." He paused, and then added, "I mean I do, obviously, but I don't."

She laughed. "Can we just talk? I need someone to talk to right now, and you're it."

"I can be that guy," he said. "Let's go for a walk."

They exited the car and walked to the baseball fields, an older pair of blotchy fields with rusty chain link backstops. A small set of wood bleachers were rotting from the Arizona sun, which was setting behind the distant mountains and casting long shadows across the fields.

"So what's troubling you, Mika Jones?"

"You. You're my troubles, Mr. Beckett."

"Ouch," he smiled, feigning a blow to the heart.

"I just don't understand how you're here. Or why you're here."

"Or why you're so attracted to me," he smiled.

She tried to ignore that comment, but she instinctively nodded. "And I'm married," she said as if this would eliminate her feelings for him.

"But not happily married," he quickly chimed in. "Or so I'm assuming."

"What makes you say that?"

"Just a hunch."

"Based on what?"

"Just a few things you've said, and how you've said them." He led her through the third base dugout and onto the field. "Oh yeah, and maybe because you've met with a strange man several times—in secret."

She just nodded. "I guess that's something." But she didn't want to talk about Todd, not with Jayce, and fortunately neither did he.

"I hope I'm not being rude when I say that I don't want to talk about your husband or your marriage," he said. "I don't know the guy, but I'm a little biased here, so it's unfair for me to judge."

"I just don't understand..." she stumbled, not sure how to articulate what she didn't understand.

"Don't understand what? *This*?"

"Right. *This*. Yes, I am incredibly attracted to you. But it's more than that. I feel connected in such a unique way. And it's really fucking me in the head!"

He laughed. "I know what you mean. The moment I saw you sitting in that auditorium, there was just something about you. And every time since, that feeling has been confirmed."

They walked along the first base path under the darkening sky and continued into the outfield. "I just don't understand why this is happening? This isn't me. I'm not a cheater. So why am I here? Why now?"

"Well, I'm not the most religious person around. I believe in God, but I don't necessarily believe in Divine intervention," he said. They had reached the outfield wall, a chain link fence covered with faded plywood signs from local businesses. He reached down and picked up a forgotten baseball that had seen its share of activity. "I guess what I'm saying is that I don't believe everything happens for a reason."

"Neither do I. I hate that expression." She did hate it when used by other people, but there had been a few times in her life when Mika secretly clung to it, hoping that her situation would improve with a positive attitude.

"But I do believe that each challenge is an opportunity to grow. Life gives you some crazy shit at times, and you either get stronger or you let it beat you down. It's your choice what you get from it. Watch this." He was gripping the ball, eying his target. "Think I can hit the backstop?"

She chuckled. "I have no idea."

He assumed a strong throwing stance, took a few steps and rifled the ball. It sailed in a low arc over the field, past first base, and landed just next to home plate.

"See, I told you I could hit home plate." He winked at her, and she wanted desperately to hold him. Fortunately, he continued walking along the outfield wall. "It's like the song says, 'you can't always get what you want, but if you try sometimes, well you might find you get what you need.'"

"So you're saying that I *need* my life turned upside down? I *need* you to just show up out of the blue and be a pain in my ass?"

"First, I didn't just show up. Things don't just happen. I'm here because of choices I've made that brought me to this spot, right now. As have you. Maybe we didn't know that this is where it would bring us, but it's not really an accident if you think about it. Sometimes we need to face tough challenges to really move forward and end up where we should be. What we need isn't always the easy path."

Mika tried to apply this to her situation. *So what's the easy path? Stay faithful? Stay in my comfort zone of a marriage? Keep falling for this guy?* She didn't know the answer, and she knew that she probably would never know for sure.

"So what about you? What choices have you made to bring you to this spot, right now?"

He hesitated. "I can't talk about it. It's protected by court order." At first she thought he was serious, and when she realized he was joking, she pressed with more direct questions.

"Ever been married?"

"Nope."

"Ever wanted to be married?"

"Yes."

"Engaged?"

"Guilty."

Oh shit. Really? "What happened?"

He continued walking, hands in his pockets.

"You don't have to tell me. I'm sorry."

"No, I don't mind." He proceeded to tell her about his two-year romance with Jacque, a pharmaceutical sales rep whom he had met at a friend's party. She was 26; he was 29 and working on his Master's degree at UVA. They shared a passion for physical activity, often taking hiking and kayaking trips on the weekends. He asked her to marry him on New Year's Eve, and she said yes.

"So what happened?"

"A month before the wedding, she told me she couldn't go through with it." He paused, but continued before Mika could interject any type of incoherent commentary. "She said she was in love with someone else."

That bitch. That stupid bitch. "She was cheating on you?"

"No. Really. Most people assumed that. When we met, she had just broken up with her boyfriend. Apparently she never got over him.

She said she loved me, but couldn't marry me when her heart was still with someone else."

This poor man. Again, she wanted to touch him, but instead said, "That's horrible. I'm so sorry."

"Yes, but in the big picture, not really. I'm glad she told me then rather than later. If someone doesn't want to be with me, that's okay. You're entitled to want what you want." He paused again and took a seat on the bleachers; Mika sat next to him. He smiled, and she could tell he was going to make a joke. "Plus, she was a vegetarian, so I don't have to deal with that crap anymore." They laughed.

"So, to go back to your statement earlier, this made you stronger?"

"Absolutely not," he said, completely serious. "I took the self-destructive path."

"Sure you did," Mika said, trying to crack him.

"This happened just before I graduated. I had already accepted a job offer in Washington D.C. More money, better position. But I took this one because I couldn't stand the thought of living in the same region as her. So now I travel, never staying in one area for more than six months, which means I've never had a relationship that lasted longer than two months. As my sister puts it, I 'hit it and quit it' before someone else can hurt me. And now, I'm pursuing a woman who isn't even available. A woman who works for my employer, which can get me fired. I'm only here for another 30 days. And she's married. Does that sound healthy to you?" He looked at her with a self-deprecating smile.

Wow! What do I do with all that? She didn't say anything as she held his gaze until it became uncomfortable. "I should be getting home."

"Right," he said. He helped her from the bleachers, and Mika would have a difficult time recalling the next several moments. She would remember his hand taking hers. She would remember pulling him back to her as they walked to the car. She would remember pressing her lips against his. But she couldn't remember how she ended up on the bench seat in the middle row of the minivan. His lips were as soft as she remembered, and his hands were as strong as she imagined as they slid across her back, from her shoulders down to her lower back, where his right hand rested and then firmly grabbed her skin—a move that in another situation with another man would have made her uncomfortable and self-conscious, but with him it made her insides tremble. Her hands also wandered and explored, pressing against the firmness of his shoulders and chest and working their way up into his hair. His hands found their way to her front, pressing into her mid thigh and migrating up. She felt her heart race, and she gasped at the mere presence of his hands between her legs. She opened her eyes, and almost on cue he opened his.

"I can't have sex with you," she mumbled.

He nodded and leaned in for another kiss.

She grabbed the back of his head for emphasis. "I can't have sex with you tonight. I swear I will have an emotional meltdown."

Jayce nodded again. "Okay."

They resumed their kissing and exploring, but it only lasted a few minutes until they were interrupted by Mika's phone ringing.

Shit!

"Shit," she said, pulling away from him. Mika looked around slightly dazed, as if being awoken from a dream. She stumbled into the front seat and retrieved her phone from her purse. It was Todd. He had sent several texts and had just tried calling. "I'm sorry," she said as she got out of the car. She didn't want to talk to Todd, and she certainly didn't want to do so in front of Jayce. She saw that it was 8 pm, which meant she had been with Jayce for almost two hours; it felt like half that. She strolled away from the car as she called home.

"Where are you?" Todd answered.

"I grabbed something to eat with Tanya. I sent you a text, but apparently I never hit send," she said, using one of her frequent alibis for ignoring her husband.

"You're the only one I know that has trouble hitting the send button." He was still irritated.

"I'm so sorry. Tanya wanted to talk about some things, so we went—" she started, but he interrupted.

"I don't care where you are, I just want to make sure you have a ride home and that you're not walking."

"No, I'm not walking," she said, slightly annoyed at the reference. "We're on our way." She hung up without waiting for his response. She hated lying, but given what else had just transpired, she didn't dwell on it. She heard the car start behind her and rejoined Jayce.

"Everything okay," he asked as they pulled out from the parking lot.

Mika simply nodded as she heard Julia Roberts begin giving directions to her house. They travelled without speaking. Mika's mind tried to sort her thoughts into different categories. *Why am I doing this? Why did he choose me? What choices did I make that brought me to him? Am I bad person? How bad of a person am I? Is my marriage over? Can I do this again?*

"So, that was fun," Jayce said as a way of acknowledging the silence. Mika laughed.

"Yes. Yes it was." And she laughed some more at the thought of the two of them groping each other in the back of a minivan like two teenagers. She watched him as he drove, and she was reminded of her daydream of him standing on the ship.

"What?" he said, noticing her gaze.

"It's just weird, but I feel like I've known you before."

"I know." He turned off at her exit. "I'm guessing I shouldn't drop you off in your driveway?"

"That would be bad," she agreed, and she thought about where to go. "There's a CVS about a mile ahead. Pull in there, and I can walk."

"You might also do something..." and he made a gesture toward her hair. She pulled down the vanity mirror and saw a slightly frazzled mess.

"Thank you." She tried fixing it with her fingers, but to no avail. Perhaps it was okay, but in her mind it was clearly a sign that she had been fondling another man in the back of a car. Unfortunately, she didn't have a brush in her purse. Jayce pulled into the pharmacy parking lot and parked in a dark corner under a mesquite tree. He looked at the GPS and saw that they were about half a mile from her house.

"Don't you want me to drop you off a little closer to your house?"

"Yes, but no. In my neighborhood, it's not the best idea to be seen getting out of another guy's car. Besides, it's not that far," she said, pointing to the GPS. "I can cut through a park. It's really not far."

"Alright then," he said, and they slipped into the uncertain land of "now what?"

"I'm glad I called you," she said.

"I am too, but I really don't want to complicate things for you."

"You're not," she said, but they both knew it wasn't true. "I mean you are, but my life was plenty complicated before you showed up."

"Well, I'm not sure what happens next, but I think that's up to you." He flashed her that smile, and it warmed her.

"I don't know either," she said, getting out of the car. "And you're right, it is up to me." She chuckled not only at the joke, but also at the idea that this was the one thing that actually gave her a feeling of control in her life. "Good night, Jayce Beckett."

"Good night, Mika Jones."

She started to close the door, but stopped just before it latched. She leaned her head in and said, "Thank you." She closed the door, went into CVS, bought a brush, and primped in the mirror on the makeup table.

The walk home was quick, and much to her surprise, it didn't feel like the walk of shame that she expected. She didn't like the thought of lying and cheating on her husband; the guilt was still there, but it was buried beneath the fact that she felt good about herself. Two weeks ago she had never even heard of Jayce Beckett, and yet in this short time she had experienced more intimacy with him than she had in almost 20 years with her husband. She felt wanted, but more importantly, it felt good to want someone.

Chapter 30

Mika entered her home, and her positive energy rapidly drained from her body. Todd was already upstairs, and Ryan was on the couch watching TV. Her first instinct was to pour herself a cocktail, but she opted instead for a bottle of water. Before leaving the kitchen, she again tried to smell herself to see if there were any remnants of Jayce still with her. The only thing she sensed was what an idiot she must look like.

Mika found Ryan sprawled on the couch, wearing just shorts and socks, and she smiled. She sat in the recliner next to his feet.

"Hey," he said.

"Hey," she grunted, mocking him. He didn't notice. "How was school?"

"Okay," he said, not looking up from *Pawn Stars*, one of his favorite shows.

"Did you get your homework done?"

"I don't have homework," he said. "I'm on the swim team, remember." He paused before cracking a smile.

"Really? Swim team has been elevated to that status level?"

"No," he laughed. "I just don't have any."

"How's Emily?"

"Good."

She reclined back in the chair. "You know, I'm going to miss these deep conversations next year."

"Me too," he said without missing a beat. He didn't move, but he looked at her and smiled. "I'm sorry. I'm just trying to relax and keep my head clear for Saturday."

"I get it. Don't worry, I just like giving you a hard time." She watched a few minutes of a guy discovering that his authentic and expensive Japanese sword was actually a replica, and she chuckled at Ryan's laugh and "fail" comment. As she did the other night, she started to take inventory of her surroundings: the coffee table she found on Craigslist, the lamp they had kept from their first apartment, and the leather sofa and recliner that would probably outlive them all. She started to feel guilty for a different reason. Was she being unappreciative? Certainly people have it worse in life. Maybe Todd could be an asshole, but he never failed to provide for them. Doesn't every relationship require taking the good with the bad? She asked herself these questions because she really didn't know how a long-lasting relationship should function. Her parents were gone before she could ever recognize the dynamics of their relationship, and she had really only been with Todd.

Then she looked at Ryan, and it hit her that maybe she was also taking him for granted. Yes, he would be leaving for college in a year, but she didn't want to let that overshadow her time with him now, and she didn't want to under appreciate what a great son he was.

Stop focusing on the negative, she told herself.

Unfortunately, there was one negative she couldn't avoid: going upstairs to her husband. She wanted to appreciate him. She wanted not to be angry with him. She wanted to want him. But that wasn't the case. She was afraid that if she went upstairs, she would feel compelled to make love to him, or at a minimum he would have trouble sleeping and ask her to help him with that. And while Mika wanted to feel differently about her life with Todd, the thought of being physical with him hours after a make-out fest with Jayce made her ill. So she stayed in the recliner for another two episodes of her son's favorite show. She thought about sleeping in the chair, but she felt she owed Todd something, even it if was just her presence. When she realized that Ryan was asleep, she stood up, woke him by kissing him on the forehead and went upstairs, where she found Todd already asleep.

She readied herself for bed, turned out the lights, and slipped beneath the covers. She didn't want to wake him, so she consciously stayed on her side of the bed, almost to the point that she was tense. She stared at the ceiling fan in the dim light created by the digital clock and moonlight seeping through the cracks in the blinds. She watched the blades spin in a blur and tried to continue her thought process from downstairs, the one that told her that her life was good. Eventually, though, all she could think about was Jayce.

Chapter 31

Mika sat next to Lisa in the bleachers of the aquatic center on a clear Saturday morning, enjoying the warmth that came with her hot tea. The Phoenix afternoons were still warm, but with the sun setting earlier, the mornings were finally starting to begin with a crisp chill. The stands were filled for the state championships, and she had mixed feelings about Ryan's swim career coming to an end. Ryan had obviously matured physically in the past four years, but Mika had also appreciated seeing him grow socially. He had become more confident and outspoken, and even though he had recently shifted his allegiance from Mark to Emily, she was proud of the young man he had become. She would miss watching him in this chlorine-scented environment. She would not miss, however, all of the stress she created for herself through her involvement with the booster club. Once the gala was finished next weekend, she was officially finished with the parent drama and minutia of high school athletics.

Now, Mika was filled with anxiety, but not just because it was her son's final competition. The previous day she and Jayce had made plans to see each other after the swim meet.

* * *

Mika woke up at 4:45 am for no apparent reason. She stared at the ceiling, hoping that she would go back to sleep, but abandoned that idea after ten futile minutes. She couldn't help but think about the night before, and she tried to connect the dots on how she ended up in the back of his minivan. She couldn't remember all of the details, but no matter how hard she tried to tell herself otherwise, she knew that she was the one who had initiated the kiss. It was so unbelievable to her that she would do such a thing that she had a hard time feeling guilty about it. Her thoughts vacillated between *Why did I do that?* and *Oh my God, am I a whore?* She knew she wasn't going back to sleep, but she wanted to clear her head, so Mika slid into her yoga pants and went downstairs to utilize one of her yoga DVDs, a remnant from her previous attempt at yoga.

She completed the 45-minute program and was surprised by her strength. She was able to hold poses much longer than when she first tried the DVD years ago. It was still a struggle at times, and she was definitely sweaty at the end, but she felt good about herself. When she went upstairs, Todd was in the shower, so she sat on the bed and picked up her phone. There was a text from Jayce.

JB: Good morning ☺

Shit! She panicked and deleted the message. Did Todd see this? If he did, would he question why she was getting a text from a 206 area code? It didn't have a name on it; would that make it more suspicious? She decided to hide his number under a woman's name. Her first thought was Tanya or Lisa, but then that might draw more attention. Jaycee? Way too weird. As she heard the shower turn off, it came to her: Julia. If Todd were ever to ask, she is an assistant in the sales department and they're working together on a project. She set the phone down as he came out of the bathroom, naked and drying his hair with a towel. She couldn't look at him.

"Hey, doing some yoga this morning?"

"I couldn't sleep."

"Well good for you," he said as he put on his boxers. "Next week I might be taking a day trip up to Flagstaff for a meeting with John." She studied her husband as he pulled a white undershirt over his head. Didn't he care what time she came home last night? She was thankful that he didn't ask, but his lack of interest still bothered her.

"Which day?"

"Not sure yet. Should know today."

"Alright. Well, I'm going to need the car quite a bit this week. I have a lot of errands for the gala."

"Shouldn't be a problem. Just let me know when."

They drove to work in their usual silence, and Mika debated sending a text to Jayce, but she decided to wait until Todd dropped her off at work. As soon as he pulled away from the curb, she replied sent her reply.

MJ: Good morning ☺

She climbed the steps to the MedCare entrance and said good morning to a few people she knew. As she reached the door, she felt someone brushing against her right arm, and a familiar voice drifted into her ear.

"I'm right behind you."

She turned to find Jayce, who looked stunning in a blue suit that complemented his grey hair. He smiled, winked, and walked past her. Before she knew it, he was ten steps ahead and waiting for the elevator. She instinctively knew that this was how it would be at work, which suited her just fine. Neither one of them could risk letting their relationship—if that's what it could be called—be known. She hurried her steps to get in the elevator just before the doors closed. Jayce was in the back, and Mika made very brief eye contact. As the elevator stopped at her floor, she said to the stranger next to her, just loud enough for everyone to hear, "I can't wait for those Century idiots to leave, right?" and she walked out. She grinned as she heard Jayce chuckle from the elevator.

At lunch, she opted out of going to lunch with her department and instead ate outside, alone, as she texted Jayce.

MJ: Can you talk?

As she awaited his response, Mika navigated through the to-do list for the gala that she had created on her phone.

God, I have a lot to do.

When she had initially texted Jayce, she was sure that he would respond, but 15 minutes later, she was starting to have doubts.

Maybe I shouldn't have said that in the elevator? He's probably busy. That must be it.

As she threw away her trash, he finally called.

"This is Jayce Beckett calling from Century Consulting. May I speak with a *My-ka* Jones?"

She smiled. "It's Mika, and this is she." His voice warmed her heart. She strayed onto one of the walking paths, where she could have this conversation in private. "What are you doing?"

"I just finished a meeting, and now I'm getting ready to eat lunch."

"Well, I just finished my lunch."

"I know."

"How do you…?" She turned around and looked up at the mirrored building. "Can you see me?"

"I sure can."

"Wow, stalker."

"No comment. So, you wanted to talk?"

I did? Oh, right.

"So, I appreciate the good morning text, but I need you to be careful with those."

"Be careful as in don't do it. Got it."

"No, no. Not exactly. Just maybe not at 5 am, when I might not be by my phone."

"Yeah, I can see how that might be a problem," he said, pausing before he continued. "But what I'm hearing is that it is okay for me to contact you."

"Yes." She smiled. "Yes it is."

"Well, then this is a better call than I thought I would be getting."

"Did you think I was going to end *this*?"

"I most definitely did."

"Good," she said. "It will keep you on your toes."

She realized that she needed to get back to her office when an idea came to her.

"What are you doing tomorrow afternoon? I have some errands to run."

* * *

Now Mika sat with Lisa, waiting for her son to compete in the state championships and for a chance to see Jayce later that afternoon.

She scanned the pool deck for Ryan and found him with Emily amidst a group of other swimmers. She followed the fence line and saw Mark sitting by himself, listening to music on his Beats headphones. Todd and Gary stood next to him, talking about something that looked like nothing to Mika. They had been there all morning.

"Does it bother you that he's been down there this whole time?" Mika asked Lisa.

"Who?"

"Gary."

"Why would it bother me? He's with Todd."

"I don't know," she hesitated. "You're not worried that it's a sign that he doesn't want to spend time with you?"

"No, that's stupid. I've been up here the entire time—is that a sign that I don't want to be with him?"

"Well, you said it," Mika laughed.

"Okay, bad example," she laughed, but then turned serious. "Why are you asking? Did he say something to Todd? What did Todd say?"

Mika waved her hands in retreat. "No, of course not. I'm just not happy with how much time Ryan has been spending with Emily, so it kind of got me thinking. What happens from their age to ours? You can't stand being apart from each other, and now we can go days, even weeks, without really spending time together." Mika hoped she had adequately turned the conversation away from Todd.

"Why are you so consumed by this? He's a kid."

"I know, but still...."

"It's called growing up," Lisa said rather simply. "We're more complicated than we were as kids. Besides, I need him down there so you and I can talk about how hot that coach is—damn, look at him." She paused to examine the opposing coach that she had ogled at regionals. He was talking to two of his female divers in the shade of the 10-meter platform. "I can't do that with Gary, and they talk about whatever the hell they talk about. Wait, why are you asking this? Do you think Todd is losing interest in you?" She became suddenly excited. "You think he's having an affair."

"No, no I don't think that at all," Mika protested in a hushed voice.

"Well don't worry about that one," Lisa said. "I've flashed my girls around him enough to know that dog ain't straying." She patted Mika on the leg for reassurance.

"I know," Mika said. *Trust me, I know.* Deep down, a part of her wished that he would.

"Listen, don't worry about Ryan and Emily. He likes her and wants to spend time with her. If that's what he wants, it's what he wants."

But at what cost?

Lisa let out a holler, interrupting Mika's thoughts. Mark approached the blocks for his first event, the 100-meter freestyle, and Mika stood with Lisa and yelled encouragement. She could see Todd and Gary watching from the deck, and past them she saw Ryan and Emily sitting against the fence, uninvolved in supporting their teammate, let alone Ryan's best friend. Her first instinct was to be angry with him, but she made the choice to let it go.

Life is short, Mika. Just let him be and enjoy the moment. Besides, who are you to judge after last night?

She spent the next few hours cheering for Ryan and Mark; Mark placed first in both of his events, and Ryan finished fourth in the 200 breaststroke. She and Lisa left the stands to meet the boys during a long stretch before their final event, the medley relay. Mika could tell that he was disappointed with his performance.

"You gave it your all today, right?" she asked, after hugging him. "And you have one more event, so put that behind you."

"Too bad you didn't swim like you did at regionals," Todd added.

Mika shook her head, but couldn't leave it at that. Her intolerance for her husband was starting to grow. "Really?"

"What?" Todd said defensively. "He had a hell of a swim that day. He knows it. It's something to be proud of." He apparently saw the resolve in Mika's eyes because he put his arm around Ryan. "I'm sorry if that came out wrong. I'm just saying you had a hell of a season, and I'm proud of you."

"I know, Dad. Don't worry about it."

Todd hugged his son, and then left to go talk to the coach. Mika noticed that Emily wasn't around, so she decided to take advantage of the opportunity.

"Come on, I want a picture of you and Mark."

Ryan resisted with a sarcastic chuckle. "Right."

"Ryan?" she said, sternly. "It's your last meet. I just want a photo."

"Mom, just forget it, okay?"

She grabbed his arm just above the elbow. She pulled him close and spoke under her breath. "Look, you might think that this is okay now. But one day you will regret it. One day you're going to realize that you totally missed out on this time with someone you really care about."

Ryan pulled away. "You don't know what the hell you're talking about mom. Just stay out of this."

Mika stood in horror as Ryan started to walk away. "Ryan, don't you—" she started, but he stopped her as he yelled, "Granola, Mom!" It was loud enough for some to look in her direction, which added discomfort to her anger.

You little shit.

As she retreated to the bleachers, she checked her phone and saw a text from Jayce. His confirmation that they were still on for later saved her from the moment. She spent the remainder of the meet with Lisa, Todd and Gary, trying hard to stay positive, which was difficult as she deflected questions about what happened between her and Ryan.

"It's nothing," she said. "He's just stressed and disappointed, and I should have recognized that."

Lisa gave her a reassuring squeeze just above her knee. "You can't be perfect all of the time," she laughed.

The medley relay team was the final event. Ryan swam the breaststroke while Mark anchored the team with freestyle. Mika pushed all of her thoughts aside as she cheered for her son and the team, which finished second after Mark came from behind to narrowly beat the Chaparral swimmer by a fraction of a second. The four parents sat in the bleachers, letting the crowd thin out before leaving. Mika started getting antsy, eager to get home and then out again—alone—to see Jayce.

"Are steaks okay for dinner?" Gary asked.

"And I've got margaritas," Lisa added.

Mika narrowed her eyes as she looked to Lisa, then to Gary.

"Is the Jacuzzi fired up," Todd asked.

"It's good to go," Gary said.

Mika was confused and frustrated. "What are you talking about?"

"Couples night," Lisa said with a sultry tone, again squeezing Mika's leg.

What? How do I get out of this?

"But I have plans," she objected, and then realized how suspicious that might sound. "I was going to run across town to pick up some of the prizes for the gala."

"But we don't have a car," Todd said, and in what must have been a response to her blank stare, he added, "Remember?"

"Remember what?"

Todd sighed. "Ryan is taking the car tonight. A group of them have a room at The Hyatt."

Mika tried not to sound frantic. "But I have to pick up the prizes. I had plans."

"Jeez, Mika. We talked about this."

"When?"

He prompted her memory by speaking in short phrases. "At dinner. The night I came home. Emily and Ryan. He asked to use the car. You said yes."

"I did?" And as she recalled the events that night, she remembered the dinner, and then being upset with Ryan and losing part of the conversation to thoughts about Jayce. "I don't remember that at all."

"That's because you were in fucking la-la land again," Todd said with an anger that made the group uncomfortable. Lisa finally broke the tension with a call for "margaritas," which she dragged out in a singsong kind of way. She put her arm around Mika and comforted her. "Whatever you were going to do this afternoon, I'll do it for you during the week." Mika let out a loud laugh, which Lisa mistook as excitement for their couples' night.

They left the stands as a group to congratulate their sons. Mika pulled back, pretending to get lost in the crowd, which went unnoticed by Todd. She sent a quick text.

MJ: Abort! Change of plans... sorry ☹

Chapter 32

Mika awoke early on Sunday and went downstairs for another DVD session of yoga. The previous night had been a disaster, and she needed something to clear her head.

After hugging Ryan and getting an unsolicited apology from him, which Mika reciprocated, she had gone home with Todd, Gary and Lisa. She had tried hard to not to let her mind drift back to her beach because she knew that Jayce would be there. While she was mostly successful, her heart was only partially invested in the evening. She listened to Lisa's stories about her new favorite restaurant and about one of her colleagues who was "wrongfully" fired for sexual harassment ("He was joking…"), and she enjoyed the New York strip steak that Todd had grilled. Mika slowly consumed two margaritas during the night, while the others drank four or five each. The night ended in typical fashion with the four of them in the Jacuzzi. Mika had spent the night trying to keep her distance from her husband, which wasn't difficult until they were in the water together. She had managed to escape his touch twice by going inside for a bathroom trip and by checking her phone for a message from Ryan. Unfortunately, she failed to elude him forever, and she eventually found herself sitting on his lap with one of his hands rubbing her back and the other fondling her breast. His touch didn't repulse her, but it felt strange and she did not like it. This man, the one who fathered her child, the one with whom she had slept with for the past 20 years, was suddenly a stranger to her. He landed sloppy, drunk kisses on her neck, and when he spun her around to kiss her on the mouth, she closed her eyes and tried to think of Jayce, but even that couldn't put her in the mood.

The night almost finished in typical fashion. Mika and Todd went home, and he groped her up the stairs and into the bedroom. He tried to pull her onto the bed, but she excused herself to go to the bathroom, where she sat on the counter with her damp swimsuit pressing through her shorts and sweatshirt. She even looked around for some magical exit, even estimating the width of the window and the possibility of her fitting through it. While she didn't want to have sex with her husband, at the same time she felt sorry for Todd. *Even he doesn't deserve to have to have sex with his wife while I'm thinking about another man.* Eventually she garnered the courage to go back to the bedroom and was relieved to find that Todd had passed out into a deep sleep.

Now, she was finishing a 50-minute intermediate yoga session in her living room, and she had struggled through most of it, which is exactly what she wanted. She had hoped that the more difficult routine would force her mind to focus on her muscles and not her life. She sat in baddha konasana with her feet pressed together and her eyes closed, taking in full breaths and listening to her increased heartbeat pulse through her body. Mika tuned out the instructor's voice; she was in her own space and wanted to stay there. For the first time in a week, she felt internal peace. Her heart rate slowed, and she felt comfortable coming out of this private world and re-entering her real life through the portal that was her living room. She opened her eyes and went to turn off the TV even though the instructor was still making some commentary about life choices. Just before hitting the power button on the remote, she took a second glance at the screen. As the instructor spoke, a quote appeared across the bottom of the screen:

> "Happiness is not something ready made. It comes from
> your own actions." –Dalai Lama

Mika dropped into the recliner and read it several times before the video ended and the screen reset to the menu page.

Why am I not happy? Of course, she could easily revisit the list of complaints she had about her husband, but she quickly asked herself another question: *Do I deserve to be happy?* After all, it was her choice to marry Todd. Could she have handled being a single parent 17 years ago? Maybe, but it was her decision not to try. She eventually landed back on her initial question: *Why am I not happy?* But here, with her heart finally close to a resting rate, Mika wasn't blaming Todd for her unhappiness; she was willing to accept that her own actions had been the real cause of her misery, and only her own actions would bring her the happiness she craved. She had always followed her mother's dying words of working hard and taking care of "him"—whether that was her father, her husband, or her son—but she had not really "loved harder." Sure, she loved her son with everything she had, and she had tried to love Todd as much as she could, but she had ignored loving one essential person—herself. This realization was liberating.

She wanted nothing more than to jump in the car and just drive away, like a newly licensed teen looking to explore her freedom, but then she remembered that Ryan still had the car. She was already feeling empowered by her thoughts, and her irritation over the car was just the spark she needed to get up and start moving. Mika went to the kitchen for some water. When she opened the refrigerator, she was so annoyed at the nonsense cluttering the shelves that she dragged the trash can over and started cleaning, throwing away baggies of leftovers from the past several weeks, food that had been stashed away with the intention of being eaten later but had been quickly forgotten. She needed to start a second trash bag to complete the job, and once everything had been thrown away that needed to be, she shuffled the remaining items from one shelf to the next while wiping down each shelf with a wet paper towel and clearing away the crumbs and random sticky ring that had accumulated under a jar of jelly or some other syrupy substance. Once finished, she looked at her work and felt a little cleaner herself. She moved on to the pantry, where she was amazed at the redundancies: multiple boxes of he same products, each of them opened and emptied to varying levels. She condensed when she could, and some she just discarded. There were even two bottles of Ketel One vodka, both opened and relatively full.

She continued this journey through the first floor of the house, clearing the cupboards of never-used souvenir coffee mugs, mismatched plastic food containers and lids that couldn't be paired, and a few manual appliances that never worked. The closet was relieved of several jackets that hadn't been worn in years, as well as board games that hadn't been touched since Todd entered high school. Bookshelves were cleared of paperback novels that weren't worth reading again, as well as some knickknacks from various vacations. As she moved from one location to the next, she felt much better about herself—that much more in control—and two and a half hours later, she had two piles of trash bags stacked by the kitchen door, one for the garbage and one for donations.

On her final trip into the kitchen, she found Todd coming out of the pantry with a box of Frosted Flakes.

"Wow, you've been busy," he said, referencing the pantry behind him. "It looks good."

"Thanks," she said, separating the two piles of trash bags.

"Any chance you're making breakfast for two?"

She knew he was joking by his grin, but she wasn't interested in playing along. "Nope," she said as she breezed past him and went upstairs, where she spent the next two hours sorting through her own closet, the linen closet, and the medicine cabinet. This time she was surprised and irritated by her discoveries, from nail polish that she had never used to clothes that she never wore again because Todd made a disparaging remark about it how it didn't fit right or he didn't like the pattern. After she took a shower, she tried on one of these forgotten shirts, a light blue V-neck that hugged her shape. She checked herself in the mirror and liked what she saw. She wasn't positive, but she felt as if her sides were a little firmer. She went downstairs, expecting Todd to say something about her outfit, but he was wrapped up in a conversation with Ryan at the breakfast table.

"Hey, Mom."

"Welcome back," she said, kissing him on top of the head. "How was the party?"

"It was great," he smiled. "We had a good time."

"I'm sure you did," she said. She wanted to ask if Mark was there, but she knew the answer. She spent the next 30 minutes sitting with her family, rehashing the previous day, from how Ryan felt "off" from the very beginning of his race to how they tried to fit too many people into the hotel elevator, causing it to get stuck for five minutes. It was a moment she chose to relish, as she knew that there wouldn't be many more like these. She even appreciated Todd when he gave their son encouraging words about trying to swim at some level in college.

"I'm going to go take a nap," Ryan said finally, pushing away from the table.

"Nuh-uh," Mika stopped him. "Not so fast. Those six bags on the left need to go to the trash."

"I'll get them later."

"Now," Mika said in a calm manner but with a tone that caught his attention.

"Mom, I'm tired. Why can't I—?"

She interrupted him with a smile. "Granola." He looked into her eyes, and then to his father for help.

"Your mom's been busy all morning," Todd said. "Take out the trash."

Ryan grunted some nonsensical words and picked up a trash bag. "These aren't all going to fit into the can."

Before Mika could reply, Todd spoke up. "Then take what doesn't fit, put them in the trunk, and take them over to the dumpster by the park."

Again, Ryan let out some kind of noise, but he did as he was told.

"Thanks," Mika said. "And I'm going to need the car when he's done."

"Alright," Todd said. "Picking up stuff for the gala?"

"Yes, and taking those bags to Goodwill," she said, getting up from the table. "And I might stop at the car dealership." She had no intention of doing so, even though she had thought about it while cleaning her closet. She had something else in mind, but she wanted to see Todd's reaction, and it was exactly what she expected.

"Why are you doing that?" he asked, almost stammering.

"Because I need a car," Mika answered with little emotion.

"I know, but I have a guy working on that. He's looking around for the right one."

"Well, I'm tired of holding my breath," Mika said, and she went upstairs to take the nap that her son had wanted. She slept soundly for 20 minutes, and when she awoke, she felt very awake, as if her world prior to falling asleep had been a dream. She went downstairs and made a turkey sandwich, but what she wanted to do was text Jayce. She wanted to meet him, even if for a moment, but she still wasn't sure of her schedule. It was already 2:30 pm, and she didn't know what time she would be able to leave. As she finished eating, Todd and Ryan from taking the trash to the dumpster.

Ryan stopped at the counter where Mika stood, took one of her chips, and said, "*Now* I'm going to bed, okay?"

"Yes," Mika answered, and she gave him a reassuring nod.

Ryan patted her on top of the head. "You're funny," he said, and he disappeared upstairs before she could ask what he meant. Todd opened the refrigerator and searched its contents before removing a jar of pickles.

"I put gas in the car for you, so it's good to go," he said.

"Thanks," she said, not quite sure if it was funny or sad that he had gassed up the car so she could see another man. She chose not to think about it.

"And I know you need it this week, so just let me know when. I can have Erick pick me up and bring me home." If she wasn't mistaken, Todd seemed a little nervous. "And Wednesday, I'm going to Flagstaff with Erick to meet with some clients, so you can definitely have it then."

"Alright. Are you spending the night up there?"

"I don't think so," he said. "It kind of depends on how things go."

Mika didn't know what to say without revealing that she would prefer that he stay out of town, so she kept quiet. She put her dish in the sink, and Todd settled in behind his laptop at the breakfast table. The silence was a signal for her that it was time to go. Mika loaded the car with the items to be donated, then went upstairs to refresh her deodorant and put on some perfume. Before she left, she stood in the kitchen doorway and watched Todd as he worked behind his computer. She finally said, "I'll be back later," and then left, taking it as some kind of sign that he didn't ask what time she would be home.

Does he even care?

She drove to the nearest Goodwill, which was about 30 minutes away. It might have been closer, but her community petitioned the city council to keep them out of their neighborhoods, a movement that Mika did not support. There were times after her mother died that she had been a shopper at Goodwill, and she didn't appreciate the doom and gloom mentality that her neighbors felt about a donation center. After dropping off her donations in the back of the building, she parked and made her way inside, where she was immediately hit with the stench of old clothes and musty air. As she walked the aisles of the store, she was amused by how the shirts were organized by color.

If I need a red shirt, I know where to go.

She remembered carefully sorting through items as a teenager, looking for something fashionable and in decent shape, and she was embarrassed to admit that she would now have a difficult time actually wearing anything in the store. Even though her teenage years were tough, an interesting question entered her mind:

I was happy then. Wasn't I?

The joy of finding a great deal on a slightly-used top or dress back then was like a discovering a buried treasure. It had provided her with much more satisfaction than buying an overpriced outfit at Macy's that she could now afford to buy at full price. The teenage Mika, she thought, was much like an explorer, always searching for another destination, another find, and—most importantly—appreciating each step of the journey. Now she felt like a passenger who had no say in where the ship was headed. But that wasn't going to be the case anymore, as she was committed to making her own happiness.

As a tribute to her old self, Mika set out to make a purchase in this second-hand store, whatever it may be. She moved quickly through the clothing racks, dragging her fingertips along the hanging sleeves that begged for attention. She occasionally stopped to study a piece of clothing, and she considered buying a black sheer top with a sequined butterfly on the back simply because it was horrid. She opted to move on because she thought she might be disrespecting the women who were legitimately shopping there. She circled through the home section. *A DVD? Better yet, a VHS tape? Wait, what would that symbolize? A past I can't access because no one owns a VHS player? Maybe I can also find a VHS player?*

She found copies of *Pretty in Pink* and *Can't Buy Me Love*, two of her favorites, and she tucked them under her arm in case she couldn't find anything better. She wandered through metal shelves filled with many of the same coffee mugs and useless appliances that she had just brought in, as well as hundreds of ceramic figures, shapes and containers, many of which expressed some kind of "home is where the heart is" sentiment. Mika made her way to the front of the store and realized she had been there for almost an hour.

I'm not sure this was a good first step toward happiness, she thought. *I'm pretty sure that happiness is not found in a Goodwill.* As she carried the two VHS tapes to the cashier, she passed a display case of jewelry, and something white caught her eye. She leaned over the glass top and scanned past the gold, bronze and silver necklaces and bracelets before finally focusing on a small ceramic flower brooch with white and pink petals. She had no idea what kind of flower it was, but it was a unique item. Even though she would never wear a brooch, she liked this one and decided that this was her purchase. She had the cashier retrieve it for her, set aside the movies, and paid $12 for her Goodwill find. She looked curiously at it and decided to fasten it to her purse strap. Mika felt a hint of the satisfaction that she had experienced decades ago after finding a good buy.

She was now headed to Tempe to pick up two donated gift certificates from the Boulders spa, and she debated whether or not to text Jayce. It took her 35 minutes to drive to the Boulders, and she still hadn't committed to calling Jayce. *Just because I can choose my own happiness doesn't mean this is the right thing to do.* Her reluctance also centered on whether or not Jayce was what she wanted, or was he what she needed?

Could he be both?

Looking at the white flower attached to her purse, she realized something: *I'm not going to be happy if I go home right now.* So she sent Jayce a text.

MJ: Baseball field?

Mika started driving, figuring that if this is meant to happen, Jayce will reply before she reaches the exit to the baseball fields. Just in case her destiny needed additional time to get its act together, she stopped at a Starbucks, even going inside to pad the time. It wasn't until she was leaving, chai tea in hand, that her phone buzzed.

JB: When?

She smiled.

MJ: 15 minutes?

Her drive to the baseball fields was the fastest 15 minutes that she could remember, mostly because it only took her eight minutes to get there. When she arrived at the parking lot, there was one car parked near the field, and Mika saw a man and his young son near the third base line. She pulled into the far corner space under the overhang of a large palo verde tree, which partially hid the sinking sun and made her feel isolated and comfortable. She cut the engine and thought about what she was going to say to Jayce when he arrived.

Between the occasional pings of a baseball hitting an aluminum bat in the background, she thought about showing him the flower she purchased and telling him about the Dalai Lama quote. She wanted to tell him about her love of raspberry and chocolate and how she had never traveled outside of the United States. She wanted to talk about her eclectic taste in music, from Eminem to Taylor Swift to U2, and she wanted to tell him that her favorite color was green. And she had an equal number of questions for him. As her mind raced through them all, trying to classify them into the most meaningful order to maximize their time together, his minivan pulled into the space next to her. Her stomach fluttered, a pleasant change from the frequent knots that reflected her pain. Mika climbed out of her car, walked around to the passenger side of his van, and climbed in.

"Hey," Jayce said, with a huge smile.

That was the only word that was said before Mika locked her lips against his and pulled him to the back seat.

Chapter 33

Mika and Jayce rolled around together for almost an hour, steaming up the windows as they explored each other. At one point, as the action heated and Mika's shirt was tossed to the back of the car, Jayce reached for a lever that sent the top half of the bench seat backward into a bed-like position. Mika was not prepared for this, and she flung back unexpectedly, hitting her head against the door panel. She laughed, and Jayce uttered the second words of the evening.

"Are you okay?" Again, Mika silenced him with her kisses, and they continued. She rolled him onto his back and straddled his crotch. She could feel his erection press into her, and she slowly pulsed her hips against him. She unbuttoned his shirt, revealing a chiseled chest and a slight outline of his abs, and she traced her fingers through his chest hair and across his sweaty skin. Jayce pulled himself up, and his abs tightened under her delicate fingers. She felt his hands slide under her arms and around her back to undo her bra. He explored her breasts, first with his hands and then his tongue, which circled around her flesh several times before landing on her nipples. She grabbed the back of his head and pressed him harder into her breast; each time his lips tugged at her nipples she closed her eyes, bit her lower lip, and grinded her crotch harder into his until she came. She sat atop him, sweaty and topless, letting her pulsations cease. When she opened her eyes and looked out the back window, she could see the father and son getting into their car. She couldn't help but laugh. Loudly. And continuously.

Jayce pried himself from her grip and leaned back and grinned. "Yeah, laughing isn't exactly what a guy wants to hear at this moment."

She squeezed him and then rolled off next to Jayce, still chuckling. "No, no. It's just the thought of *this*, us here like we're teenagers in my mom's van. And I hope these windows are really tinted, or that kid just got the show of his life."

Jayce leaned up to see the other car leaving the far end of the parking lot. He mimicked the boy's voice and said, "Dad, let's practice hitting every day!"

"Best practice ever," she added, and they laughed. She pulled herself a little closer and nestled her cheek against his chest.

"Can I just say... that was awesome," he said.

"Agreed." Mika played with the hairs on his chest, and even though the sun was now behind the mountains and they had very little light, she could tell that they were also gray. She felt him squirm under her touch, and she pulled back. "Are you okay?"

"Yes," he grimaced. "This just isn't the most comfortable position." She saw his leg pressed against the passenger seat at an odd angle, and she moved so he could stretch it. "Thanks," he said, and he pulled her back into to him. "I don't know if I should ask this, but what brought this on?"

"You did," Mika answered simply.

"But you are still married," he said.

"Yes, but that's my problem, not yours, remember?" Mika proceeded to tell him about the Dalai Lama quote and how for once she was doing what made her happy. "I don't know why or how this happened—how you happened--but I am happy right here. Right now."

"I am too," he said.

"So, what does Jayce Beckett do on his weekends?" she asked.

"You mean besides *this*?" Without looking up, Mika could feel the smile on his face, and she poked him in the stomach. She reached out and took his hand, bringing it to her lips to kiss. "I read. I work out. I like to see the city I'm in."

As he spoke, she noticed a dab of red on the side of his hand.

"You're bleeding?" She gently touched the red spot, for no other reason than curiosity, but she realized it was too smooth and dry to be blood. "Is it paint?"

Jayce jerked his hand out to see the spot, and he did so in such an abrupt way that it startled Mika. "I'm not sure what that is. Maybe I brushed against something." He pulled back his hand and reached to retrieve their shirts. "So what about Mika Jones? What consumes her time when she's not taking care of her son's swim team?"

Mika's face tightened in thought. *I have no idea.* She pulled her shirt back on, struggling for a moment to find the second sleeve. When her face finally emerged from the shirt, she found Jayce gazing at her.

"I was going to say earlier that I love that color on you," he said, "before you attacked me." They laughed, and then Mika turned to her purse.

"I found this today," she said, her tone losing some of its enthusiasm. *Why are you showing him this? He isn't going to care.* "I don't know why I'm showing you. I just thought it was interesting."

"I think," Jayce said, taking the purse and pulling the brooch closer to his face, "it's a lotus."

"I don't know," Mika shrugged.

"I'm pretty sure it is," he said. "Did you know that the lotus represents rebirth?"

"No," she said. "Wait, so you know flowers and their meanings?"

"I'm a mysterious man," he laughed. "And I spent some time around a garden when I was a kid." He went on to explain how the Egyptians believed that the lotus would close each night and retract into the muddy waters, only to reappear the next day. "It actually doesn't do that, but they thought it did because the flower can take several days to emerge from the water, and then it only blooms during the day. In Buddhism the lotus represents purity and spiritual awakening. Each color has a meaning, but I don't remember them." Mika's eyes narrowed as she smiled at him. "I also read a lot of magazines on the airplane," he said.

Mika turned her attention to the brooch, and now she appreciated it even more. "Thanks," she said, but before she could say anything else, her phone started vibrating in her purse. She took it out and saw it was Ryan calling. "Probably wants dinner." She looked at Jayce in the back of his darkened minivan, his eyes and hair highlighted by the dim light coming in from the parking lot. It was an awkward moment that he broke.

"You need to go," he said. "Will I see you again?"

"Most definitely." She leaned forward and gave him a tender kiss that they held much longer than was necessary. Then she returned to her car and called her son.

Chapter 34

Mika sat at a conference table, and for the first time in two days, she was irritated. It was Tuesday afternoon, and until this point, Mika had felt free. As Todd promised, she had possession of the car for the week, and Mika was making the most of it. After taking her husband to work on Monday, she had stopped for coffee then planned how to get her errands finished and still have time to see Jayce.

She had taken personal time to leave work two hours early on Monday so she could accomplish some of her tasks before meeting Jayce at their baseball field. Her main stop had been the entertainment rental facility, where she met with Scott, her account manager, to review the details for the event on Saturday. Mika didn't gamble much, so she put her faith in Scott that they had the right number of blackjack tables, roulette wheels, and a few other games she had never really heard of. When she had finally met Jayce at the park, it was mostly a replay of Sunday's game, with the two of them ending up half naked in each other's arms. She confirmed for him that the white lotus indeed represented awakening.

"You didn't believe me?"

"No, no, I did. But you didn't remember the colors, so I Googled it last night."

This morning had started with Mika in a great mood; the taste of Jayce still lingered in her mouth, and the expectation for more this afternoon left her smiling inside all morning. But now she sat in a conference room with Don Hicks and his team, and she was getting angry at his self-absorbed perspective. He continued to misconstrue data and use incorrect terms to describe their wellness product. Correcting him in a supportive and professional manner was sapping her energy, not only because she didn't like playing games but also because this only confirmed what she knew was inevitable: a trip with Don and the team to visit Kondike. It was not unusual for the Wellness account manager to join the sales team in visiting the client and to be a part of the formal pitch, and Mika had enjoyed a few trips to California where she could sneak away to the beach. But Mika didn't travel especially well, mostly because she didn't enjoy flying. The rough vibrations of the plane during take off frightened her, and she would spend the entire flight envisioning a sudden explosion that would leave Ryan without a mother. So Mika became very good at communicating with the sales representative and telecommunicating with the client, which minimized her need to leave the state. Don, however, was a different breed, and she couldn't trust him to accurately answer questions that arose from her program. A majority of the time that she did have to travel, it was for one of Don's accounts. He could make the sale but needed support with the details. The size of this account likely meant that Mika would be headed to Seattle soon, but she hoped otherwise. Her desires died when Tanya hurried in just as the meeting ended.

"Sorry I'm late," she said as the room emptied, leaving just Mika and Don standing by the door. "I just wanted to check in to see how things were going."

Mika knew that this was code for making sure that Don wasn't screwing everything up. It also meant she was there to make certain that Mika was going to attend the presentation visit. When it came to working with Don, Mika had a difficult time hiding her distaste for him, whereas Tanya was better able to finesse the situation. It helped that Tanya was higher on the food chain than Don, so he no choice but to listen to her.

"It's all good," Don said in his boisterous cadence. "Things are really coming together nicely, Tanya. It's a slam dunk."

"Well, as you know, just when we think it's a slam dunk, it isn't," Tanya smiled, subtly referring to a large account that Don let get away two years ago. "So let's not take anything for granted."

"No, no, of course not," Don stammered, scrambling to regain his dominance in the room. "We're not taking this for granted at all. I'm just saying that we've got some great numbers, and Mika's bringing in a solid plan."

Even though she knew what was coming, she took pleasure in seeing Don squirm a bit.

"Glad to hear it," Tanya replied. She turned to Mika. "When are you and the team leaving?"

Shit. Mika hated the question because it confirmed what she didn't want to hear, but she was impressed with Tanya's simple but effective wording. She didn't ask when *the team* was leaving. She didn't ask Don when *he* was leaving. "When are *you and the team* leaving?" Don heard it, and so did she. Mika was going to Seattle.

"In a few weeks, right Don?" Mika asked.

Don confirmed, and Tanya expressed her encouragement as they left the conference room. They went their separate ways at the elevators as Don lumbered down the hallway to his office. When Tanya and Mika entered the elevator, Mika was surprised to see Tanya hit the button for the lobby.

"Where are we going?"

"We need to chat," Tanya said sternly, but she followed with a reassuring smile that failed to reassure Mika.

Tanya led her to the cafeteria, where they ordered two coffees, waiting mostly in silence, broken only by the uncomfortable small talk about the Kondike account. Mika contributed to the awkwardness by giving short bursts of answers, which was all she could do between her thoughts of the inevitable: *Tanya knows.* She tried to convince herself otherwise, but she couldn't figure out any other reason for this type of conversation.

They went outside to the courtyard and sat at one of the tables off on the edge of the grass. Mika tried to come with a joke, a comment, anything to break the tension and divert attention away from her betraying thoughts. She couldn't think of a thing.

"So, do you have something you need to tell me?" Tanya asked.

Oh shit. She does know! But how? Never mind how, just say something. Anything!

"Okay," Mika sighed. "I have to tell you, I really don't like Don Hicks." *Did that do it?*

Tanya tried not to smile, but the corner of her mouth twitched before she got it back under control. "Seriously Mika, what is going on?"

Please don't ask me this. Please don't know.

"What do you mean?"

"You've been," Tanya started, taking a sip of her coffee as she considered her next words, "different."

She doesn't know...? Is she fishing? Be careful. "What do you mean? Different how?"

"Our whole program is built on wellness and taking care of yourself, and we encourage people to notice changes in behavior that could suggest that an employee might be in need of some prevention services."

"Right," Mika said, sounding confused. *Where is she going with this?*

"Well, I can't help but notice some change in your behavior, and I just want to make sure that everything is okay."

"What kind of changes?"

"You seem a little more withdrawn lately."

"Like I'm sad?"

"No, that's the weird thing. Withdrawn isn't the right word. More like preoccupied. You seem to be checking your phone a lot, and yesterday you left early. And I know you've been going to yoga quite a bit more."

"And that's bad?" Mika laughed. Tanya also laughed, apparently realizing how it sounded.

"No, not at all. But you know as well as anyone that people are usually motivated to change behavior when something bad happens to them."

I think I'm in the clear. "Nothing bad has happened."

"So you're not sick or anything? I know I'm not technically supposed to ask you that, but I'm just worried."

Whew. I'm clear, but say something to make sure. "No, nothing like that. I've just been a little stressed over Ryan," she said, relaxing back in her chair. "And I have a lot of swim team stuff going on, which is why I left early yesterday. And I still don't have a car, which is pissing me off a bit."

"Are you sure that's it? You know you can tell me anything. You have my support."

No, I can't tell you anything. I can't tell you that I dry humped Jayce Beckett in the back of his minivan, she chuckled to herself, and her smile must have come out as Mika saw Tanya relax. "Really, I'm good. It's just a lot going on, but nothing to worry about. But I do appreciate your concern."

Tanya reached across and placed her hand over Mika's. "We're a team."

Mika grinned, causing Tanya to raise an eyebrow.

"If you really want to help, you can get someone to replace Don on our team."

Tanya laughed. "Nice try."

They finished their coffee and talked about a few different subjects, from Ryan's performance at the state championship meet to Tanya's sudden interest to go on a cruise. As they returned to their office, Mika thought about her behavior and realized that she needed to be careful. *I wonder if Todd has noticed anything? Would he care? What about Ryan?* She had intended to leave a few hours early again, but didn't want to stir up any more questions from Tanya or anyone else, so she ended up leaving just 30 minutes early. She made sure to let Tanya know that she needed to run some errands for the gala. Unfortunately, she didn't get to as many places as she needed, so when Jayce pulled into the baseball field parking lot, Mika was standing by the entrance and got in his car.

"Change of plans," she said. "Drive."

Jayce just smiled, as if he was ready for an adventure. "I am driving."

"We need to pick up a few things for Saturday," she said. "I hope you don't mind."

"Not at all. You're not worried about being seen with me?"

"No. The few places where we're going, we won't see anyone," she said, and she directed him to a Mexican restaurant and then a cupcake bakery near central Phoenix. The trip was relatively short, and it felt even shorter as they fell into the easy conversation that occurs between people who have known each other for years. Mika tried to complain about Don, but Jayce wouldn't let her, cutting her off with a simple "Nope." Their conversation turned to food as they pulled out of the parking lot of Aunt Chilada's, and Jayce eventually brought up her disdain for pizza.

"So, who doesn't like pizza? Have you ever had pizza?"

Mika had eaten pizza, plenty of it. She explained that after her mother had died, her father dug a hole for himself. For eight months, he came home from work with a large cheese pizza from Uncle Joe's, a small pizzeria next to the lot where he parked his truck for roofing. The two of them would eat in silence while watching TV on the sofa, the pizza box and his six-pack of Heineken on the coffee table in front of them. He would manage a few questions about school, and Mika could see that he was trying. He emanated a smell of sweat and dust, and she would study his sun-drained skin that struggled to support his watery eyes. *Take care of him,* she would hear her mother's voice say, and she did so the only way she knew how—she sat with him, answered his questions, and ate the pizza he had brought. Sometimes he would drink three beers, sometimes the entire six-pack, but it usually ended with him falling asleep in a sitting position. Mika would clean up, tossing the empty cans and returning the full ones to the refrigerator, then wrapping the leftover slices of pizza in tin foil for lunch the next day. Occasionally she was able to find some money to get a few groceries to make pasta or a salad, but a majority of her weekday meals consisted of cheese, sauce, and crust.

"Then one Wednesday night, after about eight months, my dad came home without a pizza. He told me to put on my shoes, and he took me to Wendy's, which was my favorite restaurant at the time. We talked about school, and he told me how one of his coworkers had been chased up a ladder by a Doberman. Something was different. He was laughing, and his eyes were more alive. He never brought a pizza home again."

"What happened," Jayce asked. "What changed?"

"I was 11-years-old, so I didn't really care. My dad was back," she said. "When I was old enough to actually think about it, I never had the chance to ask." She stared out the window and watched the white street lines disappear under the minivan as it cruised down the street, and she felt Jayce's hand take hers. He squeezed it gently, and then lightly dragged his fingertips up and down her forearm, stopping occasionally when his driving demanded both hands. She couldn't believe the tenderness of his touch and how much it relaxed her. All of the questions she had been asking herself—and suppressing—about her involvement with the man to her left, this feeling made them all moot. This felt right.

They returned to the baseball field parking lot, and while their backseat activities may have looked very similar to those of the previous nights—two figures twisting and touching and pulsating in the back of a minivan—Mika felt much more passion. From their initial kiss to his tug at her nipple, she felt something, an energy perhaps, that made her feel more than just alive, but a part of something, a part of someone else. She straddled him, her shirt half open and his entirely off, and he sat up and embraced her. She could feel his breath on her ear as it matched the rhythm of their bodies slowly grinding on each other, and he whispered, "I want to be inside you."

Oh God.... Mika thought, and she moved her hips faster, pushing herself against his hidden erection. She looked at him and smiled, never slowing her pace. "I want you inside of me," she groaned. "But not here."

And as she finished having her third partially-clothed orgasm in as many nights, she knew that it was no longer a question as to how far she would go with Jayce Beckett, just a matter of when.

Chapter 35

Mika scanned her kitchen, as if trying to get one last look just in case it was gone when she returned. It was Thursday, and while she knew that the kitchen would not disappear, she had no doubt that she would be different the next time she saw it.

After their last rendezvous on Tuesday, Mika and Jayce had agreed to elevate their affairs from a minivan to a hotel room, or as Jayce described it, "something more legitimate." Mika's home was off limits. Not only did she not want to risk getting caught, the thought of Jayce in the same world she shared with Todd made her ill. She assumed that Jayce's hotel room would be "more legitimate," but he quickly squashed that idea because he and his colleagues had adjoining rooms. The risk of her being seen even on the same floor was too great. Instead, they had agreed upon a boutique hotel near Scottsdale and Paradise Valley, far enough from her house and any significant public activity that might include someone she knew. With Todd out of town, her only concern was Ryan, but fortunately he had asked to stay late at Emily's. Mika had worried that her enthusiasm was too obvious, but if it had been, Ryan probably didn't care. With all of the pieces in place, Mika's evening with Jayce was set to go. She had rushed home after work, quickly showered, put on a matching bra and panty set of black lace that she had purchased on her way home from work on Wednesday, and slid into a black infinite wrap dress that she had purchased a year ago but never wore.

Mika put a lot of thought into her outfit, simple as it was. She had sifted through her closet on Tuesday night, pulling out different items, each time envisioning not only how she might look in it, but also how Jayce might take it off. She favored a more casual look of jeans and a comfortable blouse, similar to the night of their first kiss outside of Plantation Jane's, but she couldn't get past the thought of her jeans getting stuck while Jayce tried to pull them off. She had spent more than an hour in and out of her closet on Tuesday night, which became even more complicated when Todd came in to get ready for bed.

"What are you doing?"

Shit! Couldn't you still be downstairs?

Mika had just slid into the black wrap dress and was studying how it fit in the mirror. It was a nice, casual strapless dress, and she liked the way it hung over her hips; she couldn't remember why she had never worn it.

"Just going through some clothes," she answered, trying not to appear startled or nervous.

"For what?" He disappeared into the bathroom, and she could hear him turn on the water.

Mika wasn't expecting this question. "I don't know, the gala?"

"You're not going to wear that to the gala, are you?"

"I don't know," Mika answered. "Why not?"

Todd stood in the entry to the bathroom, brushing his teeth. "One, it's a little too casual, don't you think?"

Mika knew that it was, but had to play dumb. "I don't know. Do you think so?"

"Yes, I do. Plus, it makes you look a little hippy. Just sayin'." He returned to the bathroom.

She then remembered why she had never worn it, but this time her husband's negative reaction was just the confirmation she needed that this was the dress for Jayce Beckett.

Now that the night had arrived, she stood in her kitchen, prepared to do something that she never imagined was possible, her stomach tightened. Before she could consume herself with doubt, she grabbed the half-filled bottle of vodka from the pantry. *I may need this*, she thought, and she quickly left her house with her purse in one hand and the vodka in the other.

The drive to the hotel calmed her, and Mika's stomach relaxed as she lost herself in a collection of songs, completely forgetting each one as soon as it ended and the next one started. She pulled into the long, winding drive of the Canyon Suites, which sat in the shadows of the Phoenician, a much larger five-star resort that sat at the southern base of Camelback Mountain, a small but picturesque set of mountains that served as a popular hiking destination for both residents and tourists. Mika had never even heard of the Canyon Suites, which assured her that she wouldn't be seen by anyone she knew. As she drove around the parking lot, she was pleased to see only a dozen or so cars, and she found a spot next to Jayce's minivan. She tried to hide the vodka in her purse as she imagined how suspect she would look walking into a hotel by herself carrying a bottle of vodka, but the bottle was too tall and the neck poked out of the top.

Mika crossed the parking lot to the entrance, and she couldn't help but notice the beautiful surroundings. The sun was setting and the lights strung along the top of the Canyon Suites helped the tiny hotel sparkle in the shadows created by Camelback Mountain and the Phoenician resort. It was quaint. *It's almost perfect.* As she stood there, the headlights from an incoming car illuminated her, and her heart pounded. She quickly reached into her purse and put on her sunglasses. She took several quick steps toward the entrance before realizing how ridiculous she must look.

Way to look unsuspecting, Mika.

She removed the sunglasses and quickly entered the lobby of the hotel, a beautiful room of darkly-stained vigas and adobe-style walls. Mika wanted to appreciate the decor, but she had one mission: *get to the elevator quickly without anyone noticing you.* She passed through the lobby far from the check-in desk where a young woman spoke on the phone, and Mika felt that the woman was staring at her.

Am I walking too fast? Slow down. No, that's too slow. Don't look over there. Oh shit, why did I look over there? Just smile. She didn't smile back. Does she know what I'm here to do? Does she think I'm a whore? Crap, can she see the vodka? Shit, why is this lobby so fucking big?

Mika finally reached the elevators and was relieved that one of them was already open, as if it had been awaiting her arrival. She entered and went to push the button, but realized that she didn't remember the room number. Jayce had texted it to her two hours ago, and she couldn't get it out of her mind at first. But now that she was here, her mind was blank. She thought she heard footsteps coming from around the corner, so she quickly pushed every button just so the door would close before someone joined her. Her heart continued to pound as the doors slowly closed. *Come on. Come on.* She kept tapping the button until the doors finally closed, leaving her alone. She fished her phone from her purse and saw that Jayce was waiting for her in room 802. Mika saw that the building only had eight floors, and now she had to wait as the elevator stopped at each floor along the way. Each time the doors opened, her stomach tightened in fear. Fortunately, she made it to the eighth floor without incident, and she found her way to room 802.

She faced the darkly stained door and smiled a little knowing who was on the other side. She knocked lightly. It felt like an eternity before she heard the handle rattle from the other side, and then the door opened to reveal Jayce. She had last seen him Tuesday evening, but it felt like it had been much longer as she absorbed his smile and the spark in his eyes.

"Well, hello," he said simply, holding the door for her.

"Well, hello," she responded, entering the room, which turned out to be a suite with a small kitchen and a large living area. Mika set her purse on the kitchen counter and explored the space.

"This is beautiful," she said. A leather sectional, half of which faced floor-to-ceiling glass doors that opened to a balcony, anchored the living room. To the left was a half wall that separated this space from the bedroom. While she wanted to explore that room too, she wasn't ready. Instead, she opened the balcony doors and stepped outside. Jayce followed.

"Nice, right?" he asked.

"Just a little," she smiled. The balcony overlooked an expansive free-form pool strategically surrounded by palo verde trees to create an intimate setting. The lights below the surface made the water glow a light blue, which illuminated parts of the surrounding landscape. Less than 100 yards away, the southeastern edge of Camelback Mountain rose from the ground, and Mika could see the start of the trailhead where hundreds of hikers began their trek into the red-tinted mountains each week. She tracked the trail—barren and white from being trampled over the years—until it disappeared on the other side of the mountain. She had never done the hike, but was curious about it. Even though she heard that it was difficult, it must be rewarding if all of these people were doing it. There were still several late-day hikers coming down the trail.

Mika felt Jayce's hand slide around her waist, and despite their previous forays in the back of his car, she became tense.

"Are you okay?" Jayce asked.

Mika looked into his eyes, and she lied. "I'm fine." She managed a smile to disguise her inner turmoil. She wanted to be here. She wanted to be with him. But she also desperately wanted a reason to leave. *Can I really do this? Is this who I am?* But before she could fully engage in this internal conversation, she felt Jayce's lips press against hers. At first, she just stood there, still tense, but as his fingertips pressed into her skin, she quickly melted and gave in to her own desires. She slid her hands along the contoured muscles of his back as his moved up from her waist to her head. One hand cupped the side of her face and the other slid up the back of her neck. His fingers combed their way into her hair, and they tightened, giving a slight pull that sent shivers down her back and through her arms. It was a feeling that told her one thing: this is right.

They made out for 10 minutes on the balcony, kissing and touching, completely unaware and unconcerned that two hikers watched from the trail head on the other side of the pool. Jayce's hands had finally made their way to the bottom of her dress and had begun to move up her thigh, lifting the dress's hem. One of the hikers yelled something indiscernible to Mika, but it opened a brief window of thought that this should move inside. She laughed and pulled his hand away before walking inside. Jayce followed. In that brief respite from Jayce's touch, doubt again found its way into her thinking, and Mika knew what she needed. She walked past the living area directly to the kitchen, where she found her purse and her bottle of Ketel One.

"Are you sure you're okay?" Jayce laughed.

Mika retrieved two juice glasses from the shelf above the sink.

"Oh, I'm fine," she chuckled. "I just need a drink." She held up one of the glasses for Jayce, but he waved it off.

"I've been drinking since noon."

She smiled at his joke. "That's what I should have been doing." She poured vodka into her glass and set the bottle on the counter. She looked into her drink, envious of its clarity. She could feel her heart pounding, not just from the past ten minutes on the balcony, but for what she was about to do. She took a deep breath.

"Hey," Jayce said, and she could see his concern peeking out through his gorgeous smile. "We don't have to do this if you're not ready."

Mika wasn't worried about being ready. She felt like she had been ready for quite some time, perhaps the entire length of her marriage. Mika was more concerned that if she didn't do this now, she never would. It would be so easy to slip back into a life of disappointment simply because it was familiar. She could think about divorce. She might even discuss the issue with Todd, but would she have the courage to do it? She couldn't say for sure, but she did know that at this moment she had the opportunity to be happy, and she wanted to take it.

"No, no. I just need…" She didn't know how to explain it, so instead she just took a long sip of her vodka. Mika was unprepared for the dull and awkward taste that hit her tongue. *What??* She spit out the vodka, spraying it on the counter, some of it hitting Jayce.

"What the fuck?" she yelled. The vodka didn't taste anything like her old friend, Ketel One. It wasn't horrible, but her automatic reaction was to spit out this strange substance.

"Are you okay?" Jayce asked for the third time in the past ten minutes, but this time Mika didn't answer. She regained her wits and started processing the taste on her tongue. There was a hint of Ketel One, but it was different. Her first thought was, *"Did it go bad? Does vodka go stale?"* But as the flavor developed in her mouth, she realized that it wasn't bad, it was diluted. *Why is this filled with water…?*

"That little shit," she said, half smiling, half angry.

"Care to tell me what's going on?"

"This is mostly water," she said, holding up the bottle to the light as if she could identify the difference between the water and vodka. "Apparently my darling son has been drinking this and replacing it with water."

Jayce let out a laugh that surprised Mika. "It's not funny."

"It's a little funny." He took the bottle and pulled a sip.

"What's funny about it? My son is drinking alcohol. He's not old enough to drink."

"He's a teenager, right? I'm not saying it's okay, but that's what they do, right?"

"I didn't drink when I was teenager," she said, which was true. But Mika also knew that her teenage years were far from the norm.

"You also don't eat pizza," Jayce smiled, and he moved around to her side of the counter. As he tried to take her hand, she playfully slapped his arm.

"This is serious."

"I know. I'm not saying you shouldn't beat him, or whatever it is you do as a parent, but I just don't know if you should get too upset about it. He's a kid, and kids do stupid things."

She knew he was right, but she couldn't help but worry about her son. Was he drinking a lot? Was he drinking and driving? He was a great young man, but now that he was less than a year away from being out of her reach, she worried about him more than ever. Jayce laughed again, breaking her from her trance.

She laughed nervously. "Why are you still laughing?"

"Because life can be funny. Think about it. Here, with me, is where you find out that your son is stealing your vodka. In the big picture, it's funny." He paused. "A little, right?"

"If you're not laughing, you're crying, right?"

"Exactly," he said. He took her hand and started massaging her palm with his. She let out a good laugh. "I'm pathetic."

"No, you're amazing."

Mika didn't feel amazing, so she offered a "thank you" without looking at him.

"As I said before, if you're not ready for this, I completely understand."

For a moment, Mika had started to think that this was a sign—possibly the type of Divine intervention that she didn't believe in—to remind her that she had a family at home and needed to reverse course. But feeling Jayce's gentle pressure on her hand, hearing his understanding tone coupled with his ability to make her laugh, she didn't want to turn back; this was where she wanted to be more than ever. She closed her hand around his and pulled herself into him. Jayce put his free arm around her, pressing her against his firm chest. She closed her eyes and could hear his heart pounding, and she controlled her breathing so that her heartbeat would match his. Like their first encounter at their baseball field, Mika wouldn't be able to remember the next several moments, only that they led to her taking Jayce Beckett into the bedroom, where she gave herself to him.

Chapter 36

Mika entered her kitchen cautiously. She knew Todd wasn't home, but she was unsure of how Ryan might receive her. Lisa always joked about someone who smelled like sex. Was it true? Did Mika smell like sex? Would her son know that she had just spent the most incredible evening of her life with a man who was not his father?

* * *

Mika and Jayce entered the bedroom, and they danced in a way that wasn't possible in the minivan. Mika pulled off his shirt as they stood next to the bed. Kissing his torso, her tongue found every crevice between his defined muscles. Then Jayce dropped to his knees, both hands caressing her calves and working their way up her thighs, eventually sliding past her dress and beneath her underwear. She ran her hands through his hair as his fingers teased her lips, and she groaned and dug her fingers into his scalp, which encouraged him even more. Eventually, he wrapped his arms around each leg, held tight for leverage, and tossed her onto the bed. He removed her black lace panties she had worn just for him and pressed his hands into her hips before kissing her pleasure zone. Mika was overwhelmed with sensations as Jayce's tongue and lips took turns seducing her clit, and as the sensation grew, she arched her back and clamped her legs around Jayce's head, banging her hands into the bed. Her dress clung to her skin from the sweat, and she climaxed at the end of her fourth "Oh God." It was the first of three orgasms she would have that night, which should have been memorable enough, but instead the night was marked by two other moments.

After Jayce had made her climax with nothing more than his mouth, Mika took her turn on him. Unprovoked and without pressure, Mika found herself around his waist, unbuckling his belt and pulling off his pants. She played with his erection in her hands, lightly kissing it several times before taking it in her mouth. She immediately noticed its warmth, and as she pressed her lips around it, she loved the way Jayce squirmed and squeezed her shoulders as she moved back and forth on his shaft. Mika found deep satisfaction in the selfless pleasure she gave him. He pulled her off before exploding in her mouth, and they ended up naked and sweaty together. Mika reached her second orgasm while on top of him and then collapsed. She almost fell asleep, their sticky bodies stuck together on top of the sheets. Later, after Mika had started to come back to reality and stood to get dressed, Jayce took her from behind, first massaging her shoulders, then kissing her neck and cupping her breasts. He worked her up again, and this time he bent her over the bed. What had been her least favorite position instantly became amazing when he entered her. He was crooked in a way that when inside her from this angle, he hit an untouched spot that made her scream. It would become her new fantasy when she thought of Jayce Beckett.

They left the hotel room together just after nine thirty, and the sound of the door closing behind them was the first step back to her reality.

"They all know we just had sex," Jayce said, referring to the staff as they passed through the lobby, their fingers touching just enough to feel each other but light enough that no one could say for sure that they were holding hands.

"Stop it," Mika said, and she purposely kept her eyes from catching a glimpse of the employees at the front desk. "Do they?"

"Probably. They're hoping we did, that's for sure." His fingers pressed a little harder into hers, and she laughed. He walked her to her car door, and she looked up into his handsome face, which was illuminated by the glow of the moon.

"So...." he smiled.

"So...." she returned, giggling at the thought: *What do you say after you just had sex in a hotel room? Thank you? Nicely done? Way to go?*

"You are amazing," he said, and their eyes locked. He started to move in for a kiss, but a car entered the parking lot, startling Mika and bringing her another step closer to reality. She gave him a quick peck on the lips. "I'll see you," she said, and she hurried into her car.

"I hope so," he said as he closed her door for her.

* * *

She hadn't thought about how to face her son until the moment she stepped into the kitchen and heard the television in the other room. Mika felt the knot return to her stomach as she imagined Ryan barraging her with questions: "Where have you been?" "What's that smell?" "Did you have sex?" That her 17-year-old son would do such a thing was ludicrous, but it was very much alive in her mind. She considered different approaches to this possible scenario, even going up the back stairs and avoiding him all together, but then she rediscovered the bottle of vodka in her purse. She had completely forgotten about the watered down Ketel One until now, and her anger shook off her insecurities and concern. She spent a moment trying to decide how to best approach her son. She wanted to simply yell at him, but she knew that would not have the desired impact. Should she just say, "Alright, talk," and set the bottle in front of Ryan? *Better yet, set the bottle on the coffee table in front of him, sit down, and just watch TV. That will make him sweat.* She envisioned him just staring at the bottle, his eyes occasionally stealing a glance at his mother. She could see the little drip of sweat starting to dribble down the side of his forehead. She would sit there for 30 minutes, an hour, as long as it took, and just when he started to gain the hope that she wasn't going to say anything, Mika would turn to him and say, "Are you fucking kidding me?" This was the plan, and she was ready.

Mika grabbed the bottle and entered the family room, where Ryan was fast asleep on the couch.

Thank God, she thought, and she quickly returned the bottle to the pantry and went upstairs.

Chapter 37

Mika drove alone to the gala on Saturday evening. After an early morning yoga routine, she and Lisa had gone to the hotel in the morning to unpack supplies and prizes, finalize details with the banquet manager, and set up the silent auction sheets. Lisa talked non-stop about how her brother was being a shit because he wasn't pulling his share of the load in helping their mother, who was recovering from a knee-replacement surgery. Mika nodded and let out occasional noises of sympathy and frustration, but her mind was focused on the fact that this was her last gala. It wasn't that she was upset that she would no longer spend her time coordinating parent volunteers and soliciting donations, it was more like, "Now what?" Any disappointment that she had with her own life was usually masked by keeping busy with her son's, and she was again trying to picture what her life would be like after he left for college. She wasn't troubled by the vision of a horrible future; it was more that she couldn't see anything at all that bothered her. Her future was a blank screen.

Now, after spending all day Friday thinking about Jayce, she was thinking about Todd as she drove to the gala. It wasn't pleasant.

Does he even get it? I've been with another man for the past two weeks, and he doesn't even seem to notice. Mika walked through several dozen moments of the past few weeks, and it became more apparent to her that he was not invested in their marriage. She really wasn't trying to justify her affair; this was an honest reflection on the state of their marriage. They hadn't had sex in almost a month, and she couldn't help but think that neither one of them missed it. Last night was the second time in two weeks when he had come home from an overnight trip, and there was nothing when he returned. No kiss on the cheek. No hug. No, "Hey, I missed you." Mika wasn't blaming him because she didn't offer any of those things either; she was just noting that he must be in the same emotional space as her. All he offered was his damn overnight bag left on the bed for her to unpack.

And now she was driving to the gala alone because she needed to arrive an hour early, but he had some work he wanted to get done. It was a borderline argument, and only Mika's fatigue kept it from becoming more.

"Why can't you just come with me now?" she asked.

"Why can't you just go alone? I'll catch a ride with Gary later."

"Would it kill you to just come a little early and help me out?"

"No, it won't kill me," he smiled. "But seriously, I'll catch up with you later."

Fuck it, she thought, and she left without saying another word. She was angry for many reasons, especially about the fact that she still didn't have her own car. She knew that this was her own fault; she could have just gone and purchased a car without her husband, but she knew that she didn't do so because it would lead to a huge confrontation. She started to question whether there was more to it than that. Had she avoided buying a car just to see how long it would take him to give in? Had she been testing his selfishness just so she could blame him for her own unhappiness. How much longer would she play this game of chicken, one that she couldn't win? Todd was clearly as emotionally removed from the relationship as she was, and Mika started to question if it was because of her, or if he was simply incapable of that type of connection with anyone.

At the hotel, Mika checked in with the banquet manager. He confirmed that everything was ready as planned, so she made a quick trip around the room. Since Mika was the first of the parents to arrive, she had to make two trips to her car for the remaining donation baskets filled that she didn't have room for that morning. As she removed the final two baskets, she heard Lisa's voice call her name. She turned to find her friend carrying her own armful of bags, as Gary followed closely behind.

"Hey...?" Mika said. "I thought Todd said he was coming later with you?"

Both Lisa and Gary looked caught off-guard, like a couple of kids who had just been caught in a lie by their parents.

"Right," Gary stammered. "I'm going to go back for him," he finally said. "Lisa just had a lot to bring in, so I thought I would help."

Mika noticed that he was only carrying one small basket. *What the fuck is he talking about?*

"And this way we only have one car with us tonight, right Gary?" Lisa awkwardly added.

Gary nodded in agreement and started to explain further, but Mika didn't pay any attention to him as she turned and walked ahead of them into the hotel. She could hear Lisa and Gary talking right behind her, but all she really heard was her friends trying to disguise the fact that her husband was an asshole.

After she unloaded her donations on one of the banquet tables, Gary disappeared, and she and Lisa started arranging the items along the table in silence. Just as several other parents arrived, Lisa finally said, "Gary went home to pick up Todd."

"Great," Mika said. "Stacey and Jenni aren't here yet. Did you hear from them?"

"Yeah, they said they would be here early so they could see what we do."

"Whatever. Next year is their problem. I'm going to go check on the DJ," and she left Lisa to explain to the incoming volunteers what needed to be done.

Mika spoke with the deejay, checked in again with the banquet manager, spoke with one of the blackjack dealers, and then went to the restroom, where she went into a stall and started to cry. Her tears were born not from sadness, but from fatigue. Physically, she was tired from running around and coordinating this event, but she was more exhausted mentally. This was her son's final high school event, and in order to make it a success, she had used every ounce of energy to stay focused on the gala and away from Jayce. Now that everything was set, she broke down, leaning against the door of a bathroom stall. She was crying, but she felt an undercurrent of relief as she thought about the new man in her life. She pictured his face and imagined the touch of his lips on her cheek. She could have stayed there for hours had it not been for the sound of someone else entering the restroom. Mika straightened up and took several deep breaths, bringing her final tears to a halt. She heard the sound of running water, and she peeked through the crack of the stall door to see an employee washing her face. Mika waited for her to leave before exiting the stall and then went to the sink to pat some cold water on her face. She checked herself in the mirror, wiped a little smudge of mascara from her lower eyelid, and took two more deep cleansing breaths.

Let's do this, she thought, and she left the bathroom to discover that a dozen or so parents had arrived, which relaxed her even more knowing that the increased activity might make it less noticeable that she had been crying. She worked her way to the bar and ordered a vodka tonic. As she took her first sip—a large one—Lisa sidled next to her.

"Starting without me?" Lisa laughed, and she directed the bartender to pour one for her.

"Oops," Mika smiled. "Sorry, my friend."

"No worries." Lisa took her cocktail from the bartender and held it up to Mika's glass. "To the gala," she said as their glassed clinked together.

"To the gala."

"To the mother fucking gala," Lisa added, and Mika almost choked as she laughed. "Are you sad?"

"About this? Hell no."

"Really?" Lisa questioned, checking her friend's face for sincerity. "It's our last one. Our boys are moving on. I'm kind of sad."

Mika took a long sip from her glass. "It is sad, but I'm ready for what's next."

"Well, you're much stronger than I am, that's for sure," Lisa said, and she guzzled the rest of her drink and ordered another.

The ballroom filled quickly over the next half hour. Ryan and Emily arrived together and spent the obligatory amount of time with Mika before joining their friends at the corner table next to the deejay. She watched from across the room as her son hugged Emily and danced awkwardly in his suit and Converse tennis shoes. She smiled, not because she was happy for him, but because it felt surprisingly good to acknowledge that she wasn't in control of him. He was with Emily--for now--and that made him happy. Mika strolled through the room, which was now filled with parents and teens standing and eating Mexican food from the buffet, while others played blackjack and craps. She pretended to look for her husband because she knew it was what she should be doing, but she was really just enjoying drifting through crowds of people, smiling and saying hello as she nursed her vodka tonic. Upon her second passing of the room, she saw Emily and Ryan sitting with a man and woman, whom she barely recognized. Emily's arm was around the woman, which led Mika to the conclusion that it was Emily's mother. She looked relatively healthy, but Mika couldn't help but see her pain. Before she could decide whether or not to join them, Emily saw her and waved her over.

Shit.

Emily stood as Mika approached the table. "Mrs. Jones, this is my mom and dad." Her father, a short and stocky man with a tired smile, stood and shook her hand.

"David," he said. "This is my wife, Elisabeth."

"I'm Mika," she said, turning to Elisabeth. As she shook Elisabeth's hand, Mika looked into her eyes and saw the same sparkle that her mother had, one that seemed to burn to spite her illness. "It's so nice to meet you."

"Here, have a seat," David said, and before Mika could object he slid he chair toward her and pulled out another one for himself. Mika reluctantly took a seat between them.

"We just love your son," Elisabeth beamed.

"He's a good kid," David added, and Mika couldn't help but feel their sincerity. Parents make comments like this all the time to each other: "You should be proud," and "Nice kid." But mostly it's just shallow flattery. Mika felt otherwise here.

"Well, you don't have to live with him," Mika joked.

"I can't imagine he's any different," David rebutted.

"He's not," Emily gushed, poking Ryan in the ribs. Mika noticed Ryan's face getting red.

Ryan stood. "Okay, we're going to go now." He took Emily's hand and kissed her giggling lips. "You kids have fun," Ryan smiled, and he led Emily to a blackjack table filled with some of the other swimmers.

Elisabeth looked at Mika and said, "Seriously, we adore your son."

"Thank you," Mika smiled with pride. "I do too."

"You know, having a daughter is rough," David said. "This whole dating thing has cost me some hair. You just hope your girl finds a guy who treats her right. You should know that your son is a good one." David excused himself to get another drink, leaving Mika and Elisabeth alone. Mika didn't know what to say. Her son was becoming a man, and it was nice to hear validation that he was on a positive path. She sat there for several moments before realizing that she should return the compliment.

"Well, Emily is just a doll," Mika said, but she worried that it sounded as obligatory as it was. "She and Ryan seem to have a great time together." She smiled an awkward smile that stayed silent for too long. *Shit, Mika. Why can't you just be normal and say something nice about their daughter and mean it? Just say something else. Quick! Now!* "So, how are you feeling?" She immediately felt horrible. She knew from her mother that some people don't want to talk about their illness. Elisabeth was apparently not one of them, as she went to explain how her pain ebbed and flowed and how different diets made things better or worse. The ease with which she spoke made Mika gradually forget her discomfort, and just as she was starting to feel a connection with Emily's mother, Lisa tapped her on the shoulder.

"I'm sorry to interrupt," she said, acknowledging Elisabeth with a nod. "We need you."

"Certainly," Mika said. "It was so nice to finally meet you." She extended her hand, and Elisabeth took it and embraced it between her two weak but warm hands.

"I know," she smiled. "We'll have to do dinner sometime."

"Definitely. That would be nice," Mika said, and she almost meant it until Elisabeth ruined it.

"Who knows, we may be in-laws someday." She chuckled, and Mika forced the same, but inside her heart stopped. *Really? Did you have to say that?*

She left the dining area, practically being pulled by Lisa.

"What is it?"

"We have some serious drinking to do," Lisa said, directing them to the bar, where Gary and Todd were in line. Mika found herself contemplating what appeared to be her only two options: staying back at the table with the woman who just joked that their children might get married one day, or get a drink with her husband. Had it been a real choice, she might have chosen Elisabeth.

"Hey, hey," Gary said, giving Mika a hug. "This is it."

"Hey, Hun," Todd added with a strange smile. He grabbed her arm and pulled her in for a kiss, which caught Mika completely by surprise; instead of a soft kiss, their teeth banged together.

"Shit, Mika..." Todd said as he pulled back and touched his teeth, checking to make sure nothing was chipped.

Mika was too overwhelmed to notice the short pain that ran through her teeth. It was the first display of affection that Todd had displayed in weeks, and it was the last thing she wanted right now. She tried to shake it off as Lisa handed her a new vodka tonic.

"Cheers," Lisa said. "To the gala," and she clinked her glass against the others.

"To the gala," Gary added. And they all drank, Todd still stewing a bit over his failed kiss.

"The mother-fucking gala! Woo!!" Lisa yelled, catching the attention of a group of parents standing in line at the bar. Mika gave her a look to settle down, which Lisa disregarded. "Fuck 'em. We're seniors! This is it!" Her melancholy had obviously dissipated after the many drinks she had apparently indulged in. They spent the next thirty minutes hopping between two blackjack tables with Gary and Todd before the guys eventually drifted off to the craps table. As Mika attempted to play blackjack, listening to the dealer and other people at the table tell her when to stay and when to hit, she saw Ryan and Emily across the room. He was leaning against the wall with Emily pulled in close, looking up at him as they spoke unknown words that Mika didn't want to know. And when she saw Mark walk past Ryan without any kind of acknowledgement of each other, Mika's stomach tightened.

"Doesn't this bother you? They're seniors…" she started to say before realizing that Lisa's attention was far away.

"Holy hell," Lisa said. "Who is that?"

Mika tried to follow her line of sight, starting first at the bar, then over to the tables filled with silent auction items, before finally landing on Lisa's target. Standing in the entryway was Jayce Beckett.

Chapter 38

What the fuck is he doing here? Mika thought, heavily conflicted between the panic over his presence and her attraction for him. While she was flustered over why he would be here, she couldn't help but notice how great he looked in his dark denim jeans, boots, and moleskin blazer. She didn't know why, but his boots made her tingle. Jayce stood just inside the doorway, his hands stuffed in the pockets of his jeans. He looked around the room with a degree of satisfaction, like Gatsby overseeing one of his parties.

Before Mika could formulate a complete thought, Lisa was pulling her toward Jayce.

"No..." she started, but Lisa plowed forward. By the time they reached Jayce, Mika felt slightly winded, and her stomach tightened. She struggled for a quick escape, but Lisa wouldn't let go of her arm.

"Hi," Lisa said. "Can we help you?"

Jayce turned and smiled, looking first at Lisa, then to Mika, and his smile twisted her stomach even more. *Don't look at me. Don't look at me.* As if he could hear her thoughts, Jayce turned his eyes back to Lisa.

"No, no. I didn't mean to intrude. I was just passing by and saw that this was a swim banquet, and thought I would check out the party."

"Intruding?" Lisa let out an awkward laugh that embarrassed Mika. "Of course you're not intruding. I mean, it is for our kids and parents... you're not one of our parents, are you?"

"No, I'm not a parent. But I have a good friend whose son is a swimmer, so I'm partial to the sport." He looked at Mika. *Don't you dare fucking wink at me.* He again complied with her thought by turning back to Lisa and extending his hand, which she eagerly grasped.

"I'm Jayce."

"I'm Lisa, and this Mika," Lisa said, but she wouldn't let go of his hand, so he couldn't offer it to Mika, which she greatly appreciated; his touch right now might destroy her.

"Like I said, I don't want to intrude, so I'll let you two go back to your party." He was being very good about not looking at Mika. When he tried to pull away, Lisa pulled back and grabbed his forearm.

"Don't be silly, Jayce. Let us buy you a drink," and she led the way to the bar, Jayce on one arm and Mika on the other.

Mika's legs felt weak. *Is this real? What the hell is happening?* Her family life and all of its dysfunctions were being invaded by this man who made her feel like a better woman—a happy woman—and he was just two feet away and connected by her best friend. *What is he doing here? Shit!* Her head was spinning, making it difficult to scan the room for her husband as Lisa led her and Jayce into the storm.

Lisa stopped off to the side of the bar, where a dozen or so parents waited in line.

"What do you want?" she asked Jayce.

"Why aren't we in line?" Mika asked.

"I'm not waiting in line. What do you want?"

Jayce smiled, amused. "Do they have Ketel One?"

Lisa let out a birdlike cackle that was obviously the product of too many drinks. "See…?" she said elbowing Mika. "He belongs with us. Wait here." Mika watched her go to the bar, and in typical Lisa fashion expressed some urgency to the person at the front of the line.

"I'm so sorry," Jayce said. Mika turned slightly so she could see his face, but kept one eye on Lisa so it wouldn't appear like she was talking to him. She did this partly to avoid any wandering eyes in the room to draw any conclusions about them, and partly to prevent herself from melting when looking at him. Jayce did the same.

"What the fuck are you doing here," she asked through a smile.

"I am so sorry," he repeated through a veneer of smiles. "This was a horrible idea."

"Are you following me? Seriously, what are you doing here?"

At the bar, Lisa laughed with the couple that had just let her order in front of them. She turned and gave two thumbs up to Mika and Jayce.

"This is my home."

"What?"

"This is my hotel. This is where I live."

"You never told me that. Did you?"

"I don't think you ever asked."

"Well, shit." The room stopped spinning for Mika, and she again scanned the room. This time she spotted Todd and Gary enthralled with a craps table across the room.

"I was heading out when I saw the sign for the swim banquet," Jayce explained, relaxing his façade and talking more directly to Mika. "I'm so sorry. I just figured that there couldn't be too many swim banquets going on tonight. I thought maybe I would get a glimpse of you and then just leave."

"Well, you need to leave. Now. Seriously."

"I know," Jayce smiled. "But it's difficult because you look drop-dead amazing right now."

"Shit. Yes, well thank you. You look great too. Now get the hell out of here." She started to direct him to the door when Lisa interrupted with three glasses of vodka.

"And here we go," she laughed, giving each of them a drink. She held up her glass for a toast. "To our new friend, Jake!"

"It's Jayce," Mika protested before thinking better of it. "It is Jayce, right?"

"Jake. Jayce. It's all good," Jayce said, winking at Mika.

Don't do that!

He took a sip of his vodka and tried handing it to Lisa. "It's been a pleasure, but I really must go."

"Don't be silly," Lisa said, sliding her arm inside of his. "Come play black jack with us." Before he could protest, Lisa pulled Jayce to one of the nearby tables. Mika stayed back and watched while her friend retrieved a handful of chips from her purse. Part of her wanted to laugh, and the rest wanted to run.

What the hell have you gotten yourself into? This is not good, Mika. Not good.

As she stood frozen in fear of every possible bad ending to this situation, she noticed Jayce typing on his phone. He broke free from Lisa for a moment to set something down on a nearby table that was mostly empty save a centerpiece and a few discarded appetizer plates and beverages. Before he returned to Lisa, he looked at Mika, held up his cell phone, and smiled.

What the hell is he doing? Did he text me? He better not have texted me!

She contemplated not getting her phone just to prove a point of some kind, but that thought vacated quickly and she hurried to find her purse under one of the silent auction tables. She fished out her phone and saw one text from Jayce: Room 812. Mika's heart pounded and she felt the air tighten around her. She leaned against the table just to make sure she didn't fall over and then finished off her drink in one gulp as she watched Lisa grope Jayce's back at the blackjack table.

I can't go there. Don't do it, Mika. Everyone will know that you're gone. And what about the Wrap Around? What if his partners see me going into his room?

What bothered Mika the most, though, was that this was her son's event. She had never missed a meet or event, and this was the last one. Was she really going to sneak out? The presentation and slide show would be in 45 minutes, and she couldn't miss that. Her guilt from just thinking about it made her want to find her son. She scanned the room and figured he was in the crowd on the dance floor, so she moved that way. She was so focused that she ignored the swim coach as he tried to thank her as she passed him.

Mika stood at the edge of the dance floor and spotted Ryan doing some horrible shoulder shake with Emily and several other kids. She laughed at his awkwardness and tried to use this moment to make her forget about Jayce and room 812. She must have had an odd look on her face because Ryan made his way to her.

"Everything okay, Mom?" He had sweat trickling from his forehead and was a little out of breath.

"Yeah, sure. Of course," Mika stumbled. "I'm just making sure that you're having fun."

"I'm good," he said, and he started to go back to the dance floor. Mika grabbed his hand.

"Did you eat? Do you want to get some food?"

Ryan stared at her incredulously. "No...? Mom, I'm dancing. Go have fun, okay?" He kissed her on the head and disappeared into the crowd. Mika caught glimpses of him moving with Emily, and she was reminded of how soon her life would be different with him at college. Unlike in the past when this thought filled her head, this time something filled the glaring void: Jayce. She turned away from the crazy lights of the dance floor and walked to the mostly empty table near Jayce and Lisa. She tried to be casual as she walked around the table, and she almost lost her cool when she found a hotel key card lying next to a partially eaten piece of chocolate cake. She approached the key, looked around the ballroom to make sure no one was watching, and set her purse down next to it. Mika pretended to fidget through her belongings in such an awkward and obvious manner that if anyone had been watching they would have certainly known she was either up to something or drunk. She swiftly scooped up the card, grabbed her purse and walked away from the table. Mika's heart raced, and her hand gripped the room card. Mika moved quickly as she navigated around a few tables, out the door, and into the hallway. She was surprised to see several groups of people in the ballroom lobby, and she tried to slide past them, unnoticed.

"Mika!"

Shit.

She turned to find Stacey, one of the new parent coordinators, coming toward her.

Shit!

"Sorry I was late," she smiled, giving Mika a hug. Mika could only feel her sweaty hand tighten around the keycard.

"Oh, no worries," Mika said. "We took care of everything."

"Well, it looks fantastic. I hope you don't mind if we call you next year when we have questions."

"Sure, but I probably won't answer." Mika laughed, but not quite enough to make it clear that she was joking. An awkward silence grew between them, which Mika tried to erase. "I left something in my car," she said, making a move away from Stacey.

"Oh, let me help you." Stacey started to walk with Mika, but Mika abruptly stopped.

"No. No. It's okay. It's just something small. Just have fun, okay?" Before Stacey could reply, Mika turned and walked away, praying that Stacey was not following her. When she turned the corner and didn't hear footsteps behind her, she relaxed and quickly turned into the elevator bay. She pushed the "up" button.

"Come on. Come on," she muttered, positioning herself with her back to the lobby so that people passing through couldn't see her face. She was buzzing hard from the drinks and the exhilaration of stepping into Jayce's room. It felt like forever for the elevator doors to open, and when they did, Mika quickly shuffled in and repeatedly pressed the button to close the doors. They closed, but then immediately reopened. *Come on you stupid fucker.* She pressed the close door button again. Again they closed and reopened. Mika leaned against the wall of the elevator, exasperated. *Is this another sign? Should I not be going to the 8th floor? Wait...* She realized that she had never pushed the button for the 8th floor. *Dumbass.* She pressed it, the doors closed, and she began her second journey that week to a hotel room to meet Jayce.

Mika slid the key card into the lock to room 812 without hesitation, but she slowed as she opened the door. What if this isn't his room? Is he somehow already here? Is he going to arrive before she has to return to the gala? She gently moved into the room and whispered, "Hello?" When she was answered with silence, she added, "Housekeeping," which made her laugh. Two table lamps revealed the living room to a spacious two-room suite, similar to the other hotel room where she had first met him. *Nice. They must be charging MedCare a good chunk of change.* Mika slid out of her pumps and immediately went to the bedroom, which consisted of a queen bed that looked soft and inviting, a flat screen television, and a dresser and desk. She opened one of the dresser drawers to find several t-shirts neatly folded. *I'll bet he looks fantastic in jeans and t-shirt!* She had a quick vision of waking up in one of his t-shirts, and she considered stealing one before thinking better of it. Mika proceeded to the closet, which contained two suits and several dress shirts that she recognized. She felt the sleeve of the blue one, which she immediately recognized as the shirt he wore during their first interview. Mika really wanted to slip into this one with the hope that Jayce would find it sexy. She took it to the bed and started to reach for the zipper of her dress, but the clock that was staring at her from the end table told her she didn't have the time. *Well, shit....*

Mika returned to the living room and noticed something by the window that had escaped her when she first entered: an easel holding a stretched canvas. As she moved past the love seat that partially hid the easel, she discovered a small artist's corner. The easel stood on what looked like an old bed sheet to protect the carpet from spills, and a plastic tray held a kit of acrylic paints and brushes. The canvas was partially filled, and Mika recognized parts of the image. When she pieced together the mountain with the setting sun, she realized that it was the view of Camelback Mountain from their first hotel encounter.

Wow, that's good, she thought. *Did he really do this?* Mika was far from an art expert, but she recognized the depth that Jayce had created in the shadows of the mountain, and she liked the combination of reds and purples. As she studied other details, she heard the door unlock behind her.

"Housekeeping," a deep voice said as the door opened, which made her grin. Jayce entered with a swagger that made Mika's groin slightly wet.

"Hi, Jake." Mika said, mimicking Lisa's voice.

"So... is Lisa your friend?"

"One of my best."

"She is an interesting one," he said, removing his sport coat and draping it over the arm of the sofa.

"You can say it. She's crazy." Mika watched with glee as he came to her.

"I would never say that about your best friend." He reached her, and they kissed. As much as she loved the touch of his lips against hers, she pulled away and pointed to the painting.

"You did this?"

"Oh, don't look at that," he said, trying unsuccessfully to turn her back to him. "It's not finished."

"It's fucking awesome," she said.

Jayce laughed at the forcefulness of her statement. "Well, I wouldn't say that," and he slipped his arms around her waist.

"I would. Seriously. That's the view from our room, right?" Jayce nodded, and he kissed her just as she started to speak again. His lips felt good against hers, so she held the kiss for several moments before continuing her thought. "You painted that from memory?" Jayce smiled at her persistence. "From just one visit? That's amazing. Fucking amazing. Excuse my language." She was still buzzing.

Jayce relented and retreated to the sofa. "Not exactly. I took a picture on my phone, and I paint from that. It's kind of cheating."

Mika joined him, curling her legs under her and caressing his shoulder. "That's not cheating. I couldn't do anything remotely close to that, even with a photo."

"Trust me, I'm not that—" he started, but was cut short by Mika's finger across his lips.

"Just say 'thank you.' You're talented, and there's nothing wrong with that."

"Thank you," he smiled and followed it with a wink.

"There's that wink."

Jayce started to lean in for another kiss, but Mika again stopped him. "I want to know more about this," she said. "What, you're some kind of secret artist? Did you go to art school at some point?"

"No, not really."

"You just learned this on your own? You just know how to paint?"

"Kind of, I guess."

"Did you watch a lot of that guy on PBS? You know, the happy tree guy?"

He laughed. "No. I have seen him, but no, I didn't learn to paint from him. You know, we can talk about this another time," and he leaned in for a kiss. Again she stopped him. She wanted him physically, and seeing his talent made her want him even more. But for some reason, right now she wanted to talk.

"I know we can," and she smiled knowing that she was driving him crazy. "But I want to talk."

He leaned away, resigned to her commitment. "Ok. My dad was a painter. A disgruntled painter. He loved art and tried to pass it on to me, but I never really liked studying it. I mean, sometimes I can look at a painting and appreciate a certain style, but I just preferred painting or drawing instead. It used to piss him off."

"But he taught you how to paint?"

"A little. He understood what to do, but he was too critical of his own abilities. He sent me to an art camp when I was six."

"An art camp?" Mika laughed.

"I wasn't exactly the coolest kid on the block," he smiled.

"I'm sure! So why didn't you go to art school?"

"I just didn't. It's more of a hobby for me, kind of a creative release to keep me sane."

"And how's that working for you?" She leaned into him and resumed caressing his shoulder. "So, you travel around the country and paint in hotel rooms?"

"Something like that," he said, slowly nodding his head in thought. "I like to find something special about the city I'm in, and then I paint it." After thinking for a moment, he added, "It kind of makes me feel like I belong there, even though I know I'm eventually leaving."

"So, what do you do with the paintings? Do you have a gallery somewhere?"

"No."

"So, you take them home?"

"No. I just leave them."

Mika laughed, and then she saw that he wasn't joking. "Really?"

"Really. I have no place to put them, and I don't need a collection of things to remind me of where I've been. I just leave them in the room."

"What do they do with them?"

"I have no idea. Maybe they keep them. Maybe they throw them away. I don't like to worry about it."

Mika stared at him, incredulously. "Throw them away? Fuck no. I'm taking that one. That's *our* view. I want it." Mika was being boisterous and confident, but then she saw the uncomfortable look on Jayce's face and dialed herself in. "I'm sorry, I shouldn't have assumed that I could have it. I'm sorry."

"No, don't apologize. It sounds strange, I know, but I don't usually give them to people. It's nothing personal, really." Mika didn't understand, but she didn't need to. In his eyes and face, she could see tenderness and concern for her feelings, and that was all that mattered to her. She was finished talking; now, she wanted him physically, so she kissed him. They made out for several minutes before his hands started to wander.

"You look absolutely stunning," he whispered between kisses, and he reached for the zipper to her dress.

"Nope," Mika said, pulling his hand away and continuing to kiss his neck. "I have to be downstairs in 10 minutes."

"And we spent all this time talking about my painting?" He laughed. "I told you we could have talked about that at any time."

"This was better. Besides, I shouldn't have even come up here," she smiled.

"I'm glad you did."

"I am too," Mika said, and she kissed him on the cheek. She took a peek at the clock and added, "But I do have time for this." She slid down from the sofa, dragged her hands down his chest and past his incredible abs, unzipped his pants, and gave him a blowjob.

Chapter 39

Mika primped in Jayce's bathroom mirror, smoothing her dress with her hands and using her fingers to tame any frazzle from her hair. Jayce leaned against the entryway to the bathroom and watched her.

"I can honestly say that I did not expect any of this when I went downstairs tonight," he said.

"Neither did I," Mika smeared some toothpaste on her tongue. "And while I liked it," she mumbled, "it was really stupid."

"I know. I know. I didn't think I was actually going to see you, and then your friend—Lisa?—wouldn't let me go."

"And what about your coworkers?" Mika brushed past Jayce and headed for the door, and he followed. "What happens if someone from your team sees me leaving your room?"

"That's the only reason I dared enter the ballroom. Everyone went home for the weekend, except for Ray—the "wrap around"—and his wife is in town, so they went out for the night. I was actually supposed to meet them at a movie about 30 minutes ago, but I became distracted." He kissed her on the back of the neck.

"Distracted? Yeah, you distract the hell out of me too," she replied.

"So, when can we distract each other again?"

She checked the clock on the wall and saw that she was already a few minutes late for the presentation. "I don't know. I have to check my schedule with the car, but we'll figure something out." She quickly kissed him and patted his chest with her open hands, admiring the firmness of his muscles. "We will definitely figure it out. But now, I have to run."

He opened the door and she hurried out. As she moved down the hall, she could feel him watching her, and it felt good. She didn't dare turn for fear of being distracted again and missing the entire presentation. In the elevator, she thought about how much she wanted to stay with Jayce and to see him again, and then her euphoria slowly turned to anger. She still had no car. She still had a husband who irritated her. By the time she reached the ballroom, she had almost forgotten the previous 20 minutes and was instead reminded of the last 20 years.

When she entered the gala, most everyone was seated and listening to coach Davey stumble through his feelings about the season. There was no line at the bar, so she ordered another vodka while scanning the room for Todd. As the bartender handed her the glass, she caught Lisa motioning to her to join her at one of the tables along the wall. She twisted and turned through the crowd and eventually landed in a seat between Lisa and Todd.

"Where were you?" Todd whispered.

"I went to the car, and then I got lost."

Lisa leaned in. "Bullshit." Mika could practically taste the alcohol on Lisa's breath. "You were looking to screw that hot guy. Jason."

Holy shit! Did she just say that? Did she see me take his keycard?

Todd gave Lisa a confused look.

"I'm just fucking with you," she laughed, a little too loudly. "He's mine."

Gary put his arm around Lisa and got her to focus on the end of the coach's speech. Mika sat back in her chair and looked around. This had been her life. These were her people, and she had been one of them, hyper-focused on practice times, personal bests, and uniform colors. She had always told herself that it was for Ryan, but now that it was over, she realized that it was really just another distraction. She sat slightly behind Todd so she could secretly study him, and her first thought was, *"Who is this man sitting next to me?"* But she quickly knew this was the wrong question. She knew who he was. The real question was, "How on earth are we still together?" Mika's body tingled at this question, like an energy running under her skin that was daring her into some kind of action. It was strong enough to make her uncomfortable, and as she squirmed in her chair, she caught a glimpse of Ryan sitting across the room with Emily and his teammates. She then recognized this buzzing energy for what it was—another distraction, a very unwanted one. This was his final event before graduation, and she wanted to enjoy it. Mika took three cleansing breaths, which didn't catch the attention of anyone at her table, and she was able to bring herself down enough to listen to the final words of coach Davey's speech.

The remainder of the gala was relatively uneventful. Awards were given for best performances, and the students recognized each other through a set of superlatives awards like most improved and best sense of humor. Mika, Lisa and the other booster parents were acknowledged for their efforts in supporting the team and organizing the gala, and all of the swimmers and divers gathered on the dance floor for one final group photo. Behind the official photographer, all of the parents gathered and held up cell phones to take their own photos. Mika had wiggled her way to the front, just next to the photographer, and she zoomed in on her only son, who sat in the middle with one arm around Emily and the other around David Zupke, one of Emily's diver friends. Mika enjoyed seeing Ryan in the crowd, a place where she herself never felt comfortable. She watched her son through the screen of her iPhone, and the past 17 years of his life flashed before her: his first day of kindergarten, watching the Princess Bride under a sheet fort in their living room, his game-winning home run in 5th grade, and his first swim meet. She was so wrapped up in the moment that she was even happy to see him with Emily. Her moment of peace came to an end, however, when the photo session was finished and the students started to disperse, most of them randomly hugging each other as they moved off the dance floor. Mika was making her way toward Ryan when she saw Mark approach him. Mark held out his arms to invite an embrace, his face looking a little defeated. Mika's heart jumped in anticipation, but instead of reciprocating, Ryan looked like he was going to hit Mark. He refrained, and Mika could read his lips as he told Mark, "Go fuck yourself," before escorting Emily away from the crowd. Mika's evening had been a range of emotions, from frustration to elation, confusion to contentment, and now it was ending with disappointment. She was sad that Ryan would walk away from a friend like that, and she was upset with herself as a mother because she felt that Ryan's actions represented her failure as a mother. Still, she tracked him down and hugged him.

"Congratulations," she said. She decided to chew his ass tomorrow.

"Thanks, Mom," he said, oblivious to her emotional state and the fact that she had seen his exchange with Mark. He pulled Mika away from his crowd. "Seriously, thank you for always being there. I know you didn't have to do all of this, but it meant a lot to me knowing that you were a part of things." Mika's eyes swelled, and she couldn't contain a few tears from flowing down her cheeks.

"You're my little boy," she smiled. "Nothing is more important." She hugged him again, long enough to contain the tears and regain some composure. "Be safe tonight, okay?"

"I will. We're just all going to Zupke's house and crashing there."

She grabbed his chin and forced him to look her in the eyes. "No drinking."

Ryan smiled. "Come on Mom, you know me." He kissed her on the forehead and returned to Emily and his crew.

Yeah, I know you.

Mika found Lisa, Gary and Todd by the silent auction tables. Much of the crowd had left already, and now she had some cleanup duties left, mostly gathering the supplies they had brought.

"Can you start gathering the signs and photos," she said to Gary and Todd. "We'll pack up the auction."

"No, Honey. We are done!" Lisa took her by the shoulders and squeezed. "Done!"

"Well, we need to pack up some things, and then we're done."

"No, the newbies are taking care of that," Lisa said, pointing to moms who were coming back into to the ballroom with empty boxes.

Todd grabbed her hand, which felt odd. "You've done more than enough. Let's go."

Mika didn't know what to feel. She had been looking forward to being "done," but now that it was here, she wasn't so sure. "Alright, let's go," she said, and the two couples walked out holding hands. Todd's hand felt cold and strange, and Mika was silent as they walked through the lobby and out to the parking lot. She tried to reflect on her conflicted feelings, but kept getting interrupted by Lisa's giggling. As they exited the building, she started heading to the right, but Todd pulled her to the left.

"I'm parked over here," Mika said.

"No you're not," Todd smiled.

Mika was confused. *Did I move the car? I swear I parked over there.* She tried looking in that direction, but Todd kept guiding her the other way. They passed one of the hotel's large fountains and turned the corner, where Todd stopped.

"Here is where you are parked," he said, and he held up a key.

Mika stared blankly at the black key fob dangling from his fingertips. *What?* She looked past Todd to discover a white Mercedes 1200 with a large red ribbon on the hood. She looked back at Todd and then to Lisa and Gary.

"It's your new car!" Lisa squealed.

Chapter 40

Mika watched the eggshells drop through the garbage disposal in her sink. She was cleaning up from an easy breakfast on Sunday morning after a difficult series of emotions on Saturday night. She had many issues to resolve in her mind, including why she was so unenthusiastic about finally getting a car—but she had committed her morning to one task: confronting Ryan about the vodka.

* * *

Mika had driven herself and Todd home in her new car the previous night. The Mercedes was not exactly new, but Mika didn't care about that. It was eight months old, a lease vehicle turned in early by an accountant who had lost his job in Flagstaff. Todd's trip earlier that week hadn't been for business; it had been to buy this car. For her. And while he had been doing that, she was *doing* someone else. But it wasn't guilt that consumed her while she drove. Nor was it the sense of freedom that the car represented. No, it was something else that she couldn't identify. She spent the entire drive home trying to figure out what was keeping her from loving this moment, and it was more than just listening to Todd drunkenly repeat what a great deal it was. When they arrived at home, she waited with the car running while Todd moved his golf clubs and repositioned his car to make room for her. He was still under the influence, so his movements were awkward and it took him much longer than it should. *You knew I would be parking there, right? Why did you leave your clubs in the way?*

As they entered the house, she dreaded the thought of having sex with Todd. It had been at least a month since the last time they were intimate, and she feared that the car came with expectations. Upstairs in their bedroom, Todd kissed her, and she returned the favor for a moment before excusing herself to the bathroom as she had the previous weekend. She killed time by taking off her makeup and brushing her hair, very meticulously. Mika knew that Todd's beer consumption meant that he would likely fall asleep soon, and she was right; he was totally asleep in his clothes by the time she returned to the bedroom. Mika stared at her husband with anxiety. She felt guilt over allowing her mouth to touch his after it had been on another man's penis earlier that night, and she wanted to sleep somewhere else. Instead, she slipped under the covers next to him and quickly realized how exhausted she was. *It's over. Holy shit!* She fell asleep before she could even begin to think about Jayce.

Mika's alarm went off at 6:30 am. *What the hell??* It was not intentional; she had forgotten to turn it off from her Saturday morning yoga workout. She wanted to go back to sleep, but she couldn't stop thinking about the previous night. Mika went downstairs for another yoga session. She hoped that it would clear her head and get rid of her slight hangover headache. As she moved slowly through her poses, her headache never completely disappeared, but she did receive a moment of clarity: she needed to talk to Ryan about the alcohol... and maybe about Mark.

During her breakfast with Todd, she wanted to talk to him about Ryan, but she never had the chance. Todd spent the time rehashing the details of the great deal he had made on her car and espousing its features. She had heard them all the night before, but since he was rather proud of himself, listening again was the least she could do. Fortunately, he was in a rush to get to the golf course early to hit some range balls before his round, so their breakfast was brief. Mika didn't mind.

* * *

Mika washed dishes while waiting for Ryan to get home, which she knew wouldn't be for a while. She decided to text him.

MJ: What time will you be home? I want to talk.

She was surprised at how quickly he responded.

RJ: An hour. Just eating breakfast. Am I in trouble?

Mika didn't know how to respond to his question. He wasn't technically in trouble since she wasn't going to punish him. *But I suppose listening to me complain about you could be considered a punishment.* She thought about not sending a reply, but she didn't think that was fair to him, so she kept it vague.

MJ: Not really.

Maybe that's worse than no response. She stopped worrying about it and finished washing the dishes and cleaning the counters. She started to go upstairs, but stopped at the pantry. She hadn't been sure about how to begin her conversation with Ryan, but she decided to just put it out there. She took the watered-down bottle of vodka from the shelf, and set it on the breakfast table where it stood alone and obvious. Then, she went upstairs to start a load of laundry.

Mika grabbed an armful of whites, mostly Todd's undershirts and dress shirts and went to the laundry room. She started the washing machine—she still had a top-load that she loved—and she slowly poured the blue detergent into the base of water that had started to fill the basin. She watched it swirl about and turn into foam, and her mind wanted to take her to the beach. She wanted to go there, but the collars to Todd's shirts needed to be sprayed before being thrown into the wash.

After she finished loading the machine, Mika wandered around the house, like a bored teenager looking for something to do, still reeling physically from the late night. She took a tour through Ryan's room, taking in the medals and photos on his wall, and it was a little more than she wanted to handle emotionally. Eventually, she returned to the kitchen, took the bottle of Ketel One, and landed on the couch, contemplating the irony of her situation. Now that she had a car, she could leave and go anywhere, yet she couldn't because she didn't want to miss her teenage son coming home. She stared at the ceiling fan, watching it spin fifteen feet above her. Before she could calculate the last time she had dusted it, she fell asleep.

She only slept for 10 minutes, but she had a vivid dream that she was on one of the historic ships that sailed along the shore in her many daydreams. She was alone at sea, and she was frantically searching the ship for laundry to put away, but her search yielded nothing. As she returned to the top deck, she heard a door slam behind her. She slowly approached the captain's quarters, unsure of who might be there with her. Was it Jayce? As she reached for the rusty door handle, another door slammed, but this one originated from her real-world kitchen and drifted into her dream world, waking her from her nap

Mika felt refreshed and alert, and she sat up just as Ryan entered the living room.

"Hey, Mom," he said, appearing chipper until he saw the vodka bottle. "Um, I'm going to go to bed. We didn't get much sleep last night."

Oh no you don't. "Not yet. Come sit down."

"Mom...."

"Sit."

Ryan complied, sitting in the recliner opposite his mother. He stared nervously at the vodka. Mika ignored the bottle and smiled at him. She enjoyed making him squirm, but she wasn't sure how long to let it continue.

"So, what did you guys do last night?" she asked.

Ryan started to answer, but then he surprised his mother by turning directly into the storm. "I'm sorry about the alcohol, Mom. I'll pay for a new bottle."

What? That was easy. Too easy. Mika had a planned attack ready to go, but now she needed to adjust her approach. She tried to create more bullet points for her conversation, but she decided to just speak from the heart.

"Do you think I'm upset about the cost?"

He shook his head.

"What were you thinking? And I don't know how pissed I should be that you thought I would be too stupid to notice."

"Mom, it's no big deal."

"Drinking alcohol is a big deal."

Ryan looked at his mother with a sharp smile. "Really?"

"We're not talking about me. You're 17. It's not legal for a reason."

"I'm not the only teenager who drinks, Mom. Isn't it normal?"

"Well, I didn't drink when I was 17, and trust me, I had plenty of reasons to drink."

"I know. I know. You were working and helping to support your dad." Until this point, Ryan had been mostly calm, but now his voice started to reveal his exasperation. "I can't help what your life was like. That's not my fault."

Mika sensed his frustration, and the tired look in his eyes pushed her into a different direction.

"So, how long have you been drinking?"

"It's not like 'I'm drinking.' I've been to a few parties and had a few drinks."

"Did you drink last night?"

"No."

Mika looked at him. *Really?*

"No. We just stayed up all night and watched *Goonies* and *Rugrats.*"

Mika couldn't help but smile. "You were watching *Rugrats*, and you weren't drinking? I started drinking just to get through that show."

"Yeah, it wasn't as good as we remembered it. But it was funny to watch."

Mika stared at him. She was still upset with him and didn't want to condone his drinking, but she had to admit that her upbringing was far from his, and she knew that experimenting with alcohol was likely a normal occurrence. Besides, she was more upset with him about Mark.

"Are you driving when you drink?"

"Of course not," he scoffed. "I'm not an idiot."

"Any of your friends? Emily? Are they driving?"

"No, it was only at parties when we were spending the night."

She thought again as he avoided eye contact with her. "So, when was your first drink?"

He shrugged. "A few months ago, toward the end of summer."

"When you started seeing Emily?"

Ryan finally looked at Mika. "I'm not drinking because of Emily, Mom. I drank because I'm 17."

"I didn't say it was because of Emily."

"Yes you were. I know you don't like her, Mom. It's no secret."

"It's not that I don't like her," she said, and she carefully selected her next words. "It's just that you spend a lot of time with her."

"Why is that bad? Aren't you supposed to spend time with people that you like?" He leaned back in the recliner and added, "And with people who like you in return?"

"But at what expense? You hardly even spend time with Mark anymore." Ryan let out a noise that was part laugh, part grunt, which soured Mika's tone. "I watched him last night. He came to you and you told him to go fuck himself. He's your best friend, Ryan."

Again Ryan let out his noise. "You don't know what you're talking about."

She leaned forward and placed her hands on his feet. "Then tell me, because I don't get it. Mark was your best friend, and for a time, you're only friend. And I don't know what happened, but I would hope that my son wouldn't just throw that away." She sat up and looked very directly at his face. "And as far as I can tell, it all started with Emily."

Ryan stood up, angry and charged. He started to walk away, but Mika stood and blocked him.

"Mom…."

"What? Am I wrong?"

Ryan's frustration grew. "Granola."

Mika shook her head and raised her voice. "No! Not on this!"

Ryan turned back to the couch and started to pace. "It's nothing, Mom."

"It's not nothing!"

"Fine!" Ryan plopped down on the couch. "You really want to know?"

Mika stood behind him. "Yes! What is going on with you?"

"He tried to have sex with Emily."

Mika walked around the couch. "What do you mean?"

"Well, Mark has a penis, and he tried to put it inside of her," he said. "He practically attacked her, Mom."

Mika sat in the recliner. "When was this? Before you were dating?"

"No, we were already dating." Ryan looked like he was ready to cry. "Emily and I had already gone out three or four times."

Mika listened to Ryan explain that when he had gone to the beach with Mika and Todd for a three-day getaway just before school started, Mark had offered to give Emily a ride home from practice. Since Ryan was out of town, Mark had convinced her to go to a party. She had texted Ryan about it so it wouldn't seem weird, and Ryan didn't mind because Mark was his best friend. When he took her home, he pulled into an empty parking lot and started kissing her and putting his hands all over her. Emily had been wearing a skirt, and he started forcing his hand between her legs. Eventually she found the door handle and pushed herself out of the car. She scrambled to her feet and ran away without looking back.

"He's a fucking asshole, Mom. When I confronted him about, he just laughed and said that he was drunk and just messing around."

Now the past few months started making more sense, and Mika assumed that Mark's black eye at regionals came from her son. She wanted to know more details, but she realized that it might sound like she was defending Mark.

"Did she report it to anyone? The police? Her parents?"

"No, she didn't want to tell her parents. They have a lot of other things to worry about."

"So, why didn't *you* tell *me*?"

"Because Mark's mom is your best friend," he said, and without trying to be funny, he added, "and you don't have a lot of friends, so it just didn't seem like something I should tell you."

Shit. Now she was feeling guilty about all of her recent animosity toward her son. She leaned across and took his hands in hers. "You're my son, and whenever you have something to tell me, that's more important than anything else. Got it?"

He nodded. "Are you going to tell his mom?"

"I don't know," she said, and she didn't know. "Should I?"

"I don't know. Probably. But here's thing, he's always been kind of a dick."

"Well, he was your friend, so let's not totally ignore that."

"He was, but he always had little ways of being mean to people, thinking he was better than everyone. It just started getting really bad this summer. Who does that to a girl? And what kind of an asshole makes a move on someone else's girlfriend?"

Mika didn't want to think about that question, so she left it with, "I'm sorry that you've had to deal with this."

They sat in silence, and Mika thought that the conversation was over, but Ryan spoke up. "I know I spend a lot of time with Emily. She's cool, and she really likes me. I feel really comfortable with her, and I know that you're worried that I spend too much time with her and that my whole life is about her, but it's not like we're getting married. Don't worry, I'm not you."

What? What does that mean? She tried to process his comment, and Ryan must have been able to see it in her face.

"I'm 17, and Emily is my girlfriend right now. *Right now*, but probably not forever. I know that. We have college to get through, and likely a lot of other people to see. I'm not going to get stuck in a relationship now that I'm going to hate 20 years from now."

Mika heard an innocent quality in his voice to know that he wasn't trying to insult her. "Is that what you think happened to me?"

"I'm not stupid, Mom. I see other parents together. I love you both, but I'm not sure what the two of you are doing. You seem like you're on different planets." When Mika didn't respond, he added, "I thought for sure you were getting divorced when I was in 7th grade. You went away for a weekend, and I wasn't sure that you were coming back."

"How would that have made you feel… a divorce?"

"I would have hated it. I cried a lot."

"You did?"

"I tried to hold it in until I was in bed. One time it happened at school."

Mika's heart sank. She knew that he had struggled during that time, but the thought of her son crying destroyed her.

"But now? I just think you should be happy. You deserve to be happy."

Mika smiled at him, stood up and kissed him on the forehead. "You're an amazing kid. Now go get some sleep." She grabbed the vodka bottle and went to the kitchen. Her legs felt weak, and she leaned against the counter to make sure she didn't fall.

Holy shit.

She snatched her purse and went to the garage. She needed to go somewhere—anywhere—so she got in her new car and drove. As she cruised aimlessly through the neighborhood and eventually onto the freeway, she only had one word on her mind: divorce. Did her son really say that? Was it really an option for her? After their last brush with splitting up, Mika had buried the notion of a divorce, figuring that her life was on a path that included being permanently unhappily married. Even after she had spent time with Jayce and lost herself in his world, she had never considered divorce as a real option, so hearing Ryan say the word had rattled her. It was like he had drugged her and she was hallucinating, uncertain of what was real around her.

She drove for an hour, contemplating life as a single person. She thought about Ryan and what his real reaction might be if she and Todd actually divorced. Whose home would he come to when he returned from college? Where would she live? Could she fix a clogged sink on her own? How would their friends react? Would Lisa and Gary side with Todd? Surprisingly, Jayce didn't factor into any of her thinking. Instead, she was asking herself the same question she had asked and answered 17 years ago: *Can I do it on my own?* She wasn't sure that the answer was yes this time, and that bothered her.

This thinking had taken her west on I-10, outside the city limits and into the clear skies over Goodyear, a sprawling development west of Phoenix. If she kept going, she would end up in Los Angeles, and the idea was tempting. *Just keep going, and don't look back*, she thought. Mika checked her gas gauge, and seriously considered the option of driving to the beach, where she could bury her feet in the sand while she explored the vastness of the Pacific Ocean. She pulled off the freeway to get a drink at the Quick Trip gas station.

Something about filling her cup with Coke Zero grounded her, and she resigned herself to returning home. Eventually. As she returned to her car, she stopped to study it. *It's nice, but why do I hate it?*

She admired the curved lines of the fenders and roofline, and the white paint was smooth and shiny. It was beautiful, yet she hated it. When she got in, she started the car and paid attention to the aerial view of the backup camera, the feature that Todd bragged about the most. She paid attention to the other interior features: the cup holders, the push-button start, GPS display screen, the room in the back that could be converted to a third row seat. It was all very nice, yet it bothered her. *Why don't I like this car?*

This became her new focus as she drove east into Phoenix. She kept thinking that maybe she didn't like it because she was angry with Todd, which made her ask another question: *Am I just an unappreciative bitch? Todd went all the way to Flagstaff to get a car that was a great deal, a car that had much more than I needed to be happy....* And then it hit her. She didn't hate the car just because it came from Todd; she hated it because it was *for* Todd.

In their shopping experiences, he had always ignored what she desired and instead tried to convince her why she should want something else. He didn't go to Flagstaff to buy her the car that she wanted; he went to buy her the car that he wanted to give, the one that was a great deal with features he could brag about. She acknowledged that it was very nice, but it wasn't for her, and this wasn't the first time he had done something like this. He often bought her bigger and better appliances, like blenders and hair dryers for Christmas, even though she never expressed that something was wrong with the old ones. He didn't talk to her for a week when she refused to accept delivery on a new front-load washer—it was semi-new and a "great deal"—but instead called a repairman to fix the top-load that she loved. Perhaps her biggest irritation came on their 10th anniversary when he gave her a new platinum wedding ring with a 2-carat diamond. It dwarfed her original ring, which was yellow gold and barely a carat, but she wanted to keep the original, the one that represented her marriage vows. Lisa convinced her that she was crazy, so she begrudgingly wore the new ring without much protest.

She had always felt guilty about not being more appreciative, but this time Mika was coming to a different conclusion: *Todd either doesn't know me well enough to know what I want, or he is too selfish to care.* It was a revelation that excited her because it made her feel less guilty about the possibility of a divorce. *I'm entitled to want what I want, and he is entitled to be with someone who appreciates what he has to give.* She meant that last part. She wasn't feeling anger toward Todd, just acknowledgement of their reality. When she had been driving west, she was feeling confused and depressed, but she now felt lucid and energized. She wanted to share her insight with someone, hopefully to get validation for her feelings.

She thought about calling Lisa because she had always been her confidant, but she was also the one who was quick with an "are you crazy?" response and would tell Mika that she was being unappreciative. She didn't want to be brought down, and she was also afraid that she might let something slip about Jayce. She ran through her other friends, but there weren't too many besides Tanya, and she didn't want to have this kind of personal discussion with a coworker. The only person she really wanted to talk to was Jayce, despite her commitment not to talk about her marriage with him. Ryan's last words ran through her head, "You deserve to be happy," and she pulled over to send Jayce a text.

MJ: Baseball field?

Mika sat in the dirt and pebble-filled parking lot of a deserted tire store just inside the city limits, eagerly awaiting a response. *What if he doesn't reply? Please reply.* As she sipped her soda, she looked at the dilapidated front of the tire store. White paint peeled away from the building, and graffiti-covered plywood covered the windows. Old buildings like this intrigued Mika. She imagined it new, filled with excitement and life, and she wondered how it had slowly died. She didn't believe in ghosts, but she pictured spirits inside trying to keep the building alive, and it made her sad. As Mika tried to make out the name from the faded sign—it was either Floyd's or Boyd's—her phone chimed with a text.

JB: Sure. When?

Mika didn't hesitate with her reply.

MJ: Now. 20 minutes?

His response came equally quickly, which made Mika happy.

JB: Yes!

Mika drove to the baseball fields where they had experienced their first intimate encounter just a week ago. Jayce's minivan was already there when she arrived. She pulled into "her spot" by the tree.

"What?" Jayce said as Mika exited her car. "Did someone finally get her own car?"

She nodded, hurrying over to embrace him. She watched as Jayce checked out the interior.

"This is nice. It's no minivan, but not bad." She must have been making a face because he followed with, "You don't like it?"

They leaned against his minivan, and she went on to explain the myriad of thoughts she had about the car and how it represented what was wrong between her and Todd. Jayce held her hand as he listened. "But do you know what I mean," she asked, eager for his agreement. "It's not what I wanted. Does that make me a total bitch?"

"No, absolutely not. It's not like you're complaining because you deserve a better car."

"No, I don't ever assume that I deserve anything. I am very fortunate to have things in my life that others can't. I actually wanted something less."

Jayce smiled at her. "We've never really talked about your husband. I'm not sure I'm comfortable with this."

"I know. I'm sorry. It's just that when I have something to say, I want to say it to you. I'm sorry, I'll stop." Mika was a little defeated. Jayce was a beautiful man who made her feel amazing physically, but she also wanted to see him as a friend. She felt him squeeze her hand.

"I will say this. You are entitled to want what you want. You can't help that, and when it isn't beyond anything that you've worked for, you shouldn't feel guilty about it." She pulled him closer, and then she heard for the second time that day, "You deserve to be happy."

Mika held on to his arm, her head leaning against his shoulder. She wanted to say something, but she felt equally content just holding him. Her new car stared at her, so she closed her eyes and breathed in the moment. Jayce cancelled the silence with a small chuckle.

"What?" Mika asked, keeping her eyes closed.

"Nothing," he said, but then he laughed again.

This time Mika turned and looked at him. "What's so funny?"

"Well, we could break it in."

Mika's face tightened. "What do you mean?"

"Your car," Jayce smiled. "We could break it in." He winked at her.

Oh my God! That would be horrible, she thought momentarily, but before she knew it she and Jayce were in the back seat of her car, twisting naked together in the cramped space and steaming up the windows. She managed to go down on him, and after he figured out how to lower the seats flat, Jayce returned the favor. They fumbled through several positions before settling on the missionary style, which was more than enough to make her cum twice. She curled up next to him, her sweaty leg draped across his, and she watched the moisture clinging to the windows and protecting them from the outside world. Her hand rested on his chest, and his heartbeat pulsed through her fingertips. She could stay here forever, except for one thing: she was getting cold. She reached for his shirt and tugged on the sleeve, but it was pinned under the seat.

"Cold?" Jayce rubbed his hand up and down her leg. He started to sit up, but Mika pulled him down.

"No, I'm fine," she said, but her teeth started to chatter, which then turned into laughter.

"Right," he laughed, and he pulled her up with him. "Besides, I'm sure you have somewhere to be." He was right; she should head home. Jayce manipulated the seats so he could free their wadded up clothes from below. They dressed in silence, which Jayce eventually broke as he finished buttoning his shirt.

"Every time I see you, I'm surprised."

Mika stopped pulling up her pants. "Why is that?"

Jayce hesitated, and Mika could see him considering his words. "You're married," he finally said. "I just keep thinking that you're going to come to your senses and decide that this isn't for you." He paused, and their eyes met. Mika was caught off guard by the comment, unsure of how to answer. "I enjoy you, Mika. I really enjoy you, and yet I can't help but think, 'why is she here?'"

Why am I here? Several thoughts raced through her head as she finished dressing. *Maybe because I don't want to be somewhere else. Maybe because I'm falling for you? Maybe because I'm crazy? How can I answer that question when I can't really explain myself?*

"You don't have to answer," Jayce said, taking her hand and pressing his fingertips into her palm, a move that cleared her head.

"Good," she said as she leaned across the seat and kissed him.

After Jayce drove away, Mika returned the seats to their upright positions and thoroughly checked the floors for any evidence of her encounter. She drove the long way home, taking surface streets when it would have been faster to take the freeway. The entire time, Jayce's question bounced around her head, and she kept trying to justify her actions: *Life is short. I deserve to be happy. My marriage is practically done anyway.* She continued making this argument with herself until she found herself at a stop light in a neighborhood she wouldn't be in if she hadn't been trying to avoid going home. She sat at the light, adjacent to a freestanding liquor store that was simply labeled "Liquor," and watched a tall, lanky man emerge from the store with a 12 pack of Bud Light dangling from his fingertips. She only noticed him because his frame and the gait of his walk reminded her of her father. It made her smile and feel sad at the same time, and then she heard her mother's voice.

Love harder.

Mika was caught off guard by the flood of tears that followed. She forgot about Jayce and about deserving happiness as she cried through a full cycle of the traffic light, only moving when a car finally pulled up behind her and honked as the green light turned to yellow. She drove home, blurry-eyed and sniffling, thinking about how her life was a mess, how she had made it so, and how disappointed her mother would be. Her mother had made tough choices in her life, ones that made her stronger. Mika's choices in life had failed to make her a stronger person. Right now she felt incredibly weak. She managed to subdue her tears by the time she pulled into her garage, but her body and mind felt wilted. As she checked her face in the mirror and tried to repair damage to her makeup from both crying and contact with Jayce, the door to the house opened.

Shit.

Todd came out and approached the passenger door.

No. No. Don't get in.

She took a quick glance around for any last second signs of her illicit behavior and then opened the door, hoping to exit before her husband joined her in the car. No such luck. The passenger door opened, and Todd popped in next to her.

"Well...?" he asked, smiling.

Mika had no idea what to say.

"Well, how does it drive?" he asked with a slightly annoyed tone.

Mika forced some enthusiasm, hoping it would mask everything that she was trying to hide from her husband. "It's great. It's really a great drive."

"I know, right?" Todd caressed the dashboard with pride. "I still can't believe the great deal I got. I didn't even get into the great safety rating." He took in a deep breath.

What are you doing? Oh my God, does it smell like sex?

Todd smiled. "And I love that it still has that new car smell."

Chapter 41

The first time Mika had contemplated getting a divorce, the marriage counselor recommended that she spend a weekend away from home and make a list of what she wanted from her husband. She had resisted because she thought it might be too weird for Ryan if she slept somewhere else for the weekend, but Todd convinced her that they would "man up" for two days, and Ryan wouldn't even notice that she was gone.

Mika had made a reservation to stay at the Tempe Buttes, but she mindlessly passed the exit and continued on the I-10 for 90 minutes until she found herself in her hometown of Tucson. She hadn't intended to go there, so she had no idea that driving past her childhood home would have such an emotional impact on her.

* * *

Mika parked across the street from the single story home that stood in a dusty neighborhood in the southeastern part of Tucson. The home was simple in its style and design, typical of homes built during the depression. As a teenager, Mika had recognized that their compact home was old, but her father's handyman skills kept it alive.

From her parked car, she immediately noticed how the previous 20 years had taken their toll on the house. The lawn had been worn down to patches of dirt with the occasional pack of weeds posing as Bermuda. Paint peeled away from the wood siding as if it were trying to leave the neighborhood, and rotted eves battled to support the weathered roof. She took inventory of the place, trying to note what had changed. The fence, while dilapidated, weak, and probably 15 years old, was "new." The bushes that lined the outer edge of the driveway were still there, but they were much more woody than leafy. The large peppercorn tree was still there where the yard met the sidewalk, its roots pushing up the sidewalk and contributing to the image of disrepair.

From the safety of her car, Mika was able to see moments of her childhood play out before her: her father holding on to the back of her bike seat as he taught her to ride in the driveway; her mother making popcorn before they sat down to watch the Sunday night Disney specials; Saturday morning dusting with her mother. Each memory filled her with sadness. They had so little compared to what her current life offered, and yet she had been so content. And she missed her parents. She had not thought this much about them since just after Ryan's birth, and tears flooded her eyes. Despite the sadness, the tears had brought with them a sense of relief, almost as if they were stripping her clean of the anxiety and stress that had been festering inside of her. She continued to scan the yard for more memories when she stopped at the peppercorn. She remembered that this was their second tree, planted after the first one had almost crushed their home.

* * *

"You need to replace it," Regina said to her husband.

Mika lowered her book to see her father using a hand planer to trim the edge of the front door. Her mother took a break from mixing a salad to watch from the kitchen.

"Why don't you listen," she continued when he didn't respond. "You know it needs to be replaced."

Denny responded without looking up from his work. "I can't just replace the door. I must replace the frame."

Mika had heard this discussion several times in the past few years. As the house continued to settle and the foundation cracked, the house's wood frame twisted everything out of alignment, and the front door in particular failed them on a regular basis. It began with a gentle sticking, but gradually grew to where one had to put a shoulder into it in order to open or close it completely. On this day the door was so badly jammed that Mika and Regina couldn't open it when they had returned from the market, so they walked around to the back door, which Regina had left unlocked for this very reason. When Denny came home, he had to throw all of his weight into the door just to enter his own house after a long day of work.

"Yes," Regina said. "So you say."

Mika heard the exasperation in her father's voice. "Yes, that is what I say. The frame is no longer square, so a new door will have the same problem."

"Then replace the frame."

"When do I have time for that? I must rip out the frame, cut the new frame, and then repair the plaster and stucco, and then it must be painted."

"It sounds like excuses," Regina said, and she returned to her salad. "But hurry and close the door. I don't want dust in the house."

Mika set down her book and hurried to the kitchen window to watch the wind toss leaves around in a jaunty little dance.

The late summer monsoons were a welcome relief from the oppressive heat of the Arizona desert. As the afternoon sun reached its peak, a wall of clouds often crept up on the city, and by nightfall, the wind would pick up and blow dust across the town. Heat lightning often flashed in the distance, briefly illuminating the overcast skies. Many nights were just filled with wind and a few raindrops, which left the humid air thick and uncomfortable. There was great joy when the rain did fall, bringing coolness across the desert to combat the sweltering afternoon heat.

Mika was in 4th grade, just before her mother became ill, and she had started to look forward to these climatic events. After lunch, she would watch the clouds form in the distance and try to predict whether or not it would rain that night. She would spend each evening watching from the window until her parents warned her to move to a safe place. This was her father's busy season, as he responded each morning to countless phone calls to repair a roof damaged by the previous night's storm.

Mika and her parents ate dinner in the kitchen that night, and she half listened to her parents talk about their day while she focused on the developing storm outside. The eucalyptus leaves rattled against each other just outside the kitchen window, and she heard the branches scrape against the eves of the roof. *It's going to rain for sure,* she thought. When she went to bed later that night, her anticipation kept her awake for hours.

Mika finally dozed off and had been asleep for almost an hour when a loud crack of thunder woke her. Startled, she cautiously sat up before realizing that the wind was still blowing hard outside, and she heard heavy raindrops assaulting the roof. An occasional blast slammed the screen against the window and gave her a jolt, but she was quickly filled with excitement. She rushed to the kitchen window because the streetlights usually afforded her a better view, but this time she saw nothing past her front yard, only the sheets of rain illuminated by a dull yellow light. It was the most powerful storm she had ever witnessed, and the sheer force of nature amazed her. She was enjoying the show until the storm shook the walls of the house. Before she could process another thought, she heard another loud crack and the outside sky illuminated several times from nearby lightning.

"Mika!"

At the sound of her mother's voice, she instinctively moved away from the window while her mother pulled her even farther toward the center of the house. Denny joined them and began chastising his daughter when the house shook again, this time followed by a large crash and the sound of breaking glass and cracking wood. Mika turned to see branches from the eucalyptus tree poking through the ceiling above the front door. The tornado-like wind had finally won the battle, breaking the tree like a wishbone and sending half of it into the front of their home. Mika cried as her mother barked orders in her native Ukrainian, which Mika only heard in times of duress. Denny pushed his wife and daughter back and started to approach the disaster area when an eight-foot opening suddenly appeared in the ceiling, the wind having ripped away a section of the weakened structure. Denny let out a "My God" as rain now poured freely into their house.

"Go. Let's go!" he yelled, pulling his family to the back door.

"Go where?" Regina asked in Ukrainian, holding on tightly to Mika's arm. "We're not going out there."

Denny responded quickly. "Right. Right. The bathtub."

Mika and her mother sat in the bathtub, where Regina tried to pacify her daughter's fears. She ran her fingers through Mika's hair and told her stories about growing up in the Ukraine while Denny recruited the help of a neighbor to secure a tarp over the damaged roof. Mika eventually fell asleep in her mother's arms.

Mika awoke to find herself in her own bed, and she followed the trail of muffled voices to the living area, where she confirmed that the storm had not been a dream. Regina was mopping water from the kitchen floor, and through the broken kitchen window Mika could see her father talking with neighbors, apparently discussing the best way to remove the tree from the house. She studied the water-soaked area and saw the broken bits of plaster, glass, and roof debris that had been scattered around. She looked up to see the hole in the roof that was covered with blue plastic sheeting, and branches of the tree poked through a nearby sections of the ceiling. The front door leaned inward and away from the wall, which struggled to stay up from the weight of the tree trunk that pushed down on it from above. Again, she cried.

Regina put down her mop and hugged Mika.

"What is wrong, my love?"

"It's all broken," she sobbed, trying to get it under control.

"It will be okay," her mother told her. "It could be worse. You could have been hurt, or me, or your father." She pulled herself slightly away so she could look into Mika's eyes. "Things could be much worse." Mika managed to stop crying, and her mother continued in typical fashion to find the silver lining. "Besides, now your father will have to fix that door properly, right?" She smiled at Mika. "Sometimes we need a storm to come along to help us get things done."

* * *

Mika was supposed to be making a list of what she wanted from her husband. Instead, she had spent the rest of that afternoon traveling around Tucson and retracing moments of her childhood—walking around the playground of her elementary school, driving past the pre-school where her mother worked, getting a drink from "her" Wendy's—before ending the day at the Tucson Botanical Gardens. It was her mother's favorite destination and the location where Mika and her father had secretly spread her ashes 25 years before. As she walked through the cactus and succulent garden, she could hear her mother's voice marvel at the agave bloom that rose 10 feet into the air and about how much she loved the herbs. But as Mika walked throughout the garden and reflected on what she thought was wrong with her life, she heard her mother's voice saying just one thing: *It could be worse.*

Chapter 42

For the first time in her career, Mika lied to Tanya, but it didn't bother her. She had sent Tanya a text just after Todd left for work on Monday morning.

MJ: Food poisoning? Staying home. Sorry!

Unfortunately, Tanya immediately called her, which didn't surprise Mika. The team was leaving for Seattle on Wednesday, and she had preparation meetings today and tomorrow.

"I'm not sure what I ate," she had said, trying to sound weak but not so much that it sounded fake. "But I need to get this out of my system before Wednesday."

She could tell that Tanya was irritated, but she recovered quickly. "Okay, I can handle today's meeting. Check in later so I know about tomorrow. We really need you tomorrow."

Mika knew that her presence at the meeting was important, but so was getting her life together. The previous night she had struggled to fall asleep as she continued to wrestle with the chaos that was her life. The visual reminder of her father outside the liquor store had lingered long enough that she tossed and turned in bed until she knew what she needed to do: make another pilgrimage to Tucson. She had mapped out the day, allowing for a two-hour drive each way, time at her childhood home and the Botanical Gardens, and a relaxing lunch. She would be home around the time she usually arrived home from work.

As she pulled away from her house, Lisa waved her down from her driveway. *Shit.* She pulled up next to the curb and rolled down the passenger window.

"How much do you love it?" Lisa smiled as she approached Mika.

"Love what?"

"Your car? Hello?" Lisa poked her head into the car, examining its interior even though she had spent 15 minutes inside it the other night.

"Oh. Right. It's fantastic. Really." She was stumbling to be sound sincere while trying to end the conversation so she could be on her way.

"Are you okay?"

"Of course. Why do you ask?"

"You just seem... different? I thought maybe you were just bothered by the gala and all that shit coming to an end, but I just want to make sure it's not more than that. Have I done something to offend you?"

"Oh God no," Mika said sincerely. *I've just been having an affair for the past few weeks. No big deal.* "Between the gala and my trip to Seattle, I guess I've just been distracted lately. Seriously, when I get back this weekend, let's get together."

Mika didn't mind lying to take the day off, but she didn't like looking at Lisa and not telling her the truth. It wasn't just guilt; she really wanted to tell Lisa everything. For all practical purposes, they were best friends, even if it was often out of convenience.

"Definitely," Lisa smiled, but her eyes suggested that she didn't quite believe Mika. "Call me when you're home."

The drive to Tucson was relatively uneventful. She listened to a steady mix of 80s music on Sirius as she worked through more memories of her parents. She recalled her previous trip to her childhood home and how she had failed to follow her counselor's suggestion to make a list of what she wanted. Instead, she had told herself that things could be worse. Given the struggles that she endured while growing up, she certainly couldn't complain about her life. She had returned from her last trip to Tucson with a certain level of contentment and in a better position to search for the silver linings that her mother had frequently identified. Mika had no idea what conclusions this year's excursion might bring; she only hoped that she would find some clarity and resolution.

After weaving through some of the ever-present construction zones in the north section of Tucson, and then stopping at a Jack in the Box to use the restroom, she navigated through town and into her old neighborhood. She was surprised by the two new shopping centers that had been erected about a mile from her childhood home. One contained a Target and a freestanding Starbucks, and the other appeared to be a bunch of little shops, including a nail salon, a pizzeria, and a UPS store. Mika and the other neighborhood kids had once used both of these lots as a short cut to school.

Pretty nice, Mika thought. *That will definitely help this area.*

Mika's neighborhood had been just a collection of 15 homes that lined a single street, which eventually became surrounded by larger developments during the building boom of the 1950s. As Mika drove through these neighborhoods, she took note of the gentrification that had started to occur. Many of the houses were now dressed in fresh paint, and their yards were green and manicured, making them closely resemble the homes that Mika remembered from her childhood. Her excitement grew at the thought that her own home might be more than the dilapidated dump it had become, and she sped through the web of side streets before skidding to a stop at the entrance to her past. She stared in disbelief at the empty street; her house was gone.

What in the hell...?

Freshly churned soil lined both sides of the street, and the road had been replaced with fresh asphalt that ended in a nicely rounded cul-de-sac instead of a dead end of two-by-fours barriers. A construction trailer sat in the corner of the development, and a large wood sign announced the impending construction of "Royal Verde" patio homes.

Mika slowly drove down the newly paved road, trying to estimate where her house once sat, but it was difficult to know the exact location as the land had been completely stripped of its former life. Instead of recalling new memories, Mika could only envision bulldozers tearing down her home, completing the job that the tornado-like winds couldn't.

Now what?

Mika drove to the Starbucks, ordered an iced green tea and a piece of coffee cake, and planted herself at a table by the window. It was not the lunch she had planned, but her day had already fallen apart. She looked out the window at the changed landscape and felt remorse. Beyond this new strip of shops was a vacant piece of land that was once her home, and she felt like she should have done something to preserve it. After her father fell from the roof of a two-story building a week before her high school graduation, and after she had spent 10 days in the hospital before her uncle agreed to remove his life support, Mika was eager to sell the house and be on her own. It had taken just two nights alone in the house for Mika to realize that the memories and emotions were too strong for her. As she now stared out the window and drank her iced tea, she recognized the irony in her current desire to revisit the home and memories that she had readily abandoned 22 years ago.

She finished her coffee cake and proceeded to the Botanical Gardens, where she hoped to channel her parents and to find some direction for her life. She looked forward to visiting the cactus and succulent gardens and hoped to see the same beauty that her mother always relished. The desert had not been her mother's native habitat, so she marveled at the uniqueness of the landscape, especially the cacti. Mika, however, had been born in the desert and failed to see what was so special about it. She hoped that this visit would help her understand it... something. Anything.

But her efforts were again thwarted at the garden's ticket office, where a sign announced the closure of several sections of the garden, including the area where her mother's ashes—and a small vial of her father's—were scattered.

Are you fucking kidding me??

Chapter 43

Two days later, Mika sat on a plane, waiting for it to leave the gate and take her to Seattle. She sat in coach, and it was a relatively full flight, which likely meant she wouldn't have an empty seat next to her. Mika didn't enjoy flying; the rough rumble of the engine as the plane peeled away from the ground always turned her stomach into knots, and a crowded flight made things worse. She watched anxiously as the last of the loading passengers passed her row, hoping that they would leave the seat open between her and the shaggy-bearded man who sat in the window seat. The stream of passengers slowed, but her hopes were dashed when an older woman with a tint of blue in her silver hair squeezed into the seat next to Mika.

At least she's little, Mika acknowledged.

She sat patiently, waiting for the flight crew to make their announcements. Out of boredom, she did something for the first time in almost three days—she checked for a text from Jayce. They hadn't communicated since Sunday, which is what she had wanted. Kind of.

* * *

Despite the closure of the cactus and succulent section of the Tucson Botanical Gardens, Mika bought a ticket anyway. She wandered along the narrow paths, stopping occasionally to read a sign or people watch. She took note of one woman who was likely with her own mother as she pushed a stroller—three generations of family out for an afternoon. Her mind never settled on much until she landed at the butterfly center, an area covered by mesh netting to keep its occupants contained. Mika remembered that as a child she enjoyed watching the butterflies through the netting, but she only dared to enter the exhibit one time. During her first visit to exhibit, she had taken just a few steps in when she saw a man being swarmed by fluttering butterflies. Although the man had been laughing, Mika freaked out, pulled free from her mother's hand, and ran a safe distance away. Despite visiting the gardens with her mother at least a dozen more times, she never again attempted to enter the butterfly exhibit. She knew that butterflies weren't dangerous, but the thought of being surrounded by them was too overwhelming, too messy, and just too uncertain. This was the only new memory to jar itself from the recesses of Mika's brain, and she appreciated how her parents never pushed her. They had asked her each time if she wanted to try going into the exhibit, but they seemed perfectly okay to let her establish her own comfort zone.

Maybe I should go in, she thought, standing there as an adult. But in an odd tribute to her past, she decided against it.

Mika returned to Phoenix earlier than planned. During her drive home, she felt disappointed and more alone than ever. It was her hatred for this feeling that sparked her one and only conclusion for the day.

Get your act together, Mika. Stop this foolishness with Jayce and get your act together.

She didn't know exactly what this meant, but it was her goal. Could things be worse? Did she need to love harder and try again to make her marriage work? She didn't know, but she knew she couldn't deal honestly with her marriage or her life if she were acting dishonestly with Jayce. She needed to end things with her lover. She had debated sending him an email to let him know, but she feared that it would spiral into another conversation, leading to another naked rendezvous in the backseat of her car. No, it was best to just not contact him anymore. Ignore his texts, and don't send him anything. It was a simple plan, but it wouldn't be easy. Checking her phone for a message—or sending one when she had something to share—had become habitual, and it was a challenge to keep him out of her head. She would do her best to keep her phone out of arm's reach, leaving it in her purse or in another room as much as possible. When she did need to use it, she tried to convince herself that she didn't want to see a text from him, generating a false sense of relief each time her phone was "Jayce free."

At work on Tuesday, Mika's mind was tied up in meetings and polishing the Kondike presentation, and she roped Tanya into having lunch delivered to the office to minimize her chances of running into him in the building. This proved easy because Tanya wanted to share that she had decided against investing in the restaurant. At home, between cooking dinner and packing for her trip, she actually tried to engage in a conversation with Todd, which mostly focused on his parents coming in for Thanksgiving next week.

She had one moment of weakness before going to sleep on Tuesday night. Lisa had sent her a message to enjoy her trip. After responding to it, she stared at the screen.

Why the hell isn't he sending me anything?

She immediately hated herself for giving in to her instincts, but she found a way to turn this anger toward him.

Fuck him. Maybe this didn't mean anything to him.

* * *

The flight attendant's voice carried across the plane, asking passengers to turn off their phones. Mika took one last look at her messages: nothing. *Just be done with it.* She turned her phone to airplane mode and slid it into her purse. Her anxiety started to build when the plane made a small movement, and she found some comfort in staring at the lotus brooch, which was fastened to the strap of her purse.

As much as she hated flying, she was looking forward to this trip. In her effort to "get her act together," she made a commitment to use this time away to make a decision about her marriage. Either she needed to fix it or get out. Jayce or no Jayce. She was hopeful that a trip away would allow her some "Mika time," and that everything would become clear. Even though she would be working alongside Don Hicks, she hoped that being engaged in her job would bring her more confidence and clarity. Plus, she had arranged for a different flight than the rest of the team so she wouldn't have to spend all of her alone time around Don.

Mika settled into her seat and prepared for the takeoff that she dreaded, closing her eyes and taking a deep breath. She started a second deep cleansing breath when she felt a tap on her shoulder. She opened her eyes to find Sarah, a middle-aged flight attendant smiling at her.

"Ms. Jones?"

"Yes…?"

"We're getting ready for take off, but you've been upgraded to first class."

What?

"Really?"

"Yes, so if you would like to move now, you should go ahead and do so. Or you can wait until after we are at cruising altitude."

"No, I'll go now. Thank you." She fished her purse from below the seat and followed Sarah to the first class section.

Awesome! See, this is going to be a great trip!

As she cruised past the other coach passengers, she couldn't help but feel a little cocky. *That's right. I'm a big deal.* They passed through the blue curtain, and Mika saw two available seats. Sarah led her past the first empty seat in row 5 and then stopped at row 2.

"Here you are, Ms. Jones."

"Thank you," Mika smiled. It wasn't until she actually started to sit that she noticed the gray hair in the occupied seat next to hers.

Shit.

"Welcome aboard," Jayce said, and he winked at her.

Chapter 42

Mika stood in the aisle of the plane as she contemplated going back to her other seat.

"Ma'am," the flight attendant said. "You need to take your seat now."

Mika wanted to groan, but she already felt like an idiot, as she was sure that all of the first-class eyes were on her.

"Come on," Jayce said. "Have a seat. Please."

She begrudgingly sat down. She didn't want to look at him, but she could feel him staring at her, probably smiling and winking.

"What are you doing?" she asked, finally acknowledging him.

"I almost didn't see you when you got on. I had to check with Sarah to make sure it was you. It was." He smiled.

"Who is Sarah?" Her stomach tightened as the plane started to back away from the gate.

Jayce pointed to the flight attendant who had brought Mika to her new seat. "She let me transfer some of my mileage so you could sit up here."

"What if I didn't want to sit up here with you?" Mika tried to laugh, but it didn't hide her irritation over his radio silence.

"Are you angry with me?"

The plane jolted to a stop, sending Mika a shot of anxiety that made her face tighten.

"No, I'm not upset." She sat back in her seat, clutched the armrest on each side of her, and took a deep breath as the plane started to roll forward.

"You're not a good flier, are you?" Jayce asked.

"I could be better," she said before taking another deep breath. She was fairly sure that Jayce had said something else, but she didn't hear it. She was focused on the increasing rumble from the jet, and she closed her eyes as the plane's momentum pulled her into her seat. Just as she felt the lift of the plane, she felt something else: Jayce's hand on top of hers. The vibrations increased, and she instinctively let go of the armrest and intertwined her fingers with Jayce's, squeezing tight. And just like that, she felt a noticeable relaxation in the rest of her body. She was still afraid of crashing, but it would be okay because her final moments would be spent holding his hand, her delicate skin pressed against his. She still felt the heavy vibrations of the plane, but she tuned out the noise and forgot that she was angry with him. Her mind flashed between scenes from her beach and a variety of images of Jayce, from ones of him in his suit to those of his naked body on top of hers. She didn't quite fall asleep but she had definitely drifted away, and before she knew it, the plane settled in at its cruising altitude and Sarah was asking if she wanted something to drink.

"Mika?" she heard Jayce say, and she opened her eyes to find both of them smiling at her. "How about two vodkas on ice," Jayce said to Sarah.

Mika realized that she was still squeezing Jayce's hand, and she let go, slightly embarrassed. "Yes, thank you."

"You really zoned out there."

"It's the take off. Once we get past that rocky start, I'm okay." Mika tried to settle in but was uncomfortable in her new seat. More specifically, she was uncomfortable with her new travel partner—the man she was trying to avoid, the man she knew she should avoid, the man she knew she didn't really want to avoid. She envisioned spending the next three hours not saying anything to him, but she knew that wouldn't work. "You're really on this flight? You're stalking me." She tried to be light and funny, but her anxiety and tension were difficult to mask.

"No," he laughed. "Really. I'm heading to Vancouver to follow up with one of our clients tomorrow, and then I'm driving back to Seattle for the twins' birthday on Saturday." Mika's eyes narrowed in confusion. "My nephews are turning five."

"Your nephews' birthday?" Mika was flustered. Was this another sign? A test? Or was it simply a terrible coincidence, or a fantastic one?

"I told you my sister still lives in Seattle, remember?"

"Yes, I remember." She did, kind of. "It's just a crazy coincidence, right?"

"Yes it is," he said, taking her hand again. Mika almost pulled away, but instead held tight. "And earlier I sensed that you were upset with me. Was I right?"

Mika felt stupid contemplating how to answer this. She decided to be honest, with herself as well as with him.

"Yes... but no. Not really. I was more disappointed. I haven't heard from you since Sunday. I guess I was just assuming that you were done with me."

Sarah interrupted them with their drinks, which only took a moment but felt like forever to Mika as she waited for Jayce's reply.

"Thank you," she said, taking her glass of ice and travel bottle of vodka from Sarah. Jayce did the same.

"Can you I get you anything else?"

"No thank you, Sarah," Jayce said, winking at her.

Don't do that to someone else!

Sarah moved on to the next aisle, and Mika emptied her vodka bottle over the ice in her plastic cup. She was half hoping that her last comment was forgotten and they would avoid the conversation.

"If I'm not mistaken," Jayce said, "I haven't heard from you since Sunday either. I figured you were done with me."

Good point, damn it. Let's not talk about this anymore. Change the subject. Change the subject. "I am," she stammered. "I think. I mean, I am."

He squeezed her hand and pulled her closer to him, which forced her to actually look into his eyes. "What's going on?"

"I don't know," she said, relaxing and deciding to just open up. "I'm a mess. A huge fucking mess." She cringed as she realized that she had spoken loudly enough for others to hear. She lowered her voice. "I want to be with you, but I know I shouldn't. And then you tell me that I should come to my senses, and I don't know what that's about, and now here I am sitting next to you on a plane, and I'm not sure what hell is going on. All I know is that I tried really hard not to contact you, and yet all I wanted was to hear from you, and then I didn't."

"You're right; you're a mess." Jayce winked at her.

She slapped him on the arm. "I'm serious. What is wrong with me?"

"First, I didn't tell you to come to your senses. I told you that I kept thinking that you would come to your senses."

"What does that even mean?"

"I have a job that I love, and that's at risk here. But you have much more at stake. I guess I just expected you to realize that I'm not worth risking everything. Your family. Your marriage. Your reputation. So, when I'm checking my phone ten times a day to see if you've sent me something, I keep preparing myself for the end."

Their eyes locked and Mika wanted nothing more than to kiss him, but she resisted the urge. She simply smiled. "Can we not talk about this right now?"

"Sure," he said. "But just know that I don't want to be done with you, Mika Jones."

Shit piss.

Chapter 43

Mika looked across the table as Don Hicks explained details about the proposed contract between MedCare and Kondike. It was Friday morning, and the team was answering some final questions from the director of Human Resources, with whom they had spent most of the day on Thursday. As Don spoke, Mika could barely listen. Ordinarily, she didn't care much for what Don had to say, but this had been a good trip. Don showed an unusual amount of respect and deference to the client and to Mika in Thursday's presentation, and the team felt as if they had secured a new client. But her disdain for Don was not what distracted her; it was her plans for tonight.

* * *

Mika spent most of the flight to Seattle curled up next to Jayce, watching *Shawshank Redemption* on his iPad. She had not seen it before, and while it wasn't her favorite movie, she was so disappointed that she didn't get to finish it that she tried to order it through several online resources in her hotel. No such luck.

When the pilot's voice announced the beginning of their decent, Jayce closed the iPad.

"Hey!" Mika said, looking up at him for the first time in more than an hour.

"I have an idea. It's a crazy idea, and I totally get it if you say no." He paused. "What are you doing on Friday?"

"We have a morning meeting, and then I fly home. Why?"

"Any chance you could postpone your flight to Saturday? We could spend Friday together. You know, just have some fun."

Just have some fun. Mika didn't know how to comprehend those words. She felt like she never just had fun, and she wasn't exactly sure that she was capable of doing so. Between the death of her mother, the subsequent death of her father, and being a mother and wife, Mika always had been the grown up. *Or have I always just made that my choice?*

"Let me know," Jayce had said as the plane touched down. "I'm not leaving until Sunday, so let me know."

Mika spent Wednesday night getting settled into her room, calling Don Hicks to confirm their morning meeting, and taking a long walk around the hotel's neighborhood while considering Jayce's offer. More specifically, she debated *how* to accept Jayce's offer. She had no doubt about wanting to spend time with him away from work and without the constraints of a home to go to. What would it be like to truly spend a timeless night with this man? She felt a little silly thinking about it, like a teenager spending the night with her boyfriend when her parents are away. But that silliness excited her, so she searched for a reasonable excuse to spend another day in Seattle, one that wouldn't cause Todd to think twice about it. The simplest excuse was to make it work-related—they needed to stay an extra day for another meeting—but she had this horrible vision of Todd running into Don Hicks in Phoenix.

"Aren't you in supposed to be in Seattle," Todd would ask.

"No, but I think your wife stayed behind to bang some guy," Don would say.

Would Todd ever run into Don? *Of course not.* Even if he did, would Todd even recognize him from one of the company Christmas parties? Probably not, but she couldn't shake the fear, so she eventually decided on the truth. Kind of.

"It's beautiful here, and I wouldn't mind taking some time just to have some fun," she told him. "Do you mind if I switch my flight to Saturday afternoon?"

Todd was so agreeable and nonchalant with his "of course not," that Mika had two thoughts: *See, he doesn't even care about spending time with me,* and *Shit, I should have tried to push it to Sunday.*

She had the green light, but she spent the next few hours filled with trepidation, guilt, and disappointment in herself. *What happened to getting your act together, Mika? Are you really doing this again?* After beating herself up, she came to a surprising resolution and sent Jayce a text letting him know that she was available on Friday, and she followed it with a bold statement that helped appease her guilt.

MJ: No sex.

She had no idea how Jayce would respond, but she never expected him to agree:

JB: Good idea ☺

What the fuck does that mean? Why is that a good idea? Stop over-thinking, Mika!!

* * *

And now, as the Kondike meeting concluded and she slid her laptop into her bag, her phone buzzed with a text from Jayce.

JB: Pick you up at 3?

MJ: Yes ☺

Outside of the Kondike building, she said her goodbyes and congratulations to the MedCare team, who were on their way to the airport to return to Phoenix. Only Shelly, Don's sales assistant, asked about Mika's return flight.

"Oh, I'm returning tomorrow," she smiled. "I have some friends here, so we're going out tonight."

Mika took a green Prius cab back to her hotel room. She stopped at the café in the lobby for a piece of cinnamon coffee cake and an iced tea and headed for her room, where again she felt like a school girl getting ready for prom. She had two hours until Jayce arrived. She relaxed in child's pose before moving into a few yoga poses to stretch and clear her mind, and then she took a shower. Mika put on her bra and underwear, grabbed her lotion, and sat in the leather high back chair by the desk. She finished off the last of her coffee cake, and before she rubbed a lavender tree oil lotion into her skin, Mika removed her wedding ring. And then she waited, sitting in her underwear alone in her room. What would they do? Where would he take her? She laughed a little, realizing how far her pendulum had swung this week, from trying to avoid him to this moment, waiting for him to take her away. Her phone buzzed, and her heart swelled, but it was not Jayce. It was Ryan.

RJ: I got a job!

MJ: Great! Where??

RJ: Planet Fitness. Front desk.

MJ: I am so proud of you! ☺

And she was. For whatever reason, this made Mika feel better about staying in Seattle for another night. *He's going to be all right,* she thought.

RJ: Now can I get a car?

MJ: Ask your father.

RJ: Grrr...

As far as Mika could recall, she had never used that phrase before: *Ask your father.* Not once, and it felt good—almost liberating—to pass off a parenting duty to her husband.

Her phone buzzed again.

JB: Room #?

She sent him the room number, and then panicked as she realized that she was half naked in another city.

MJ: Wait! I will come down.

Mika slipped into her only pair of jeans and the top she purchased at the nearby Macy's the previous night. She heard her phone buzz, but before reading the text, she took her wedding ring and dropped it into her cosmetic bag on the bathroom counter

JB: Good idea. ☺

Chapter 43

"It's a personal tour," Jayce said as they exited the hotel and entered the parking garage.

When she saw him in the lobby, she was struck by how amazing he looked in his jeans and green and white gingham shirt, and she immediately regretted the "no sex" condition. *Do I kiss him? Shake his hand?* She settled for an awkward hug.

"A personal tour? I'm honored," she said.

"Well, I wouldn't get too excited," he cautioned. "I just thought I would share some of my favorite spots around the city."

They walked past several cars before stopping at a 1987 Jeep Wagoneer.

Mika smiled. "Is this your car?"

"You know it," Jayce smiled and opened the door for her. Instead of getting in, she walked around the car, studying its details: forest green paint that looked original but well cared for, wood paneling that was badly faded in spots, squared corners, edges and headlights, and chrome bumpers and accents. Mika didn't notice these features because she knew anything about cars; she noticed them because the vehicle was so different from today's cars, and it wasn't at all what she expected Jayce to drive. She loved it.

"I'm speechless," she said, returning to Jayce and the open door.

"Impressive, right?"

"Totally," she said.

As they drove along the damp streets and headed north on the I-405, Jayce explained how he had bought the car when he turned 18. It had been his first major purchase after he graduated from high school, and although there were times when he needed money, he just couldn't bring himself to sell it. Although he could certainly afford something else right now, "Why get rid of something that you love if it still works?"

They wound through the interchange to get on the 520, which soon became the Evergreen Point Bridge, a mile-long floating bridge that crossed Lake Washington.

"Have you ever been to Pike Place Market?" Jayce asked?

"No," Mika answered, but she was familiar with the place that was famous for vendors tossing fish through the air. "Are we going there?"

"No," he smiled. "You'll have to see it another time. We're going somewhere else."

"Fine by me," she said, and it was. At that moment, driving with Jayce into the setting sun with water stretching to each side of her for what appeared to be miles, she didn't care where she was headed. As she watched the water ripple outside of her window, she caught herself drifting away to her beach. *Not now! You don't need to go there.*

They ended in East Lake, parking near a tiny park just next to Lake Union. When she exited the car, her senses were overwhelmed by the smell of the ocean, the chill in the air, and the intense greenery that seemed to be winning the battle for space against the neighborhood homes. Jayce took her hand, intertwining his fingers in hers, and his touch was too much for her system as her skin tightened with goose bumps.

"Are you cold?"

"A little," she said. "I forgot my jacket." He let go of her hand and retrieved a denim jacket from the back of the Wrangler.

"Thanks," she smiled as she slid into the jacket, which dwarfed her. Her fingertips barely reached the opening of the arms. Mika put her hands on her hips. "I look like an idiot. I'm okay being cold." She started to remove the jacket, but Jayce stopped her by pulling her close, and she thought he was going to kiss her. She wanted him to.

"You look fantastic," he said, "as usual." He bent down and folded the cuff back on each jacket sleeve so her hands were visible, which Mika found endearing.

"Thanks," Mika said. "Now I only look kind of like an idiot." They laughed, and Jayce took her hand in his and led her to a small stretch of grass bordering Lake Union.

"Are you okay with this?" he asked, referring to the handholding.

She didn't quite know the answer to that. She loved holding his hand, but she was still remembering her commitment to get her act together. But damn, it felt comforting. She squeezed his hand as her answer.

"There you go," he said, pointing across the water. Mika followed his finger to see the Space Needle reaching above the surrounding buildings of downtown Seattle.

"Is that the Space Needle?"

"Yes, and it's the only touristy thing you will see on tonight's tour," he said, pulling her close to him. "But at least now you can say you saw the Space Needle, just in case anyone at home asks."

"I could have said that anyway," she said.

"Yes, but now you can say it and it's true. You don't strike me as a good liar."

Really? Isn't everything I'm doing a big lie? Mika wanted to explore this comment more, but dropped it instead. "So, what are we going to see?"

"Let's go," he said, and he walked her north along a small, winding road that ran parallel to the shore. On her left was a wall of trees and shrubs shielding her from Lake Union and the rows of floating houses that lined the shore, which she couldn't believe was real.

"That's crazy," she giggled, amused by her own wonder. On her right was an eclectic mix of houses of varying sizes, colors, and architectural styles; the only consistency in the neighborhood were the towering trees and shrubs that seemed to be taking over the land.

"This is just so gorgeous," Mika said.

Jayce looked around, almost as if he needed to take a second look to remember where he was. "I guess you're right."

"You guess? Look at all of the color. Nothing in Phoenix turns this green; everything is drab."

"Well, as with all things, it's easy to take things for granted."

Mika thought about her mom. *"Things could be worse."* She didn't want to think about this now, so she pushed it from her mind.

"I suppose. It's also not usually this sunny, right?" The sun was nearly set, but the daytime skies had been clear each of the previous two days.

"No, not usually," he said, turning onto a street that took them away from the lake. "It's usually pretty gray. The gloom can really get to some people."

"I can't imagine," she laughed. "In Phoenix, we dance for joy when it's an overcast day."

"And we dance for joy when we have days like today. Too much of a good thing, right?" They walked for a few more blocks before transitioning out of the neighborhood and onto Eastlake Ave., a rather dirty stretch of offices and the occasional shop, most of which were closed. A homeless man sat on a USA Today machine.

"Help me out?" he asked. Mika's stomach tightened, a conditioned response to the countless times that Todd had been confrontational and rude to someone asking for a handout. From the more benign "Go find a shelter" to the belligerent "Get a fucking job," Todd had embarrassed and frustrated Mika several times. Mika didn't even know how she felt about giving money to someone on the street; she had never been given the chance to form an opinion.

Jayce stopped and removed a five-dollar bill from his pocket, and he handed it to the man.

"God bless," the man said, and Mika couldn't help but notice the appreciation in the man's voice. Jayce walked her into the corner entry to Captain's Pub, a small dive joint hidden in its own obscurity. The dark grey exterior paint flaked to create a spotted pattern, and two of the windows were covered with posters for various beers, a faded menu, and a health inspection that revealed they had earned an A. *I'm sure that's a forgery,* Mika thought as she entered the bar. She took a look around, and it was definitely not an establishment that she would have explored on her own. Everything appeared clean, but it was old and eclectic—from the mahogany bar in the center of the large room to the mismatched blue and green Formica tables. One wall contained at least 100 neckties and a faded sign explaining that the ties had been cut from patrons and proudly displayed here to reinforce their no necktie policy. And while Mika questioned Jayce's sanity for taking her here, she noticed that most of the seats at the bar were occupied and many of the tables were filled with people dining. *And they look normal,* she thought.

"Over here," Jayce said, and he led her to a table against one of the poster-free windows.

"This is an interesting place," Mika said. "Definitely not 'touristy.'"

"No, it's definitely not touristy, and they have some amazing food."

"Really?" Mika was quickly embarrassed by her snobbish comment. It didn't seem to faze Jayce.

"You wouldn't think so, right? But it's good."

"I'm assuming you've been here before?"

"A few times," he smiled.

Before Mika could probe further, a woman's hand appeared on Jayce's shoulder. Mika's eyes followed the hand up a tattooed arm to an attractive blond waitress in her 30s.

"Hey stranger," the waitress said.

"Hey beautiful," Jayce said, standing and hugging the waitress, which was all Mika needed to dislike her. *Hey beautiful? Who is this whore?*

"Char, this is a good friend of mine from Phoenix, Mika."

A good friend? I don't know what that means. Wait. Stop being jealous, you idiot. Smile. Am I smiling? Smile.

"Nice to meet you," Char said with a large toothy smile.

"Yes, nice to meet you," Mika forced out.

"Char's parents own this place," Jayce explained. "How are they doing?"

"They're still causing trouble. You just missed Mom."

Mika tried to suppress her jealousy of this conversation, but she felt Char's eyes as they gave Mika a lookover in between sentences. *She's probably thinking the same of me: Who is this whore?*

"That's too bad. Give them some love for me."

"Will do. Are you in town long?"

"Just the weekend. Birthday party for the twins."

Mika wanted to feel confident—*After all, he's with me*—but she was stricken with the realization that Jayce had a life outside of her, one likely filled with desirable women. More importantly, *single* women. She had lost the last few moments of the conversation and was surprised to find Jayce and Char looking at her.

"I'm sorry, what?"

"Can I get you something to drink?" Char asked, apparently for the second time.

"Oh, sure. I'll have whatever he's having."

"Alrighty. I'll be right back and get your orders."

As Char turned, Jayce grabbed her wrist. "Wait."

Don't touch her in front of me! Mika felt her face get hot and her stomach started to knot.

Jayce looked back to Mika. "Do you trust me?"

"What?"

"Can I order for us?" He smiled. "Or are you particular about that sort of thing?"

Mika was too flustered to process a complete thought. She could only offer a shrug and "Sure," and then as Jayce gave their order to Char, she muttered, "I need to use the restroom." Char pointed the way to a door on the wall of ties, and Mika hurried off to the single-user bathroom and locked the flimsy door behind her. Her face was burning and her stomach was angry. Mika took several deep cleansing breaths, which helped her regain a small degree of control.

She stared at herself in the dingy mirror. *What the fuck is your problem? You knew that none of this was real. You're just here as friends, right? Stop being an idiot.* Mika understood that her time with Jayce wasn't reality. She was married, and he would soon be moving away. But this weekend was supposed to be a break from her life, an opportunity to play a game of "what if" without her reality getting in the way. She had never considered the possibility of his reality crashing her party. Her breathing was more under control, and her stomach had loosened its grip. She rinsed her face with water and continued to study herself in the mirror. Her anxiety had morphed into embarrassment. *Now what? Can I sneak out and just go home?*

276

Maybe if I stay in here long enough he will forget about me. Maybe he already left. With Char. Char the whore. She almost chuckled at her own insecurity when someone knocked on the door. Mika didn't move. *Go away. It's occupied.* The knock returned, this time followed by Jayce's voice.

"Mika?"

Shit. She contemplated not responding but quickly decided to just face the truth of the moment. She opened the door to reveal Jayce's concerned face.

"Hey," he smiled. "Are you okay?" He gently touched her face with his fingertips. "You look a little clammy." Mika smiled at the realization that she hadn't dried her face after rinsing it with cold water. She grabbed a paper towel from the dispenser and patted her forehead and cheeks.

"No, I'm fine," she said, tossing the paper towel in the trash. "Let's go sit." She tried to brush past him, but he took her hand and pressed her body against the flimsy bathroom door. Before she knew what was happening, his lips were pressed against hers. He slowly let go, winked at her and then led them back to their window-side table, fingers intertwined. Mika wanted to move on as if nothing had happened. She thought about ignoring her freak out moment, but that would be the real-world Mika, the person who suppresses her feelings and works to avoid disappointment and confrontation. But this wasn't her reality, so why not just go all in and play a new role?

"I freaked out. Sorry." She took a sip of the beer that had appeared on their table while she was gone.

"You freaked out? About what?"

Mika didn't hesitate in her response; she just put it out there and explained in a surprisingly matter-of-fact way that she didn't like seeing him talk to Char, and how she had been living in this fantasy where it was just the two of them. "I was just naïve. And overwhelmed. I'm not sure why other than the fact that I really like you, and I was jealous. I really do like you, Jayce Beckett, and that's not a good thing."

He took a long sip of his beer and wiped the bit of foam that lingered on his upper lip before reaching across and taking her hand, pressing her fingers between his. "Well, Mika Jones, I really like you too. I didn't mean to do anything to upset you."

"You didn't do anything. It was me. That was all me and my stupidity."

"Your stupidity makes you even more beautiful." He winked again as he brought her hand to his lips. "And just to clarify about Char—."

"You don't have to clarify anything—."

"Char is like family. We went to elementary school together. Our parents were good friends. Nothing is going on between us. Never has."

Mika shouldn't have cared about this, but it made her smile as she took another sip of her beer. "Like I said, I'm an idiot."

"No, you're not," he said, and he sipped his beer. "After my dad died, Char's mom and dad helped us a lot. My mom almost had a meltdown, and we spent a lot nights with them while she had her fits."

"How old were you?"

"Eleven," he answered, and he went on to explain how Char's dad had taught him how to make a few basic repairs around the house, as well as how to tune up his first car, the Wagoneer. As he talked, Mika was able to dismiss all of her anxiety and forget that this night was only temporary. It felt good to watch him talk, and the sound of his voice both soothed and excited her. Char brought them a dish of lobster ravioli and a po' boy sandwich.

"Can I get you another a beer?"

"Definitely," Jayce nodded before explaining their dinner selections to Mika. "Lobster ravioli in a sherry cream sauce. It's spectacular. And this is far less fancy, but it's my go-to meal every time I'm in town. Best po' boy I've ever had."

"And what's in it that makes it special?"

Jayce poked at it with a fork, examining its insides. "Fried oysters... and stuff?"

They both laughed. "So, you're not exactly the food connoisseur then?"

"Not at all. But her dad used to make it for me all the time. It was his claim to fame in the neighborhood."

Mika cut one of the large raviolis with her fork, and her mouth instantly watered as she took a large bite. If she had any kind of palate, she would have said that the creaminess of the sauce set her mouth at ease, and the lobster was buttery and rich, balanced by hints of tarragon and lemon. But she wasn't quite that articulate.

"Holy shit." It was definitely nothing that she would expect from a place that looked like this.

"Right?" Jayce reached across and stole a bite for himself. Mika wanted to take another bite, but she just sat and let the flavors continue to linger in her mouth. "That's on the elegant side," Jayce said. "But if you're feeling a little dirty...." He placed half of the po' boy on an empty plate and set it in front of her.

"Hmmm," she said somewhat seductively, and she bit into the sandwich, which was indeed messy as the spicy remoulade sauce dripped onto her fingers. It was delicious, and Jayce was right. Whereas the ravioli was clearly a sophisticated dish, the only word to describe the po' boy was "dirty."

"Yeah, I like it dirty," she mumbled while still chewing.

"I knew you would." He smiled, and she playfully kicked him under the table. As she took her next bite, she found herself staring out the window, almost drifting away to her sandy beach when the homeless man walked past the window.

"So, tell me your philosophy on giving money to people on the street," she asked without shifting her gaze away from the man, who was now just standing on the corner rocking back and forth slightly as if debating whether or not to cross.

"You mean, do I think I'm enabling them by giving a handout?"

She sensed a defensive tone in his voice, and quickly turned to him. "Yes, but I'm saying you are. I don't know the right answer, but Todd...." She tried to stop herself from talking about her husband, but it was out there. "Todd is just so adamant about it, so it was just a refreshing gesture."

"Well," he said, pausing to wash down a bite of ravioli while formulating his thought. "Is there a good chance that he will use it to buy beer or drugs? Probably. But everyone hits rock bottom at some point. You hope that someone who is down on his luck can turn it around, right? But that doesn't happen overnight. He doesn't go from being on the street to applying for a job tomorrow. So maybe he has hit rock bottom, and maybe my gesture helps him move in the right direction. If there's even a small chance that I'm helping him, I'll take that chance." He finished off the last of his beer. "I don't know, though, maybe I'm wrong."

"I don't think so," Mika said. "I mean, is he going to run out and get a job just because I didn't give him money? That's always been my dilemma. It makes sense to me that if no one gives him money, he will more likely turn to stealing to get what he wants. When someone is on a destructive path, it's difficult to get off."

"Agreed," he said, taking a look out the window as he talked about the horror stories he has heard about some of the homeless shelters and the need for better mental healthcare. She was pained by the words he shared, but she found another level of beauty in his face while he watched their homeless man asking another passerby for money. The concern in his eyes matched the gravity of his tone, and it made her feel safe. They spent the rest of dinner making the connection to the behavioral health component of MedCare's wellness plans, and the importance of recognizing when someone might be headed for a downward spiral. They agreed on the importance of having a potential lifeline to throw them. Mika was so excited about the topic that she didn't realize that it was their first conversation about work that actually took place outside of the MedCare facility. As they finished, Char joined them.

"How was everything?"

"That was fantastic. Seriously, I am in love with that ravioli," Mika said.

"Thank you. I'm so glad you liked it. It's a neighborhood favorite...." She was stopped at the site of Jayce leaving several twenty-dollar bills under the edge of his plate. "Get that flippin' money off the table."

Jayce looked resigned, like a boy caught taking an extra cookie after dinner. "Let me at least pay for Mika's dinner."

"No. You know my dad would kill me if I took your money. Besides, you finally brought someone back to the neighborhood. We want to make sure we see her again." Mika saw Jayce's cheeks turn red, which she hoped overshadowed the shade she felt washing over her own face. "Sorry, too awkward?" Char smiled at Mika and placed her hand on Mika's shoulder. "It was a pleasure having you here, and I hope to see you again. You," she said, turning to Jayce, "not so much. Give your sister some love for me."

"Will do," he said, and he stood to give her a hug. Char stacked two of the plates and took them with her to the kitchen.

"I kind of like her," Mika laughed.

"I thought we would head over to this garden…" Jayce started to say as the stepped out into the night, but Mika suddenly stopped, her mind reflecting on elements of their recent conversation.

"Are you okay?" Jayce asked.

"If you two went to elementary school together," Mika smiled, "then this is the neighborhood where you grew up?"

Jayce sighed. "Affirmative."

Mika giggled. "This is all I want to see, the beginnings of the one and only Jayce Beckett."

Jayce balked. "There's not much to see here, really. I thought we would…"

"Nope. We can do that later." Mika tingled with excitement. "Show me the house where you grew up."

Jayce stared at her.

"Please." Mika jokingly batted her eyes in a way that she would definitely never do in her real world.

Jayce squeezed her hand and let out another sigh. "This way," he said, leading her back down the side street that had brought them to the pub.

Chapter 44

Mika and Jayce stood at the edge of a crumbling sidewalk, staring up to a 1970s split-entry home that sat fairly close to the road. The sun had completely set, but a streetlight helped illuminate the house. Unlike the condition of Mika's childhood home, this one had been maintained and loved.

"It's a good family that lives here," Jayce said. "Two kids, and they're both accountants."

"Do you know them?"

"No, but my sister stays in touch in the neighborhood, so she keeps me posted on what's going on."

"Does she live close by?"

"About three or four miles that way," he said, gesturing past the house. One of the second floor windows came to life with light. "That was my room."

Mika looked at the window and saw shadows interrupt the light, and then the window went dark again. She looked to Jayce, who appeared to be lost in thought, and she was frustrated. She wanted desperately to see the memories that were filling his head, just as her childhood had revisited her when she stood before her home. She wanted to see him playing and reading and having dinner conversations with his parents. Mika wanted to experience everything about the man next to her, and it pained her to know that she didn't have access.

"So," Jayce said, leaving his trance, "that's where I grew up."

"That's where the magic happened?" Mika smiled.

"I wouldn't use the word 'magic.' Now, for the rest of the tour...." But before he could finish, Mika interrupted.

"Where did you go to school?"

"Umm, yes, I went to school." He smiled.

"I know you went to school," Mika smiled back. "Where? I want to see it."

"But I had this tour planned. We were going to drive up to..."

Mika pulled him close and interrupted with a kiss. With their lips still touching, she whispered, "Where is it?"

And just as he did before, he grabbed her hand and led her down the street. "You know," he laughed, "you're not being a very good guest."

"Is that a polite way of saying that I'm a pain in the ass?"

"Yes."

"You're right."

They walked hand in hand through the neighborhood as Jayce pointed out which homes belonged to his childhood friends, including Char. He shared his stories, like William Chainholt riding his bike through a screen door in third grade, and seeing a neighbor completely undress in front of her window when he was in sixth grade. Mika was so taken by his voice that she didn't notice that they had walked half a mile when Jayce abruptly stopped. They were standing at the edge of a grassy field lined on both sides by tall maple trees. The moon provided enough light for Mika to see the outline of two soccer goals in the middle of the field. Beyond them was a patch of darkness, from which rose two brick buildings about two hundred yards from where they stood.

"This is it?" Mika smiled.

"This is it. Bronson Public School." He paused, squeezing her hand a little tighter than before. Finally, he relaxed and smiled. "Ready to go?"

"Not so fast!" Mika said, pulling him across the field. "I want to explore."

Under his breath but loud enough for Mika to hear, Jayce again chuckled, "Not being a good guest."

"Deal with it." They passed the soccer goals, and she asked. "Did you play soccer?"

"Not formally. It was kind of a heard mentality. Whatever the group was doing that week, we played it. Sometimes it was soccer, sometimes it was football, and we played a lot of tag."

Mika chuckled as she envisioned a miniature version of Jayce running around on the field before her. She pictured mini-Jayce with his same stylish clothes, muscular build and gray hair, and she imaged that all of the girls were checking him out. Now that they were closer to the buildings, she saw that the one-story building to the left had signage close to the roofline that read "elementary" while the two-story building was labeled "middle school."

"Did you like going here?"

"Sure," he said, pensively. "It was a good school."

Mika saw his eyes drift across the campus, and he took a deep breath as his eyes darted away from the left edge of the yard, where playground equipment hid in the shadows of some taller oak trees. Her first instinct was to head to the swings, but Jayce was slowly walking the other way, and she realized that he didn't really want to be there. She caught up to him and took his hand.

"Well, I've seen enough," she joked. "Are you ready to continue the tour?"

Jayce squeezed her hand and chuckled. "I haven't been here in forever." She thought he was going to say something else when his phone rang. He smiled at Mika. "I'm sorry; it's my sister."

Mika waved him off and stepped aside. She could hear his voice, but her attention was lost in the shadows of the playground. She caught glimmers of chain metal from the swings, and the moon broke through the canopy of the tree to catch the edges of the slide. Mika smiled again at the thought of Jayce playing here as a child, and she wished that she could have been with him then. Her tranquility was broken by Jayce's hand on her shoulder.

"Change of plans."

Chapter 45

Jayce turned the Wagoneer into the Montlake neighborhood at the southern end of Portage Bay. The development was built in the 1940s and the homes now sold for upwards of $1 million. Mika smiled at the irony of Jayce's old car pulling a beat-up trailer from "Jump Around" into this gorgeous community.

"I could have taken you back to the hotel," Jayce said, sympathetically. "We were right there."

"Not a chance. I didn't stay an extra night to spend it alone in my hotel."

When Jayce had answered his phone, his sister was frantic. The owner of "Jump Around" called just after dinner to tell her that his son had been in an accident with the company truck, and he wouldn't be able to bring the bounce house to the party in the morning. It was a father-son operation, one that Jessica had used the previous two years, so she had been able to convince the father to let them pick up the bounce house themselves. But she and her husband didn't have a car with a trailer hitch, so she called her brother. After Jayce had talked to his sister, he and Mika walked back to the car, drove back across the floating bridge into Bellevue, where they met Carlo, a short, stocky man in his mid 50s. Carlo apologized several times for the inconvenience, which Jayce dismissed.

"We're just glad that your son is okay," he said.

Carlo helped Jayce connect the trailer to his Wagoneer, and then he talked over some hand-written directions for setting up the bounce house.

"Don't worry, it's not rocket science," Carlo concluded.

As Mika and Jayce approached the front door of his sister's home, Mika's stomach knotted slightly. She was excited to meet his family and curious to dig deeper into the life of Jayce Beckett, but she was also nervous as she envisioned his sister's reaction to Mika. *Who the hell are you? Why are you here? You're married?* Jayce squeezed her hand.

"Relax," he said, and he winked at her. Jayce knocked on the door and then opened it without waiting for a response.

"Hello...?" Jayce called out as he entered the foyer. Mika reluctantly followed. Before she could get a look at the interior, Jessica came around the corner and gave Jayce a huge hug.

"Jay-cee!" she squealed in a hushed voice.

Mika immediately sized her up. She was a petite woman, several inches shorter than Mika, with auburn hair. She had skin that looked soft, but Mika noticed the kind of crow's feet that is typical of people who smile a lot. As Jessica pulled back from Jayce, she revealed the same brown eyes of her brother. It was the only physical trait that connected the two.

"Thank you," she whispered to her brother. She turned to Mika. "I'm so sorry for screwing up your night, but I didn't know what else to do."

"Jessica, this is Mika Jones," Jayce said before Jessica shushed him.

"The boys are in bed. Come on." She led them into the kitchen. Mika took inventory of the decor as they passed through the family room. The furniture was sensible and well cared for, and Mika felt that it somehow represented the opposite of her own home. The kitchen looked as if it had been recently redone with the ubiquitous granite countertops and stainless steel appliances, but it looked more comfortable than it did pretentious.

"Where's Tom," Jayce asked, leaning against the small island that separated the cooking area from the breakfast nook.

"He's in the yard moving stuff around," Jessica said as she turned to Mika. "Nice to meet you, Mika. Again, I am so sorry for this."

"Don't worry about it. I've had my fair share of bounce house birthdays, so I get it." Mika thought about what she had just said and quickly added, "For my son, not me."

Jayce and Jessica chuckled. "How old is your son? You have just one?"

Oh shit. Should I have said that? What does she know about me? Can she tell I'm married? Does she think I'm a whore?

"Yes, just one boy. He's seventeen, a senior in high school." Mika smiled mostly because she didn't know what else to do or say. "I guess he's not really a boy anymore."

"Ugh, teenagers. When the boys get there, I am going to drink heavily," Jessica said. "Speaking of which, can I get you a glass of wine?"

Mika felt stupid standing there, a few feet away from Jayce, wondering what she could and could not do. *Can I hold his hand? Can I be myself with her? Should I just keep my mouth shut the entire time?* Jayce forced the issue.

"Sure, we'll have some wine," he said, looking to Mika and again winking. "I'm going to go get Tom and get the bounce house laid out."

What?? Don't leave me.... But before she could think any further, Jayce had disappeared through the French doors that led to the back yard. *Just relax, Mika. Just be yourself. Wait, don't be yourself...*

"Jayce said you're from Phoenix. Do you visit Seattle often?" Jessica handed Mika a glass of wine.

He told you about me?

"Thank you. No, I've only been here a few times. I was here for a business meeting on Wednesday and Thursday. Kondike. I work for MedCare, which is where I met Jayce. In Phoenix. It sure is beautiful here. Everything is so green." She took a sip of the Pinot Grigio to stop herself from rambling.

"It is very green," Jessica chuckled as she leaned against the island across from Mika, and she winked at her.

Oh, it's a family thing, Mika thought, but it was a gesture that reminded her so much of Jayce that it helped her relax.

"You're lucky with the weather, though," Jessica continued. "We don't get a lot of days like this. It's usually grey skies." Jessica moved to the breakfast table, which was covered with party gift bags, trinkets, and candy. "So what have you seen? The Space Needle?" She unfolded a bag and set it on the table.

"Yes, I did see that," Mika smiled. *Thank you, Jayce.* "We also went to a restaurant, The Captain?"

"Captain's Pub. Did you meet Char?" Jessica kept opening bags, lining them up in a row.

"Yes. She was really great. Can I help you with that?" Mika joined her at the table. Her years with the booster club and PTO wouldn't allow someone else to put together the details of a party without offering to help.

"That would be great. I'm just putting one of each in the bag," she said, pointing to the piles of plastic whistles, toy cars, candy, and other small items. "Yes, Char is great. She's practically family."

Mika followed Jessica's lead and filled each bag one at a time, which seemed inefficient to Mika. In any other situation, Mika would have taken over and suggested doing it her way.

"We also went by your old house and school. It was fun." Mika kept filling a bag, but she noticed Jessica's hand had stopped moving. Mika looked up at her and smiled.

"Bronson?" Jessica asked with a quizzical smile.

"Yes, the elementary and middle school. That's where we were when you called."

Jessica smiled and returned to filling a party bag. *Did I say something wrong?*

"That's great," Jessica said. "I haven't been back there in forever." The awkwardness that Mika had just felt disappeared as Jessica quickly changed the topic. "So what do you do for MedCare?"

Just as she had with Jayce several weeks prior, Mika explained the wellness program and its importance to the insurance industry. And just as her brother had done during their initial conversation, Jessica nodded in agreement throughout and brought in her own experience as a yoga instructor, which led to Mika asking questions of her own. Before Mika knew it, the party bags were stuffed and Jessica was giving her a tour of the house while telling her about their remodeling plans. Mika felt surprisingly relaxed as she stood next to Jessica, who pointed to the exterior wall and explained how they were going to replace the two smaller windows with pocket sliding glass doors. But as Mika listened, she became fixated on the large painting that hung on the wall that Jessica was talking about renovating. It was a 20 x 30 canvas with an abstract blend of colors that seemed to represent a mountain. Mika stepped closer and was captivated with both the mix of grays and blues, and the subtle brush strokes. Her eyes fell to the bottom-right corner where she saw the initials: JB.

"This is fascinating," Mika said.

"It's Mt. Rainier."

"Did Jayce paint this?" Mika pointed to the initials.

"No, that was our dad, Jack Beckett. He was a data processor, but he painted quite a bit when he wasn't working." Jessica let out a small sigh as she studied the painting. "This was what he really wanted to do."

"I don't know much about art, but this is wonderful. I can see where Jayce gets his talent."

"What do you mean?"

"Well, I haven't seen everything he's done, but your brother is pretty good too. He was painting a scene of Camelback Mountain in his hotel room. I loved it." Jessica paused, and again Mika felt a slight discomfort in their conversation. This time she addressed it. "I'm sorry, did I say something wrong?"

"No, no, not all. I'm sorry. Yes, Jayce has some great talent. I just didn't know he was still painting." Again she paused, which made Mika nervous.

What the hell is going on? What did I say?

Jessica then surprised Mika by taking her hand and giving her a smile. "Let's go see how the boys are doing." She guided Mika back through the house as if they had been childhood friends. Jessica's touch instantly calmed Mika and erased any remnants of tension. As they passed through the kitchen and into the back yard, Mika processed this strange phenomenon that had brought her instant comfort. Jessica's hand was cold and thin, and its gentle squeeze brought back a distant memory. It reminded Mika of her mother.

"How's it going?" Jessica called out to the dimly lit yard.

In the glow of the moonlight and the makeshift work light, Mika could see Jayce and another man driving spikes into the ground at the corners of a flattened, deflated bounce house. Jessica finally let go of Mika's hand, which slightly disappointed her.

"We're pretty much done," Jayce said. He and the other figure approached.

"I didn't know you were going to set it up tonight," Jessica said, finishing her glass of wine.

"I didn't want to be rushing in the morning," the mystery figure said, coming into the light. He was tall and lean with broad shoulders, and his dark hair was cut close and tight. "I didn't know how complicated the setup would be."

"Tom," Jayce said, putting his arm around Mika. "This is Mika, a friend from Phoenix."

A friend? Mika knew there wasn't really a more appropriate word to describe her, but she still felt slightly disappointed. *Lover? Sex Goddess?*

Tom smiled and wiped his hand on his pants before extending it to Mika. "Nice to meet you, Mika. Terribly sorry to interrupt your evening."

"Don't apologize," Mika smiled, squeezing his hand. "A bounce house is a big thing for five-year-olds."

"Well I appreciate someone who understands that," Tom said. "Are you two hungry? Did you eat?"

"They went to Char's," Jessica said.

"Fantastic," Tom said. "Well, I'm having a beer. Can I get you one, Jayce?"

Jayce agreed, and the four of them returned to the house, where they chatted over drinks in the kitchen. The conversation was so natural and comfortable that it never occurred to anyone to go sit somewhere. Mika enjoyed hearing about Tom's experience as a pilot for Alaskan Airlines, and she appreciated Jessica's occasional interjection to provide more insight into Jayce.

"Now that he travels everywhere, he is organized, but growing up, his stuff was everywhere!"

As Tom finished his beer, he asked Jayce if he wanted another.

"No, we need to get going," he said, and for the first time since they entered his sister's house, he took Mika's hand. "We have one more stop tonight, and then I want to get Mika back to her hotel."

"Alright then," Jessica said. "You never responded to my text. Are you sleeping here? I'll leave the door unlocked if you are."

Please don't say you're sleeping here. You're not sleeping here. Please say you're not.

"No, sorry to disappoint you, but I'm at a hotel for the night. I figured it might be a little crazy here for you, so I thought I'd stay out of your hair."

What?? You have your own room? I shouldn't have told him "no sex!"

"Bullshit," Jessica said. "You just want to sleep-in without your nephews jumping on you."

"I like her," Mika smiled.

"Well, the feeling is mutual," Jessica said, and she gave Mika a hug. "Can you join us for the party tomorrow?"

"That's very nice, but I have a one o'clock flight, so I will have to miss it."

"If you're up and want to join us for breakfast on your way out, feel free," Tom said. "Jayce, you can come too."

Mika laughed and put her arm around Jayce as they walked to the car. "I really like them. I mean, I really, really like them." And she did. In a way, they reminded her of Lisa and Gary. *Only normal*, she thought. She also loved the connection between Jayce and his sister, something she wished she could have provided for Ryan.

"There's a lot to like," Jayce smiled. "But this is the thanks I get for saving the party?"

Chapter 46

Jayce pulled the Wagoneer to the side of the road in another heavily-wooded neighborhood. They had only driven for about 10 minutes before he stopped.

"Is everything okay?"

"This is our last stop," he said, and he gazed into her eyes. She expected a wink, but it never came. "I think you'll like it."

They exited the car, and the chill in the air slapped Mika in the face. She had stopped feeling stupid in Jayce's jacket and instead was thankful to have it. She watched Jayce unload a large canvas bag and a small soft-sided cooler that he tucked under his arm.

"This way." He took her hand.

Mika followed him across the dark and quiet street, which had a slight incline to it. As she looked ahead, she realized they were near the bottom of a hill that rose quickly above them and was filled with towering evergreen trees. Toward the top of the ridge, about 100 yards from where they stood, she could see an occasional house light twinkling through the trees.

"Is this a park?"

"Not exactly." He led her down the street a few blocks, and at the intersection of another side street, the trees gave way to a clearing. A six-foot tall chain link fence separated them from Freidrich-Mayer Public Garden, a two-acre stretch of shrubs, flowers, and trees that hugged the hillside. Low-voltage lighting dotted parts of the garden, illuminating chunks of cobblestone steps and worn pathways. At the top of the hill stood two lone houses, one at each end of the garden.

"It's a hillside garden," he said, as they approached the gate. "One of my favorite places."

Just past the gate was the start of a winding brick staircase that invited her to explore the garden, but the padlock on the gate suggested otherwise.

"It looks amazing," she said. "Too bad it's closed."

"For most people," he said, and he led her along the sidewalk to where the garden ended and the forest continued. They turned and followed the chain-link fence into the trees.

"What are you doing?"

"There should be a spot," he said, mostly to himself.

She was glad he was holding her hand, as it helped her stay balanced on the rough terrain under her feet, and it was a fairly steep climb. Eventually, he stopped where the fence ran past a small collection of cement blocks and water pipes that rose several feet above ground. Jayce tossed the canvas bag over the fence and stepped onto one of the lower pieces of cement. As he took a second step onto a heavy steel pipe, Mika could see that the mixed levels of the water junction could serve as a stepladder.

"They should have put this inside the fence," Jayce said, reaching his hand back to help Mika. "Come on."

"You want me to climb that fence?" She had several horrid visions, beginning with an embarrassing fall and ending with a trip to the police station for trespassing.

"I'll help you over," he said, hanging the cooler on a fence pole. In a quick move, he popped over the fence and was standing on the other side. "Come on, it will be fine."

Mika laughed as she navigated the steel and concrete footholds. *This is crazy! Whatever you do, don't fall!* "I don't think this is a good idea."

Jayce laughed with her. "Don't take this the wrong way, but it seems like good ideas haven't been our specialty recently."

"True. So true." She stood atop the water structure and leaned against the top of the fence. She popped one foot next to her hands, and she visualized her next move. It seemed so simple: *just bring the other foot across, shift your body and drop to the ground.* But when she brought her second foot across, she froze. Her hands gripped the pole, and the edges of her feet dug at the other end. She balanced perilously in a plank-like yoga pose, afraid to move, afraid she would get hurt no matter which direction she went. Finally, she said something that she rarely said.

"I need help."

She felt Jayce's hands grab around her pelvis, and she could feel herself stabilize.

"I have you," he said with reassuring confidence. "Just come this way."

Mika slid her feet off the fence and rolled her weight toward Jayce, who slowly lowered her to the ground. She took a deep breath.

"Sorry about that," Jayce said.

"No, I'm good," she laughed. "I just had this terrible thought that I would break my neck."

"Yeah, that would be bad." He winked at her, retrieved the cooler and canvas bag, and proceeded up a dirt path that was dimly lit by the moon. Mika followed, and her heart rate rose quickly as they climbed the winding path.

"Exercise and trespassing," she huffed, "no wonder you're still single."

"I know, right?" He came to a stop where the path leveled off among a small stretch of viburnum.

"I just want clarification," she said, draping her arm around his waist. "We are technically trespassing, right? I mean, that was a locked gate, right?"

"Yes, but we're fine. Trust me."

She was glad that she did trust him because when she looked out, she saw the twinkling landscape stretch into the dark horizon, which included a glimpse of Lake Union and the illuminated Space Needle.

"Wow." Mika felt a little stupid, but it was all she could say.

She followed as he continued along the path that wound up and down through flowerbeds and around bushes.

"The garden was originally two separate ones," he said, pointing to the two houses at the top of the hill. "The Meyers started theirs in 1962, and then the Friedrich's followed a year later. Eventually, they met in the middle and continued to expand."

"And they still own it?"

"Yes. It's kind of a cool story. Their children, Katrina Friedrich and Delco Meyers, grew up together working these gardens, and eventually they married. They still live there," he said, pointing to the house on the left. "The other is a bed and breakfast." He stopped again, just short of the garden's lone tree, a 10-foot Pacific Dogwood, which almost looked like a tall bush with three thin trunks climbing from the ground. "In the spring, this is covered with white flowers. It's just fantastic."

Mika smiled as she tried to imagine not just the tree covered with flowers, but also at the thought of Jayce admiring it. She followed him around to the front of the tree where they settled on a small cobblestone landing with two old concrete benches at each end. He set down the cooler and removed a sleeping bag from the canvas bag. Mika looked back up to the two houses.

"Are you sure we're not going to get caught," she said. She grabbed one edge of the extra-large sleeping bag and helped him spread it out.

"We're good," he said, sitting on the sleeping bag and opening the cooler. "We're hidden behind the tree." He removed a bottle of Merlot from the cooler and an old-fashioned corkscrew attached to a carved wooden handle. "Care for some wine?"

His confidence and comfort helped push aside her anxiety, and she sat down next to him.

"Of course," she said, and she watched his strong hand twisting and pulling the cork from the bottle. She laughed when he took two red plastic cups from the cooler.

"Nothing but class," he said, and he winked at her. He poured the wine and handed her one of the cups.

"So, is this one of your routines? How many women have your brought here?" She sipped the wine and appreciated its warmth on her tongue.

"You're the first," he said, and almost as if reading her mind, he followed with, "Really."

Even if it weren't true, she wouldn't have cared. But Mika studied his face and believed him.

"I spent a lot of time here after my dad died," he said. He took a long sip of his wine and then lay back on the sleeping bag. Mika did the same. "It was my secret place where I could escape. Sometimes I came during the day and just wandered around, reading about the plants and flowers, but occasionally I would come at night and just sit here, getting lost in the stars. Look."

Mika had been watching Jayce as he spoke, but she turned her head to look into a vast chasm of blue and black filled with stars, more than she could ever see in Phoenix. "Wow." Again, she felt slightly stupid for having such a minimal response. She felt his hand fumble between them before finally finding her hand and placing it in his. They lay on their backs, both staring above them. "Were you friends with the owners? The two who were married?"

"No. I only know their story. It's a bit of legend around here."

"So how did you end up coming here?"

"I don't know for sure," he said. "I came here once with my dad when I was six or seven. I remembered him looking at this tree and saying, 'This doesn't fit in here. It doesn't belong.' He seemed agitated."

"What did he mean by that?"

"I'm not entirely sure," Jayce said, and she felt him shrug his shoulders. "The best thought I had was that he felt like a misfit himself, so he identified with this tree. The funny thing is that it's a native tree, so it actually does belong here. Eventually, I stopped trying to figure out what he meant, and I just came here to clear my head."

Mika stared into the night sky, and while her body melted into the sleeping bag, she felt like she was floating, unburdened by the weight of her daily life with Jayce's hand tethering her to the earth. As she traveled among the stars, she found her mother and father, smiling down at her from above, holding hands. It was a vision that reminded Mika of what was missing from her life, and suddenly the night sky opened her mind to possibilities, opportunities, and questions. How would her life be different if her father hadn't fallen from the rooftop? What if she hadn't stayed with Todd just because she had been pregnant? What if she divorced Todd now? It was her first genuine thought about him in weeks, and it was the first time in a long while that it didn't make her stomach tighten. As she stared into the sky, she had no anger or resentment toward him. He wasn't a bad man; he was the wrong man. She returned to earth with a hard question that she wasn't sure she really wanted to ask.

"If I weren't married, would we be together?" She felt Jayce squeeze her hand.

"Well, that's a big question. I'd like to think so." He paused and shifted onto his side so he could look at Mika. "What do you think?"

"What do I think? I think I wouldn't leave you alone if I were single. You might need to get a restraining order." They laughed.

"Seriously though, you don't know that," he said, tracing his hand along her thigh. "We came together because of our individual situations. You're unhappy in your marriage, and I've had my own history. If you change either one of those, who knows if we're still looking for the same thing, right?"

"That's pretty existential," Mika smiled.

"It's like when people ask, 'What would you do if you won the lottery?' It's easy to say that you would give this much to your family and that much to charity, but put the money in front of me, and then I'll know what I would really do with it."

"You're kind of a buzz kill at parties, aren't you?"

"Reason #7 why I'm single." They laughed, and then their eyes locked and he became more serious. "I don't want to assume that I know what you're thinking, and I haven't really talked to you much about your marriage, but I think it's important to say this. You can't leave him for me. We don't know what *this* really is. If you leave him, it has to be for you."

Mika shifted her focus back to the stars. She knew he was right. She would have loved to hear him say that he wanted her no matter what, that they would be together under any condition, but she appreciated the dose of reality and honesty. Strangely, it made her feel even closer to him.

"I hope I didn't disappoint you."

"Not at all," she said, and she rolled onto her side, curled her head into his shoulder, and draped her arm across his chest. "Thank you."

"For what?"

"For being you."

They snuggled on the sleeping bag, and when the cold air started cutting through her clothes, they slid inside it. Her mind raced with more random thoughts about Ryan and Todd and MedCare. She wanted to let them all go and enjoy what she knew should be her last moment alone with Jayce. She took a cleansing breath and found herself focusing on Jayce's chest as it moved under her arm. Soon, their breaths rose in unison, and they created a spiritual rhythm that made her feel like they were one being. The feeling produced the urge to ask a question that she had wanted to ask before.

"How did your dad die?" She could feel a stutter in his breathing, and she suddenly regretted asking. "Never mind. You don't have to answer."

Without skipping another beat, he told her. "He committed suicide."

Mika's own breath stopped for a moment. "How old were you?"

"Eleven."

Oh my God! This poor man. She instantly thought of herself losing her mother around that age, but she knew that the cause made it even more difficult to deal with. She was ready to let the subject go, but he continued.

"It was the day after his 36th birthday," Jayce said, staring into the sky. "We went out to dinner at some Italian place. It was a Friday night, and we came home and had cake and presents... the usual stuff. When we woke up, he was gone."

Mika felt incredibly guilty for her next thought: *What did he do?* She mustered the control to not ask.

"The sad part—I guess it's all sad—is that we didn't realize he was truly gone until late that morning. He often got up early and ran errands. My mom assumed he was just out and about, but she figured something was strange when we hadn't heard from him by lunch time."

He paused, and Mika felt compelled to fill the void with something, but this time she didn't exercise the restraint that she did moments earlier. "What happened?"

"They tracked his credit card usage, and based on when he got gas, our guess is that he left the house around 4 am and drove down to Longview, where he grew up."

"Where is that?"

"On the Oregon border." Again, he instinctively answered the question that rested on the tip of her tongue. "I don't know if he was planning to do it there, or was just visiting, but at some point he came back and parked his car about half a mile from Pike Place. Then, I guess he wandered the streets for most of the day." He paused and took a deep breath. "I can't shake the image of him just walking around. Did he look okay? Did anyone notice that he needed help? Was there anything anyone could do to help him?"

Mika didn't want to ask the question that immediately filled her head. She knew it was strictly twisted curiosity, yet she wanted to know everything that Jayce experienced. "Where did they find him?"

Jayce let out a quiet noise that Mika was certain was a chuckle. "Less than a mile from our home, on the slide at my school's playground."

Oh my God. Mika thought back to how distant he seemed as they approached the school. *I made him go there.* "I'm so sorry."

"Thank you, but you didn't know." He took her hand off his chest and kissed the back it. "One of the neighbors later reported hearing a loud noise around 2 am, but had assumed it was a car backfire. An older couple were walking their dog on Sunday morning and found him."

Mika stayed silent, clutching his chest and unsure of what to say. The deaths of her own parents at a young age heightened her sensitivity to his pain, but the experiences failed to generate any words of wisdom or comfort. Eventually, he broke the silence.

"I asked you a question before, but you never really answered it."

"What question was that?" She thought back to what questions he had asked, but she couldn't remember any that she hadn't answered.

"What are your dreams, Mika Jones? Is your job at MedCare really where you want to be?"

Mika remembered the question now, and she recalled her frustration in not knowing the answer. She stared out into the stars and let her mind drift back into the darkness as it had done moments before. She again saw her parents, and for the first time in her life, she knew what her dream had always been: to love someone as her mother had loved her father, and to feel that same love in return. *Love harder* had not just been her mother's dying command, but her own spirit pushing her toward her dream. Despite her realization, she chose not to share this with Jayce.

"That's a good question," she said. "I still don't know."

Mika expected a follow up question, but Jayce remained content with her answer, so Mika turned the question on him.

"And what about Jayce Beckett? Is traveling around the country, living city by city with Julia Roberts... is that how you expect finish your life?"

She felt Jayce's chest rise under her hand as he took a deep breath. "I don't think so," he said. "I mean, I love what I do, but do I think there will be a day when I just want to settle down in one city? I think so." He paused. "I hope so."

Chapter 47

Mika awoke to an odd sound. It wasn't the alarm on her phone, but the very subtle snore drifting from Jayce's mouth. She smiled as she studied his peaceful face. She looked at her phone to discover that she had awoken almost 30 minutes before her alarm was set to go off. She settled back into her hotel pillow and thought about the previous night.

After Jayce had finished telling the story of his father's death, they cuddled in silence for nearly 20 minutes before their mouths eventually found each other. They kissed for a while, which helped warm her body, but they never moved beyond that. When they left the garden, they did so in silence, but they both knew that he was going to spend the night in her bed. During the drive to the hotel, her mind had tried to avoid thinking about one of Jayce's statements: "You can't leave him for me." He was right, and she knew what she needed to do when she went home. But for that one final night, she was in another world with Jayce, and she knew that the journey was about to end. Tonight was about them, and she once again convinced herself that she had the right to be happy, even for just this one moment. When they arrived in her hotel room just after midnight, she tossed aside her commitment to not sleep with Jayce Beckett and gave herself to him.

Now she sat in her bed, feeling like a woman getting ready to end her vacation and head back to work. It would not be pleasant or easy, but she finally accepted that divorce was a part of her future. She planned to bring it up with Todd that night. She wanted to believe that Jayce would be there for her when it was over, but she knew that his statement, "You can't leave him for me," was probably his subtle way of telling her that he wasn't in it for the long haul. *It's not about him. This isn't real,* she convinced herself. *This is awesome, but it isn't real life.*

Mika took her phone and sent a text to Todd.

MJ: Let's talk tonight after dinner

She didn't expect his immediate reply.

TJ: Ok. Golfing this afternoon... will be home around 6

Mika felt relief; her flight was scheduled to land at 4:00 pm, so she might have a small window of time alone before Todd came home. She left the bed, walked to the window, and opened the curtains to reveal overcast skies. *Oh no, it's going to rain on the party.* She went to the bathroom and started brushing her teeth. She found it odd that she hadn't even met the twins and she was upset about the rain ruining their party. Jayce entered the scene, leaning against the doorframe in his black boxer briefs.

"You're up early," he smiled.

"I know," Mika said after spitting her toothpaste into the sink. "I couldn't help it."

As Mika went to rinse her toothbrush, Jayce snatched it from her hand and put it in his mouth.

"What are you doing?"

"I just need a quick brush," he said with the toothbrush moving along his teeth.

"That's disgusting," Mika said, yet she found it somewhat endearing. "You can keep that brush."

"I will," he said, and he tucked it in the waistband of his underwear. He again leaned against the doorframe, this time in an exaggerated pose to emphasize the toothbrush extending from his hip.

Mika laughed. *Damn it! Stop being so adorable.* Her spirits dropped a bit as she again realized that their time was coming to an end, and she brushed past him. "Come on, I need to pack." She took her suitcase from the closet and tossed it on the bed. "It looks like rain."

"That's Seattle," he said.

"Care for breakfast with my sister? She invited."

She thought for a moment as she tossed her clothes in the suitcase without regard for their care. *No. I just want to get home and get this over with.*

"I think we have time, but it's up to you," he added.

"Sure, if you think I can still get to the airport on time."

"Definitely," he said, pulling on his jean. "I'm going to run downstairs and get some coffee. Do you want anything? Tea?"

"I'm good," she said.

She felt herself wanting to pull away from him, an instinctive desire to protect herself from the pain of their inevitable breakup. He kissed her on the back of the neck and left. When the door closed behind him, she quickly jumped in the shower to cleanup so she wouldn't be tempted to invite him to join her. She wanted this morning to last; yet she wanted it to end quickly. Just when she thought she found her balance between these two desires, Jayce returned with a coffee and a hot tea.

"Just in case you changed your mind," he said with a wink and smile.

Damn it! She not only appreciated his thoughtfulness, he was right as she had indeed changed her mind.

She finished packing, and as they left the room, Jayce took her suitcase in one hand and her hand in the other. Mika felt that she should pull away, but she didn't want to, and they held hands until they reached his car. The drive to his sister's house was shorter than she had remembered from the night before. She spent the trip trying to listen to Jayce talk about his nephews, but she was really trying to find something to not like about him, anything that would make their separation easier. She failed. *He's kind of cocky. Yes, but you like that. His forehead is kind of big, isn't it? No, it's actually a normal sized forehead. He talks too much. You like listening to him talk, you dumbass. He's bad in bed. Uh, hell no he isn't.* Before she knew it, Mika found herself hugging Jessica in the doorway of her home.

"So glad you could make it," Jessica said. "Come on in."

They were no sooner in the door when Jayce's nephews, two shaggy-haired lightweights, attacked him. "Uncle Jayce!"

Jayce scooped them up and kissed each one on the forehead. "Missed you guys."

Yeah, this isn't helping me.

"What's going on today? Anything special?" Jayce asked the boys.

Michael, the slightly skinnier one on Jayce's right hip, cocked his head. "Like you don't know."

"Right," Jayce said, winking at Mika. "We're doing yard work."

Oh Lord, this is definitely not helping me.

David, the calmer of the two, said, "It's our party, Uncle Jayce. Stop kidding around."

Mika laughed, causing the boys to look at her. Michael loudly whispered in Jayce's ear. "Who's that?"

"Michael, David, this is my friend Mika." Again, he winked at her.

"Nice to meet you," she said.

"Nice to meet you," they said in unison, and Michael giggled.

"Let's stop standing around," Jessica said. "Are you hungry?"

"I am," Jayce said as they followed Jessica to the kitchen.

"Mika, I hope you're hungry," Jessica said.

Mika didn't initially plan to eat, but the smell of cinnamon and bacon coming from the kitchen made her realize that she was famished. "I definitely am." When they entered the kitchen, the familiarity of the room captivated Mika, and Jessica's voice enveloped her with comfort.

"Can I get you some coffee? Juice?"

"I'll have some coffee," Jayce said.

"Me too," said Michael.

"And me," said David.

"Nice try," Jessica said. "Go find your dad and tell him that Uncle Jayce and Mika are here."

Jayce dropped them from his hold, and they ran off in different directions, yelling, "Daddy!"

"Boys!" Jessica called out to them, and she laughed as they disappeared. "Boys are so loud. Mika, coffee?"

"No, I'm fine thank you. Maybe just some water?"

"Water it is." Jessica removed a glass pitcher filled with water and poured some into a glass for Mika. "So, did Jayce show you any more highlights of Seattle last night?"

"She was with me, that's the highlight," Jayce smiled.

"You poor girl," Jessica said, and she sent Mika what was clearly a family wink. "I hope you like French toast, scrambled eggs, and bacon. It's not the healthiest, but you have to indulge sometime, right?"

"It all sounds fantastic," Mika said. "Anything I can do to help?"

Tom entered the kitchen, "Nope, we're all good." He kissed his wife on the cheek and gave a fist bump to Jayce. "Good to see you again, Mika."

Jayce leaned into Mika and whispered loud enough for everyone to hear, "She doesn't like help in the kitchen, but don't worry, she'll probably rope you into something later."

"Where are the boys?" Jessica asked, removing a casserole dish filled with bread slices soaking in an egg batter from the refrigerator. She set it next to the stove and started setting slices on the hot griddle. The sizzle made Mika's mouth water.

"Making their beds," Tom said, taking a tray of bacon from the microwave and setting it on the island in front of Mika and Jayce. He took a piece. "We gave them bunk beds for their birthday, and they're pretty excited for you to see them, Jayce. I told them to clean it up before showing you."

"Can't wait," Jayce said, taking two pieces of bacon and handing one to Mika. Just as she bit into it, the boys scurried in.

"Uncle Jayce, come on! Wait until you see what we got," David said, pulling on Jayce's arm.

"Yeah, come on!" Michael echoed.

Jayce put his hand on top of Mika's. "Want to see?"

"No, I'll stay down here." Mika felt weird saying that because she wouldn't normally feel comfortable staying behind in a kitchen with two people she had just met, but this was different.

"Alright guys," Jayce said in a booming voice. "Let's see what you got!"

He disappeared, leaving Mika alone with Tom and Jessica.

"They are very cute," Mika said.

"Thank you," Jessica replied, flipping the slices of toast to reveal a golden brown side "They are taxing at times, but we love them."

"So, what time does your flight leave?" Tom asked.

"One-thirty. Jayce said we would leave here just before 11 so he can get back here for the party."

"That's about right," Tom said. "Too bad you can't stay. We'd love to have you."

"Thanks," Mika said. "I really appreciate that." And she did. She felt an unexplained level of comfort. "I hope it's not going to rain until the party's over."

"We're used to it," she said, nonchalantly. "Not much we can do about it. So, what did you end up doing last night? Anything fun?" Jessica stacked French toast on a platter and stirred scrambled eggs that were sitting in a skillet.

"We went to some garden on a hill, not far from here. I don't remember the name, but it was fantastic."

Jessica stopped for a moment and appeared to be in thought. "Freidrich-Mayer? The public garden?"

"Yes, I'm pretty sure that's it. We don't really have gardens in Phoenix, so it was a refreshing change."

"You left here kind of late. Were they open?"

"Not exactly. We hopped the fence." Mika spoke without hesitation, but then quickly regretted it. *Do they think it was my idea? Shit, I shouldn't have said that.* But her fear was quickly pacified by Tom's laugh.

"Only Jayce," he said.

"And teenagers looking for a place to drink beer," Jessica laughed.

"Is that why he knows so much about it?" Mika asked, innocently. "He told me he used to go there after your dad passed away." Mika could see a slight pause in Jessica's movement, and she again regretted opening her mouth. "I'm sorry, I feel like I keep saying things that I shouldn't."

Tom placed a reassuring hand on Mika's shoulder. "No apology is necessary; you're good. I'll go get Jayce and the boys," he said, and then he left the kitchen.

Jessica set the platter of French toast next to the bacon, and she smiled a warm, safe smile. "You definitely don't need to apologize. It's just that Jayce used to disappear a lot after our dad died, and we never knew where he was. He would never tell us, and it worried our mom to death. She would freak out that she would lose Jayce too. I hadn't thought about it in a long time, so it's just interesting for it to come up now."

Mika didn't know why she said the next words that came out of her mouth. "He's a fascinating man."

"That he is," she smiled, just as Jayce, Tom and the boys entered the kitchen.

They filled their plates and sat around the same breakfast table that had been used the previous night fill party bags. Mika's stomach and taste buds loved the French toast, but her soul enjoyed a comfort that it hadn't felt since she was a child having breakfast with her parents. Jessica and Tom asked her questions about Phoenix ("Can you really fry an egg on the sidewalk in the summer?") and she asked about the rain and all things Seattle. While the conversations made her slightly sad that this family wouldn't be a part of her future, it further articulated what was missing from her life. Thankfully, it reconfirmed what she knew she needed to do when she returned to Phoenix.

When they finished eating, Mika insisted on helping Jessica clean the kitchen, to which Tom commented, "Jayce, she likes to live dangerously. We should go." Jessica quickly stopped fighting as it became apparent that Mika wasn't going to give in, and the two of them awkwardly moved around the kitchen before finding a smooth rhythm of putting dishes in the sink and returning perishables to the refrigerator. Jayce, Tom, and the boys went to the backyard, and Mika occasionally looked out the window to see them shuttling coolers around and inflating the bounce house. As Mika washed the dishes and handed them to Jessica to dry and put away, they made comfortable small talk about mother-son relationships and sharing funny stories about their children. Mika told her about "granola," which impressed Jessica.

"If my boys tried to cut me off like that, I would lose it," she laughed.

When the sink was empty and the last dish put away, Mika spotted the clock and saw that she only had 30 minutes before she had to leave.

"Come on," Jessica said. "Let's go sit." She led Mika to the living room, and they each sat in a leather armchair next to the painting she had seen the night before. Through the window Mika could see Jayce and Tom keeping the boys at bay while the bounce house finished inflating.

"I do hope you'll make it this way again," Jessica said. "We don't see Jayce nearly enough, but you are welcome here anytime. Heck, you can come without him if you want."

Mika felt such a strong connection to this new person that she suddenly felt guilty and deceitful, and she blurted out her confession for absolutely no reason. "I'm married." She stared out the window, wanting to avoid Jessica's reaction. It was a painful moment, yet one of relief. Mika had long wanted—perhaps needed—to share what was happening in her life, and what she couldn't tell her closest friends at home she had now told someone who was practically a stranger in another city. She had no idea how Jessica would react, but she never expected her reply.

"I figured."

Mika shot her a confused look, and she immediately checked her finger to make sure that she wasn't wearing her ring. *Shit.* She panicked for a moment before remembering that it was in her cosmetic bag.

"It's what he does," Jessica explained.

It's what he does? What the hell does that mean? Her face felt flush.

"Don't worry, I'm not going to judge you," she continued, perhaps in reaction to Mika's pale face. "You have to decide what's right for you. It's just disappointing because I like you."

Mika didn't know if she wanted the answer, but she asked the question anyway, "What do you mean, 'it's what he does'?"

Jessica looked out the window to make sure they were still outside. "My brother's a great guy, but he's broken."

"Broken? Aren't we all?" Mika grinned.

"Yes, probably," Jessica said, and Mika could see her face relax a bit. "My counselor said he has abandonment issues. He stopped seeing a counselor a long time ago, but I still go, and we spent a lot of time talking about my brother. He's afraid of people leaving him, so he tends to find himself in situations where he knows it has to come to an end anyway. I think it's why he likes his job. He gets to know people in a company for awhile, but he knows it won't last, so he doesn't have to worry about getting emotionally invested."

They sat it silence while Mika pondered this new information. *It's what he does? Has he slept with other married women? Am I just part of a long line of cheaters that he leaves behind in each city?* And then her mind settled on Jayce's words from the previous night: *You shouldn't leave your husband for me.*

Jessica broke the silence. "I'm sorry, I shouldn't have just thrown that at you."

"So, he's done this before?"

"Yes, but I really don't know how much. A few years ago he told Tom about a married woman in Dallas—and a few others--and I lit him up, so he doesn't talk to me about it."

Again silence. Mika felt stupid.

"Here's the weird thing, though," Jessica said in a sincere and reflective tone that caught Mika's attention. "He's never brought anyone home before. Ever. He had a serious girlfriend near the end of grad school that we met."

"His fiancée? The one who left him?"

"He told you about that? That was bad, but you're the first woman we've met since then. I mean, he hasn't even talked about women since I yelled at him about hooking up with a married woman. I was kind of hoping he was gay; at least that would give me hope that he wasn't still stuck on our dad."

"Your dad? I assumed he was hurting from his broken engagement."

Jessica sighed. "That was big, but it really just reinforced what he already felt. He took our dad's suicide personally."

"That's terrible," Mika said, "Why would he take it personally?"

"Did he tell you how he died?"

Mika nodded. "He told me some things, but maybe not everything."

Jessica returned the nod and stood. "I'll be right back." She ran upstairs, and Mika looked out the window to see the twins jumping in the inflatable castle while Tom and Jayce watched through the cargo netting. She saw a slightly different man in Jayce than she had before. She didn't know if it was worse, just different. Jessica returned, carrying a slim canvas bag.

"The night before my dad... we had celebrated my dad's birthday. Before we went to bed, Jayce gave him a painting, one of his own. He wrapped it tight in brown butcher paper so it would look professional. Jayce was so excited to give it to him, and when my dad opened it, he just stared at it, and then he let out a little smile and said, 'It's nice, Jayce.' The next morning, the painting was on the kitchen table, but our dad was gone. Something about the way the painting sat made us think that he had been staring at it before he left."

She opened the bag and removed a 12 x 12 canvas with a painting of a tree covered with white flowers emerging from a garden. Mika instantly recognized it as the dogwood from the garden.

"Jayce doesn't know I still have it. I keep hoping that he'll ask about it one day."

"He was 11 when he painted that?" Mika's amazement momentarily overshadowed her disappointment that she may have been just another number to Jayce. The painting was far from perfect, and Mika could see a few areas where Jayce had painted over his mistakes, but it was impressive for an 11-year-old.

"He was good, and he really wanted to make our dad happy. I think Jayce thought that the painting somehow made our dad do what he did, like maybe if it had been better, Dad would still be alive. Jayce threw it away, and as far as I knew, he never painted again... until you told me otherwise last night. He had a rough time and was emotionally distant for a long time, but college seemed to open him up, and then his fiancée kind of drove him back into a hole."

They stood side-by-side and studied the painting, two women who each possessed different pieces of the puzzle known as Jayce Beckett. Mika almost lost herself in the cluster of white flowers on the dogwood when Jessica took her hand.

"I'm not sure you wanted to hear everything I just told you. I'm not even sure why I just told you, and yet I feel like I should thank you."

Mika was confused. "Why would you thank me?"

"For loving him. It's clear that you do."

Mika wanted to cry, and she used all of her energy to withhold her tears. She had not identified her feelings for Jayce as love, but deep down she knew that's what it was. Now that she was finally feeling an emotion that she had not truly experienced in a long time—if ever—it was going to end.

"For what it's worth, I think he may feel the same."

Mika struggled with a reply and ended up avoiding the topic. "I'm sorry about your dad."

"Thank you," Jessica said, and she let go of Mika's hand. "I better get this back upstairs. They should be coming back in." As if on cue, Jayce and Tom entered just as Jessica disappeared up the stairs.

"Where's Jessica?" Jayce asked.

"She went upstairs. She'll be right down." Mika did her best to shake the fog that had enveloped her, but she still felt off balance.

Jayce approached her and took her hand. "Are you ready to go?"

"Yes, I think it's time." She looked Jayce over and saw a broken man. She felt sorry for him, but she was also confused. *Am I just another symptom he is ignoring?*

Jessica descended the stairs and said, "You're going?"

Jayce led Mika to the foyer, where they all met. "Yes. I should be back for the start of the party."

"It was a pleasure meeting you, Mika," Tom said. "I hope to see you again."

"Definitely, Tom. Thank you so much for everything." She faced Jessica, and they embraced like lifelong friends saying goodbye. Mika whispered in her ear, "Thank you."

Chapter 48

Mika rode the airport tram to the west parking lot of Sky Harbor International Airport, and she walked with strength and intention while looking for her car. She was so determined to get home, unpack, and meet with Todd that she forgot to turn on her phone and retrieve her wedding ring from her suitcase.

The ride with Jayce to the airport had been difficult. She tried to be talkative, but her mind raced with random thoughts, feelings, and comments from the previous 24 hours. Her heart wept for him now that she knew more about his father's death, and yet she felt like another casualty in the life of Jayce Beckett. *But if he doesn't care about me, why did he take me to his sister's house? Why did he show me the garden? Why me?* She wanted to hold him and hit him at the same time; instead, she struggled to keep up with the small talk until they reached the airport. Despite her objections, he had parked the car and carried her bag to the security checkpoint, where they awkwardly stood and stared at each other, both aware that this was likely a permanent goodbye. Mika wanted to say something poignant, but all she could utter was "thank you" before hugging him. She paid close attention to how it felt to have him squeeze her before finally pulling away. He looked at her, and she could see sadness in his eyes. She didn't want to try to interpret what that meant. She made her way through the security lines and never looked back.

Mika was numb as she sat on the plane, dreading the impending rumble at takeoff. Unlike the flight to Seattle, this time she didn't have a hand to squeeze. She sent Ryan a text saying she was on the plane, and then she turned off her phone. After takeoff, her mind kept returning to Jayce's statement: *You can't leave him for me.* She knew he was right, and now she could move forward with that. In the course of the next few hours, Mika's mind gradually shifted away from Jayce and toward the next step in her life. Her biggest debate was when to do it. She had told Todd that she wanted to talk that night, but Thanksgiving was next week and Todd's parents were flying in. *Perhaps I should wait and pretend to enjoy one last Thanksgiving as a family. One traditional, dysfunctional, unhappy family.* Ultimately, she knew it couldn't wait. *If I wait, I will chicken out. I know it. Thanksgiving will just have to be different.*

Even though her feet were now on the ground, Mika felt like she floated through the parking lot, a balloon filled with anxiety and excitement. She ended up passing her car twice because she had momentarily forgotten that she had a new car. When she found the white Mercedes nestled between a Prius and a Tahoe, she was reminded of everything that frustrated her at home. Finally, she felt grounded.

Let's do this. You're a big girl, Mika.

She drove home, calculating her plan as if she were preparing a presentation for work. She would outline her frustrations, but also address his. *This isn't about you; it's about us. It's not you. It's not me. It's us. We're not working.* In her mind everything went smoothly. She would be calm and rational, which he would appreciate, and in her crazy mind, he would agree that this was best for both of them. Her only obstacle was Ryan. She knew she could justify her decision to him, and based on what he had told her, he wouldn't be devastated. But she couldn't imagine a setting where she didn't get emotional in front of Ryan. *It's his last Thanksgiving before going off to college.* She looked at the clock on the dash and saw that she still had an hour before Todd would be home from golfing, which was more time to continue getting her mind right. She looked forward to taking a shower, perhaps the last shower she would take in that house. *Am I moving out? Is he? I should... no, he should. Ryan and I will stay in the house until he graduates, and then I can get something smaller when he's at college.* Then she thought about Lisa and Gary. *Will they understand? Will they pick Todd over me? Or can they be friends with both? Do I really care? Maybe I need to get rid of everything in my life.*

Mika filed all of these thoughts into different compartments in her mind, returning to each one every few minutes. Then she tried to set them all aside as she turned onto her street. She was surprised to see Todd's car in the driveway.

What the fuck?

She was irritated not only because he was home and altering her plan, but also because his car was in the middle of the driveway, forcing her to park in the street.

This is the kind of shit I won't miss.

Mika left her bag in the car and approached the house. She paused for a moment and took a deep breath. *Just be strong.* She passed through the open garage door and opened the door to the kitchen, where she saw Todd slumped in one of the breakfast chairs with his laptop. Ryan sat beside him, and she could tell that both were upset. Todd immediately stood and rushed to her.

"Thank God," he said, and he embraced her. It took a moment for her to realize that he was crying. He pulled back and said, "Why haven't you been answering your phone?"

"What's going on? What happened?"

"It's my mom," Todd said.

Chapter 49

Mika sat on the boardwalk wall of Pacific Beach, bundled in a sweatshirt and staring out into the ocean. The waves were small but choppy, crashing on top of each other before rolling in to the shore. She had been right; Thanksgiving was definitely different this year, but this was not where she expected to find herself.

* * *

After Todd regained his composure, he told Mika about his mother's accident. She had been taking a Silver Sneakers fitness class for seniors when she lost her balance and tripped, tumbling headfirst into the mirrored wall. Todd didn't know the details, only that his father had said, "It's not good."

"I'm going to catch a flight tonight," he said, and while Todd searched online for airline tickets, Mika sat down next Ryan at the breakfast table.

"We'll all go." She reached for Ryan's hand and squeezed it.

"You don't have to do that," Todd said, appreciatively.

"Yes, we do," Mika said, looking at Ryan. "It's a short week at school and a slow week for me at work."

"I want to go, Dad," Ryan said.

"Alright," Todd said, and he continued clicking away at his keyboard.

Mika appreciated that Ryan wanted to go. Laura Jones had been his only grandmother, and since he was her only grandchild, she had done a nice job of doting over him. And while Mika had hoped to be doing something else, she wanted to go too. Mika had met Laura after she and Todd had been dating for six months. They had flown to Cincinnati to meet his parents, and Mika was instantly taken by Laura's warmth. In some ways, she reminded Mika of her own mother: confident, outspoken, and a little spunky. When Mika announced that she was pregnant, Laura became a confidant and mentor, calling regularly to check on Mika and to share the latest prenatal advice that she read in a magazine or heard on a morning talk show. While Mika knew that many women would resent the mother-in-law for this type of meddling, it gave Mika strength. There were times when Mika felt as if Laura enjoyed talking to her more than with her own son. When Mika was later exploring the idea of a divorce, Laura must have picked up on the vibe because she mailed a letter that simply said, "You're a strong woman... everything will work out." Mika never mentioned the letter to Laura, which she regretted. Instead, she started to withdraw during the past few years, partly because she was embarrassed that her marriage to Laura's son still wasn't working, and partly because life just got in the way. When Laura and her husband Dave retired to San Diego two years ago, Mika and Todd should have visited more frequently. Sitting at the table with Ryan and Todd, she was flooded with guilt and remorse.

"Are you okay?" she asked Ryan.

He nodded and squeezed her hand.

Mika looked at Todd and saw the frustration and pain in his face as he stared at the computer screen. He grunted each time he clicked on the wrong tab, and Mika finally offered to help.

"Do you want me to look it up?"

"No," Todd snapped. "I'm not an idiot."

Mika took a deep breath, got up, and poured herself a glass of water. *He's suffering,* she told herself. Todd's phone rang, and he jumped out of his chair to answer it.

"Hey Dad. What's going on?"

She watched him pace along the kitchen wall filled with family photos. Her stomach knotted at the realization that just a few moments earlier she was going to ask for him a divorce, but not now. *I can't do that to him now.*

316

"Mom?" Ryan said, startling her because she hadn't noticed that he left the table and was now standing next to her. "Can I run to Emily's real quick?"

"Sure," she said, kissing him on the head. "Drive carefully, and be home in an hour." When he left, Mika was now alone with her husband, and while she knew she should to be there for him, she needed to get out. She retrieved her suitcase from the car, and she passed through the kitchen, Todd was still talking to his father, so she continued upstairs. She dropped the suitcase on her bed, opened it, and emptied it of her dirty laundry. She entered the closet in search of clothes to pack for this next journey, and she lost herself in the swirl of colors that radiated from her shirts, blouses, and dresses. Again, her stomach tightened, she felt light-headed, and before she knew it, she was on the floor of her closet crying.

They landed in San Diego early Sunday morning. His mother was in the intensive care unit at Scripps Mercy Hospital, and when they arrived at the hospital, Dave immediately embraced his son. Mika could see the worry in his tired eyes and was amazed by how much Todd now looked like his father. There had always been a resemblance, but now that Todd's face was getting softer and weathered, the similarities were much more pronounced. Dave came over to Mika and Ryan and gave them a group hug.

"I'm sorry," Mika said, realizing that she was really apologizing for a few of things: Laura's injury; her recent lack of contact; her desire to divorce his son.

"What's going on?" Todd interrupted. "What's the latest?"

Dave explained that his wife had a brain hemorrhage, and the doctors weren't sure that they could stop the bleeding.

"Is she awake?" Todd asked.

Dave shook his head.

Laura remained unconscious for two more days. Then, Dave and Todd agreed to remove life support on Tuesday evening. She held on for several hours, but eventually passed just after midnight. It was three days of futile hope, yet time spent preparing for the worst. When they weren't at the hospital, they were at Dave and Laura's small home in Normal Heights, the closest to the ocean that Laura would live; a compromise to her husband's desire to live on a boat. Todd and Dave spent time going through her living will and their finances, and a few times Mika took Ryan out for lunch or a drink.

There wasn't going to be a funeral; Dave wanted her cremated so he could take her ashes home to Cincinnati, but they agreed to stay with Dave through the rest of the week.

* * *

The cold ocean breeze numbed Mika's face as she sat on the retaining wall, but she didn't care. She was alone for the first time since Sunday, a moment of solitude before going to a nearby Italian restaurant for Thanksgiving dinner. She stared out to the rolling waves of the Pacific Ocean, and she looked for the vintage ships of her daydreams. Mika was sure they would come, and she was desperate to be taken away. She slipped off her shoes and slid off the boardwalk wall. Sand kicked up behind her as she trudged closer to the water. When the sand became wet and hard, she kept walking until her feet were underwater. The water was biting cold, but Mika didn't feel it. She kept plodding along until she was knee deep and the bottom half of her jeans were soaked. Then she stopped and watched the glassy waves roll into pounding foam. She tried to tell herself that this was just a momentary speed bump in her plans. She tried to calculate how much time would be appropriate before leaving Todd. Two weeks? One month? Could she withstand two months? But even as she worked through her options, she could feel her balloon deflating, and deep down she feared that she would never regain the courage and momentum that she had upon her return from Seattle.

Chapter 50

"What time will you be home?" Todd asked. It was a simple question, but one that irritated Mika. Two weeks had passed since their return from San Diego, and she was trying to be supportive, but she felt sick that morning and didn't want to expend the energy to be nice.

"I should be home by 5," she said before she took a bite of toast at the kitchen island. "Why?"

"I thought maybe we could go out to dinner, invite Gary and Lisa."

The death of his mother had made a small dent in Todd's behavior and attitude, but it rubbed Mika the wrong way. He was being more social, and he kept talking about how life is short: "You have to enjoy your family and friends while you can, you know what I'm saying?" *He acts like he's the only one to lose a parent,* she thought, which made her feel like a bitch. At his suggestion, they had gone out with Lisa and Gary the previous weekend, as well as with one of his business partners. He had also become more affectionate at home, kissing Mika before she left for work each morning, and they had had sex three times. It felt incredibly awkward for Mika to have her husband's hands on her body again. For the most part, it was a good change for Todd, one that Mika would have appreciated years prior, but now resented.

Why now? Why couldn't you have changed earlier? These thoughts came with a side of guilt, as she knew she was watching a man grieve. In her professional life, when a person reaches medical or emotional rock bottom and finds a reason to change, she applauds the effort. Why couldn't she do the same for the man who was the father of her son?

"Dinner sounds great," she replied.

He grabbed his briefcase and kissed Mika on the cheek. "I'll text Gary and see what they're up to."

"Perfect," Mika smiled.

As Todd left, she noticed that Ryan had entered the kitchen and was staring at her. He had an odd look on his face, one that almost looked like a smirk.

"What?"

Ryan shook his head and headed for the door. "Nothing. Just… nothing."

She abandoned the idea of trying to figure out what he was thinking; she was afraid of the answer. "Can I give you a ride to school?"

"Emily's on her way."

"Invite her to dinner tonight," Mika called out as he closed the door behind him. "Please!"

On her way to work, she mapped out her day. She had several emails to respond to, and a meeting with Don Hicks to finalize some details in the Kondike contract. She thought about lunch in the cafeteria, but the uneasiness in her stomach made her dismiss that idea. *Stick with a smoothie today.* She parked her car in the MedCare garage, and it marked a major milestone in Mika's recent life: she made it to work without thinking about Jayce. It had been a strange and difficult two weeks as she tried to sort out the chaos of her life. She had spent much of her time continuing to negotiate the appropriate waiting period for a divorce, while also acknowledging that she was losing momentum, and she occasionally sprinkled in a decent dose of Jayce. She knew that their relationship was over, but subtle reminders came in the form of a radio commercial for Plantation Jayne's and flipping past Julia Roberts in *Pretty Woman* on TV. The previous Friday, she had even driven to their baseball field and looked for their spirits, as she had done at the abandoned tire shop a few weeks back. She tried to make sense of it all, but it felt like such a distant memory that she almost believed that it never happened. Each day became less and less taxing, and today she finally spent a morning where Jayce Beckett didn't cross her mind.

Her morning was uneventful, and the office was filled with some of the usual Friday chatter about plans for the weekend. She was proud of herself as she joined the conversation with her coworkers about a new arcade-game bar in downtown Phoenix. She only contributed with a simple comment, "That sounds awesome. I'll have to check it out," but it was enough to make her feel like a legitimate social creature.

As the day was coming to a close, Mika was tired and looking forward to the weekend. Todd had texted a confirmation for dinner, and she was contemplating ways to cancel when Tanya hurried in. She leaned over Mika's shoulder and whispered, "We need to walk." Mika looked up to see Tanya halfway to the door, and she scrambled to catch up. Tanya didn't say anything until they were out the elevator, through the cafeteria, and on the walking path behind the MedCare building. They walked for several minutes before Tanya stopped.

"We're done."

"What does that mean?"

"The Century report. I just met with Dominik Moon. Century is recommending that the Wellness Division be eliminated."

That fucker. "They can't do that. They aren't going to take the suggestion, are they? They can't. We're a big part of MedCare's contracts." She stammered, looking to argue with the person she didn't need to argue with. "The clients will be pissed."

"Dominik said a bunch of crap about the importance of the program, but that it can be outsourced."

"Outsourced? That's bullshit! I'm going to go talk to him."

Mika turned, but Tanya stopped her.

"No. I'm not supposed to tell anyone, but I had to tell you. It won't be official until next week, so you can't say anything until we have all the details."

"What other details are there? A sack of shit for a Christmas bonus as we get pushed out the door?"

"I don't know. Maybe I have all the details. As he talked, I stopped hearing everything he was saying."

They stared at each other, unsure of what to say. Mika felt like she was on the receiving end of a divorce notice, and it made her queasy stomach even worse. She hurried over to a sage bush and vomited all over the tiny dusty green leaves. She felt Tanya's hand caress her back.

"Wow, I didn't expect that."

Mika wiped her mouth with the back of her hand. "I'm coming down with something. I'm okay." She looked up to the windows of the MedCare building and wondered if anyone had just seen her puke her guts out. She wondered if *he* was watching. For good measure, she held up her middle finger, which Tanya quickly swatted away.

"Mika, don't! I told you because I trust you. You need to not let on, okay?"

"I'm okay. Thank you for telling me. I think."

They hugged, and Tanya held on for much longer than Mika typically would have, but given the circumstances, it felt right. They returned to their office in silence. Mika contemplated the news, and while she tried to find a positive handle to hold onto, she couldn't avoid one thought: *Can I really get divorced while I'm unemployed.* As she packed her laptop and tidied her desk, she found a strange level of peace in the fact that her life wasn't hers right now, and it may never be. The best thing to do was go home, have a dinner that she wasn't in the mood for, and get drunk. She left the office with what she thought was a smile, but was more likely a smirk to anyone who saw her. As she approached her car, her inner peace shattered at the sight of Jayce Beckett standing next to her car. *You mother fucker.* She proceeded with force, brushing past him to get to her door.

"Mika, I need to tell you something. Can we talk?

She rested her hand on the door handle, and she badly wanted to just get in, but she couldn't control herself. "You need to tell me something? What, that you fucked me?" Suddenly, she didn't care about anyone knowing about their affair, and she raised her voice so it would carry though the garage. "And I don't just mean in the back of my car."

Jayce took a deep breath and stared at the ground.

"What? What is it? Go ahead, tell me."

He looked at her with a softened face. "I wanted you to hear it from me, and there's so much to explain."

"What's to explain? You told me that you agreed with everything we did—and you did so rather convincingly, mind you, so congratulations on that—and then you sunk the program. You sunk *me.* You pulled me in, and I trusted you, and then you betrayed me."

"It wasn't personal...."

"It was completely personal! This is my life!" She yanked the door open and climbed in. Jayce moved forward and blocked her from closing it.

"Mika, please. Let me explain. It will be okay."

"I don't need an explanation. Save that for the next married woman in the next city." Mika shoved him back and slammed the door closed. She started the car and squealed out of the spot, leaving Jayce Beckett behind. She cruised past the MedCare entrance, barely tapping her breaks as she exited the compound and turned onto McDowell Road.

Her anger floated inside her head and took turns beating up both Jayce and herself. *Are you fucking kidding me? He is unbelievable! And how could I have been so stupid? He never really cared about me!* The turmoil in her mind now surpassed the chaos in her stomach. *Do I go to Dominik? What would I tell him? Hey, I fucked that guy, so now he's just fucking me over? No, you dumbass! Just make an argument. Fight for the program. Plan your strategy and meet with Tanya on Monday! Why on Earth did you sleep with him!*

A text came through her phone and distracted her, mostly because she thought it would be Jayce. She considered ignoring it, but eventually glanced at her phone. It was Todd.

TJ: Pick up some beer on your way home?

Can't you pick up your own fucking beer? I can't take this anymore.

Her mind was in such disarray that she didn't notice that she had run a red light at Scottsdale Road, nor did she see the Toyota Tundra that plowed into the passenger side of her car, sending her tumbling several times down the road.

Chapter 51

Mika's eyes open. She is sitting on the sand at the beach, waiting for the ships to come in, but she is not alone. Her mother is sitting to her right, and her father to her left. The cool breeze washes over each of them, and Mika smiles as it cools her soul.

"Where are the boats?" Mika asks.

"I don't know," her mother answers. The sound of her voice sends a tingle through Mika's body.

"Sometimes," her father says, "sometimes, the ships don't come in."

"If they don't come in, what do we do?"

"We can just sit and wait," her father says. "Maybe they come, maybe they don't."

"If they don't come in, is this so bad?" her mother asks.

Mika silently agrees. "There are definitely worse places to be," she thinks. Her mother's bony hand rests on Mika's knee and squeezes gently.

"But if you really want the ships, then go look for them," her mother says.

"Where? How?" Mika is confused.

"Don't challenge your mother," her father says, and he places his arm around Mika's shoulder. "Just do what she tells you."

"But I don't understand...?"

"You think too much," her mother adds. "Just close your eyes."

Mika starts to question her mother, but she stops herself and closes her eyes.

Mika's eyes slowly opened, fluttering as they adjusted to the soft lights of the hospital room. Her vision was foggy, but she could see an array of colors at the end of the room, and a series of tubes coming from above and disappearing into her arm. She looked left and could make out a male figure sitting in a narrow recliner. Her vision slowly and slightly improved, and she could see it was Todd. He was sitting up, but appeared to be asleep. She knew she was in a hospital room, but she had no idea why. She tried to look right, but the morning light peaking through the blinds was too bright. Suddenly, the blinding light was cut off as a blurry nurse stepped in and bent over her.

"Mika? Good morning. Can you hear me?"

Mika nodded as she felt the woman's hand take her wrist. Mika looked into her tight but pleasant smiling face and found it comforting.

"How are you feeling?"

Mika thought about this and suddenly realized that she felt horrible. As she tried to move, pain shot through every joint, and her face hurt at the slightest movement of her mouth. *What the hell happened?*

"Like shit," she mumbled.

"Do you remember what happened?" The nurse continued checking tubes and fluid bags and pressing buttons on a monitor.

Mika shook her head just enough for the nurse to register her response.

"Well, you were in an accident. It was pretty bad, but you're lucky. Your car did a pretty good job of protecting you. Just a broken arm, but lots of bruising."

She shifted her eyes toward her left arm, which was bandaged in a cast. Then she heard Todd's voice.

"Mika? She's awake? Oh, thank God." He leaned over the left side of the bed and gently kissed her on the forehead. "How are you feeling?"

"Been better." She tried to smile, but it hurt her face too much. She mustered the strength to ask, "What day is it?"

"Saturday."

Mika felt herself drifting and mumbled a final few words before returning to her slumber. "That's nice."

Mika spent the next eight hours in-and-out of a deep sleep, wakened momentarily by random and faintly familiar voices talking about her, as well as the regular check up from the nurse who forced to Mika answer some questions before letting her fall back asleep. She finally opened her eyes for good just after dinner. The sunlight had disappeared from behind the blinds, and she smelled Chick-fil-A. In the corner of the room, Todd, Lisa, and Gary sat, eating from their laps. She watched silently, listening to their conversation.

"It hasn't been your month," Gary told him before popping a piece of chicken in his mouth.

"Just thank God it wasn't worse, right?" Lisa said. "She is really, really lucky."

Todd nodded in agreement. For the first time that day, Mika started to have coherent thoughts. *I am lucky. They're here for me.* She studied Todd and his disheveled hair, unshaven face, and wrinkled clothes—the look of a man who had spent the last 24 hours in a hospital chair. She felt horrible for him. *He isn't a bad man. There are worse places to be.*

Lisa looked at Mika and saw her eyes open. She hurried over to Mika and placed her hand over Mika's. "Hey, girl," she whispered. "You're awake?"

Mika nodded and tried to smile. Her mouth was too dry to talk, and Lisa instinctively held a cup of water to her mouth. Mika sipped it, and it felt cool as it slid down her throat. Gary and Todd came around to the other side of the bed.

"You gave us quite a scare," Gary said. "How are you feeling?"

Mika nodded as she took another sip of water. "Not so great." She had more energy than she had the last time she had answered that question, but she definitely felt more pain than she did earlier. "What happened?"

"You were t-boned by a Toyota Tundra. You rolled a few times."

"Why?"

"What do you mean? He hit you hard."

Mika took another sip of water. "Why did he hit me?"

"You ran a red light."

I did? Mika's mind started to scramble through the previous day's events. She remembered talking to Don Hicks, and then she remembered meeting with Tanya on the walking trail behind MedCare.

"Do you remember anything?" Lisa asked. "Were you being chased or something?"

Then Mika recalled her exchange with Jayce, and she remembered being upset. *I just keep fucking up.* "No, I don't know what happened."

"Are you hungry?" Gary asked. "I'll go get the nurse." He left without getting a response from Mika, but she was hungry.

"Where's Ryan?" Mika asked.

"He was here most of the night," Todd explained. "But I told him to go home and sleep. I just texted him and told him that you were awake, so he should be here in a bit."

Gary returned with the nurse, a different one than she remembered from the morning. This one, Yazmin, was an older Hispanic woman in her late 50s. She moved her short, stocky frame with confidence as she brushed Lisa aside.

"Good to see you awake," she said with a slight accent. She checked the monitor and swiped a thermometer across Mika's forehead for her temperature. "Are you hungry?" she asked. "Food is on the way." Just as she spoke, a young intern carried in a tray and set it on the rolling bed table. Yazmin wheeled it to Mika and adjusted her bed so she was sitting up completely. When Yazmin uncovered the food to reveal meatloaf, a small salad, and applesauce, Mika was surprised that it didn't look that bad.

"I'll let you eat, and then I'll come back later." She patted Mika on the hand, and while it was somewhat comforting to Mika, she found it strange.

Lisa offered to cut Mika's food into small pieces and proceeded to do so before Mika could agree or disagree. The meatloaf had little taste, but Mika wasn't sure if it was the food or her condition. The applesauce was her favorite, as it was easiest to consume without chewing, and she appreciated the cool feeling as it went down. Todd and Gary finished eating their chicken and fries, and Ryan eventually appeared, looking sullen. He stayed in the doorway.

"Ryan!" Lisa rushed over and gave him a hug. "How are you doing, kiddo?"

Ryan shrugged.

"Come here," Mika said, forcing a smile. "Give me a kiss."

He approached, but hovered cautiously. "Is it okay to touch you?"

"Yes. Just kiss me on the head." He did, and again she smiled through the pain in her face. "I've missed you." Ryan's eyes turned glassy, and Mika reached for his hand. "How's Emily?"

Ryan was visibly surprised by the question, perhaps as much as Mika was. "She's good. She's in the lobby."

"She can come in."

Ryan's face lightened a bit. "Are you sure? I didn't know if it would be too many people in here."

"No, it's okay," Mika said, but then she saw Gary and Lisa and wondered if their presence would make it too uncomfortable. "But it's up to her."

"Go get her," Lisa said. "The more the merrier."

Ryan left and returned shortly with his girlfriend. Mika paid close attention to the interaction between everyone in the room. To her surprise, Ryan and Emily were friendly toward Lisa and Gary, and she respected that her son—and his girlfriend—were big enough to not hold Lisa and Gary responsible for their son's actions. As Mika finished her applesauce and a few bites of the meatloaf, the room became livelier with chatter about college and Ryan's new job. Mika took it all in. She mostly enjoyed seeing her son, but also found appreciation for the entire group. Again, she thought, *I am lucky. Maybe I hit rock bottom and this is my second chance.* She thought about how fortunate she was to have all that she had in her life, and she considered the possibility that her unhappiness had been more about her attitude. *Maybe I should try to love harder.* Eventually the group returned their attention to Mika and started telling her about her visitors and the text messages they had received. Tanya and Dominik Moon had been there that afternoon, and many of the swim parents had reached out to send prayers and positive thoughts. Just as Mika was starting to lose her steam, Yazmin entered and looked at her plate.

"You ate some. That's good. Are you finished?"

Mika nodded as she snuck one last bite of meatloaf. Yazmin pulled the cart away and started directing the group.

"Alright, I'm going to need some alone time with Ms. Mika here."

"We need to go?" Todd asked.

"Well, I need to run some tests and get her into the bathroom. Some things we want to do alone. It won't take long, okay?" She asked it as a question, but it was more of a statement.

"We're going to take off, Hun," Lisa said, and she pulled Mika's hand to her lips. She leaned in. "I love you so much. I'll be back in the morning."

"Love you too," Mika smiled.

"We're going to go, too, Mom," Ryan added. "I'm going to take Emily home. Do you want me to come back?"

"No. You have fun. I'll see you tomorrow."

"Love ya," Gary said, and he patted Todd on the shoulder as he and Lisa left, followed by Ryan and Emily.

"I'm going to go home and grab a shower, then I'll be back," Todd said.

Mika saw the concern on his face, and she felt guilty. "Just stay home and get some rest. I'm probably going to be sleeping anyway."

"I'll be back in a few hours to check on you, and then I'll go home to get some sleep."

Mika nodded, knowing she wouldn't be able to convince him otherwise. Yazmin waited for him to leave before speaking.

"Do you want to go to the bathroom?"

Mika wasn't sure that she needed to go, but decided she should try. "Yes, please."

"Do you want to try to get to the bathroom, or just go where you are?"

If she had to pee, Mika didn't want to use the bedpan, so she had Yazmin help her out of bed. It was painful, and she ached throughout, but they eventually made it. She spent more time trying to get off the toilet than she did using it, and it reminded her of the pain she was in after overdoing it at yoga, only much worse. She chuckled, which reignited a rhythm of pain throughout her body.

"So, I imagine that your head is hurting quite a bit?" Yazmin asked as she repositioned Mika on the bed.

"You could say that."

"Those airbags can save your life, but they can cause a lot of pain. I'll give you another dose of Tylenol in about 20 minutes." She fidgeted with the tubing and monitors, efficiently checking and recording numbers. Mika liked her, but felt that she was stalling.

But for what?

When Yazmin was finished, she sat on the corner of the bed and smiled at Mika. "I think there are some things that are primarily women things," she said.

What is she talking about?

"So I didn't want to ask this in front of anyone." She paused. "Do you know you're pregnant?"

Mika's entire body went numb, and she said nothing. *What was that?*

"I'm guessing that you're early enough that you might not know, and I didn't want to spill the beans in front of your family."

"Are you sure?"

"Sure as daylight. They ran a blood test before they gave you medicine." She must have seen the turmoil on Mika's face, because she followed with another question, "Congratulations? I'll leave you with that while I go get your meds."

Shit piss.

She looked around the empty room, wanting to laugh and cry at the same time. Her eyes settled on the table across the room, recognizing that the color blurs she had seen that morning were actually several bouquets of flowers. She scanned them from left to right before focusing on a picture leaning against the wall behind one of the smaller bouquets. It was a 24-inch canvas with swirling blues and greens in the background and a beautiful white lotus painted on it. It was her lotus, and even though she couldn't read the initials in the corner, she knew they were "JB."

Chapter 52

Mika waited outside her townhouse for her Uber driver to take her to the hospital. She wasn't looking forward to the actual process of giving birth, but she was eager to meet her second son. More importantly, she was tired of being pregnant in Phoenix in August. Carrying an extra 35 pounds in 110-degree heat was more punishment than anyone should endure. The previous eight months had been a roller coaster, physically and emotionally. So, she was somewhat relieved when the heavy contractions started a week earlier than expected.

She had no choice but to come clean with Todd, since she obviously wouldn't be able hide her pregnancy. He was surprisingly calm through much of the conversation. He had retreated at first, but then brought to the table rather levelheaded comments like, "I deserve to be with someone who wants me for who I am," and he made no attempt to reclaim the relationship. Save for one moment when she heard him crying in the bathroom, he had kept his emotions in check. He did offer a few biting words when he said, "It doesn't really surprise me. Of the two of us, it makes sense that it would be you who would cheat." While it was hurtful, Mika didn't hold it against him. She actually thought that he had let her off easy. Within three weeks, they had agreed to the details of their divorce, and she was shopping for a new house.

Ryan had been a different story. Mika had insisted on being the one to tell him the news, and she had wanted to own it all. The day after New Year's, she took him to lunch.

* * *

They walked into Goliath Burger, one of Ryan's favorite places to eat, and Mika immediately regretted this decision. The restaurant was much smaller than she remembered, and it seemed to be much more crowded than it really was. After ordering their food at the counter, Mika was relieved to find an open table in the corner.

"Any new year's resolutions?" Mika asked.

"This year," he smiled, "I am committed to staying awesome."

"Nice. If by awesome you mean getting good grades and cleaning your room, I think it's fantastic."

"Well, I think we might be operating under different definitions."

"As usual," she laughed. Their number was called, and Ryan brought back both their meals. Mika picked at her fries as she contemplated her next move. "So, getting scared for college? Excited?"

Ryan forced down a bite of his burger. "No, not really. It will be cool." He took a sip of his Coke. "Are *you* ready for me to go to college? I'm more worried about how you're going to do?"

"Why do you say that?"

"Are you kidding me? You've been moping around for the past year, worried about me leaving. And I'm sure you're not crazy about being home alone with Dad."

Mika watched him eat. He said it so matter-of-fact that she decided now was as good a time as any.

"Well, speaking of that, I have something to tell you."

Ryan put his burger down, as if he knew what was coming.

"Your father and I are getting a divorce." Mika couldn't stand the thought of silence, so she continued. "I know you're almost out of the house, but I still expect this to be confusing and difficult at times for you."

"Mom," he interrupted. "I'm not surprised. We kind of talked about this. I'm sad, sure. Nobody wants to see their parents split up, but nobody wants to see their parents unhappy."

She was struck by the maturity in his face as he spoke, and he looked at her with concern.

"I'll be all right if you will," he said.

"I'll be fine," she smiled.

He returned to his burger and said while chewing. "I do expect to take advantage of the whole 'two Christmases and two birthday' thing. I'm not too old for that."

Mika nibbled on another fry, and the silence must have been noticeable.

"Mom," Ryan said, staring at her. "I'm okay. And for whatever it's worth, I think it takes courage to make this decision."

Courage? I didn't make this decision; I let it happen.

She wanted to be slow and deliberate with the entire message, but instead she just blurted out the rest. "I'm pregnant."

Ryan continued to chew a bunch of French fries, but at a much slower pace as he processed what his mother had just told him. "What?"

"You're going to have a brother or sister. I'm pregnant." She smiled, as she had genuinely come to recognize what a miracle and blessing this child would be, but she tried to tone it down for Ryan.

"You get pregnant, and then you and Dad decide to get divorced? I don't get it."

Mika contemplated her response, but Ryan continued.

"I thought dad had a vasectomy?" he said, confused.

"It's not his."

"What's not his?"

"The baby. Technically it will be your half-brother. Or sister."

Ryan's face tightened as he processed this information. "You had an affair?"

Mika nodded.

"You had an affair?"

"It's nothing I'm proud of, and I don't expect you to understand, but I wanted you to know the truth and hear it from me."

"I don't understand," he said, raising his voice. "You fucked some other guy?"

Mika felt other people look her way, and she tried hard to keep Ryan calm. "Ryan, I know you're upset, disappointed, confused, but listen...."

"Fucking right I am."

"Ryan, please...."

"What? You can get knocked up by some guy, but I can't use profanity? Whatever." He stood up to leave, and she tried to stop him, but he turned and yelled, "Granola, Mom," as he stormed out. "Fucking Granola!"

That went well.

* * *

The next two months had been horrible for Mika as Ryan refused to talk to her. She never anticipated that he would choose to live with his father, which was the only real regret she had in her new life. Fortunately, Todd had a conversation with Ryan—the kind that Mika didn't think he was capable of having—and he convinced Ryan to re-establish a relationship with his mother. They started by having a weekly dinner together, which eventually led to Ryan living with his mother on the weekends. It was short-lived as he would be off to college in the fall, but it still pacified her soul.

Lisa and Gary had their own unique reaction to Mika's news. They had expressed their desire to stay friends with both Mika and Todd, but time would reveal that most of their couple events would only include Todd. Mika couldn't identify a good reason for her feeling, but she sensed that Todd had been disappointed that he wasn't the one that Mika had chosen to fool around with. Mika had lunch with Lisa regularly, and the first few had been filled with Lisa asking for the sordid details about the affair. She found pictures of Jayce on the internet and confided, "I'd hit that."

* * *

Mika and Tanya sat across from Dominik Moon. This was only her second time in his office, and she had forgotten how sparse it was. He had a conference table for a desk, and none of the knickknacks that adorn many offices. Mika had returned to MedCare two weeks after her accident, and the news had already been announced about Century's recommendations. Dominik had scheduled the meeting for Mika's first day back.

"How are you feeling?" Dominik asked.

"I'm feeling good," she said. "I'll be better when I get this cast off, but I'm good."

"Well, I know you know the news, and I wanted to discuss the timeline and make sure we're all on the same page, alright?"

"Thank you, Dominik. I really appreciate this," Tanya said.

Appreciate this? We're being fired.

Dominik went on to explain that the Wellness Division would continue to operate the existing contracts until June, when the new vendor would assume control of the accounts. Until then, the Wellness Division would operate on a skeleton staff. "Just enough to maintain support for our clients. And Tanya, we're still on for your final day in two weeks, right?"

"That's correct."

"And you two will work out whatever you need to do for Mika's time here."

What the fuck is he talking about? Do I have pregnancy brain already?

"We'll keep you posted. Thank you, again, Dominik."

Thank you?

Mika struggled to say something, but couldn't.

"It can't go past June, though. Understood?"

"It won't be a problem."

Dominik looked at Mika and must have seen the confusion on her face. "Are you okay, Mika?"

"I think so," Mika said. "I'm just trying to...."

"She's just catching up on some of the details," Tanya interrupted. "She's fine."

Mika trusted Tanya enough to leave it at that. "My head is just spinning a bit, Dominik. I'm good."

Mika waited until she and Tanya were alone in the elevator to say, "It sounds like there are a lot of details to catch up on."

"You have no idea," Tanya smiled. "Tomorrow we have a meeting with our partner."

* * *

Mika and Tanya sat at a table of Cien Agaves, a trendy tacos and tequila joint in Old Town Scottsdale. Mika had never been there, but Tanya knew the owner through a friend of a friend.

"I could have invested in this place," she said, sipping on a late afternoon peach margarita. "Good thing I didn't, huh?"

"I don't know. It depends on how this works out."

"It will work out. It has to."

Yes, it does.

* * *

After they had left Dominik's office, Tanya explained the many details that Mika was missing. She knew one of them: the Century report recommended outsourcing the Wellness Division because the overhead involved in employing that many people was too costly. MedCare could purchase the services from a company that offers and maintains wellness product packages with less risk to the company, and they wouldn't be stuck with employee overhead when the economy shifted. The problem was that there weren't that many companies that provide and maintain wellness product packages for insurance companies. There were a few start-ups, but none with an established history to prove they could handle the clientele of MedCare. Jayce Beckett had convinced Dominik Moon and the Board that their best bet was to go with a start-up company that was already familiar with the MedCare brand and clients, a company soon to be started by Tanya Halvord.

* * *

"In case I'm hiding it really well," Tanya said, "I'm scared shitless."

"You should be," Mika grinned. *You're scared? You should be in my shoes.*

"Thanks. I knew I could count on you." She paused. "It's a good scared, though, you know? I can't say that I ever expected to be doing something like this, but it's exciting. It's just funny how life brings you to a certain point, and there you are."

Mika chuckled. "You got that right."

Tanya checked her watch. "I hope this isn't his typical style," she joked. "I expect a partner to be on time, although I suppose I can forgive him when he looks like he does."

Mika became increasingly more nervous as she knew it would be moments before she was sitting face-to-face with Jayce Becket, and she wasn't sure that she would be able to separate her emotions from her professional obligation. "Are you sure you can trust him?"

Tanya took a deep breath. "I don't know that I have a choice, but I think so. I mean, look at what he's done so far. He convinced the Board to give us time to get the company going, he's bringing investors to the table, and he's quitting his job to join us."

"Eventually."

"Yes, eventually, after he fulfills his next assignment with Century. But even then he's going to work around that to be a part of things. I mean, why would he go through all that if it wasn't legit?" She took another sip from her margarita. "You don't trust him?"

"I trust you," she said. "If you're in charge of the product, it's going to work."

"If *we* are in charge of the product," she corrected. "We're a package deal."

At that moment, Jayce approached the table, and his voice sent Mika's stomach into a knot. "Hello, ladies." He shook hands with Tanya, and then extended his hand to Mika. She reluctantly took it. "Mika, great to see you. How's the arm?"

How's the arm? How's the arm? Shit, this isn't going to work.

"Broken." *Oh, and I'm pregnant. And the baby is yours.*

Mika fidgeted in her seat as she listened to Jayce and Tanya strategize the beginning stages of their new company. Jayce gave her a list of contacts, including attorneys and accountants, and they established some deadlines for specific actions. Mika's thoughts kept her quiet. *What the hell am I doing here? Can I really work with him? Does Tanya suspect anything? Damn he looks good.* And as much as she no longer wanted to be attracted to him, listening to him speak with confidence heightened his sexiness.

Jayce ordered a round of tequila shots, which Mika brushed aside.

"I shouldn't, not with my medication," she explained.

Jayce held up his shot glass for a toast, and Tanya joined in. Mika held up an almost-empty water glass.

"To our new venture," he said. "To good people."

They clinked their glasses and drank. "Mika, you've been rather quiet. Do you have any thoughts or questions?" Jayce asked.

Where do I begin? Did I even matter to you? Was I just another married conquest? Do you even remember what we had together? Can you tell that I'm pregnant?

"Not really. I'm just wondering when this all happened? When did you two come up with this idea?"

Tanya spoke first. "I bumped into Jayce after I saw you in the hospital. I was leaving and I ran into him the parking lot."

"I don't remember the specific moment that I thought of it," Jayce said. "I just believed in what you were doing and wanted to be a part of it."

* * *

Mika walked to her car, which was parked on a side street in Old Town Scottsdale. As she approached her car, a slightly used Kia Sportage that she had purchased two days prior, Jayce called to her from behind. She slowed and allowed him to catch up.

"Can we talk?" he asked, brushing up next to her.

"Sure," she said, but she didn't know what she would say. She had worked hard at moving on without him, and she didn't want to trust him. She had already given up on him, and she was ready to experience this pregnancy alone. The only question she continued to wrestle with was whether or not to tell him that he was the father of her baby.

"Seriously," he asked. "How are you feeling? Physically…?"

"I still have a few bruises," she said as they passed her car and continued walking through the winding streets. "But I'm mostly feeling pretty lucky."

"You are lucky," he said. "It could have been a lot worse."

They made small talk as they wound their way to a landing alongside the canal, which glistened in the night from the streetlights and Fashion Square Mall across the street. They stopped and leaned against the railing.

"I have to tell you something," he said. "I wasn't completely honest."

Uh oh. Here comes the confession. Mika didn't want to hear it, but she was ready.

"When I said back there that I believe in what you were doing, that wasn't the entire truth."

"Wait? You don't believe in our program?"

"No, no, of course I do," he smiled. "What I didn't say—what I couldn't say in front of Tanya—was that I believed in *you*. You are the most impressive woman that I know, and I say that without intentions or expectations."

Mika didn't want to look at him, but she had a difficult time turning away from the sincerity she saw in his eyes. She tried to remain firm.

"And so you felt like you had to rescue me by creating this company with Tanya? I don't need to be rescued, Jayce."

"I know. This isn't rescuing you; it's rescuing me. For the first time in a long time, I'm inspired to pursue those things that I've deprived myself of. Stability. Passion. Love."

Don't look at him. Don't look at him. She looked at him, and she saw all of the features that made her fall for him before.

"I know," he continued. "I'm not asking for anything. You're still married, and that's not what this is about. I just needed to thank you."

* * *

Mika's delivery was easier than when she had Ryan. She had hoped that she could go without an epidural, but quickly gave in and took the shot. Two hours after stepping into the hospital, she was holding her baby. Ryan was on his way down from Northern Arizona University and would be there shortly to meet his brother. Mika enjoyed the solitude and used it to bond with her new son. Her eyes swelled as she looked into his cherub face, free and innocent from the challenges of life.

"May you always know that you are loved," she whispered, "and may you always find time to love."

Mika was about ready to close her eyes when she heard a light knock on the door, and she smiled when Jayce Beckett entered.

"You're supposed to be on a plane?"

He kissed Mika on the lips. "I was able to switch flights during the layover in Vegas. I wanted to surprise you and get here in time."

"Well, he just couldn't wait."

Jayce studied his son, and Mika loved seeing the wonder in his face. "Can I hold him?"

"Of course," Mika said, and she maneuvered their baby into his hands. "Jack, this is your daddy."